YOU ARE NOT LIKE
OTHER MOTHERS

Angelika Schrobsdorff

YOU ARE NOT LIKE OTHER MOTHERS
THE STORY OF A PASSIONATE WOMAN

*Translated from the German
by Steven Rendall*

Europa
editions

Europa Editions
214 West 29th Street
New York, N.Y. 10001
www.europaeditions.com
info@europaeditions.com

Translation by Steven Rendall
Original title: *Du bist nicht so wie andre Mütter*
Translation copyright © 2012 by Europa Editions

Library of Congress Cataloging in Publication Data is available
ISBN 978-1-60945-075-5

Schrobsdorff, Angelika
You Are Not Like Other Mothers

Book design by Emanuele Ragnisco
www.mekkanografici.com

Cover photograph © H. Armstrong Roberts/Getty

Prepress by Grafica Punto Print – Rome

Printed in the USA

You are not like other mothers,
You don't have old hands
Or white hair,
And don't envelop me
In heavy care.

The first stanza of a poem by Peter Schwiefert
dedicated to his mother

CONTENTS

YOU ARE NOT LIKE OTHER MOTHERS

THE COMPLETELY DIFFERENT

T oday, June 30, her birthday, I have taken the tall, slender little book out of the chest in which I keep the past. It is bound in heavy boards with black-and-gold edging and gilt lettering. On it is written:

The Life
of our child
Else

The corners of the book are a little battered, but otherwise it appears to be new. It is ninety-eight years old. The first locks of Else's hair preserved in it are ninety-eight years old and look as if they had they had been cut the day before yesterday. They are brown, and then honey-blond, and finally, in 1897, copper red. Is hair imperishable? Does it never crumble into dust? It feels silky under my fingertips. When I first saw Else, my mother, her hair was bronze-colored and as thick as a horse's mane. She always looked unkempt, even when she had just come back from the hairdresser. Her heavy, short-cut locks could not be tamed. That was not the only thing about her that could not be tamed. I would love to have inherited her hair and her vitality. But in these areas—and in a few more—I take after my father.

Lord, the absurd ideas that occur to me when I look at this small, red book, the memories, the longing! Longing for the past that I lived, longing for a past that I did not live. Berlin at the turn of the century. What meaning does that have for me? Probably a world that is intact and thus past: tramways and horse-drawn double-decker omnibuses; cobblestone pavements and gas-lamps; solid, café-au-lait colored apartment buildings and "grand" villas surrounded by large gardens; hurdy-gurdies and flower-and-fruit stands, sausage-and-newspaper sellers; the first big department stores; dance halls, cafés with violinists, elegant eating places with waiters in tailcoats, variety shows, the theater; parks in which green was piled on green, somber, magnificent buildings, bronze monuments; the Kurfürstendamm and Unter den Linden, along which gentlemen in morning coats and ladies with muffs, flower-bedecked hats, and high-laced bosoms strolled up and down; and all around the city lakes, the Spree, fir forests to which people drove in horse-cabs, picnicked, rowed, and drank wheat beer and ate meatballs in garden cafés with military bands.

My mother's childhood world. Was that what it was like? Was it intact? It looks that way. That is what she wrote:

> I was the little, beloved girl of affectionate parents, Jewish parents, who are the most affectionate of all. We— Friedel, my brother who was three years younger, and I— were happy children who lacked for nothing.

The entries made by her mother Minna come off as sketchy, and I can imagine why. Minna had severe literary tastes, and the book, which had probably been given her by one of her many relatives, was studded with embarrassing poems, such as: "Outside it's blooming so splendidly / All is effulgence and fragrances / Around the rocking cradle / A troupe of angels dances."

She called this kind of thing "exaggerated." She used that word a lot. A hat could be exaggerated, and so could a person, a dessert, or even a concept. For example, the ideas that quite a few people, especially the young, formed of love were completely exaggerated. Love between a man and a woman was nothing but a figment of the imagination. The one great love and the only true happiness for a woman was children, and to this end she entered into marriage, a reasonable marriage carefully considered and planned by her parents. What did the world matter if you had a family in which you felt secure, that needed you, and for which you had to be there and wanted to be there, from the first day to the last?

That was how Minna saw things, and it was also the assumption on the basis of which she married the jolly, warmhearted Daniel Kirschner, who had a little potbelly, eyes like drops of water, and a wholesale firm for dresses, blouses, and dressing gowns. Two years later Else was born.

The birth announcement, which certainly appeared in a Jewish newspaper and was glued to the first page of the little red book, is modest:

> Filled with joy by the fortunate birth
> of a lively baby daughter were
> DANIEL KIRSCHNER AND SPOUSE MINNA, née COHN
> Berlin, June 30, 1893

I wonder how she might have looked then, the small, delicate Minna, whom I never knew otherwise than in black dresses from which only her hands and face emerged, a long, narrow face clouded by skepticism and melancholy, but that immediately brightened and shone as soon as she had her grandson with her. She still mourned her son, my mother explained to me, and couldn't get over his death. Siegfried, who was mercifully called Friedel, had died of the Spanish flu in 1918. I have never seen a photo of him or heard my grandparents say a word about him, because even mentioning his name would have had a devastating effect on Minna's state of mind.

So I can hardly imagine how she looked as a young woman, wearing light-colored clothes and a pert smile on her face. No, she was probably never pert, but she was certainly satisfied, because her life, for which she had no exaggerated expectations, had been fulfilled by a reasonable marriage with a good, kind man and by the birth of a healthy child. Perhaps she was even cheerful, or at least more cheerful, since she had probably always had a predisposition to melancholy.

Her ancestors came from Spain, and her Sephardic blood had put its stamp on her outward appearance: the light olive hue of her skin, the almost black, almond-shaped eyes, the splendor of her thick, wavy hair, which when I knew her she wore pinned up in a large, iron-gray braid. The Gothic hand in which she recorded her daughter's most important developmental stages in the red book is as delicate and orderly as she herself was. She noted down increases in weight, immunizations, the first tooth, the first words. From pages bearing the title "Diary" I learn that little Else already wore her first dress at the age of two months, threw her first tantrum at nine months, was photographed when she was one year old—it's a good photograph—sang "Anna Marie," "Fox, You've Stolen the Goose," and "Now Rub your Little Eyes and Wake" at one and a half, could say by heart the whole book of *Struwwelpeter* when she was two and a quarter years old, and at four and a half was sent to playschool and did her first needlework, which was quite dainty.

These notes already allow us to clearly discern young Else's prescribed future life. From babyhood on she was being prepared for a well-situated marriage in which she was to be nothing other than a little wife and mother.

It was no doubt Minna who set the tone in the family, and Daniel let her do it without protest. He loved and respected his wife, who never gave him the warmth and tenderness he would have valued more than flawless fulfillment of her wifely duties.

He recognized that she was smarter and more cultivated than he, because she came from a far better family than he did. Sigmund, her father, was a physician in West Prussia. Aaron, his father, was a baker who lived on the Polish border. She had five siblings and a good education; he had nine siblings and had had to leave school at the age of fourteen. She had read books and played the piano, he had delivered bread with his eight brothers and sung in the synagogue choir. His mother had died young, after giving birth to her eleventh child, and his father, an orthodox Jew, had worked all day in the bakery and read the Torah and studied the Talmud far into the night. After leaving school early, the nine sons were sent out into the world so that they could learn a craft somewhere, somehow. All nine of them had ended up in the very promising city of Berlin, and had built themselves a solid middle-class life there. In his old age the pious father also moved to Berlin, where he lived with one of his sons. He saw to his dismay that his children, who had been brought up in strict observance of the Law, neglected the Lord's commandments in the worst way and allowed themselves to be seduced by the godless age.

I know only one story about my great-grandfather Aaron. With its grave consequences, it was probably the only one that Else never forgot. She must have told it to me sometime after I turned thirteen, because before then I had heard of only one Jew—mentioned by my father—and that was Jesus.

So here is the story: When she was four and half, Else started going to the so-called playschool, and thus came into contact with Christian children for the first time. They were just like her, they played as she did, got up to mischief just as she did, spoke as she did. But as Christmas neared, a change took place. The children spoke in a different way, now spoke only about things of which she had never heard before: about the Christ child and Santa Claus, about Joseph, Mary, and the three Magi, including a Moor. They spoke of gifts, Christmas trees, angels, poinsettias, cribs, and all that went with them: little Jesus, the Holy Family, the ass and the ox.

"Just stupid stuff," Minna said when her daughter besieged her with information and questions, "don't listen to it."

But Else did listen, thought of nothing else, dreamed about it. Shortly before the great holiday a Christmas tree was set up in the playschool and splendidly decorated by the children with colorful, glittering ornaments. They stood before it with clasped hands and sang one Christmas carol after another. Else, who had been able to sing "Fox, You've Stolen the Goose" when she was only one and a half, immediately learned the song and sang it for her parents at home. They were shocked by the "fair child with curly hair" and decided not to let Else go to the playschool during such dangerous holidays. But the damage had been done. The child absolutely wanted a Christmas tree. She clamored and sobbed so long that her parents, who were worn down and themselves almost in tears, brought home a little tree and a few balls and tinsel. There were no candles, because Daniel was deathly afraid of a fire, and was firmly determined not to yield to the "indulgent Goyim" on this point. When the tree, meagerly decorated, stood there and Else was singing "Silent Night, Holy Night" in front of it with her hands clasped, the doorbell rang. Daniel, sensing trouble, ran to the door, looked through the peephole, and saw a broad beard and a large black hat. If that wasn't a sign from the Lord, what was it! He ran back into the room, grabbed the little tree, and threw it into the broom closet. Whereupon Else fell to the floor and screamed for her Christmas tree. The grandfather, who was finally let in, stood on the threshold, gravely and silently taking in the scene: his granddaughter, possessed by the Evil Spirit, his son, his brow covered with sweat, his daughter-in-law, white as a sheet. The little one's behavior was exaggerated, Minna finally said, adding that it was no wonder, with all this fuss about the Christmas tree.

Christmas trees are everywhere, Daniel said, and now the child is feverish and is imagining things.

Else was put to bed, and Minna sat down beside her and stroked her hot, distraught little face. There were things more important than a Christmas tree, she told her, and tomorrow she could light the Hanukkah candles.

The next day Daniel took his daughter on his lap and initiated her into Judaism. He told her about a temple in the faraway East that had been destroyed, and about a people that had been scattered around the whole world. He told her about the one true God, who didn't have a white beard and certainly not a son. And he was her God.

Else found the story of the Christ child more beautiful, and she also wasn't much taken with a God who had no face and no family members.

It was little Else's first leap into religious life, and if she had understood anything at all about it, it was that she was, for curious reasons, different from the children in the playschool, and would therefore never again have a Christmas tree in her own home.

The Kirschners lived in Charlottenburg, in the Bismarckstraße, a typical street in central Berlin: broad, straight, long, neither beautiful nor downright ugly. Of all the old buildings, I have been able to find only one, a sedate gray townhouse with a blue-tiled fishmonger's shop on the ground floor. At that time, the houses probably all looked about the same, and the street may have been narrower, with fewer trees. The apartment in which Else lived from the day she was born until she was twenty-one was certainly not very different from the one I knew later in Grolmanstraße, which was for me the quintessence of protective coziness. It might have been somewhat larger and not on the ground floor. But the heavy, dark furniture decorated with scrollwork, which was made for sedentary generations, the glass display cases with more or less valuable porcelain figurines, crystal goblets and silver religious objects, the embroidered quilts and ruffled drapes must have already been there. The kitchen was in a rectangular backyard planted with a little grass and a couple of trees, and the oven in which Minna roasted her goose or baked her shortbread crepes filled with jam was fueled by briquettes. At that time the Kirschners still had a maid, but she was not allowed to touch the oven. What did a Christian maidservant know about good Jewish cooking! Minna was a dedicated housewife, and I will never understand why she didn't convey at least part of her dedication to her daughter. All her life, Else was incapable of frying an edible schnitzel or holding a broom the right way. The only housewifely activity I ever saw her engage in was washing out a handkerchief, which she then laid out on the bathroom tiles to dry and flatten out. This way of doing things made such an impression on me that even today I deal with my handkerchiefs the same way, and every time laugh at myself and shake my head. Minna must have been thoroughly convinced that her daughter would make a match that would ensure her a permanent salon-lady's life and never force her to do any kind of housework whatever. Oh, how wrong she was!

Thus Else grew up as a Jewish young lady in a warm, secure nest over which her parents spread their wings and which they guarded with wary eyes and sharp beaks, alongside her beloved and pampered little brother, in a clan with countless uncles, aunts, and cousins. She was and remained a cheerful, healthy, uncomplicated child bursting at the seams with love of life and excess weight. But for Minna and Daniel, every pound she lost was a harbinger of an ominous illness, and so they anxiously saw to it that their little Else got in abundance everything she especially liked to eat. "A young person has to eat," was their motto, and thus they laid the foundation for Else's later figure.

However, Else's chubbiness did not diminish her charm. Under the baby fat could be glimpsed a lovely face with broad, clear planes, enormous dark eyes, and a beautiful, prominent nose. Her bronze-colored hair was woven into a braid as long and thick as a giant serpent and caused her no end of trouble.

"Pull your braid forward!" her mother called to her every morning as she was going to school. Minna was constantly worried about her crowning glory, because in Berlin at that time a rascal was creeping up behind girls and cutting off their braids.

Else took piano and violin lessons, had private tutoring in French, was taken to the opera and the theater, and received as gifts many books by classic German authors. She went to a Christian school for girls, because it was nearby and her parents were more afraid of the many perils that a young girl might encounter in a large city than of an un-Jewish education. She learned easily, and was a good pupil much beloved by her teachers and classmates. At a time when a girl from a good German home showed the highest degree of genteel reserve and feminine sweetness, Else must have been a revelation. She already paid little attention to rules of behavior and was the epitome of naturalness, candor, and impulsiveness.

One of the few stories about her life that she herself told me so impressed me that I still remember it word for word: "My class," she said, "organized a little show for our graduation ceremony. Each girl had to do something, and I decided to sing my favorite song, 'It was in Schöneberg, in the Month of May,' because it wouldn't take me long to prepare it. The big day came and I put on my prettiest dress, with lots of frills, ruffles, and flounces, which made me look even fatter than I was. On top of that, the thick braid and a floral wreath on my head. Well, I was sixteen, and wasn't afraid of anything. The hall was full of teachers, parents, relatives, and friends. Just before I came on, a beautiful blond girl had performed "Gretchen at the Spinning Wheel," and I felt a little uneasy because I found her so impressive and beautiful and thought to myself: Compared with that, you don't have much to offer, kid! When she finished, the audience clapped, but only for a short time and without great enthusiasm. Afterward I sang my little song and danced a few steps. It was very cute, but nothing special. I still don't understand what got into people. They applauded wildly and shouted 'Bravo!' and 'da capo!' I had to sing the whole song again, and at the end I took off my wreath and threw it into the crowd. Now, that was something!"

This is a typical story, a kind of leitmotif that ran through the first half of Else's life. People—men, women, children—were attracted to her, wanted to be near her, sought her warmth, her love, her friendship. She gave these to many people, all too many, gave fully, without reserve, lavishly, often imprudently.

Over and over, I have asked myself what the secret of her fascination was, and I have asked people who were friends with her about it. But none, including myself, could pinpoint it. To be sure, she had a beautiful face, she was clever, witty, overflowing with love, vitality, and generosity. She recognized no conventions, kept no accounts, had no pretensions. But that alone was not the secret. She had a charisma that cannot be explained by her beauty, generosity, or intellectual gifts.

When I try to describe her to myself or to others, I repeatedly come back to the word "genuine." She was, in a world characterized by self-deception, disguise, and hypocrisy, genuine and basic as only a creature of nature can be. At the same time she had an acute intellect and was much quicker, more flexible, and more independent in her thinking than other women of that time. Yes, she was different—not only because she was a Jewess and thus exercised on her German fellow-citizens a certain exotic and perhaps even forbidden attraction, but because she was independent and far ahead of her time.

Shortly before her death she wrote, in her last letter to me:

"As a woman of my generation I was something new, unusual and suspect. I fell outside the box, so to speak, and had to be very strong and make my own rules. No one helped me do that; on the contrary, I was seen as being at best strange, and at worst degenerate."

The Kirschners observed their daughter's development with pride and concern. The girl attracted too much attention, showed an excessively intense interest in her Christian surroundings, and frequented people of whom Minna did not approve. What, for example, was she doing spending so much time with that overrated Lilly, an earlier classmate, about whom she then told weird stories: Lilly wore an Indian robe at home, lighted incense sticks, and declaimed poems of which she, Minna, had never heard a line. And Lilly's brother wrote novels.

What did she find so wonderful in all that, her mother wanted to know, the Indian rags or the novels, which were certainly bad?

The artistic quality, Else replied, the free, the completely different. Minna, bewildered, just shook her head. As if Else didn't have enough cousins, young, decent people who were also not stupid. One of them was even a linguistic genius, and Selma, a very pretty girl, had a splendid voice and was already singing at private events. They were all far more obedient than her daughter, and didn't have her crazy ideas in their heads.

Daniel, who was always trusting, thought Else would grow out of it; she was, after all, only seventeen years old and was very lively and curious about life, like every young person.

It was true that Else was curious about life, but mainly about that of Christians. She knew her own milieu all too well, and the older she got, the less it appealed to her. It was the milieu of the so-called ready-to-wear Jews, considered socially unsuitable by the Jewish upper middle-class, and philistine by Jewish intellectuals. About them Else wrote: "I couldn't stand the people in our circle. They all dealt in fabrics, leather, or furs, spoke in such an atrocious jargon, and were crude and uneducated. They told me that I had to make a good marriage. I got furious when I heard that. Marry, certainly, but out of love. The good match—that was so Jewish, and I couldn't bear Jewishness in that respect."

Had her parents known what terrifying thoughts had taken root in their daughter's head, they wouldn't have had another minute of peace. But there was no question of their knowing, or even vaguely sensing. For them, it was simply not conceivable that Else, whom they had kept so distant from Christianity and had educated as much in conformity with Judaism as they could, could move closer to the former and farther from the latter. Many things that their daughter was to do in the coming years were for them simply inconceivable, and during their lifetimes they were spared a complete revelation of her way of life. Else, who cared not at all what people thought of her, made an exception for her parents and daughters.

But at that time, when she was seventeen and still a good Jewish daughter, the broad, free, Christian world also lay for her in the realm of the impossible, and the pull of another camp exhausted itself in fantasies and dreams. She would never have seriously considered breaking away from her milieu, even if it did not suit her and even if she objected to it in many ways. She loved her parents and her now thirteen-year-old brother, a gentle, quiet boy with an unusual gift for mathematics; she was fond of her warmhearted uncles, aunts, and cousins; and if she made so little use of the Jewish religion, she was nonetheless bound to the God that her father had called "her God." What she lacked, and what she mistakenly thought she could find only on the Christian side, was a stimulating intellectual atmosphere. She read straight through the lending library, and was encouraged by her parents to do so, but then, in her need to talk about what she had read, to discuss it, to be taught, she was left alone. Minna read exclusively Shakespeare and Goethe, and Daniel read only the newspaper. Minna wanted to see plays only by her favorite poets, whereas Daniel preferred comedies or plays with Jewish subjects. Minna liked to go to concerts, Daniel to the opera. Often they couldn't agree and didn't go at all.

Else would have preferred to go to an opera, a concert, or a play every evening, and she would have so much liked to roam all the way across Berlin for once.

Berlin, which was growing at a rapid pace, spreading further and further into the surrounding countryside, had a constantly changing, increasingly exciting face: new streets, boulevards, and avenues; new neighborhoods, new structures, new artworks, new bars and fleshpots, new cultural buildings, new kinds of transportation, new sounds, new smells. A city of two and a half million people engaged in ceaseless activity, two and a half million people each of whom led a different life, had a different destiny; people who strolled through the streets, walked, bustled about, hid secrets behind their windows, dramas, births, death, love affairs, boredom. Else had grown up with this city and felt related to it; she wanted to explore far beyond the boundaries her parents had set.

What did she already know about Berlin? Charlottenburg and its immediate neighborhood, the famous streets along which people promenaded, the sights they went to see on Sundays, Potsdam and Grunewald, where they went for leisurely walks, the castle, Charlottenburg Park, the Zoo, the garment district where her father had his shop, her parents' favorite café, a gigantic, two-story establishment in which boring music was played and boring people ate pastries. If she had for some reason to go to a more distant area unknown to her, she was accompanied by her mother or father, uncle or aunt, and they went straight to their destination, without looking to left or right, and returned the same way. Sometimes she dared to make secret excursions into the lively shopping streets, which were crowded and noisy: people of all classes, from streetwalkers to fur-bedecked wives of commercial councilors, from beggars to stout industrialists; vehicles, from the horse-drawn cart to the automobile; shops, from junk stores to pala-tial department stores; places to eat and drink from beer tav-erns to elegant restaurants.

Life, which displayed itself in ever new forms, fascinated Else: she was pleased by the glances young men gave her. Sometimes she looked back, briefly, confused, and with the apprehensive thought: Uh-oh! If mother knew how depraved I am.

I have a picture of her at this time. A young, pretty, still grow-ing girl whom the photographer has put in a coy pose: her heavy braid falls over her right shoulder, her head is inclined to the left, she's smiling and clutching a posy to her breast. Minna probably found the picture a good one, because it expresses the idea she had of her daughter: a sweet girl, innocent and somewhat imp-ish, who would soon sail into the safe harbor of marriage and thus give her love, grandchildren, and thus new happiness.

Men—Jewish men, of course—began to court Else. One of her cousins fell head over heels in love with her and thereby put the Kirschner clan in an uproar. A young rabbi wrote poems in praise of her eyes. Two "good matches" made her marriage proposals.

Else felt flattered by all this, found it diverting, interesting, sometimes comic, and waited for love.

"We still have time," Minna said to Daniel, "it gets urgent only after she turns twenty."

Else was nineteen when she met Fritz Schwiefert and thus the greatest love and the worst match of her life.

In a long, undated letter that she never sent—when she wrote it, I still don't know—she recalls once again how this love began: "You were a Christian, a poet, a young man without a real profession and no money. You were a man whom a girl could love, an artist, but not a husband. Husbands looked completely different, offered entirely different things—material, not intellectual things." In other words, Fritz, the chosen one, was for Daniel and Minna a catastrophe, as Aaron, the pious grandfather, could have told them. But they discovered the whole extent of this catastrophe only two and a half years later, because up to that point Fritz and Else succeeded in concealing their love.

It began in the summer, on a Saturday afternoon in the Kirschners' regular café, in that gigantic, two-story establishment in which boring music was played and boring people ate pastries.

Else had at first refused to listen, for the hundredth time, to "Shine, glowworm, glimmer, glimmer," but when her parents said that her favorite cousin, Emanuel, was also going to be there, she went along to the café. Disgruntled, she had looked at the stuffy people there and imagined that in a few years she would be sitting there too, a fat matron filling her emptiness with whipped cream alongside a "good match." Emanuel appeared in the company of a tall, slender man about twenty-five years old, whom he introduced as his friend and former classmate Fritz Schwiefert. The five of them sat at the round table with a gray and white marble top and made polite conversation. In the course of the conversation, it emerged that Herr Schwiefert played the piano, spoke Russian, and wrote poems, in addition to theater criticism and, at the moment, a book on Rilke. While Fritz spoke, gaily, graciously, and a little ironically, he kept his eyes fixed on Else, and his looks, and still more what he said, were like the strokes of a huge bell that made her placid inwardness tremble.

"And there you sat," she wrote in the same nostalgic letter, "a true poet, and I ate you up with hungry eyes: your fine, intelligent face with the gray eyes, the big nose, the beautiful, somewhat mocking mouth; your long, brown hair that constantly fell over your forehead, your slender, light hands."

Minna chatted, Daniel cracked his usual little jokes, the orchestra played a medley by Paul Lincke, and Emanuel, the only one who noticed that something disastrous was afoot, tried to waken Fritz and Else from their spell. He failed. The two of them sat there, spoke not a word, and just looked at each other.

"A very nice and cultivated young man," Daniel said on the way home, and Minna asked Else why she was so quiet; she hadn't caught a chill, had she?

Else replied that she did feel a little tired, and went to her room. She looked into the mirror for a long time, but did not find persuasive what she saw there. She was pretty, yes, but that was all. A man like him, a poet, an artist, had requirements that she, a naive, middle-class girl, could never fulfill. He had been a mirage, a hallucination, which her longing for the "completely different" had conjured up. Never, she thought, would she see him again.

The next day she received the first poem from him. "I found it very beautiful," she wrote, "but did not entirely understand it. There was something serious, melancholic about it. Wasn't love cheerful?"

Fritz Schwiefert did not come from a middle-class home. His father, who had already been dead for a few years, had been a musician, and his mother, a petite, brightly made-up lady, came from France. Luzie, his sole, elder sister, was the mother of three children, and had divorced her husband after he had infected her with syphilis.

Fritz, a high-strung intellectual, a talented dreamer, and a charming, witty, and educated scatterbrain, was allowed to do and not do whatever he wanted. He often did what was wrong and not what was right, but in view of his intellectual and artistic gifts, that did him no harm. Least of all with Else, who, in naive adoration of everything "artistic," far overestimated the callow Fritz.

"What I tried with all my strength to figure out," she wrote, "what my thoughts constantly revolved around, was artistic talent. Nothing could move me more deeply than a work of art, nothing commanded my respect and veneration more than a person with talent. He intimidated me because to myself I seemed small and inferior, and over and over I asked myself: What is it like to be a person who can compose music, paint, or write poetry? What does he think? How does he live?"

This question was in the long run to be answered for her by Fritz. But too late.

For both of them, this was their first love, and although it ran very deep in Fritz, his was not comparable to Else's. His love was typically male: demanding, impulsive, jealous, selfish, easily wounded, often impatient. In contrast, for Else, who had remained a child caught in the trap of parental love, care, and principles, it was the fulfillment of her life. Fritz was not only the beloved man who showed her how to kiss and tried to teach her the joys of sex, he was also the pedagogue who told her which books she had to read, which music she had to hear, which plays and pictures she had to see; he was the intellectual guide who initiated her into the form, the artistic movement, and the content of a work, taught her to judge and criticize, further developed her instinctively sure taste; in short, he was the one who opened for her the door to the broad, marvelous world of Christian love, art, and culture.

They met secretly for the hour or two that Else could keep secret from her mother; they met in small confectioners' shops and parks, sat hand in hand on the worn-out plush, stood entwined with each other behind bushes, squatted, like large birds, on snowy benches. They wrote each other daily general delivery letters, sometimes only notes in which they reaffirmed their love:

"My Pitt, I won't write much, I just want to tell you that I'm thinking of you. Pitt, I love you so much! Kisses!— Your Babushka.

PS: it has now been exactly 49 hours since we last saw each other!"

Else had become Babushka, Fritz had become Pitt, two new names, two new people born in the greatest secrecy, and nameless for the rest of the world.

Fritz, and especially Else, had a hard time of it. They, who would have preferred to shout their love from the rooftops and speak with everyone solely and always about it, were forced to keep silent. They had no confidant, no escape, not even enough money to provide their limited time together with a better atmosphere. And each rendezvous was like an obstacle course and cost Else lengthy reflection, ingenuity, guile, and trickery.

About a year later, on a cold, rainy day in the park, Fritz began to ask how long this was supposed to continue, whether they really wanted to spend the rest of their lives in confectioners' shops and on park benches?

Else, who got frightened whenever he became impatient, did not know what to say. She tried to take his hand, but he withdrew it and put it in his pocket.

He did not understand, he said, how her parents could be so backward. They were, after all, adults and lived in twentieth-century Berlin, and not in some sixteenth-century Polish shtetl, into which he had ridden like a saber-swinging Cossack. Or did she, Else, approve of her parents' behavior?

She shook her head.

Then she should come with him to his house, to his room, and not give a damn whether her cousin Emanuel found out through his mother or his sister. Or else she should take him to her apartment and tell her parents that they had had enough of sitting in the rain. He no longer found this whole business with Jews and Christians amusing at all. The latter were behaving in a more or less normal way, the former crazily and backwardly.

Else began to cry. She was constantly afraid: afraid of irritating him if she joked about everyday matters, afraid of disappointing him when she had no clever answer to a profound question, afraid of annoying him when she kept him from unbuttoning her blouse, afraid of irritating him when she had to cancel a rendezvous, afraid of his irony and his tetchiness, afraid of his cajoling and desiring, afraid of his constantly changing moods.

"You were always different," she wrote, "sometimes a little boy, sometimes a stern teacher, sometimes a dreamy poet, sometimes a hilarious comedian, sometimes an understanding friend who could all at once become moody, malicious, unbearable. How dreadfully I then became aware of your tremendous superiority, how helpless I was and how desperate. But I never rebelled against it. Artists had to be like that, I told myself, and not understanding the extraordinary processes going on in them merely increased my admiration and love."

What was there for Else to do, except to weep? She couldn't leave the Jewish world of her parents, and she couldn't give up the Christian world of her beloved. Two worlds in one body. Two heads growing out of it. A monstrosity!

Fritz took her in his arms, kissed her, stroked her wet hair, and told her that he loved her and no Christian or Jew could separate them. Else, happy about what he'd said and inspired by the courage with which he intended to stand up to Christians and Jews, decided to take him to her apartment the next time, and tell her parents that she had happened to run into him in the street.

A new phase began and at first went unexpectedly well.

Minna and Daniel had no objection whatever to their daughter frequenting this nice, cultivated young man. He played the piano so splendidly, recited wonderful poems by Goethe and sonnets by Shakespeare, carried on long philosophical conversations with their son Friedel, brought Else first-class literature, played four-hand pieces with her on the piano, took her to the theater and concerts. And he could be so imaginative and clever, so amusing and witty, that even Minna laughed until she cried.

"He's really lovable," she said, and Daniel added, with a sigh: "Too bad he's not Jewish."

Yes, Fritz was a great asset for the Kirschner family, a guest heartily welcomed every day, and moreover a young, much too slender man who had to be fattened up. They saw with joy that Else now seldom left the house and was turning into such a beautiful and happy woman that there was no lack of marriage candidates. And although she rejected all of them, that was not bad insofar as Minna and Daniel had not yet found the right one among them, either.

Her parents' naïveté and credulity seemed to Else very odd. Was their trust in their daughter's Jewish conscience so unshakeable that the obvious remained hidden to them beneath the motto: "Because what must not be cannot be"? Sometimes she felt sorry for them and promised herself: up to that point, and not a step farther! It was a seriously meant vow, from which she did not deviate. Yes, she would deceive and betray her parents a little, that did them no harm, but really hurting them, that she would never, ever do.

In August 1914 war broke out and the Kirschner house was in a panic. Else, who had just turned twenty, had still not entered the safe harbor of marriage, and in wartime men were in short supply or had more urgent things to do than get married. Their son, Friedel, who had just completed his high school degree, was old enough for military duty, and therefore in danger of being called up. His parents couldn't imagine anything worse. What, for heaven's sake, should they do in order to prevent their son from being called up and to accelerate the marriage of their daughter?

"And this whole mess because of a trifle," Minna said, referring to the murder of the heir to the Austrian throne.

Minna and Daniel were apolitical, peace-loving people who, in contrast to the sophisticated Jewish middle class, had not gone astray on some German nationalist path. Their patriotism was correspondingly minimal. Germany was their homeland, German was their language, their culture was German and their religious and familial consciousness was Jewish. They respected the Kaiser just because he was a Kaiser, and in addition a person under whose rule they lived, worked, and studied in peace, acquired money and high positions and yet were able to preserve their Judaism. That had happened seldom enough, and they treasured it, were thankful for it. But chauvinism was alien to them. To be sure, one had to protect his country and his people when they were attacked, but when the honor and glory of a country were at stake—even if it was one's own—then it was unimportant to them in proportion as the welfare of their children was important to them.

Else shared this healthy attitude. She wrote: "I do not admire the Kaiser, and I have many feelings about my fatherland, but not patriotic ones. I am against the war and I will never understand how anyone can have the power to send young men to their deaths."

That is, moreover, her only comment on the subject. In the many letters from this time that she left behind her, the war is never mentioned again.

I wonder to what extent Else even noticed it. Since it was waged outside the borders of Germany and did not, as is now usual, spread death and devastation in civilian life, she could safely put it aside in order to invest all her time, her strength, and her feeling in Fritz. From my own experience of world war I know that no war can be as disturbing, no peace as blissful as one's first love.

Because of his extreme short-sightedness, Fritz was exempted from military duty, while Friedel, Else's brother, was called up. However, since it was recognized that his abilities lay less in the military than in the mathematical domain, he was not sent to the front, but remained in the administration in Berlin.

The Kirschners, whose concern had for days deprived them of appetite, sleep, and speech, thanked God with a daylong fast and then went back to the normal way of life. Else was part of this way of life. A suspicion had suddenly flared up in Minna. Perhaps her fear for her son had made her senses more acute, or her innate skepticism may have finally overcome her unshakeable confidence in her daughter's Jewish conscience—whatever it was, she began to watch Else and Fritz like a hawk about to sweep down on its prey. And she discovered the obvious. Else was profoundly uninterested in the young man's advanced education and artistic gifts alone, and Fritz did not come to their home to see the whole family, but rather a single member of it. The harmless friendship was a classic love affair. And even if Else had certainly not done anything wrong and wouldn't dream of marrying Fritz, nonetheless there was a danger that she might waste her best years in a hopeless relationship.

Daniel, who had not gotten so far as to form suspicions and saw only—for whatever reasons—the squandering of Else's best years, took his daughter aside and asked her if she intended to ruin her life and end up an old maid. Young people think they'll always be young, he told her, but it isn't so; after twenty, things go very fast.

Else's parents agreed that a husband must be found for her as soon as possible, and at this critical point fate intervened and bestowed Alfred Mislowitzer on them. Like Daniel, he was in the ready-to-wear trade, had made a name for himself in Frankfurt as a first-class businessman, and had recently moved, along with his mother and sisters, to Berlin, where in his branch of business one could, as he put it, make it to the top. He was, as became clear in the course of their conversation, already well on his way, and an idea began to form in Daniel's head. This Herr Mislowitzer made an all-around positive impression: he was a rather large, heavy man who was clearly a good eater, a good tailor, with robust health, an unfailing business sense, and a solid, conservative way of life. What more could one ask for!

Daniel asked about the family status, age, and political views of this all-around positive manifestation and was not disappointed there, either: a thirty-five year old bachelor loyal to the Kaiser.

They smoked cigars, talked business, lamented the war and the rising prices. Daniel invited Alfred Mislowitzer to Friday night dinner.

Minna spruced Else up, and Daniel urged her to play something on the violin after dinner, something "for the heart."

Alfred Mislowitzer appeared in a dark suit of excellent cloth, a golden watch chain on his swelling vest. He saw Else, and his decision was made. Such a match would not be offered to him twice.

During the meal, in preparing which Minna had spared neither effort nor her best ingredients, Alfred already began to court Else. He laughed loudly and ate abundantly, giving her deep looks out of round, clay-colored eyes, was lavish with his compliments, passed her the various dishes, seeking each time to touch her hand. They talked not about textiles but rather about the advantages and disadvantages of living in

Berlin, about Jewish consciousness, good cooking, and family. Minna told stories about Else's childhood, Daniel entertained their guest with jokes. Alfred Mislowitzer was seduced. He was even more seduced when after dinner Else played something for the heart on the violin. On leaving, he kissed her hand. The evening was a complete success, and Else's fate was sealed.

She didn't know whether she should consider this new development as a comedy or as a prospective tragedy, whether she should laugh or cry. And above all, she didn't know how she should tell Fritz about all this. So she decided to keep quiet and wait. Perhaps a miracle would occur, and Alfred Mislowitzer, who had reached the age of thirty-five without marrying, would suddenly get cold feet and decide to wait a few years longer. But the miracle did not occur. On the contrary! Both Alfred and Else's parents considered preliminaries superfluous and headed directly toward their goal. After two further visits, and a common excursion to the Kirschners' favorite café, Herr Mislowitzer asked Daniel for Else's hand, and was granted it. How could anything better happen to her, or to him? She had made a brilliant match and he had won a first-class business partner, because Alfred had decided to join his future father-in-law's firm. Two fat flies with one swat.

Alfred Mislowitzer appeared with ceremonial seriousness. He gave Else a diamond ring and a kiss. The ring was as precious as the kiss was insipid. She was engaged.

I knew my grandparents only as the most loving, indulgent people in the world, and my mother as the woman who went her own way regardless of the consequences. The unbending parents who put economic interest above their daughter's human happiness and practically sold her are unknown to me and an enigma. So is the daughter, who was about to let her parents force her into a marriage that would have destroyed her life. Even taking into account the period, Jewish tradition, and the conviction that the goal and presupposition for a happy marriage, as Minna saw it, is children, or, as Daniel saw it, financial security, I still find it difficult to understand their behavior. But I find it even harder to understand that of the young Else, who had found in Fritz everything she loved, and saw in Alfred everything that repelled her. So how could she consider, even for a short time, making such a mistake? The lines she wrote about this reveal nothing other than the child who was yielding to the temptation of a comfortable life and wanted to avoid becoming an old maid:

To tell the truth, at first I didn't think this was so bad. It even flattered me. Here was a mature man, respected by my parents' friends and associates, who was courting me and admired me, who had given me a valuable ring and offered me a secure, carefree life. I found tempting the idea of being an envied young wife, wearing expensive clothes, living in a beautiful apartment, traveling. And it was truly hopeless with Fritz. He couldn't marry me because he had no money, and I couldn't marry him because he was a Christian, and even if we were able to overcome these obstacles, my parents would never allow us to marry. So what was left? Afternoons in shabby confectioners' shops, walks in the Grunewald, fear and secrets, and finally the fate of an old maid.

Yes, she was a child who obediently parroted her parents' words, and perhaps even endorsed them. For if through Fritz Else also discovered the "completely different" and had opened herself up to it with enthusiasm, she was nonetheless not capable of living it. The umbilical cord linking her to her parents had not yet been cut, and the roots of her Jewish upbringing were still as strong as the newly grafted sprouts of the Christian way of life were weak. Only a shock, a violent uprooting, was to make the little Jewish maiden dependent on family and tradition into an independent woman. But before arriving there a long road paved with constantly renewed attempts and setbacks remained to be traveled.

The engagement with Alfred Mislowitzer could no longer be kept secret, and Else was finally compelled to tell Fritz the truth. She met him in the Charlottenburg castle gardens. Fritz, who was in particularly high spirits on that day, came up to her imitating the actor Alexander Moissi, greeted her with the latter's high, cracked voice and dramatic gestures. Else, who felt she had died in body and soul, had only one thought in mind: to put a quick end to the torment. Thus she threw herself headlong into telling him that she had become engaged and would marry within half a year. He froze in the middle of a jaunty gesture, stared her in the eyes, recognized that she was serious, and covered his face with his hands. He stood before her and wept, sobbed like a little boy, and she, not being able to bear his pain, fled.

She did not sleep that night, and the next day she remained in bed. Minna wanted to call the doctor immediately, but Else, more wrathful than her mother had ever seen her, shouted that she wanted no doctor, no cold compress, no milk with honey, she wanted only to be left in peace.

"Completely exaggerated," Minna murmured, and went away.

That evening the doorbell rang, and Fritz stood there. He was warmly greeted by the Kirschners and asked to come in. Else came out of her room. She looked very pale and was shrouded by her copper-colored hair, which she had not put into a braid.

"Ophelia in the last act," Minna said, and went into the kitchen, shaking her head, to prepare the evening meal.

Fritz took Else's hand, led her to the piano, pulled her

down next to him on the bench and played the waltz from the *Rosenkavalier*.

"My Babushka," he sang softly, "my Babushka . . . "

From then on they both came, Alfred Mislowitzer, the fiancé, twice a week, and Fritz Schwiefert, the beloved, almost every day. The Kirschners, in the serene certainty that Else's engagement had eliminated any other danger and that Fritz was now truly only a platonic friend and an intellectual enrichment, were glad to allow it. They even found it delightful that Alfred was now also part of the pleasure of artistic evenings. And while Minna sat at her sewing table and embroidered, Daniel sat in his armchair and smoked a cigar, and Alfred, overcome by the heavy meal, took a little nap in another armchair, Fritz and Else played four-handed pieces on the piano, snuggled each other, and whispered words of love. As time went on, they took increasing pleasure in their cunning deception, in which Fritz saw a just punishment and Else a final rebellion before the gate to the wide, free world slammed shut. Fritz enjoyed making Alfred look ridiculous in front of Else, exposing him to a gentle, devious irony, confusing him with complicated observations, or attacking him with malicious mockery that the poor, stodgy man could not counter. Else felt sorry for him, but she couldn't repress an insidious joy. Soon she would share a bed and table with him, listen to his platitudes, have to drown in the still waters of boredom. So he would just have to suffer a little before her incomparably greater suffering began. From the time of this peculiar ménage à trois I have two poems that Fritz Schwiefert and Alfred Mislowitzer wrote in the guest book of Paula and Bruno Kirschner—one of Else's cousins. They tell us everything we need to know about these two men and their relationship to one another.

Alfred Mislowitzer wrote:

In the year of the World War everything was depressed
And still gray is the hope that lies before
I am happy to be the Kirschners' guest
And forget that the world is still at war.

Franz Schwiefert replied:

Woe is me! Can't write such splendid stuff!
I'm a stupid, oafish creature;
Know no stories good enough,
Was the despair of my teacher.
My Pegasus is a lame old jade
Can't do much with that sister!
O! If only intelligence came to my aid
As to Mister Alfred Mislowitzer!

When Paula Kirschner, who had been living in Jerusalem since 1936, gave me these poems, she was ninety years old. She no longer had any idea who Alfred Mislowitzer or Fritz Schwiefert were. But Else, her cousin by marriage, she remembered very well: "She was the most lovable person," Paula remembered enthusiastically, "a real little wild child!"

The little wild child was exceptionally difficult to tame, and Alfred Mislowitzer—not surprisingly—was dissatisfied. He asked whether the young, extravagant good-for-nothing couldn't freeload off a home other than that of his future parents-in-law.

To appease him and get rid of the stubborn Fritz for a while, the Kirschners decided to travel to the Baltic with Else and Alfred.

Fritz, who had taken Else's engagement and impending marriage less seriously with every day and had become increasingly sure of her, did not break into tears this time, but instead got angry: If that's how it was, he shouted, he would no longer stand in the way of their unhappiness; he grabbed the books and scores he had lent her and left.

They traveled to Hiddensee, and Else was diverted from her misery by the trip. She loved every kind of water, but the sea, though she knew only the Baltic and the North Sea, was for her the most beautiful. And then when the sun came out as well, she could not help feeling happy even in the midst of unhappiness. "When I'm not feeling well," she used to say, "I only need water and sun, and then I'm healthy again."

It was midsummer. The sun shone, lay floating like a sacred nimbus over the flat island with its dunes, meadows, and white, thatched-roof farmhouses. A light wind fanned the leaves on the trees, made serpentine lines on the sand, rippled the sea. Else walked barefoot along the beach, her skirt hitched up, looking out into the blinding, endless blue, her feet sometimes buried in the warm sand, sometimes washed by the water. Her hair came undone and fell down her back, and on her tanned face was an expression of ecstatic abandon. She unbuttoned her blouse to the place where her breasts started, pushed her sleeves up to the elbows, lifted her skirt as high as her knees, took a few steps into the sea, laughed, whooped for joy. Water, sun, air—her body, always wrapped up and tightly bound, longed for them as it did for love.

Minna, Daniel and Alfred sat in beach chairs. The men smoked cigars and talked business. Minna embroidered and kept a worried eye on Else.

"What's she doing now?" she asked.

"She's catching fish," Daniel joked.

"Running off a little energy will do her good," Alfred remarked.

When Else returned, tousled by the wind, the hem of her skirt soaked through, her feet covered with sand, Minna frowned.

She told Else to button up her blouse, put on her shoes, comb her hair and put her hat on, she looked like a wild thing—brown and half-naked. And furthermore, she'd catch cold.

She wanted to go swimming, Else said, really go into the water, like the other young people on the beach.

Yes, that's all we need, Minna shouted, and Daniel added: Goyim swim.

The happy little family's trip was preserved in a photograph: jammed into a beach chair we see a gay Daniel, a mistrustful Minna squinting toward the camera, and a smiling Else. At their feet lies Alfred—resting on his hips and elbows, a kind of seal in a saucy straw hat.

They returned to Berlin a week later. Else's first outing took her to the post office. But there was no letter from Fritz. It was a significant disappointment, but now that there was a telephone, he would certainly call in the course of the day. He didn't call. So he had to come that evening. He didn't come.

Else, who had taken Fritz's threat not to continue to stand in the way of her unhappiness no more seriously than he had taken her engagement, suddenly saw herself confronted by the possibility of never seeing him again. This was such an inconceivable possibility that she immediately excluded it. Here was a man who had at every turn accepted obstacles, secrets, and tribulations, rain and snow, her parents' prohibitions, her mother's soups, her father's jokes, and finally also her engagement, who had written poems to her, kissed her passionately, and found the most tender words for her, loved her. And a man who loved her had to come back. So she waited, waited until her muscles hurt from the tension and her head hurt from brooding. She used all the power of her wishing to bring him back, and then all the ardor of her prayer. When these did not help she tried superstitious tricks: if I get the mail without having blinked a single time, there will be a letter for me; if in the next half hour ten men with beards pass by my window, he is on his way to me; if my game of solitaire plays out, the telephone will ring and it will be him. But even if her game of solitaire played out, ten bearded men passed by, and she did not blink, he did not write, did not come, did not call.

After a week had passed, in the course of a sleepless night she admitted the truth to herself: he had seen the hopelessness of the situation, was tired of her kisses that went nowhere, her backward parents, and her unreasonable fiancé, and had given up. And even if she were to write to him or call him, what would she say? Come back, but don't expect anything to have changed. Or: Please don't leave me until I'm married! Fine offers!

With the recognition that she had lost him, a time of deep and genuine suffering began for Else.

"The world into which you had introduced me," she wrote, "that completely different, broad, splendid world full of poetry and music, was now closed to me again. No one brought me books, no one wrote letters to me, no one read poetry to me, no one played the Rosenkavalier waltz on the piano, no one took me to the theater. No one was there with whom I could talk. All that remained alive in me was the longing for you and for that world."

So why doesn't Fritz come anymore, her parents wanted to know. Because he no longer wants to, Else said, bitterly.

Minna and Daniel were sad about that. Such a charming, educated, intelligent man! They had taken him into their hearts, and they missed him very much.

The only one who didn't miss him was Alfred Mislowitzer. Finally he had driven the freeloader off the field! As Alfred bloomed, Else wilted. She hardly ate, she hardly slept, and she didn't laugh at all anymore. She lost weight. Her eyes, even larger than before, retreated into their sockets, her strong, Slavic cheekbones became more prominent, her cheeks grew hollow. For the first time the beautiful shape of her face became visible, the high, curved eyelids, the concave line that ran from the tip of her cheekbones over her cheeks down to her chin. This was the face that she was to have in later years. But Alfred didn't like it at all. He had wanted a fat, cheerful, pleasant-natured wife, not a haggard creature with a shrunken face who poked at her food and played sad songs on the piano.

That will never do, he declared firmly, and before the marriage she had to become just as plump and merry as she used to be.

He took her to meet his family who, having recovered from the strains of moving to Berlin, now wanted to get to know his fiancée as soon as possible.

"They lived in a dingy apartment stuffed with tasteless furniture," Else wrote, "and his mother was just as dingy and tasteless. She spoke a German tinged with Yiddish. It sounded awful. The sisters were no better than the mother, and all three of them asked me stupid, indiscreet questions. Here I encountered, in its worst form, the Jewishness that I rejected with all my heart and from which I wanted to escape."

Else's mourning for her beloved and the wide, wonderful world that he had offered her was accompanied by hatred for her fiancé and the narrow, ugly ghetto life that he expected her to embrace. In addition to losing her ampleness and gaiety, she acquired a new attitude that expressed itself in contemptuous remarks, slights, and mockery. Alfred Mislowitzer thought his little Else had met the Dybbuk. Her parents feared that their child might become seriously ill.

Daniel asked whether she didn't like Mislowitzer just a little. And Minna, taking her daughter's side for the first and last time, declared that the man was a bore.

It was now November, damp, cold, dark gray days, endless nights. The war was making itself felt. Coal and food shortages, more and more people in mourning, increasingly disturbing news from the front. Else didn't care. Inside her there was also winter and war, and she was losing.

On a stormy day she was overcome by a need to go to the Charlottenburg castle park. The storm corresponded to her mood. She wanted to feel it on her face, through her clothes on her skin, she wanted to run with it and against it, she wanted to moan and howl with it.

Her mother stood there, wringing her hands. Else should, for God's sake, be reasonable and stay home. She would catch her death!

What she caught was not death but life.

On one of the broad, empty lanes of the park she saw a tall, slender figure, hatless, his upper body bent forward, his head down. The storm slowed his pace, but Else, who was behind him, rushed up to him. He didn't see her until she was standing in front of him.

"Babushka," he said, without surprise, and threw his arms around her. She hung on his neck and wailed with the storm, wept with the rain.

There it was again, the world of poetry and music, the world of anxiety and secrets.

For the first time in their two-year-long relationship Fritz asked Else if she would marry him. Without hesitating, she said she would, and only afterward, as she lay in bed, reflected on the consequences of her answer. For her, it was as if she had stuck her head into a wasps' nest and a swarm of maddened insects were whirring around her with their poisonous stingers. She was tempted to take a sleeping pill, in order to escape her thoughts. But that would have been tantamount to running away, and if at the outset she tried to wriggle out of her promise, she would be married to Alfred sooner than to Fritz. But the one thing of which she was certain, the starting point for all her thoughts, was that that must not happen. So she had to draw the conclusion and face up to what it meant: shocking her parents, scandalizing the Kirschner clan, humiliating her spurned fiancé, breaking with her milieu, taking the step into a world that was as seductive and desired as it was alien and uncertain, enduring the tribulations of a life without financial support, without the slightest training in a profession or in housekeeping, without help or counsel, and with Fritz's more than questionable abilities in practical life, his unworldliness, absentmindedness, and irritability, and her own inexperience, ignorance, and self-doubt.

Oh, God, how were they to clear all these hurdles, cope with the vexations, overcome the fear, stand up to God and the world? Where were they to live, what were they to live on, how could they feed themselves, since she didn't even know how to cook? How could they make the necessary preparations in perfect secrecy, under constant pressure, and fearing discovery? Where was she to find the strength to look her poor old parents in the eye, sit across the table from them with apparent unconcern, gaze at them calmly, as they prepared for her marriage to Alfred? How could she maintain this two-facedness, bear her sense of guilt, win the race for time? And what if her parents were faster and she, Else, ended up, not at the registry office with Fritz, but under the chuppah with Alfred? Here she came back to the starting point of her thoughts, and the certainty that this must never happen extinguished all doubt, fear, and feelings of guilt. She fell asleep, but the next morning her *nudjes* were all there again.

This grueling state of being pulled this way and that lasted for months, and put Else's and Fritz's relationship to a severe test. They were both sure of their own love, but not of the other's. Each suspected that the other would not be able to put up with the problems and would regret their decision. Moreover, Fritz feared that Else, under the steady pressure of her parents and her own uneasy conscience, could relapse again; Else feared that Fritz might suddenly realize that he had bound himself to a woman that couldn't hold a candle to him.

When I read her letters written at this time, it becomes clear to me what a panic the leap out of "Jewish narrowness" into the "broad Christian world" must have aroused in her. Narrowness had at least offered protection and care, whereas the breadth of the Christian world had no boundaries at all. It was not only the complete difference of this world but the completely different life in it, her completely different personal sphere in this life, and the completely different, because male and not middle-class, creature in her personal sphere. How should she do justice to all that, she who had always been kept on a leash and had grown up in an atmosphere of physical sterility that had left her entirely ignorant of the sexual side of marriage?

"What is it like?" she had once dared ask her mother.

"Completely unimportant," her mother replied.

Thus I can vividly imagine what was going on in her when she wrote the little letters in which her self-doubt amounted to a surrender.

Once she wrote: "I try not to believe that you no longer love me, and yet the thought keeps occurring to me. And I have still worse thoughts, for example, that I can't really offer you anything important, and that you love me only because I'm pretty . . . "

Another time: "Don't think badly of me, Pitt, please? I couldn't bear it if you were disappointed in me. I love you so much, and I don't want to have any thought that you don't know, any feeling that I don't lay openly before you . . . "

And again: "What is it then? Are you angry? And if so, why? I'm sad, I've waited up to now, thinking you would call. I yearn for you, and you must console me, because I feel so disconsolate. And there is so much between us that has not been expressed, and I don't know what you really feel for me . . . "

Suddenly she thinks she knows, and writes: "Lately, I've been nothing more than a toy for you; you must now be disappointed in me. I can't bear thinking that I'm too small and unimportant for you. Now I doubt myself, and since the day before yesterday I've been worried sick . . . "

At the next moment she assures him: "My feeling for you has not diminished, it can't, because otherwise everything indecent we are doing wouldn't be worth it. Sometimes I myself no longer know who I am, Pitt. I want to be good, tell me that I am! I love you as much as ever, nothing can change that."

And finally, on her birthday: "A little morning gift from your Babushka, my only one, my love. I wish you all imaginable happiness, and wish for myself your still great, ever new love. Pitt, now we have to wait a little more, but no longer indefinitely. You mustn't suffer, I'll give you and be for you whatever I can."

During this time, Fritz seldom went to the Kirschners, and never on days when Alfred, Else's second fiancé, dined there in the evening and then took a nap in an armchair, puffing and blowing slightly. Else and Fritz were very careful; they wanted to avoid any unpleasantness, any further crises. When they met secretly, it was no longer in parks or confectioners' shops, but rather in buildings that rented out rooms, and in shops that sold cheap furniture. Often they looked at each other worriedly over a monstrous marriage bed or the head of a grim landlady, but when they moved on to the next apartment, the next shop, Else consoled herself and Fritz by saying: What do we need to live together? A bed, a table, two chairs, and a great deal of love.

Fritz began to look around for a steady job, and Else spent a lot of time with her mother. She often watched her mother cook, went shopping with her, and thus learned how to tell a good stewing hen and what yarn to use to darn stockings.

Minna was delighted by her daughter's interest in these things, and saw in it a sign that she had finally made up her mind to marry a bore. And in view of the children soon to be expected and the financial security, a boring but Jewish husband was still better than an intelligent but Christian one. She often talked about the wedding, which threatened to become a problem, for where and how were they to get the ingredients for a suitable meal for about a hundred guests? But she was nonetheless cheerful. Aunt Betty had given her some beautiful satin for the wedding dress, and she, Minna, had already found the right seamstress, a rabbi respected in their circle, a large hall, and a dignified set of bedroom furniture.

During these days, Else did not know who was the guiltier: her mother, who was prepared to sacrifice her daughter to her principles, or the daughter, who did not hesitate to deceive her mother in the worst way. Sometimes her anger at her mother prevailed, sometimes sympathy with her mother and horror at herself. Then she threw her arms around her mother, kissed her, and silently asked her forgiveness.

"You'll see, Else," Minna said, "he's a good, responsible man, and you're a good daughter, and your father and I love you more than anything."

There were days when Else, whether out of caution or out of the wish to give her parents as much joy as possible, made no arrangement to meet Fritz. Then he immediately became distrustful, and feared that Else might once again cave in and suddenly marry Alfred Mislowitzer behind his back and behind the backs of her parents. He accused her of fickleness and blamed her for spending more time with her grotesque fiancé than with him, her true love.

She got angry and wrote: "Pitt, you've never more unjustly suspected me than this time; your emotions have really completely deceived you! I can't force the truth on you, I can only ask you to believe me, and do what is right; and even if you've gathered together a hundred reasons, throw them away and believe me! It's so terrible when one feels unjustly blamed, one is completely defenseless . . . "

Or else she tried to calm him down by giving him precise accounts of her day: "On Saturday at noon I went with my parents to my uncle and aunt Thoman's, where there's always a great deal to eat and very little to hear, and we spent the evening all alone at home. I read Ranke and slipped into bed at 11:00. On Sunday morning I went for a walk with mama and my brother, and in the evening, just imagine, we went to the theater. It was a play by Henri Nathansen, *Behind Walls*, and I would much rather have seen something else, but my father insisted on it. It was about a problem that no one will resolve— not even Herr Nathansen—namely the conflict between Jews and Christians. Do you want to know its content? It is not exactly new, but I'll tell it to you anyway: A girl whose parents are not modern but strictly Jewish and a Christian young man love one another and want to marry. Both fathers are against the marriage . . . "

Else described for him the drama's development right up to the happy ending: the fathers give in and accept their children's love. The Jewish daughter is allowed to marry the Christian son on the condition that the marriage is not Christian and that she remains a Jew.

Behind Walls was the last play that Else saw with her parents. Daniel found it very good. Minna thought it too shallow and said she would have preferred Shakespeare. The poor Kirschners had no inkling that their daughter was about to break through the walls and provide them with a drama that had much more content than Herr Nathansen's.

Fritz got a job as a librarian in the Berlin State Library. In addition, he continued to write theater criticism. He had still not finished his book on Rilke.

Else found two rooms and the bed, table, and chairs. In her

last letter from her parents' house, she wrote to Fritz: "I want to be a wife. I want to be your wife! Maybe I'll never be able to do it, or can I, after all? Perhaps now you're smiling at my letter and the fact that I attach so much importance to all this. Please don't, and don't show me how superior you are. Tell me how you want me to be, and I'll be that way. I want to make our marriage beautiful, great, and strong. I want to be a wife whom you have to love and respect."

One morning in February 1916 she left her parents' apartment. On her pillow she had left a letter in which she told them that she had married Fritz. She begged them to forgive her.

The most tender of all mothers and the kindest of all fathers did not forgive their daughter. They banished her from their home and their hearts. They erased all trace of her. It was no longer permissible to mention the name "Else" in their presence.

What did one need to live together: a bed, a table, two chairs, and a great deal of love. That's what Else said before she married, and she had believed it. She'd made the purchase, for her and for Fritz, and she'd named her parents as guarantors for the loan. Naturally, she'd foreseen a quarrel with them, sharp words, accusations, tears, threats, a short period of separation and a longer one of discord. She'd even considered it possible that her parents would refuse to pay her dowry and forbid Fritz to enter their home. But that they would be capable of rejecting their daughter, simply cutting her out of their life, as if she no longer existed—that she had never imagined. And she had also never imagined it because for twenty-one years she'd known her parents as the best people in the world, inexhaustible in their love and their readiness to make sacrifices for their children, and constantly concerned about her. And then suddenly, from one day to the next, all that had evaporated? What had triggered this incredible hardness in them? Was it the scandal to which she had exposed them, her disloyalty to them and to Judaism? Was Judaism more important to them than their daughter, to them, who had never considered anything more important than the happiness of their children? She couldn't understand it.

Fritz and Else now lived in two small rooms in one of those typical Berlin apartments that seem to consist chiefly of long, dark corridors, high walls papered with dizzying patterns, and decades of dirt. They shared the bath, toilet, and kitchen with the apartment's owners, an elderly couple who were grouchy but indulgent and whose name was Pusche. For Else, their name was the only amusing thing about this arrangement. The view of the back courtyard, with its sole, winter-bare tree was certainly not amusing.

But what did that matter! She had Fritz, she was his wife for better and for worse, she loved and was loved, and soon spring would come, and perhaps also the end of the war, perhaps even her parents' forgiveness. Life, love, marriage lay before her, and she was determined to make something beautiful, great, and strong out of it.

At first, Fritz, who after three years of patient and difficult waiting, finally shared four walls and a bed with his Babushka, had no complaints. Certainly, he'd have liked to eat a real meal and wear a properly washed shirt from time to time, but Else was not forced to provide them, since in the meantime food and soap had gotten exceptionally expensive. And if other women managed to conjure up a clean shirt or hot soup despite the shortages, that was their affair. He was not a bourgeois but a Bohemian, and was concerned with more important things. But at that point the physical was more important than the intellectual, and so for the first time a kind of balance emerged in the young couple's relationship.

Fritz was in the library all day, and sometimes he went to the theater with Else in the evening, and then wrote a critique of the play. For her, these evenings were the broad, splendid world. Else spent most of her days reading or practicing her violin. Fritz assigned her a large daily quota, and she took it very seriously. Some day, she sensed, they would move back toward the intellectual, and when that happened she wanted to be up to snuff.

Sometimes she visited her brightly made-up French mother-in-law and her sister-in-law Luzie, who had been infected with syphilis but had recovered from it after enduring torments. Luzie was delighted by Fritz's marriage and had heartily welcomed Else. Else talked with the mother in French, made trivial jokes with the good-hearted but not very intelligent Luzie, played with her children, especially Ellen, an impetuous little girl of whom she had grown very fond.

Sometimes she received a visit from a former schoolmate who was curious, or secretly from one of her few daring cousins who had not distanced themselves from her, like the rest of the Kirschner clan, or from her brother Friedel, to whom she had since childhood been bound by a close and loving relationship. He was still in the army, but since Else had left the house, he now spent most of his off-duty time with their parents.

They suffered a great deal from the break with her, Friedel told his sister, and for God's sake, they mustn't learn that he saw her from time to time.

Else said she couldn't understand their parents' behavior, and Friedel, with talent of a little wise man, smiled and said it was based on reciprocity. She had, in case that was still not clear to her, violated their parents' most sacred principle, that of loyalty to the family and to Judaism.

And her parents, Else replied, had violated her basic principle, freedom of choice.

Friedel understood both sides, but approved of neither what his sister had done nor his parents' arbitrary acts. For him, their effort to drive Else into marriage with a man she did not love was just as irresponsible as Else's secret marriage to a man who was unacceptable because he was a Christian.

Else got cross: she was first of all a German, and as a German, she had married a German man. She was wrong about that, Friedel replied, and as soon as she had her first child she'd realize that she was not a German who had married another German, but a Jewess who had married a Christian. Had she ever thought of that? Did she know what the child was to become: a Jew, a Christian, or a mishmash that belonged to neither one world nor the other? A child would belong to her and to Fritz, Else said, and they didn't care whether he became a Christian, a Jew, or neither.

You may not care, Friedel said with a sigh, but someday the child might.

In April, two months after the wedding, Else discovered that she was pregnant. Oh, what happiness! A child! A child by Fritz, the beloved husband! It was the fulfillment of their love. It was also, of course, the fulfillment of their marriage. Although she did not see it as starkly as her mother, who always said that children were the sole purpose of a marriage, she had no doubt that the single obvious, natural, and true path for a woman led from love through marriage to children. On that point at least Minna would have recognized in her daughter the good Jewish girl whom she had raised to be a wife and mother.

Today, when I consider that my mother first found herself pregnant at a time when any reasonable woman would have reacted to such a discovery by breaking into tears of distress rather than joy, I can understand her elation only through something she said during her third pregnancy: "A woman must have a child by every man she loves." That was her conviction, and she stuck to it. For better or for worse, in wedlock or outside it, but in each case under the most unfavorable circumstances. Fritz faced these unfavorable circumstances far more reasonably, that is, more or less with tears of distress.

A child in two rooms, a nursing infant who wakened him with its cries in the middle of the night and would deprive him of the rest he so urgently needed, when fatherly love and care were not his strong point, a creature that cost money, when the money he earned was hardly enough for two to live on, a little monster who didn't give a damn whether there was a war, a shortage of the most necessary things, whether they shared the bath and kitchen with the Pusches, whether his Jewish grandparents were not reconciled with them, whether he wanted to go to bed with Else and have her all for himself. A catastrophe!

Else laughed at Fritz's exaggerated fears. She would hardly have expected middle-class reactions from a man like him. She explained to him that the restrictions that a baby would put on her were really enrichments, and that she would have enough love, strength, and courage for both the father and the child— in fact, for him and five children. Fritz shuddered and kept silent.

Spring had come, but not the end of the war, and not her parents' forgiveness. On the contrary! On the Western front, the battle for Verdun was under way, leaving hundreds of thousands of dead and fear and mourning among the civilian population. And so far as Minna and Daniel Kirschner were concerned, they did not allow their daughter's pregnancy, which they learned about through Else's favorite cousin Emanuel, to soften their resolve. Else was depressed for a while, but since depression might have a negative effect on her child, she resolutely put away all dark thoughts, read cheerful books, played lively violin sonatas, and went for walks in the lush, green park that was as fertile as she was.

Since the child had to be nourished as well as the times allowed, she now took her midday meal with Fritz at his mother's home. She swelled up like a leavened cake, but her face, soft and relaxed, was very beautiful. Her attention was directed inward, and she seemed to perceive the outside world as only the vague background for the enormous act of her creation.

Fritz wavered between affection, when he looked at her face, and worry, when he looked at her body. Was the young, impetuous woman, his beloved, who had concentrated on him all her attention, admiration, and tenderness, already to become a brood animal? Her constant concern with the embryo that was stretching her belly and that had to be fed, amused, taken for walks, and protected from his passionate embraces began to get on his sensitive nerves. And the first time he caught her knitting, an art that his sister had taught her, he asked whether she intended to turn into her mother as quickly as she could.

Else was appalled, and all her old doubts about herself were reawakened. Her increasingly heavy body had dragged her down to the level of everyday banalities. There she sat, fat, sluggish, clueless, and knitted, while he, an artist, an aesthete, a dreamer, floated away from her into the empyrean. He must be disappointed in her, perhaps already regretted that he'd bound himself to her. And rightly so! Was it for this that she'd broken away and trampled on her parents? Hadn't her goal been the wide, free world, a life alongside an unusual man who expected something from her other than baby rompers she'd knitted herself? She had to rise above her belly, above herself.

Fall came and with it the rutabagas. My mother told me about the rutabaga winter when we were in Bulgaria during the Second World War and for two years had almost nothing to eat but white beans.

"Don't complain," she said, "white beans are still more edible than rutabagas! And especially one can't make jam or ersatz coffee out of them. We had to smear the stuff on our bread and drink it and I don't know what else. Show me a rutabaga and I'll still throw up."

At that time she even learned to cook white beans, a feat she seems never to have achieved with rutabagas. Or perhaps it was Fritz who kept her from standing in front of the stove in the Pusches' kitchen, stirring a pot of the indigestible roots. However that may be, the reek of rutabagas and the cold were inescapable during that winter.

Else, in her eighth month, freezing and disheartened, just wanted to be finally freed of the burden of her belly. It hadn't gotten any lighter, and the unruly child banging around inside her, along with the rutabagas, did not allow even her to give the act of creation such a sacred meaning.

Often she longed for her parents, for her mother's experience and tender care, for her father's kind looks and silly jokes. Under other circumstances, they would have been delighted by their daughter's pregnancy, seen to it that she didn't catch cold or get tired, found a stewing hen and a basket of briquettes for her, been excited and busy as they waited with her for the baby to be born, encouraged and calmed her when she felt afraid. She could not and must not expect all that from Fritz. He was already overwhelmed even without such demands, thin as a skeleton, always tired, often suffering from headaches and dyspepsia. He did what he could to earn the necessary money for his wife and coming child, and thus gave up what he really cared about: poetry, music, art. No, she mustn't expect still more of him, and thereby risk losing his love. All that mattered was to keep his love alive through this difficult time.

The child, a boy, was born on January 5, 1917. He had light-colored down on his head and an astonishingly smooth, well-formed little face. Else held her son happily in her arms, and Fritz examined him gravely and at length.

"The kid looks intelligent," he finally said, "can't ask for more than that for starters."

Else's former schoolmates, the bold cousins, and her brother Friedel came to visit her. Her parents didn't come.

Else asked Friedel whether their parents knew that she'd had a boy.

They knew, Friedel said, and had asked that no more be said about it.

Else, the child at her breast, began to cry, and Friedel, who couldn't bear tears, swore on his life to do all he could to bring about a reconciliation.

The family of three's life in the Pusches' two rooms became chaotic, and the little Peter was not at all the enrichment Else had predicted. In any case not for his father. The infant did precisely what Fritz had feared: he screamed his lungs out, or slurped noisily at Else's breast, or bubbled to himself. He was seldom entirely quiet, and when by chance he was, Else became afraid that he might fall sick, and fumbled around with him until he began to scream again. She had, Fritz thought, become almost as unbearable as the child: jumpy, unpredictable, and uncoordinated. Their rooms reeked of sour spilled milk, soiled diapers, coal dust, and rutabagas. To limit their use of heating fuel to a minimum, the little bit of warm, damp air must not be let out of the room—and no fresh air must be let into it. When Fritz came back from the library in the afternoon and opened the door to their rooms, he was always surprised that the mother and child had survived another day in this stink.

But for the most part it was not only the stink, or Peter's angry or happy cries, that welcomed him home, but rather the most diverse people: admiring school friends, helpful and delighted cousins who bent over the baby, billing and cooing, making faces to wring a precocious smile from him, who hung did diapers to dry on his chair and did jumping jacks over Peter's bed to amuse him, brought useless gifts such as a silver spoon or an ivory napkin ring, and asked Else whether she had enough milk, whether the child was gaining weight, and was producing the absolutely necessary burp after nursing. Frau Pusche had even acquired the habit of coming in and out of the room and helping Else with the obligatory words: "After all, I've raised three kids."

Fritz told himself that he must love Else very much in order to put up with all this. For her part, Else asked herself how long he would still put up with it.

His temper worsened with every day, and his moods, which had always been very volatile, now drove him from frantic restlessness to glimmers of sparkling testiness and finally to the deepest despair. He went to the library earlier and earlier and came home later and later. If when he got home he found Else's brother Friedel or her cousin Emanuel there, he didn't even take his coat off, but pressed the visitor to go out somewhere with him—anywhere. He also went increasingly often to his mother's apartment, either to write a piece of theater criticism or to work on his book on Rilke, which didn't seem to want to come to an end.

Else didn't stand in his way, didn't reproach him, just sometimes looked at him sadly. She understood only too well why he wanted to escape this miasma of evil odors, this chaos of female clothing and baby things, unwashed dishes and damp mops, this medley of shrieks, rattles, squeals, warbles, and babbles.

"You were a man," she wrote at that time with wise foresight, "whom one loved—a Christian, an artist, but not a husband."

When she married him, the beloved man and the artist were more important to her than the husband. And nothing had changed in that regard. She still loved him as idolatrously as she had before, admired him, respected him, took it for granted that he was on a "higher level," from which he could not descend into a "shallow" existence. She blamed their poverty on the war, her parents, and her incompetence, not Fritz. Were they living together under other, more favorable circumstances, with her husband and son she would be the happiest woman in the world.

Spring came, and then summer. It was no longer necessary to heat their rooms, and they could open the windows and hang the diapers out to dry in the courtyard. Else went for walks in the park with Peter. Fritz usually accompanied them. He had become cheerful again, sometimes even boisterous. His son had grown thick, blond locks, had big brown eyes and finely drawn eyebrows, which he raised when someone spoke to him or played with him, when he was swaddled or washed. This gave him an arrogant appearance, as if he found foolish everything that was said or done to him.

"I believe the boy will someday become very difficult," Fritz said with pride.

In the little wine-red book with the gilt title "Our Child," Else wrote down, as Minna had in her time, her child's stages of development. I found nothing odd there—apart, perhaps, from the fact that he was disgusted by teddy bears and howled with rage at the tinkling of his music box. The locks of hair are much lighter than Else's were at his age, but they feel just as fresh and silky.

During that summer the Spanish flu broke out, a viral epidemic that killed umpteen thousand people. Else, terrified, thought of nothing but saving her family from the deadly attack of the disease. She took every possible and impossible precautionary step, hardly left the house, allowed no one to visit her in the apartment, and when Fritz came home from the library, she made him wash himself from head to foot and leave all his clothes in the corridor.

When the epidemic subsided and no longer caused many deaths, her cousin Emanuel appeared. He was pale and distraught, and when he spoke, he stared over her head into the darkness of the long corridor: her brother Friedel had been in the hospital for days with the Spanish flu, but had insisted that she not be told because of the danger of contagion. But now . . . His voice broke, and he took his cousin in his arms.

They drove to the hospital in the taxi that was waiting downstairs. Else huddled on the seat, her arms pressed to her body, her face distorted. The pain that radiated from her heart was like birth pangs, birth pangs that brought the end, not the beginning. Friedel, her little brother, Friedel, who had not yet lived, not yet loved! Why hadn't she thought beyond her family, had she sensed nothing, done nothing, simply let him go to meet death. And what if she were now too late, if she were never to see again his soft, bright eyes, and if he could not hear her words of love? She sprang out of the car even before it had come to a complete stop, ran up the stairs and down the corridors. The room was white and brightly lit. She saw the dark outlines of her parents, who drew back to make room for her at the bedside. She saw her brother's little head on the pillow, his delicate boy's hands on the sheet. As she bent over him and kissed his cold forehead, he had his last clear moment. He smiled and gestured toward his parents with a hardly noticeable movement of his head. What he had sworn to do while he was alive and had not achieved, he now achieved through his death.

That same evening the lost daughter returned with her son to her parents' home. She laid the child in her mother's arms and threw herself into her father's. They wept, tears of mourning, tears of regret, tears of forgiveness, tears of happiness. Their son had been taken away from them, their daughter and a grandson had been returned to them. Death and life, pain and happiness, God had cursed them, God had blessed them—the circle closed.

Else remained in her parents' home throughout the seven days of mourning. She sat with them in the living room on the moss-green sofa and received the guests. The door to the apartment stood open, and uncles and aunts, cousins, friends, and acquaintances streamed in, unpacked baskets and bags, warmed up the dishes they'd brought with them, cut the cakes, made tea or coffee, served it, washed the dishes. They spoke, as it is usual to do among Jews, not about death and the deceased, but about life. And life in the form of Peter sat on the laps of everyone in the Kirschner clan, was hugged to ample breasts and starched dickeys, kissed and fondled, fed chocolate and showered with gifts. The little prince could hardly lower his eyebrows. He found what was done around him foolish, but not exactly unpleasant. He quickly understood that people were acting out of affection for him, that they loved and admired him. This knowledge became the focus of his life, shaped his being and remained with him for twenty years.

At the end of the seventh day, when the last guests had left, Fritz appeared to pick up his wife and son. Else, holding Peter in her arms, opened the door, took him by the hand, and led him to her parents. He stood there, crestfallen and mute, holding a piece of paper in his hand. Minna stroked his arm, Daniel put his hand on his shoulder.

He could not say, Fritz murmured, everything he felt; it was in the poem.

Daniel took the sheet of paper from his hand and began to read it aloud. It was such a beautiful, sad poem that he couldn't go beyond the first lines. The whole family broke into tears, and Peter began to scream.

"The child!" Minna and Daniel said in unison, and the fear that they had caused their grandchild pain repressed their own suffering. Else tried to calm the boy, but Peter, who had in the meantime realized that there were things in the world better than words of consolation, went on screaming.

Minna took him out of her daughter's arms and with an infinitely tender smile, rocking him and softly humming a song, she began to walk up and down the room. Daniel, a chocolate bar in his hand, followed her. Peter fell silent, held his head up and raised his eyebrows. To Fritz and Else it seemed that he was looking triumphantly at them. The cornerstone of his upbringing had been laid.

A new life began for the young couple, a fairy-tale life. Gold pieces that had been laid away long ago for their daughter's dowry and for the birth of the first little Mislowitzer, who had now become a Schwiefert, fell from heaven. In the little wine-red book Else noted: "Our child received as dower: from grandfather Kirschner a life insurance policy, from grandmother Kirschner a savings book, along with many other gifts from uncles, aunts, and cousins."

But those were trifles compared with the dowry Else received. It consisted of a house in Dahlem, the most exclusive residential neighborhood in Berlin.

I must have been about one year old when my mother left this house, and during the ten years I lived in Berlin as a child, I didn't see it again even once. Only in 1948 or 1949, when I was making a short visit to Berlin, did I go out to Dahlem in search of the past. The bombing spared this area, and so its rural character was preserved: narrow streets paved with cobblestones, large gardens with tall, old trees, feudal villas that stood far apart from one another and that, though undamaged, looked the worse for wear and thus made a remarkably melancholy impression. But maybe it was only my own melancholy that I projected onto them on that gray, overcast morning.

The house in which my mother finally came to know the wide, free, splendid world impressed me more by its size than by its beauty. Perhaps it was more beautiful back then, when it was painted white with bright yellow shutters and colorful curtains, with a table and chairs under a large, blue-and-white striped umbrella on the terrace, flowers in the garden, shrubs and a children's swing. That's how I'd imagined it. The turbulent life, the never-ending series of celebrations, parties, and artistic evenings, the joys, madness, and drama of love, could hardly have taken place in this gray box with limp drapes and a bleak garden. During the Nazi regime it had been expropriated, of course, and given to an actor named Matterstock. After the war, an American officer lived in it with his wife and seven children. It was big enough, and my generous grandfather Kirschner had presumably foreseen an ample progeny. His blouses, skirts and morning coats must then have been selling very well, or during the First World War houses were not worth much, or else he had taken out a large loan. In any case, my grandfather must have found nothing too good or too expensive for his beloved, brave daughter and his charming and hardworking, even if Christian, son-in-law and his one and only grandson.

Gray under a gray sky, or as it had then been, white under a blue sky, the proof lay before my eyes. And I also saw her, with her tanned face, high cheekbones, flashing, fawn-colored eyes. Young and crazy, carried away by the feverish 1920s and carrying others away with her.

"You're right," her second husband wrote to her first, "when you say that even today it seems incomprehensible that this vital person is no longer alive. When I go to her grave, I often have a feeling of unreality, as if part of me were buried there. She was too much the human center of our group for us ever to forget her . . . "

The household was set up. Daniel had a large number of friends and acquaintances who dealt in furniture, lamps, fabrics, and housewares, and they all wanted to help him build a comfortable nest for his daughter. The best-quality goods were brought out of the storehouses, prices were reduced, he was given interest-free credit. Why are we Jews? To stick together and help each other.

Else didn't find it easy to keep the eager businessmen in check, to stop them, to make it clear to them that they didn't want any valuable "stylish furniture" with scrollwork and plush upholstery, heavy chandeliers, or fake Persian carpets, just simple, friendly things among which they felt comfortable. Neither did she want a ponderous marriage bed, wallpapers, or curtains of white lace. Not her father's daughter, these dealers said, and brought her things that no one else wanted. Else liked them.

While she set up her household and Fritz worked at the library, Peter was at his grandparents' home, and when his mother came to get him every evening, they were able to report new events: a tooth had broken through, he'd walked from the table to the sofa all by himself, he'd said four new words, and they were "alaphump," "gigaga," "shockens," and "ankarshuf," that is, "elephant," "Tiergarten," stockings," and "handkerchief." But his grandparents greatest triumph was that they were able to inform Else that the clever boy was afraid of decorated Christmas trees. Their grandson was, in contrast to their daughter, a Jewish child. Hardly had that been established before Else and Fritz had their son baptized a Protestant.

I do not believe that it was only Peter's fear of Christmas trees that led her to take this step, but what it was I cannot say with any certainty. Perhaps it was the glittering Christian atmosphere that spread over the city and seeped into people's minds, rekindling Else's inclination toward Christianity; perhaps it was the old childhood trauma of the Christmas tree disappearing into the broom closet, which had apparently been transmitted to her child; but it may also have been only

Fritz's Christian mother, who wanted to save her grandson's soul. However that may be, Peter was, as is recorded in the little wine-red book, baptized by Pastor Rudolph in the Luisenkirche. I can say with certainty only that the Kirschners learned nothing about it.

In the first days of the following year the little family moved into the big house. Now each of them had at least three rooms in which to pursue his or her favorite occupations. Peter could scream and make a racket, Fritz could write, reflect, and sleep, and Else could read, practice her violin, and receive guests. Since the house had to be cleaned, the laundry washed, and the meals, which were, thanks to the grandparents, more lavish, had to be prepared, a maid was hired. Fritz and Else were happy. Their love, which they had not been able to live out in the Pusches' two rooms, developed in the villa in Dahlem into a regular fireworks show, whose consequences Fritz was cleverly able to avert. Now life was finally what Else had expected from it: full of music and poetry, merry and boisterous.

Their first party was a housewarming, and among the many invited and uninvited guests was Grete, a young woman somewhat older than Else and her opposite: tall and well-developed, with sleek, blond hair and strong, blue eyes. A thoroughly decent, beautiful person, Else thought; a fascinating woman, Grete thought about Else.

The house and the party were a great success. Else and Grete became fast friends. What they admired in each other was exactly what they themselves lacked, whether in the physical domain or in that of character.

Grete, conscientious, quiet, and capable, came from a family of Prussian high officials, and had many talents. She was a teacher at a school for girls: she could cook and bake, do acrobatics and swim, drive a nail into the wall and cut out a dress. Moreover, she lived alone in a small garret apartment.

Else was deeply impressed. Here she had met for the first time a woman who had made herself independent, and if necessary, could get along without any man. She found that very admirable, but could not imagine any case in which she would need to get along without a man. Grete, on the other hand, was deeply impressed by Else's lifestyle: a happily married woman with a bewitching son who lived entirely for love and the fine arts, played the piano and the violin, and maintained a large household. With Peter in his carriage, Else and Grete took long walks on which they conducted just as long existential conversations. They went to museums together, read plays out loud, taking the various roles in turn, listened to phonograph recordings of classical music. Grete taught Else to do gymnastics and to swim, Else cultivated Grete's conventional taste in music and literature. They called each other Hansel and Gretel, were one heart and one soul, and were a great mutual advantage to each other.

Fritz took a neutral attitude toward this friendship. Women sometimes needed the company of other women, and what the two of them did could do no harm. He found Grete very pretty, rather boring, but not disturbing. Grete paid no attention to Fritz. In time, that began to irritate him, and he paid more attention to her, to which she reacted only by blushing deeply.

One day he asked her if she found him so uninteresting. Grete replied that she'd never thought about it, and blushed right down to bottom of her modest V-shaped neckline.

The three of them often went together to the theater or to concerts, and once they even went into a music hall to dance. Fritz asked Grete to do the tango with him, and after she'd resisted a bit and Else had persuaded her, she followed Fritz onto the dance floor.

They danced, and Else looked on, smiling and happy. She was glad that her husband and her friend were establishing a somewhat warmer relationship with one another.

In the spring of 1918, the decisive battles began on the Western front. They continued into midsummer, and then the Allies made a breakthrough. The war was moving toward its end and thus toward Germany's defeat. The German army was still putting up a stubborn resistance on the Western front, but its allies had already capitulated. The country collapsed more quickly at home than on the battlefront. With the mutiny in the navy, the November Revolution broke out. The Kaiser abdicated and the Republic was established. On November 11 the armistice was signed with the Allies. Peace. And in Berlin, there were street battles, political murders, machine-gun fire, hunger rebellions, mutilated war veterans, down-at-the-heels unemployed men. Misery.

Only a politically adept person would have understood what was going on and what was at stake. Fritz and Else, their relatives and friends, had only a vague notion. They were people without history. Some of them lived in a solid bourgeois world and were loyal to the Kaiser, and then became conservatives. The others lived in the world of art and humanism and were nothing at all. For them, politics was banal and ugly, and they did not waste their time on it. The concept of socialism, which was usually confused with communism, frightened them. They knew industrialization and its bitter consequences, the starving proletariat living in tenements and hovels in back courtyards, only through the books of Gerhart Hauptmann and the drawings of Käthe Kollwitz, but that was literature and art. They did not see it with their own eyes. Similarly, Minna, Daniel, and their large families never set foot in the Scheunenviertel, a slum in central Berlin where eastern European Orthodox Jews led their ghetto life with their side-locks, shtreimels, and caftans, and were a disgrace for these other, assimilated Jews with German citizenship. They paid a certain attention to major political figures like Rosa Luxemburg and Karl Liebknecht, and were also enraged by their murder, but they quickly forgot them while listening to a symphony directed by Furtwängler or a performance of Max Reinhardt. They skipped over the political articles in the newspaper, and then gave close attention to the business section, while others turned to the art and literature pages. On the radio, they listened to music.

At that time, the world was still so overwhelmingly large and news coverage so narrow that people could be unaware even of what was happening in their own country. They were unaware of it so long that they became ignoramuses.

In Dahlem, the pastoral residential quarter far from the city center, people did not hear machine gun salvos, screams, explosions. The only time bomb ticking there was in the house of the young couple. But it was still ticking so softly that they could not hear it, could not defuse it, and so Fritz and Else lived in short-lived harmony.

Under the influence of his grandparents, Peter made rapid progress. He now ate only tender, white chicken breast, which Daniel and Minna bought at very untender black market prices. A little later he ate his chicken only if his grandfather put on a top hat, climbed to the top rung of a ladder, and sang a little song. His grandparents, who adored the little domestic tyrant, were prepared to do anything. Fritz laughed at his son's fancies, but Else found his misbehavior and caprices less amusing. Thus for example he coined the dictum: "Stand here forever," and in fact implemented it in the most impossible situations. "He wants to be different from other people under all circumstances," Else wrote in the little book. She didn't guess that he would be different throughout his lifetime.

I have a photo of her and Peter that dates from that year. She is slender and smiling, sitting on a chair in a richly decorated dress, with Peter, completely naked and his eyebrows raised, on her knee. He called her "dear Mummy," and then only "dear," while he called his father Pitt.

As I said, it was a harmonious life, and Else's only worry was Gretel. She had become peculiar, appeared less often, and when Fritz was at home, not at all. When she did visit, she was so distracted and dejected that one could no longer carry on a serious conversation with her or read plays out loud with her. When they listened to music together, she often broke into tears and violently rejected Else's attempts to console her.

One day, Else, her wisdom and patience at an end, asked Grete what in God's name was wrong with her. After all, they were the closest friends and confidants and had never kept secrets from one another. The way she was suddenly acting was hurtful, in fact almost cruel!

The independent Grete, who was blessed with so many admirable qualities, broke down and turned into a blubbering, wailing pile of misery.

She was suffering from phase of depression, she sobbed, as her mother did. A family curse! For months things went well, and then suddenly . . .

Else, shaken, wanted to take her in her arms, but Grete pushed her away and ran out of the house.

That evening she told Fritz what had happened. They now had to take special care of Gretel, she said, and pull her out of this condition. Perhaps all three of them could go on a picnic in the Grunewald the following Sunday or go back to the music hall to dance?

God save us, Fritz groaned, he had an aversion to hysterical women.

Else, left alone to deal with the delicate task of pulling her friend out of her depression, failed. Gretel's condition just worsened, and took increasingly irrational forms. Sometimes she seemed almost to hate Else, and then returned with flowers in her arms and tears in her eyes, and made convulsive professions of friendship and loyalty.

At the end of her rope, Else asked advice of her parents, who had a high opinion of the capable young teacher.

Daniel and Minna agreed that it was very sad, but certainly not surprising. A single woman had to go crazy sooner or later, and if Grete couldn't find a husband, she should return as soon as possible to her parents. A crying shame for such a good girl!

Then, suddenly, a turning point came. Not that everything was better afterward, but in any case it was more amusing. Gretel went wild, told frivolous stories, laughed a lot and shrilly, dressed provocatively, and was not interested in anything more than going to cafés with Else and there behaving, in the most embarrassingly unsuccessful way, as if she were a femme fatale.

She'd overcome her depression, she said, throwing back her head like a horse trying to shake off a fly. Now she wanted to live.

It was at this same time that Fritz brought an attractive young woman home and introduced her to his wife as the Baroness Eugenie von Liebig, a colleague of his at work. Eugenie, or Enie for short, had fiery red hair cut short, light, freckled skin, and dark salamander's eyes in which a tiny spark glimmered. She was as small and compact as Else, but less well padded, and therefore seemed more delicate.

She certainly has Jewish blood, this baroness, Else thought.

Enie remained for dinner, and the conversation was so easy, cheerful, and interesting that it was as if they had been attuned to each other for years. The two young women laughed at the same things, especially at the sparkling, droll Fritz, they loved or hated the same music, the same books, or theatrical performances, they despised petty bourgeois values and chauvinism, buttermilk and hiking, they had the same capacity for fascination when something pleased them, and the same strong reactions when something rubbed them the wrong way.

"You're really two chips off the same block," Fritz said at midnight, and walked his colleague home. Enie became a frequent visitor whom Else was always glad to see. Now, since there wasn't much to be done with Gretel, she needed a substitute and found it in the lively, intelligent baroness. However, her relationship to the baroness was not as harmonious as the one with the blond, unresisting teacher, who had venerated Else. Enie was critical, sharp-tongued, explosive, and although Else shared many qualities with her, she did not have her refinement and worldliness. They often argued and slammed doors on each other, and then reconciled a few days later, laughing and embracing each other.

Once Enie and Grete happened to meet in the house in Dahlem, and gave Else a grim hour. Grete, the epitome of inhibited high spirits, never ceased to chatter, squeal, and fidget; Enie, a model of haughty nobility, either observed her with silent disgust or humiliated her with a well-aimed biting remark. Else found both of them obnoxious and felt as if she were sitting on hot coals.

It was the teacher who quitted the field first. As she went out, she asked Else how she could let such a malicious person enter her home. She should realize that someday this criminal woman would bring a catastrophe upon her.

When Else returned to the room, the baroness asked how she could have such a witless biddy for a friend. She could take the next one straight from the loony bin.

Else explained that Gretel was unfortunately in an imbalanced phase, but she was normally an absolutely decent and good person.

Then, Enie said, long live indecent, wicked people! At least they remain balanced. And she broke into demonic laughter.

Enie was the daughter of a half-Jewish chemist who had received the title of baron as recompense for his achievements and a seamstress from Munich who worked in an elegant dress salon for ladies and was a beautiful, proud, strict woman. The couple was not married. The father lived in Berlin; Enie grew up with her mother in Munich and at the age of twelve entered a posh convent school. There she received a first-class, puritanical education, which she completed at the age of eighteen, when she was awarded her diploma. At this point the baron considered it appropriate to marry the seamstress and bequeath his name and title to his daughter. Enie moved with her mother to her father's home in Berlin.

Little Enie, who had no doubt suffered from her parents' unmarried state, her father's absence, her mother's strictness, and the lack of freedom and excessive piety in the convent school, suddenly became Baroness Eugenie von Liebig, who lived in a magnificent villa and was recognized and courted by people who used to treat her with disdain. But her past had left marks on Enie's character. The aggressiveness and lack of scruples with which she had earlier made her way, her craving for admiration and her distrustfulness, could no longer be extirpated and became increasingly visible as she grew older.

I knew her for some eighteen years, knew her very well, and she genuinely liked me for a certain time. As a child she found me badly brought up, unbearably so, and I feared her fits of rage, which were still more terrible than those of her friend Else. When I was a young woman who had just returned from emigration, she rightly reproached me for having left my mother in the lurch and no longer wanted to see me or hear from me. Then one day—I believe it was in the same year that I looked up the house in Dahlem—I stood before her garden gate in Wannsee, and when she spotted me there from her lounge chair, she leapt up, ran crying to me, and embraced me. "Else," she sobbed, "I thought it was Else standing there."

From that day on we were bound by a relationship that extended far beyond her joy at finding part of Else in me, and my joy in having found part of my mother in her. We were confidants and accomplices who told each other everything without reservation. Enie was then leading what was for her an unusual life, which she shared with her seventeen-year-old son, Michael, and three men: Fritz, her husband, for whom she now felt only loyalty mixed with contempt; Leon, a former miner and prisoner of war who had been living with her for years and had even been her support after the war, as her lover; and Wolfgang Jacobi, a wealthy, retired Jew with whom she went on luxurious journeys. All three of them loved her; she no longer loved anyone.

In the 1960s she moved for two years to a suburb of Munich, in order to be near her mother, who was then well over eighty years old and waiting for death in a convent. In the meantime, Fritz and Wolfgang Jacobi had died, Michael had moved to Switzerland, the property at 20a Am Kleinen Wannsee, where she had lived for over thirty years, had been sold, and Leon, who had remained behind, was living out in one room a sad existence that consisted chiefly of alcohol and cigarettes.

Enie lived in seclusion, with her books and her cocoa-colored poodle in a small apartment with some of the beautiful old Wannsee furniture, carpets, and pictures. We then saw each other regularly. On Saturdays I drove out there and stayed over Sunday. On these quiet weekends, which we spent in the deepest harmony, my mother was always present. Enie spoke very openly about her for hours, and one day she gave me two boxes with the writings my mother and my brother had left behind.

After old Frau von Liebig died, Enie returned to Wannsee, rented the ground floor of a stately villa with a large garden, and finally felt happy and at home again. She tried to establish a new, purely friendly relationship with Leon, but it just wouldn't work, because he loved her as much as ever and, full of alcohol and jealousy, provoked wild scenes. Three years later Enie was informed that the villa was to be torn down and an apartment house built to replace it. She refused to leave the apartment. Shortly before the bulldozers crashed into the garden, she swallowed thirty sleeping tablets and the contents of a bottle of champagne. Leon found her twelve hours later. She was taken to a hospital and lay in a coma for a week. When she awakened, the first word she said was "Shit!" Then she resumed her life.

She was seventy-one years old, had a small, wrinkled, lizardy face with dark, flashing salamander's eyes, false teeth, thin hair dyed fox-red, which she supplemented with a hairpiece, and spoke in a "turkey voice." She was plump, but had never become fat, wore clothes made in wonderful exotic fabrics by a seamstress, a fur-lined cloak, little caps and hats with veils, valuable old jewelry, delicate shoes with high heels, and the best French perfumes. Her elegance was unconventional and therefore perfect and inimitable. Then her aggressiveness and need for admiration reached its apogee. She fell out with the last of her longtime friends, and also with me, without my having understood what the problem was. She made heavy and pointless use of her father's name and title. At seventy-three, she set out on a trip around the world on a large freighter. The passengers and crew were fascinated by her personality, her vitality, and her charm. The bartender, a good-looking Italian, married and thirty years younger than she, fell in love with Enie, and she experienced her last great romance with him. He was, she told me, the only man who had ever made her happy in all respects. With Fritz it had been only her head and her heart, with Leon, only her body. Two years later she made another, no less successful trip around the world on the same freighter and with the same bartender. When she returned, she declared that her life as a woman was over. Decline set in promptly and inexorably. She, who up to that point had been bursting with health and intensity, ate, drank, and smoked unscathed, ran like a weasel, swam like an otter, and traveled like a girl, lost all her strength. New problems constantly arose, depressions that gave way to brief manic phases and turned her into a malicious poltergeist. Her son Michael tried to persuade her to come live with him, his wife, and his two daughters in Switzerland.

"That's all I need," she screamed. "Live with my son and his family in that dreadful Switzerland!" She hardly left her apartment, which she hated because it was in a bourgeois building with no garden. She read and listened to music on the radio. Leon, now really a true friend, took care of her.

I was then living in Paris, and we talked on the telephone at least once a week. I asked her to visit me. She loved Paris, the French, their cooking, and their language, which she spoke fluently. She said that Paris was for the living, among whom she no longer counted herself.

One night she called to tell me that she now had a hundred percent effective pill and planned to kill herself. She said that I, who had a "healthy" attitude toward suicide, was the only one with whom she could speak about it. I said she should wait at least until we had seen each other once more, and the next day I flew to Berlin.

I spent three days with her in Wannsee. She looked like a plucked little bird in a beautiful, exotic robe. She smelled like an open bottle of the finest perfume. She cooked my favorite dishes for me. We talked, drinking cognac and smoking cigarettes, late into the night. She was sparkling with charm, wit, and intelligence. She gave me a valuable pearl ring, long black-and-white kid gloves, laces and Indian kerchiefs that I still have. She made saying farewell as difficult as she could. She didn't kill herself. At Christmas she called me in an exuberant mood and told me that her son and his whole family were with her and that they were having a splendid day. Afterward her telephone calls, which came mainly at night, grew ever more bizarre. She began to insult and accuse me. I was, she said, treating her just as badly as I had treated her friend Else, my mother. She ordered me to give the pearl ring to my sister, who, as kind and disadvantaged as she had always been, deserved to have it. Her son, with whom I got in contact, received similar calls. He said that now nothing more could be done.

At the age of eighty she committed suicide in the most gruesome way. She stepped into a full bathtub with a plugged-in hairdryer.

I knew Else as a mother, and that I also came to know, understand, and love her as a woman I owe first of all to Enie, to her honesty and openness, and to the two jam-packed cartons that she handed over to me with the words: "Take that and make something out of it."

Nothing about Else remained hidden to Enie, neither her weaknesses nor her strengths, neither her highs nor her lows, neither her fears nor her passions, neither her fleeting affairs nor her serious love relationships. She shared her husband with her and lived under the same roof with her for two years. She hated and loved her, often fought with her and just as often showed her the most genuine friendship. For twenty years.

Thus I also learned from Enie about the tragedy that overwhelmed Else like an earthquake, shook to its foundations her life as a loving and beloved wife and mother, smashed her world-view, whose roots were still deeply anchored in Jewish tradition, and allowed her to rise from the ruins and ashes of her illusions only months later, as a fundamentally different woman.

"It was the hour of truth," Enie told me, "and it had to come sometime. But I wish for Else's sake that it had not come so suddenly and drastically, and I wish I had not behaved like a swine. But I've told you a hundred times: I'm a nasty person!"

In her little lizard-face, the regret that she was a nasty person gave way to the satisfaction of admitting it, and she continued: "I really don't know any more how the bomb was set off—perhaps Fritz had left one of my letters lying around, or something of the kind. In any case, there was plenty of fuel, and it's amazing that Else didn't smell fire much earlier. So one beautiful morning she burst into my office at the library, looking like a Fury, and screamed—and you know how she could scream!—that I was the most infamous, degenerate, deceitful creature in all God's world. I had treacherously crept into her home, she said, in order to catch Fritz, her husband and the father of her child and to lure him into an affair. I was so much taken by surprise and confused that I couldn't even deny what she said. So I adopted a commanding tone and reminded her that we were in a library, and ought perhaps to discuss the matter elsewhere, at another time, like civilized people. Was I to be counted among civilized people, she shouted even louder, I was nothing more than an unscrupulous, crafty slut and neither civilized nor a person, and her friend Grete, with her sharp intuition, had foreseen all this and warned her about me.

Had she not mentioned this Grete and her sharp intuition, who knows, I might have been able to continue to control myself. But that was simply too much for me. I blew up, and it was terrifying! I bellowed: Your good, decent Grete with her sharp intuition was my predecessor with your husband, and there were probably a couple of others in between. I lured your faithful husband into an affair, my ass! Don't make me laugh!

You know, Angeli, it still makes me sick to think about it. I knew how much she loved her Fritz and believed in her marriage. Really, she was convinced that she would remain with him and he with her, happily married, for all eternity. And then, from one moment to the next, she learned that her wonderful Fritz, for whom she would have done anything, constantly betrayed her, lied to her, and played her for a fool: with me, his platonic colleague at work, with Grete, her bosom friend who was certainly honorable, and with every Jane and Jill. Can you imagine what was going on in her? An earthquake that suddenly swept everything away. She looked so bad that I was afraid she would faint dead away. I rushed over to support her, to embrace her, to ask her forgiveness. But she held up both her arms . . . like this . . . and said: Don't touch me! I don't want any of you to ever touch me again! And then she left.

Enie was looking at me as if I were Else: tears in her eyes, her mouth trembling, her arms still outstretched. "I swear to you, Angeli," she said to me in a low, penetrating voice, "I already knew at that time that we would never again see the Else she had been up to that point."

The Kapp putsch that threatened to turn Berlin into a battlefield, the twenty-four hour general strike by the socialist labor movement, which turned it into a dead city, the galloping inflation, which people sought to keep up with by means of boxes full of worthless currency, and the unemployment that wound through the city in long gray lines of people, all these life-threatening storms that were battering Germany were already preparing the way for the coming disaster. That was the background against which Else's personal drama was played out.

At first, she was numb and incapable of clear thinking or unambiguous feeling. She was like a bird who has just escaped the fangs of a cat and, lamed by the shock, crouches motionless in one place instead of using its wings. She felt the pain like a muffled rumble, and knew that it would break out into raging torments as soon as she awoke from her numbed state. She wished she could sleep forever, never have to think about all that her husband and her friend had done to her.

Explaining that she thought she was coming down with the flu, she took Peter to her parents' home for a few days, walked for hours back and forth through the Grunewald, and finally sat down on a bench and stared blindly in front of her. A pair of lovers strolled by her, a microcosm of blessed togetherness in the hurtling universe. They stopped at a certain distance from her and kissed. Remembering the bliss of her own, lost microcosm, Else began to cry. Oh, the happiness that she had felt in those stolen hours in rain-drenched parks and stuffy confectioners' shops, her unshakeable belief in love, her trust in Pitt, the confidence that they could make their marriage something beautiful, great, and strong! And he, he had dragged everything through the dirt, had deceived, humiliated, shattered her in the most dreadful way.

Red-hot rage rose up in her, dried her tears in an instant, and drove her home. Fritz was working on his *Dionysian Joys*, a play he had been writing since he'd completed and published the Rilke book. Else, standing behind him in the doorway, said she had to speak with him.

Couldn't he at least finish writing this scene, he asked, irritated.

He could finish writing his scene when she had finished hers, she replied. Then he'd have more than enough time for that.

Surprised, he turned around to face her. Never had she spoken to him so harshly and sarcastically, not to mention insisting that he interrupt his work, on whatever ground. Her eyes were enormously large and dark, and her cold gaze was as disturbing as her voice.

Had something happened, he wanted to know.

In fact it has, she said, and watched his expression turn from uncertainty to apprehension, and from apprehension to terrible certainty.

Yes, she said, she knew everything. About his fling with Enie, his affair with Grete, and she didn't want to hear about all the others.

He'd gone green and pale, and his large, impressive nose protruded from his tense features even more prominently than before.

He could explain everything, he said, lit a cigarette with shaking hands, and began to pace up and down the room, preparing his defense.

She was eager to hear his explanation, Else said, and he'd better come up with something convincing.

He wasn't searching for ways to deceive her, Fritz replied, he just wanted to explain to her what went on in a man, an artist, an intellectual. An artist, an intellectual, wasn't a normal, average sort of person who could sit peacefully at home with his wife and child. He was a searcher, an uneasy, often tormented spirit who needed freedoms, stimulations, and impetuses that domestic life could hardly provide. He didn't mean by that that he did not value this domestic life with a beloved wife and a magnificent son—no, by God, that was the alpha and omega. But love couldn't be allowed to become a fetter, marriage a prison, otherwise he'd run the risk of losing his creativity.

Now, Else said, she finally had the answer to the question that she'd asked herself, with a reverent shudder, ever since her youth: what is it like to be an artist? What does he think? How does he live? So that was how he thought and lived, and she had actually imagined it rather differently, as something more spiritual, more metaphysical, and not focused on erotic adventures. To be precise, she no longer found his behavior so awesome, and in fact, if it was to cause her to suffer as well, she found it quite annoying.

Else fell silent, and Fritz, standing before her and taking her face in both hands, asked if she understood him.

She replied that she understood him, but if he'd told her all this before the wedding, she would also have realized that she couldn't marry him. Her conception of love and marriage was not at all an artistic one, but rather that of a normal, average woman who absolutely did not want to owe her husband's creative power to her women friends. So now he must decide: either Enie, Grete, Jane and Jill, or her.

He chose her, of course, Fritz insisted, because she was the only one he loved. The rest were sporadic adventures, and it would be positively ridiculous to think that they took anything away from her and affected his love for her, his marriage to her . . . On the contrary, they only strengthened his feeling for her and enriched their marriage by adding a third dimension to it.

That was too much for her, Else said, and she personally could and would live without the strengthening and enrichment.

She moved out of their shared bedroom, and Fritz began to fear the fetters of her love, the prison of his marriage.

The discovery of Fritz's infidelity had far-reaching consequences and led to much devastation. Fritz broke off his relationship with Enie, who was then found to have gotten pregnant at this most unfavorable of all times; Else broke off her relationship with Grete, who then had the long-impending nervous breakdown. The baroness and the teacher received medical treatment, the one to give birth to a child, the other to rid herself of feelings of guilt. Else, in order to think over the whole debacle in peace, traveled with her mother, her son, and her maid, Hedwig, to a spa near Heidelberg. Fritz, who had suddenly been relieved of a wife, two lovers, and one born and one unborn son, plunged into his *Dionysian Joys*. Perhaps that was why he wrote to Else, explaining how one could and must, even in her precarious case, overcome pain and achieve true joy.

She replied: "All this that you have thought up and demand of a woman is not possible for any real woman. It's admirable—

and yet: for me this moving beyond pain to joy, this final insight, has an unpleasant aftertaste. It is so lifeless, noble, and full of angelic goodness. You know I always find women of that kind a little appalling; that kind of thing doesn't suit me. When I think about such women, I always imagine them as being rather like Faust's Gretchen, looking vacantly up toward heaven . . . "

And a few lines farther on: "I believe that a woman, even if she is an artist, never has such an abundance of egoism as a man does, even if he is not an artist. For a woman, love always comes first, for a man, never—or only so long as he has not yet conquered the woman. That lies in the nature of things, and one has to come to terms with it or never let oneself be 'had,' at least not with body and soul. Well, all right, the next time!"

Mentally, Else had already made the leap, but not yet emotionally. Fritz's irresponsible behavior had destroyed her picture of the world forever and struck her a wound that would never completely heal. But her love lived on, and the thought of giving up the artist and the intellectual was harder than that of giving up the husband and beloved. Perhaps after this scare he would change, perhaps she would have the strength to live in accord with his ideas, perhaps she could love him, beyond herself and her needs. Yes, but perhaps he would never change and would make her desperately unhappy, perhaps a life in accord with his ideas, even if she adapted to it, would destroy her marriage, perhaps she should tell him to go to the devil.

She was in state of tormenting conflict, constantly swinging back and forth between apathetic depression and euphoric hope, between submission and rebellion. She feared the nights when she couldn't sleep, the eyes of her mother, who mustn't know how things stood with her and her marriage, the countless questions of her son, who stubbornly insisted on an answer. She had to feign cheerfulness and calm, and she found nothing more difficult than feigning. This dilemma caused her to have an attack of tonsillitis. Now she was officially allowed to feel badly, to be grouchy and impatient. Now Minna had an explanation for her daughter's erratic behavior, because for her, only what was visible was valid. She tucked Else into bed and immediately called the doctor. Fortunately, he was a Jew, a jovial fellow familiar with tonsillitis, and who joked with the mother and daughter for a long time, praised the books that Else had piled up on her night-table, and then prescribed "gargling water," aspirin, and Adalin to help her sleep.

Now everything fell into order. Else could sleep at night and think in peace about the future all day long—the future that would lie before with or without Fritz. Her mother treated her with cold compresses, chicken soup, and gargling water; Peter was allowed to come only as far as the bedroom door, for fear of contagion, and usually went for his walk with Hedwig; the jovial physician came every day, unsummoned, looked at her throat, said she was getting better, and chatted an hour with the mother and the daughter.

Else, pretending to be asleep, made her way bravely through the thicket of her changing thoughts and feelings, and one fine morning she found herself in a pristine clearing where everything was so bright and clear that she could not explain why she hadn't found the path there immediately. The path to forgiveness, the path beyond herself and her needs.

She got up, sat down at the table and wrote to Fritz in the exuberance of her newfound knowledge: "No, this will change nothing at all between us. My heart is big, and another new bit of love for you has come into it. I am afraid of nothing, nothing except the feeling that I'm hindering and restricting you, that you can't grow because of me. And please, don't keep silent about anything out of fear, out of sympathy, or out of convenience. Promise me you won't do that! When I see that it's not too serious, I'll soon get over it. I'm flexible, you know that, and not a person who passively gives in to sadness. I need happiness so much and never close myself to it . . . "

She felt as if she'd been reborn, but the doctor and the mother ordered another week of bed rest. A relapse must not be risked.

She lay comfortably on her soft, white cushions and read stories by Gogol, fairy tales by de Costa, and Flaubert's letters, which enchanted her.

"One always finds similarities between artists," she wrote to Fritz, "listen to what he says to his beloved: You need normal, desired things. You need proofs, facts. You love me enormously, very much, more than anyone has ever loved me or will love me; but you love me as another would love, with the same concern about secondary things and the same incessant miseries. Or: you complain so much about my morbid personality and my lack of devotion that I end up finding it grotesque; my selfishness simply doubles when it is constantly held before my eyes. Now, Pitt, aren't there some similarities there?"

Peter was allowed to come back into her room. He sat on the floor and played noisily with his blocks, or lay alongside her on the bed and asked questions, his eyebrows raised; the most interesting of these questions Else wrote down in the little red book:

"Mummy, how is a person created? Where did the first person come from? Where did God come from? Where do words come from? Where did language come from? How do people who have been buried get from the Earth to heaven? Mummy, why can't I be naughty, if God made me that way? Just think, Mummy, such a tiny little ant against the whole big world! How does it do that?"

Yes, how? And she, how did she do that? And Peter, how would he do it?

Else took him in her arms, her too handsome, too intelligent son, whom Fritz had produced and to whom she had given birth. She kissed him with wild tenderness.

"Mummy," he said, "I love you so much that I have to marry you. Then we will move into our house and live together, and Papa can find another woman."

Fritz's play, *Dionysian Joys*, was moving forward, and not only on paper. Else's letters, her desire to neither hinder nor restrict his creativity, lent him wings. He loved his wife and certainly did not want to lose her. However, he had never seriously thought that she could leave him. What he had feared was that she would make life miserable for him with jealous scenes, threats, rebellions, and resentments. He had not dared to consider too much the possibility that she might swing from one to the other, or that she might impose the fetters of love and the prison of marriage on him. On the one hand, he'd always thought her a clever, strong woman, but on the other hand he'd feared that she would not be able to tear herself away from the middle-class way of life that her milieu and her upbringing had implanted in her. That she had so suddenly and radically succeeded in doing so struck him as miraculous. He treasured and exploited this miracle, which made it possible for him to lead his life in his own way. For here was a young woman, pretty, innocent, and shy, who now kindled new impetuses in him and fueled his urge to conquest. She was not to be compared with that heavy lump Grete, who had burdened him with love corroded by guilt, and certainly not with the wild, demanding Enie, with whom he had, however, been in love, or rather, was still in love. She was plainly and simply a young woman who had steadfastly refused to become his lover, and thus attracted him.

Since Else had lifted the prohibition on telephoning, he called Enie often, and she was consistently affectionate, cheerful, and relaxed. So much that over time it began to wound him. She was behaving with him, he thought, as she would with a retarded child of whom she was especially fond because of his handicap. It annoyed and depressed him all the more when the young woman treated him increasingly as a dirty old man whose suspicious behavior had to be met with lips and thighs firmly closed. In his extremity and in accord with Else's urgent demand, he told her about his problems with the young woman and his suffering. She was not shocked by this revelation and offered him consolation and advice:

Oh, Pitt, what do you expect—and what a little boy and a great dreamer you are—you were like that at eighteen, and you'll still be like that when you're sixty. Always disappointed by women who don't correspond to your wishful image of them, and usually fall by the wayside on the way from pain to joy. Tell me, why are you laying all this on the poor girl? Why are you so impatient and turbulent and why do you want to have her body and soul right at the start? How importunate you'll become for her in the long run, if she doesn't truly love you. You can be borne only if one loves you, and with me you were just lucky. I accepted everything and absorbed everything and opened myself to you right away, but I also loved you. Don't think it always has to be that way. And please don't think that I'm hostile to this girl. She is certainly attractive, and I could surely like her very much, precisely because you like her. I'd like to get to know her, if she's willing. I'm taking a flying leap into the new order. This is not the first time and certainly won't be the last time . . .

There was no question that Else had changed. Whether the change was also connected with this period, or even compelled by it, and was playing a role in her life for the first and last time, or whether she really had already distanced herself so much from her husband's sexual adventures that she saw them less as dangerous than as ridiculous, is hard to say. I believe she still suffered more than she laughed, even if she was already like a snake shedding its skin: a few bits had already fallen away from her, but the rest still clung to her.

Fritz also seemed not yet entirely convinced that she had actually "moved from pain to joy and thus to the ultimate insight," because when Else suggested that he visit her, he found a meeting premature. Of course, he feared that her new frame of mind was not yet sufficiently established to withstand his presence, the physical proximity, the shared bed. But Else thought otherwise.

She wrote to him: "My love, you know what I would like to say to you: Oh, don't talk, don't talk so much nonsense, none of it is true! Letters are dreadful, written words are still more dangerous than spoken ones. They can't be denied, they stand there black on white and never go away. And I know you, you hothead. Always out with everything, and always radical, on top of the world and then down in the dumps. Essentially, you're almost as much a woman as I am. Or am I masculine? So now point by point: seeing each other again would be painful? No, it will be heavenly. You have become reasonable? No, you were never reasonable. You don't long for me? But you do, just as dreadfully as I do for you. My love, I'm not at all afraid, I just want to be together and laugh and at first not talk about anything important. I won't make it hard for you, I'm just happy that you're coming . . ."

When Fritz finally got up his courage and went to see Else, she kept the promises she'd made in her letters. She didn't make it hard for him, she didn't talk about anything important, and she laughed a great deal. So seeing each other was not painful. But it was not heavenly, either. Fritz, as Else had predicted, had not become reasonable, and cared more about the wife of a certain Herr Hecht than he did about his own. The little woman, as he called her, or the Hecht woman, as Else called her, was vacationing without her husband and had succumbed to the poet's charm on the spot. Fritz couldn't for the life of him see what there was about her that appealed to him, but her admiration and infatuation were enough to amuse him.

Outwardly, Else did not seem annoyed. Fritz and the Hecht woman could have their silly sentimentality. But she was certainly bitterly disappointed.

She'd wanted to celebrate this meeting, which was so significant for her: saying farewell to her dollhouse world; forgiving his disgraceful act as a husband, and recognizing his rights as an artist and an intellectual; the beginning of a new phase in life, to which she'd fought her way through pain and despair, to the insight that a woman's love is more altruistic, and that men are selfish by nature, and that one has to simply accept that.

She hadn't said this to him in so many words, she'd tried to make him feel it through passionate nights and tender days, through gay laughter and indulgent smiles. And he came, a distracted, charming, irresistible poet, not at all changed, and caught a Hecht woman in his web. It wasn't the flirtation with the little, insignificant woman that hurt her, it was the banality of the situation, in which the husband didn't give a damn what had happened and might continue to happen to his wife. It was the arrogance of a man who was so sure of a woman's love that he didn't think it worth the effort to consider her. And that was the moment at which Fritz lost his wife.

Neither he nor she knew that. Her behavior toward him did not change, but her behavior with regard to life changed mightily. She now had to live up to the words she'd written to him in her first letter, after the "ultimate insight": "I'm flexible and not a person who passively gives in to sadness. I need happiness so much and never close myself to it . . . " If she was not to be granted happiness at the side of her husband, then she must and would find it elsewhere.

Three days later, Fritz went back to Berlin, and Else began life without him. The first step was to cut off the long thick braids, the last, outward relic of the good Jewish girl, and replace them with a short, bushy cut. Next she bought a fash-

ionable cigarette holder and learned to smoke. Then she pow-
dered her face and put on a bit of lipstick. She looked at herself in the mirror, the cigarette holder in her hand. She was
twenty-seven years old, had lost a few pounds from worry and
tonsillitis, and her new attitude toward life made her more
seductive.

"You'll laugh at me, my love," she wrote to Fritz, "I'm just
letting you know that the men here are courting me very assid-
uously. They all find me very pretty, and I am, too. Yesterday
we danced until midnight, and I could have danced until five
o'clock. It was heavenly!"

A man turned up—a poet, naturally—who reminded her in
many ways of Fritz, and thus fulfilled the most important pre-
conditions. However, he was also, as she wrote to her husband,
a man she could trust. What strikes me as remarkable is that in
five years of marriage, he was the first man for whom she had
had more than a purely friendly inclination, and perhaps even
granted a few kisses and promises.

Her letters to Fritz grew steadily lighter and more ironic,
and hardly ever touched on the subject of their life together.
About her admirer, who had in the meantime left, she wrote:
"Today I have received another letter from my poet, with photographs, this time showing his face. It's still not the answer to
my letter. That one will probably contain ten photos and
twenty pages. But I was pleased, very pleased, and the picture
is pretty . . ."

Or regarding the "little woman": "I believe the Hecht
woman is longing for you, she looks pretty bad. She asked
whether you're coming back. I said no, and she replied: 'What
a shame! But there's nothing to be done there anyway, your
husband is such a serious person and certainly faithful to you.'
She really knows you very well, my love. Should I tell her the
truth?"

And when Daniel Kirschner visited his wife, daughter and

grandson one weekend and took them to Baden-Baden, she reported: "Baden-Baden is a very beautiful place, so elegant. One has everything, tennis courts and a swimming pool, dancing and theater. I think I'd like to spend a few weeks there and at the same time I'm not sure I'd really want to do that. It's ultimately very superficial, isn't it? But that's how it is, unfortunately—I find solitude stimulating, and I'm also stimulated by the easy life with lots of gaiety and lots of clothes. My sole consolation is that I got bored after two weeks. Father enjoyed it all very much, but Mother observed dryly that she could live without such fuss and bother, strangers meant nothing to her, and she felt most comfortable at home with her family. Sometimes I wish I were like Mother, she never has the feeling that she's missing something, and I have it so often and so painfully."

New tones, new self-knowledge, new temptations. Would they have never emerged had Fritz behaved differently? Would she really have remained all her life a loving, faithful wife entirely devoted to her husband and children? Wouldn't she, the woman hungry for life, curious, capable of enjoyment and enthusiasm, have been tempted by something else, seduced and thrown out of her traditional role?

I will never receive an answer to these questions, and even my mother, who asked them ever more urgently as she grew older and more miserable, seems not to have found an answer. But then, after the collapse of her marriage, which she still did not recognize as such, she didn't ask any questions. She began to drift, following only the pull of happiness.

After being away for four weeks, Else returned to Fritz in the Dahlem house. Joy and concord seemed to prevail. The two nameless ones, the trustworthy poet and the rebellious young woman, were recognized as unproductive and summarily dismissed. Fritz had become more domestic and easy to get along with, Else had become more self-confident and independent. She no longer took her husband so seriously, was less awed by his artistic gifts, and was indifferent to his human weaknesses. Her life no longer belonged to him, she'd cut off a large part of it for herself.

She often went out alone, met relatives and acquaintances, strolled along the Kurfürstendamm in the afternoon, went to the theater and concerts, and had neither time nor inclination for Fritz. In all these undertakings she missed her friend Grete and recognized, to her surprise, that what was past no longer hurt her and that she felt no resentment toward her husband's former lover. "To err is human," and Else now had a great deal of insight into human weaknesses. She called Grete. The two women met in the Grunewald, walked arm in arm through an autumn idyll and carried on a long, serious conversation about the complex relations between men and women. Their friendship had overcome the pitfalls of love, and they let Fritz know it with little pokes in the ribs.

If that's how it is, he said to himself, then maybe the group can be enlarged to include the second lover.

He saw Enie every day in the library, and had, after a long period in which she treated him with acid contempt, gained ground again, centimeter by centimeter. It had cost him an enormous amount of charm and intellect, arts of persuasion and protestations of love, but now the ice was broken and the wild little baroness had been tamed. Just as friendship between Else and Grete bloomed anew, so it did between Fritz and Enie.

Else was well aware that Fritz and Enie met at the library, but she had never asked him about it. She didn't want to know anything about it. In this case, the past still hurt, because Enie was something entirely different from Grete. She was not a good-hearted person, not a true friend, she was a dangerous rival who had not hesitated to cut the ground out from under her, Else, and who would not hesitate to take her husband away from her. Else was thus unpleasantly surprised when Enie's name suddenly reappeared in Fritz's vocabulary. Enie, he said, whom he met now and then in the library, had invited them both to a private ball. Wouldn't she like to go? It would surely be a nice party.

Else always wanted to go to nice parties, and because there was in any case nothing to prevent Fritz and Enie from meeting from time to time in the library, and probably not only there, it was perhaps advisable to remember this serpent and appear at her husband's side.

They went together to the ball, Fritz in a tuxedo, Else in an evening gown. It was the prelude to a period that lasted for three years and whose end Else considered a fiasco. Fritz owed to this era his great success as a writer, a comedy that is still performed in boulevard theaters under the title *Margherite and Her Three Uncles*. Else drafted an enlightening libretto on the same subject. When I was seventeen, my sister Bettina and I found this libretto in a box full of books, letters, and documents.

That was in Sofia, shortly after the end of the war. Our mother was taking her afternoon nap in our only bedroom, which I shared with her, and Bettina, who had long been married, had come by for a short visit. We had gone out to the roofed veranda that we used as a storage space, and out of sheer boredom opened the box and poked around in it. There I found a very ordinary writing tablet that had been completely filled with our mother's hasty scribbling.

"Mama wrote a libretto," I said. "We have to read it!"

How exactly I remember all that: the oppressive humidity of the afternoon, the buzzing of countless flies, Bettina's dress, which she had had made out of a blue-and-white checkered eiderdown cover. I sat on a chair and she sat behind me on the edge of the box and read over my shoulder. We giggled. How strange that Mama had thought all that up! But then, with the progress of the action, which she had divided up into tableaus, I began to feel uneasy. The characters struck me as all too familiar, and if they were taken from life, why should their behavior, which I found extremely embarrassing, have been invented?

We came to the twenty-second tableau, which concerned a private ball. She wrote, without making an effort to find appropriate words or even a particular style:

"Festive, bright, an orchestra, many flowers. Elegant young people dance, sit at small tables, drink, laugh, Friedel (Fritz) and Esther (Else) enter. Eva (Enie) runs to meet her, shakes Friedel's hand with a telling smile, greets Esther politely. Eva follows in her wake, turns delicately this way and that, flirts, beams, displays herself. Dances flamboyantly. Esther talks with Eva's parents. Fearful and unsure of herself, she constantly looks over at Friedel. He goes up to Eva, speaks to her, and dances exuberantly with her. People wag their fingers at him. Groups stop and watch Friedel and Eva, whisper, murmur, laugh. Esther stands awkwardly in a corner, her eyes fixed on Friedel. Helmut, a friend of the house, asks Esther to dance with him. He dances wonderfully. Esther wakes up, her movements become lively, her eyes sparkle. Now and then she looks over at Friedel, who is now sulking on a sofa with Eva. Eva's face becomes angry and mocking. Esther is about to seduce one of her friends, and that was not what she had in mind. Old ladies and gentlemen, sitting together and watching what is going on, shake their heads indignantly at Esther's and Helmut's uninhibited dancing. Helmut leads Esther to a chair. Bending over her, he asks her if he might see her again."

At this point I threw the tablet back into the box. "Such nonsense," I said, "it's totally boring."

Bettina, laughing, agreed with me, and said: "Our mother always did have a fertile imagination."

Suddenly it was all clear to me, clearer than I wanted it to be, and I had realized that in the next scene a revelation was going to be made that might have caused even the trusting Bettina to have doubts. Where did this intuition come from, since apart from a few anecdotes about her childhood, I'd never heard anything about my mother's earlier life or about the wonderful dancer Helmut, whose real name was Hans? I don't know. Twenty-five years later my sister said to me: "I was always the naïve country girl, but you—you'd already known for a long time, hadn't you?"

After the ball and its unpleasant revelations—for Else her husband's relapse into his affair with Enie, for Fritz his wife's obvious readiness to deceive him with another man—it was Fritz who tried to save their marriage.

Else's transformation into a confident woman who granted him, the husband, artist, and intellectual, the freedoms he needed for his creativity—that was one thing, and it was welcome, but that this transformation should go so far that she, the wife, mother, and normal, average person, also thought of taking advantage of it—that was quite another, and it was unacceptable. He had not reckoned with that possibility, could not have reckoned with it, since he'd never doubted that she loved him as only a woman could, strongly, loyally, in a down-to-earth and modest way. Not that he doubted her love now, after a night of provocative dancing with a ridiculous beau; no, he continued to be confident of his superiority, but it wouldn't hurt to be a little careful. He'd never seen Else so wild, and at that in the arms of man whom she didn't know and who shamelessly displayed his steadily increasing infatuation and desire for her. Naturally, it was a kind of revenge on her part, an understandable reaction to his recent lapse, a way of showing him: what you can do, I can do too. But he was not a writer for nothing! He knew that a woman's acts of revenge were never very inventive, and that for the most part they threw themselves into the bed of a man whose interest in them was proportional to their husband's neglect. And he also knew that he had devoted himself more to his sporadic adventures than to her. That had to stop, because it was clear to him that she was more important than his little affairs, more important even than the great romance with Enie. On the basis of these reflections he decided to take a position as literary editor that he had recently been offered by a large newspaper in Breslau. He would leave all the temptations of Berlin behind him and begin a new, more responsible married life in Breslau. He detested the provinces, but that was the sacrifice he was making for Else, and it would prove that she was more important to him than anything.

Else was decidedly startled by his sacrifice and the proof of her importance, but not, as he had expected, in a positive way. She found the idea of moving to Breslau simply appalling.

She loved Berlin, she shouted, Dahlem, her house, her life, her friends here.

He did too, he said, but that was precisely the sacrifice he was making.

She'd never asked him to make a sacrifice, she replied, and especially not one that would cause her more suffering than it did him. He would at least have his work there, and he would soon have a Breslau girl, whereas she would have only the Oder River into which to throw herself.

Was Berlin more important to her than he and their marriage were? he asked. She was not afraid to reflect for a moment, and then she said: If there was a compelling reason for having to choose between him and Berlin, she would naturally choose him. But there was no such reason, and therefore she did not understand why they should make themselves miserable.

Wouldn't a new beginning for their marriage be a compelling reason? Didn't happiness about that outweigh the unhappiness of living in the provinces?

She said she didn't think it was moving to another place that was decisive for the success of a marriage, but rather one's inward attitude. The causes of a problem had to be eliminated, not its symptoms.

So she was refusing to try it with him in Breslau?

They could try it if he saw in it his and her salvation.

Offended, Fritz said that earlier, she would have been happy to go to Siberia with him.

Yes, earlier . . . Else replied sadly.

Fritz recognized that a move and a new start were much more urgent than he had thought, and went to Breslau for a trial period.

She wrote to him: "Little Pitt, it's still not better. It's pouring, snow fell last night, and now it's all thawing. The trams can no longer make their way through the sludge, Peter has a cough, and the telephone is out. Very nice! Inside me it looks no better than outside on Berlin's streets. Sludgy. The day has no high point, everything equally boring. And anyway . . . Well, I always have the violin and books. I'm reading Renoir, Spengler, Otto Braun, all the books that we ordered. Oh, Pitt, we could have had such a good life. We had so much: a sweet son, a fine house, friends, music, theater . . . but '*tu l'as voulu, George Dandin.*' Now we have Breslau."

Thus she'd chosen Fritz, but without a spark of joy, without the belief or even the hope that life in the provinces could save their marriage. How could it? How did Fritz imagine it? Was he thinking that they would suddenly start leading a life turned away from the world and inward, toward their "home, sweet home?" He, the good husband and father who went to the editorial office early in the morning and came home punctually at five? She, the busy wife and mother, who spent her days doing housework and raising children? Evenings on which they sat—hand in hand—beside each other, reading, nights in which they lay—head to head—alongside each other, happily, Sundays on which they, with Peter between them, walked along the Oder or made a little excursion into the countryside? He, the artist and intellectual, who needed the stimulations and impetuses that a domestic existence could not provide; she, although a normal, average person, a woman who suffered painfully from the fear of missing out on something; Peter, who was so attached to his grandparents that a separation from them would have unimaginable consequences.

It just made no sense. First, Fritz had staked everything on teaching her, a good middle-class girl, that love didn't have to be a fetter or marriage a prison, and then, although in the meantime she'd fought her way from pain to joy and thus to the ultimate insight, he tried to reverse course and exile her to the provinces and the domestic hearth. He'd deliberately destroyed her most sacred principles, and now he wanted to revive them in Breslau. A crazy idea, but since for him there was no question of their separating, she found herself forced to follow him.

She had not seen the marvelous dancer again, but he had awakened wishes and desires in her that she could no longer silence. She had danced with him during sleepless nights and bleak hours, nestled in his arms and against his body, and felt a glowing sun rise within her. What atavistic fears had prevented her from taking the final step into the wide, free world? Had she lost her chance forever? Would she never see him again? She found that idea heartbreaking.

And then, a few weeks before the new start in Breslau, fate gave her another chance.

"Guess whom I ran into on Unter den Linden," she wrote to Fritz. "It's not so hard to guess: your red fox, little Enie. We greeted each other and then had a civilized conversation. However, I had to filter out the slightly prickly, acid tone that had lodged in her voice when she talked to me. Astonishing, that it has persisted after so many months. Today I sent her a letter asking if she would like to go with me to the Reimann Ball at the Academy of Arts. We'd talked about it, and when I told her that I could get tickets cheaper, her eyes became very hungry. I also wrote to Herr Huber and asked him if he would like to come along. You remember Herr Huber, he's the handsome man I constantly danced with at Enie's fatal ball. You didn't like that, and you promptly declared that the man was as boring as he was handsome. Now what if I were to say that about your little girl! As usual, up to now he hasn't called. Either the red fox, who can't bear it when a man in her circle takes an interest in another woman, has worked against it, or the telephone was already out when he tried to call. It doesn't matter! But I'm curious to see whether I'll meet him 'accidentally' at the ball."

They danced through a second night, the pretty, petite lady of the harem, Else, and the tall, handsome Spaniard, Hans. They danced in a dream world of fairy-tale decorations, dazzling lights, bizarre, fantastic figures, and sweet music. Else nestled in the arms and against the body of the marvelous dancer, and the sun glowing within her never set. They drank champagne, clinked their glasses, and looked into each other's melting eyes. They kissed in the secluded corridors and reeled under the attack of an untamable passion.

It was one of those nights to which one turns back later on, when everything is over, with wistful longing for the ecstasy of love and with embarrassment about the cause of this ecstasy.

Hans went home with Else in the early morning hours. It was January, and Berlin had decorated itself with snow—a white, virginal bride. They didn't feel cold or tired, they were sleepwalking in a silent, glistening fairy-tale world.

Dahlem was asleep. The house was asleep. Peter and the maid, Frieda, were asleep. Hans followed Else up the path from the garden gate to the front door, from the entry hall into the living room, from the bedroom door to the bed. Then she followed the last bit of the way into the wide, free world.

I know little about Hans Huber. First nothing was said about him, and then he was dead. He must have died relatively young, but even Enie, the only one who told me about him, didn't know the cause. She'd already broken off her relationship with him in the late 1920s, when he joined the National Socialist party.

Hans Huber was the son of the standing Bavarian minister of agriculture, and came from a wealthy, long-established Munich family. After the war, in which he had bravely spent three years at the front, he went to Berlin, in order to study law there.

Enie, enraged by his political views, had torn up letters and pictures of him, but one "historical" picture, as she called it, still existed. In it one saw three men, arm in arm. The first was smiling ironically, the second manfully, the third absently: Fritz, Hans, and Erich, in highly questionable harmony. The manfully smiling one in the middle was Hans, and so far as one could tell from the small, faded photo, he was an attractive man.

In the draft of her libretto, Else describes him as tall, dark-haired, passionate, very good-looking, wonderfully developed. In terms of character, straightforward, honest, stable, thoroughly decent, primitive in thinking and feeling, steadfast in his love.

Enie's description of him was limited to one sentence: "He was dumb as an ox and became a Nazi big shot."

There is nothing to add to the two women's account. Except perhaps my hunch that of the three men he was probably the one my mother really loved.

Fritz, following his sixth sense, soon returned for a weekend in Berlin. He had a bad feeling. Else's letters had grown steadily shorter and less informative, and he'd not been able to reach her by telephone.

She received him in an affectionate, noncommittal way, rather as the owner of a pension receives a guest whose room is not yet vacant.

Her joy was overwhelming, Fritz said. Did he already smell so much like Breslau that she couldn't approach him?

She laughed, gave him a light kiss, and solemnly declared that she was always glad to see him, nothing had changed in that regard, and would not—ever!

Her soft kiss and her meaningfully pronounced words had ominous overtones. Fritz scrutinized her. She was wearing a simple black dress with long sleeves and a white piqué collar. Her face, with its smooth olive-colored skin, high, almost lashless eyelids, and delicate mouth reminded him of an icon of the Madonna.

The new dress was very becoming, he told her.

The new dress was three years old, she replied.

This was a marvelously farcical dialogue, he grumbled. Where was Peter?

He had decided to spend a few days with his grandparents.

She had made a fire in the fireplace and put a bottle of wine of the table. For Fritz, the wine had a still more ominous overtone than her greeting. Else cared nothing for alcohol of any kind, and drank it only in small quantities on very special occasions.

His absence had worked wonders, Fritz said, now she was even drinking wine.

Yes, now and then. She had acquired a taste for it, and besides, they could talk better over a bottle of wine.

Fritz was getting impatient. The situation really had a hell of a lot in common with a mediocre boulevard play. She should skip the preliminaries, he said, and tell him loud and clear what was going on. He was neither naïve nor unsophisticated nor senile, and he had sensed all along what would happen. She had decided not to move to Breslau, that was probably it.

That's part of it, Else said amiably, and the other part was: she had fallen in love with a man and was having a sporadic adventure—as Fritz would call it. Loud and clear, that was it.

Fritz felt himself pale, inwardly and outwardly. For him, Else was like the sun, the center of his life, bright, warm, and energizing. She followed her course, she rose, she set, she was hidden behind the clouds, but she was always there. Suddenly in her place there was a black hole, a terrible void, into which he would be sucked.

Else had expected hurt pride, protest, bitter words, but not the genuine pain that she now saw in his face.

She went to him, put her arms around his neck, and pressed her cheek to his.

It wasn't so bad, she told him, and moreover, it would spare him Breslau.

It would spare *her* Breslau, why *him*?

It would spare them both Breslau, since he probably wouldn't want to stay there without her.

Instead of where?

Here, of course, in Berlin, at her home.

He would have to think that over first.

During his sporadic adventures he had obviously never had to think about that.

Who was this man, anyway, Fritz said, changing the subject. Did he know him?

It's Hans Huber.

Now he really had to think about it.

Why was he making such a problem out of this, Else asked. She loved him, Fritz, and he loved her, and after all, nothing else really mattered.

Fritz returned to Berlin. She made it as easy and pleasant for him as she could, spared him meeting Hans Huber, but insisted on separate bedrooms. He was deeply depressed. His play, the *Dionysian Joys*, had been rejected, he felt unappreciated, scorned, abandoned, and Else, as affectionate and discreet as she was, glowed from within. His wife's inner glow got on his nerves terribly, and constantly reminded him that its cause was not him but a ridiculous beau with a lot of body and not much brain. He had now known Else for eight years, knew the little Jewish girl, the recklessly loving woman who had become a mature and wise partner, but he really didn't know the adulteress who struck him with his own weapons and did not even take the trouble to conceal her infidelity. And since he was concerned only with himself and had not realized that Else's metamorphosis from a larva into a butterfly had taken place slowly and painfully, he found himself confronted by a riddle. He no longer knew how he should behave toward this unknown person, how he should deal with her. It seemed to him that she grew stronger every day, as he grew proportionately lamer and weaker. He was not a fighter, a powerful person who lived from his gut. He was an aesthete, a pure intellectual, and he was a wimp. He submissively let Else take the reins from his hand.

She saw how unhappy he was, and that pained her. Now that she had welcomed his having a little or a big love affair with someone else, anyone, he didn't seize the opportunity. In the morning he went to the library, where he'd resumed his work, and returned punctually in the afternoon. He spent most of his evenings at home, sat in a chair, read and smoked, and no longer wrote a single line. When she went out and said good-bye to him, he looked at her mutely with veiled eyes. His face had become narrow and pointed, and his nose seemed all the larger. He looked like an oversized bird with broken wings. She stroked his head and told him that she loved him. He nodded and kissed her hand.

Else, caught between a husband who needed consolation and a madly jealous lover, ended up in difficulties. The situation was unpleasant, so she decided to quickly find a better, more satisfactory solution. And it would be found only in a woman who reestablished the balance between her fulfilling love life and Fritz's dull one. Irresistible poets have never lacked for women of this kind, and if, for unfathomable reasons, he was now making no effort to find one, then she would do it for him.

She arranged a little party with a lot of wine, music, and parlor games. She invited Enie, Grete, and the most attractive women among her acquaintances. She invited Hans Huber.

They were now all supposed to act like adult, intelligent people for once, she said to Fritz, and as such tolerate one another.

It worked. Enie looked ravishing, and Else let her take priority, saw to it that she was always at the center of things. To her relief she didn't have to blow on the embers very long before they began to crackle, flicker, and then blaze.

The guests left in the early hours of the morning, and Hans and Enie remained. They simply couldn't separate, they loved each other. Not only the two couples, but also the two men and the two women. They lay by turns in each other's arms, danced, kissed, and drank to each other:

"To love!" Else cried.

"To life!" Enie cried.

"To friendship!" Hans cried.

"To Else," Fritz said.

They threw the glasses against the wall.

Fritz sat down at the piano and played the Rosenkavalier waltz. Enie sat beside him, as Else once had, and looked at him, enchanted. Else lay in Hans's arms and smiled at a distant memory. She'd come a long way.

It was beginning to get light. A clear morning, which bore

within it the first promises of spring. A still, peaceful morning in which, until the city woke, hope slumbered. A new day was born and still lay whole and innocent before them. No, they could not separate. And why should they? The house was so big and their love, their friendship, were no smaller.

From then on they were a four-leaf clover, and in general that brings luck.

Enie left her parents' house, Hans Huber his small apartment. There was ample space in the Dahlem house, and if the Kirschners hadn't foreseen its use for this specific purpose, at the proper time they would see that the house could be used to accommodate dear friends. But the proper time had not yet come. First they had to settle in, sniff out, determine whether the morning pregnant with hope that had brought them together would keep its promise.

Until then, Peter, on some pretext, had to be left with his grandparents, and the grandparents kept in the dark. But certainly not for long, because life as a foursome was shaping up well.

With the prevailing balance, Fritz's depression, Hans's jealousy, and Enie's prickliness had disappeared, and Else was delighted by the enrichment that the two new residents of the house brought to their everyday life. Fritz recognized that Hans was not merely a ridiculous beau with a lot of body and not much brain, but rather a person whose generosity, openness, and honesty were impressive, and even sometimes put him, Fritz, to shame, while Hans ungrudgingly admired Fritz's intelligence, wit, and knowledge. As for the two women, they had fallen entirely under the spell of their respective loves and helped each other in a sisterly way. Moreover, the household now functioned much better, because Hans was a practical-minded man who could hang a picture and repair a wobbly chair, and Enie was a talented cook, who could make tasty meals that cost little and even knew how to manage large groups swiftly and skillfully. Nothing could now really go wrong, and on that optimistic assumption, Peter was brought home.

He found the new arrangement very amusing, and immediately figured out that he mustn't go too far with the aunt, and that he could do anything with the uncle. He found the latter much nicer than his father, who had never played so well with him and had always given him only distracted answers. With Uncle Hans he could frolic, gallop piggyback through the streets, travel on the U- and S-Bahn, eat ice cream, annoy people; and if he asked a hundred questions, he got a hundred nearly satisfactory answers.

"Uncle Hans, are you Mama's new husband, and is Aunt Enie Papa's new wife?"

"No, Peterkin, your mama and your papa are man and wife and Aunt Enie and I are their friends."

"Do you all sleep in the same bed?"

"Good heavens, child, how did you get that idea? We've never slept in the same bed, each of us sleeps in his own bed."

Peter told his grandparents what he had learned, and they could not understand it and called Else. The child was once again completely overexcited, they said, and was imagining some crazy business about new uncles and aunts and sleeping in the same beds. How did he get that idea?

A clarification could no longer be avoided.

Daniel and Minna were invited to dinner. They came with a pot of goose giblets and dozens of shortbread crepes. Else introduced her and Fritz's best friends: the enchanting baroness and the splendid son of a Bavarian minister.

"Delighted," the Kirschners said, and they were.

It was a successful evening. The baroness had prepared an exceptional dinner, and, to Minna's amusement, announced that it was kosher. The minister's son pleasantly surprised Daniel by asking many serious questions about the morals, customs, and laws of Judaism. Else and Fritz seemed happier and more intimately connected than ever before. There was absolutely no reason for concern. At some point, the fact that for the time being Hans and Enie were living in the Dahlem house was woven into the conversation. A temporary financial lull, such as unfortunately occurred in noble and ministerial circles as well.

Daniel and Minna nodded sympathetically: yes, of course, the war had put many people in difficulty.

When the Kirschners, full of praise for the splendid evening, had left, the remaining four were a little embarrassed, agreeing that they were nice people and lamenting that they had to deceive them this way.

Unfortunately, it's not the first time, Else said, and it may not be the last, Fritz added, to Hans's displeasure.

The first troubles, which very quickly grew into upheavals, occurred only a short time later. Enie, her eyes blazing and her head drawn in as if she were still in the midst of the event, told me:

"Quarrels and turmoil over nothing at all, again and again! It was unbearable! Hans asked Fritz to buy a screwdriver, and he forgot to do it, I looked all over for my comb and found it on Else's night table, and then we had terrific fights. Completely crazy, and naturally these were only safety valves that provided an outlet for the anger that was raging inside us for entirely different reasons, at least in Hans and me. We loved more than they did, and were therefore weaker. Hans idolized Else and I idolized Fritz, and we had only one wish: to get rid of the others and have our idols all to ourselves. But Fritz did not want to marry me, and Else did not want to marry Hans. They were not even thinking of that. Else already knew that her straightforward, kind Hans, her German oak, would some-day get on her nerves, and Fritz basically wanted just to be left in peace. Besides, Else and Fritz were still one heart and soul, even if they no longer slept together. And then there was their son and their common past—he was her first love, and she was his, and so forth. Hans and I sensed that, of course, and we felt . . . how should I put it . . . well, somehow humiliated. I was the mistress, Hans the lover, and when the excitement was over, it would all be over, and Fritz and Else would get together again. And that certainly would have happened, had Erich not entered this muddle and remained caught there like a fly in a spiderweb. Else didn't give a damn what damage she did so long as she had her pleasure. Without concern for the losses—Hans, Fritz, Peter, me, her parents . . . and then there was also the baby!"

In September 1921, Else realized that she was pregnant. Uh-oh, once again at such a bad time!

To think things through she went for a walk in the Grunewald, as she always did when there was a crisis. She walked and thought, but no inspiration came to her. She knew only what she would not do: she would not get divorced, she would not marry Hans, and she would not have an abortion. Everything else she could handle, and when she'd come to this conclusion, she gave herself up to the joy of being pregnant. How delightful to feel a child growing within her again, to experience the act of giving birth, to hold a warm, wonderful little creature in her arms, to quiet it, kiss it, lick it, to see it become a little person. No one could deny her that happiness or spoil it.

For weeks, she kept her condition secret in order to enjoy it in peace, because she knew that when she revealed it she would provoke storms that would require all her fortitude and willpower. Only in December, perhaps in the hope that the Christmas season would produce a gentler, more benign mood, did she announce the good news, and thus destroyed peace in the Dahlem villa once and for all.

At first, Hans was delighted, and convinced that Else would now marry him. Fritz was upset, and thought that Else had finally gone too far. Then Hans demanded that Else get a divorce, and Fritz demanded that she terminate her pregnancy. Thereupon Hans called Fritz a criminal who wanted to murder a child, and Fritz called Hans a scoundrel who had gotten Else into this situation with criminal thoughtlessness and devious motives. Hans declared that if Fritz didn't like the situation, he could leave the house, and Fritz indignantly replied that it was his house, and if anyone was going to leave it would be Hans.

Else—who had remained neutral up to that point and had tried to appease the men with such lapidary phrases as: we'll see . . . we mustn't make any hasty decisions here . . . —lost her composure for the first time and shouted that they should both leave the house. They were swearing at each other like peasants and wanted to decide without consulting her what should happen to her and her child. She, Else, was the only one who had the right to make decisions about herself and her child. Basta.

In that case, Fritz said bitterly, she might, at least in the name of friendship, take both her husband and child's father into account. Or was there perhaps still some doubt about that?

No, replied Else, whom anger at the two men had given the necessary courage, there was none. She would kill neither her child nor her parents, and that meant that there was no question of either an abortion or a divorce.

Was the poor little thing to be a bastard? Fritz asked.

Certainly not, she replied coldly. She was, after all, still married. Hans and Fritz looked at each other, silent and bewildered, and Else, who saw that she'd gone too far, said soothingly that they were all upset, and should first calm down a bit and take things as they came.

They stood in front of the Christmas tree, Hans holding Peter in his arms, with Else on his right and Enie on his left. They sang: "Silent night, holy night, all is calm, all is bright . . . "

Fritz accompanied them on the piano. The candles burned

and glimmered in the little boy's rapt, wide-open eyes. Else, moved, looked from one to the other.

Oh, how she loved them, her beautiful son, her clever husband, her upright lover, and the baby in her womb! She would never leave them, none of them, they belonged together, they had to find the "open sesame" that could lead them to a happy life together. They would find it.

Enie's face did not suggest that she was moved; instead, she looked downright angry, and the voice with which she sang the words binding people together was clear and sharp. She was the only one who foresaw it all: Else and Fritz would not get divorced, Fritz, who just wanted to be left in peace, would give the child his name, and Else would deceive her parents again and claim that the child was Fritz's. Hans, in his slavish love, would ultimately accept everything while not abandoning the hope that someday he would be able to marry Else. And what would she, Enie, do? Probably the same as Hans, since she still preferred to live in the group of four—and soon five—with Fritz than without him. So everything would go on as before.

Enie went into the kitchen and basted the goose. She'd have preferred to see Else in the roasting pan. She detested that woman, who would succeed with a shameless lack of consideration in bringing husband, lover, and two children under one roof, whereas she herself, a fifth wheel at the age of twenty-six, was doomed to wait, without a husband or a child. What an injustice, what an outrageous injustice!

Else came into the kitchen and took her hand. "Presents!" she cried.

"I think I've had enough presents," Enie exclaimed, and slammed the oven door shut.

Else broke into laughter. She laughed with the pleasure and abandon that characterized everything she did, and Enie couldn't remain serious and standoffish. The two friends embraced and shook with laughter.

It became a merry Christmas party, with fine presents, a delicious goose, and deliriously happy Peter.

"Oh, Mummy," he said as he lay in bed and Else bent over him, "Life is the best thing of all, and death is the worst. I would like to never die, I want to always have my life." He had it for twenty-seven years.

Things happened just as Enie had foreseen. A few quarrels and reconciliations later, Fritz declared that he now wanted his freedom and was prepared to give the child his name, and Hans, in his slavish love, accepted everything. The Kirschners, whom their daughter had deceived again, were delighted about the second pregnancy, and Else, happy to have gotten what she wanted, carried her growing belly with pride.

The baby, a daughter, was born on June 8, 1922, and was named Bettina. Hans, beside himself with joy, was the first to rush into the hospital with a bottle of champagne. Else, the infant in her arms, looked at him with teary, affectionate eyes: "Your daughter," she said. He kissed her face, her hands, the dark-locked head of the child, and asked if he could hold her. She gave him the baby, and he took her skillfully, like an experienced mother, walked with her to the window and looked with an expression of fervent love at the miracle of the hardly hatched little face.

"My child," he said softly, "my beautiful little daughter."

A wave of uneasiness suddenly swept over Else, a mixture of guilty feelings and fear. Here was a man, a proud, devoted father, whom she had condemned to keep quiet about his child, a man whose feeling, unfiltered by reason, broke forth from him with elemental force, a force that might wrench the tiller out of her hand. She impulsively stretched out her arms to the child, and Hans obediently laid her back on her breast.

The grandparents came with malt beer and chicken soup, Fritz came with Peter, and Enie with a bouquet of colorful summer flowers. Minna and Daniel embraced their son-in-law and congratulated him on his new daughter. Fritz smiled sourly, Hans hastily excused himself and left the room. Enie shot Else a wild glance. With an innocent face, Else held up to her the swaddled, black-haired package. Peter gazed at it, as he had his teddy bears, with undisguised disgust.

Wasn't he happy that she'd given him a little sister? Else asked.

"I'd have liked a black and white puppy better," he replied, hurt.

Fritz, giving Else a kiss on the forehead, whispered that he too would have preferred a black-and-white dog.

"The next time," Else promised, and laughed.

The child had Fritz's dark hair, Enie cried, clapping her hands with greatly exaggerated delight.

And a nose like a button, Fritz said.

It would grow soon enough, Daniel opined.

For a girl, it would be better, Minna declared, if it didn't grow into Fritz's big nose. Enie laughed shrilly, and Else rolled her eyes and fell back on the pillow.

But now they should drink the champagne that the good Hans had thought to bring, Fritz said, and reached for the bottle.

The cork popped, the champagne flowed onto the floor, the baby began to scream, Peter jumped joyfully into the puddle, Enie shrieked, Daniel hurried over with two toothbrush glasses, and Minna grabbed the baby and held her protectively in her arms: "Exaggerated," she murmured, "completely exaggerated."

They drank to little Bettina Schwiefert, the newborn, who was to learn only forty-five years later, as the result of an unfortunate accident, that she was the daughter of Hans Huber, a man she did not know.

For Bettina's first years, there is no little memory-book with locks of hair and comments on her physical and mental development. But Enie told me that she was a charming child, particularly good-natured, trouble-free, always contented and gay, and so ludicrously like her father that their genetic relationship could escape only the most naive and imperceptive persons. The Kirschners were among the latter.

For Hans, Bettina became the focus of his life, his connection to Else, who was increasingly slipping away from him, and the bait he threw her in the hope that she would yet declare herself, in the interest of her daughter, willing to marry him. But Else didn't bite. She salved her conscience with the idea that defrauding the father was less damaging to the child than an unhappy marriage to him would be. Ultimately, the primary consideration for a mother was her child's happiness.

She called the baby her bundle of joy and covered her fat little ankles, bulging belly, and plump cheeks with kisses and gentle nibbles.

She asked Peter, who looked on peevishly, whether he wasn't delighted to have such a beautiful little sister.

He was not at all delighted. He couldn't stand this disgusting teddy bear who was seducing his beloved Mummy away from him.

Else told him that he must always be very nice to little Bettina.

"Why, if I poke her in the eye with my finger will she scream?" he said with disgust.

He should behave! If he poked the baby, she'd spank him.

"All this isn't the way it should be," Peter said with a deep sigh.

No, in fact, it wasn't.

Bettina was baptized Protestant behind the grandparents' backs, with Fritz appearing as the father and Hans as the godfather. The baptism was one of many occasions preceded by a major quarrel and several hours of silence, bitter on Fritz's part, suffering on Hans's. Both men felt miscast in their roles, and for both of them the child was a calamity: for Fritz because he didn't want to have her, for Hans because he wasn't allowed to have her.

Else was irritated both by Hans's idolatrous love for the child and his constant insistence on his claim to her and by Fritz's disowning coldness and endless references to the injustice that had been done him. Had she not given these two men the best that one could give? Love, children, a fine house in which they could live however it suited them? Other husbands would have considered themselves lucky—and would gladly have accepted a little unpleasantness in return—if their own wives had put a mistress in their beds. Other lovers would have been grateful to be spared having to serve as father for a child that they had thoughtlessly produced. But these two were incapable of seeing what was positive in all this, or unwilling to do so, and virtually intent on spoiling the best years of life for her and for themselves. She was young, pretty, and healthy. She needed happiness so much, as she had written in one of her earlier letters to Fritz. And after all, why were they living in Berlin, the center of art, literature, and theater, of extravagant parties and international salons, of brilliant men and beautiful women, of vices and intellect? Why had Fritz good connections to theater people and journalists, and she a large house? Why was Enie a charming baroness and Hans a wonderful dancer? So that they could sit around a table arguing, or insulting one another in a bedroom? That was simply absurd!

Else declared that she'd had enough of Strindbergian tragedy and wanted to enjoy life. She threw herself into the "golden twenties," and Hans, who wanted only Else and the child, Enie, who wanted only Fritz, and Fritz, who wanted only to be left in peace, followed her.

I imagine the twenties as a kind of comet that left a bright, luminous trace on the short, starless night between the two world wars.

Born in the late twenties, that is, at a point when they seemed already extinguished, I only heard people talk about the enormous glamour and greatness of that time. Those who told me about it, and they were many, both in Germany and in Israel, seemed still to be under its spell. They spoke about those years in the voice of a storyteller, with an intimate or mischievous smile, with melancholy or sudden excitement. One old gentleman, who was no longer steady on his legs and weighed every step carefully, even danced the Charleston for me, to my alarm. He'd done it on the dance floor of the Jockey Club, with a bobbed blonde in a green dress, and the memory must have lent wings to his legs. A woman who was just as old sang me the hits of that time, and with each one her voice grew younger. This took place here, in Jerusalem, and today they are both gone. Almost all of them are gone, the lucky ones who saw the comet, and the golden twenties, who were born out of the bitter end of the First World War, perished in the bestial prelude to the Second, and became legends.

I grew up with much that had been produced by the twenties, and no doubt I was also influenced by them. But only decades later, when I unlocked the past, did it come back to me and mix with what I had heard, seen, and read. A clear image never emerged from the puzzle. My memory is haunted by the names of writers, critics, painters, and architects, composers and conductors, directors and actors, theaters and cinemas, nightclubs and dance halls, restaurants and cafés, newspapers and publishers, melodies from *The Threepenny Opera*, the refrains of hit songs, fragments of texts and poems by Mehring and Tucholsky, Kästner and Ringelnatz, Klabund and Brecht, impressions of paintings, drawings, caricatures that I saw here and there.

I learned nothing about the twenties from my mother. When we were in Bulgaria, in exile, she never spoke to me about the past. Probably she feared that it would disturb me and re-awaken the sleeping dogs of homesickness. Only once, when *Dreaming Lips*, with Elisabeth Bergner, was shown in Sofia, did she break the taboo. For her, as for many women of her generation, Bergner was an idol, and she had already seen the film a few times in Berlin. As we were entering the cinema, she was as excited as a young girl going to her first rendezvous.

"I went to every play Bergner was in," she confided in me. "She was the greatest! I can still see her as Puck in *A Midsummer Night's Dream* directed by Max Reinhardt. What good luck I had, to have still been able to see all that . . . No one can take that away from me, no one!"

"When was that?" I asked.

"In the twenties, the so-called golden years."

"Were the twenties really so golden?" I later asked Enie.

"They were fantastic," she said, "no question about it. The beginning of a new, modern, emancipated time that had no chance. A grandiose dance of death! The number of great artists and intellectuals that Berlin spit out at that time—overnight, one might say—is simply incredible. Half of them were Jews. Well, we succeeded in killing it all: the Jews, the art, and intellect."

And so Else threw herself into the golden twenties, which were soon being eaten away by rust. She accepted everything that went with them—culture and vices. The short, eruptive heyday, a mixture of renewal and decadence, which often pre-cedes decline, transformed the city not only into a metropolis of art and intellect but also into a Sodom and Gomorrah.

Berlin was no longer an imperial residence with strict eti-quette, prudish morals, and Prussian discipline, it was the heart, the darling, the seat of its inhabitants who, finally released from restrictions, acted in accord with their own taste and stamped their face, their character on it. It was a bold face, a character open to the world. New, clear forms, new tauter lines, new free morals, a new, franker tone emerged. The Bauhaus style was considered chic, sport, nudism, movies, the fox trot, night clubs, serialized illustrated novels, six-day races in the Sportpalast, sex-appeal imported from America. The quick-witted, versatile Berliner was born along with the saucy, level-headed Berlin woman who had "a certain something." It was the great age of women who, suddenly unleashed, were able to take part as autonomous individuals in the world of men and give expression to their suppressed or repressed feelings, thoughts, expectations, and needs. They shed their aprons and corsets, their saccharine femininity, their sexless submissiveness, and dressed themselves in light, loose-fitting clothing that left their knees uncovered, had heart-shaped lip-sticked mouths and man-style haircuts—seductive gamines, much looser in both senses.

They sat in bars smoking and drinking, stood on cabaret stages singing frivolous songs, danced half-naked in variety shows, went swimming in skintight bathing suits, displayed themselves in the seediest dives, flirted their way through the nights, were enchanted by the black topless dancer Josephine Baker and the heavyweight boxer Max Schmeling; and if a man appealed to them, they didn't say no.

Else swam comfortably in this world that had become a rushing torrent. Now she was no longer swimming against the current, but rather at the van of a school of like-minded people. Her charm had become provocative, her intelligence sharp, her vitality frenetic, and her gaiety too loud. She set the tone, she carried people away with her or imposed herself on them.

Hans was desperate and raging with jealousy. Like a faithful German Shepherd he trotted along at her side, did not let her out of his sight, tried to pull her away when one of the many men who swarmed around her got too close. He got terribly on Else's nerves with his ponderous love, which had made her so happy, his light Bavarian dialect, which she had found so cute, his dependability, which had so impressed her. Why couldn't he become looser and be wild and exuberant with her? Why couldn't he amuse himself with another woman? Why did he have to overwhelm her with his Teutonic integrity and scare away men who were much wittier and more interesting than he was? She tried not to think about the future, which loomed before her like a thick, grayish-yellow wall of cloud and threatened her. She could only see from one day to the next, and had to plan out every hour so that it offered her change and gaiety and prevented her from reflecting.

Her house became a favorite meeting-place for people eager for life, who always found the door open and Else always ready to do something. She organized musical evenings and dances, soirées during which literature was discussed, and parties that Lotte, one of Else's cousins, claimed were orgies.

Lotte, one of my mother's few relatives who survived the Holocaust, thanks to her emigration to Palestine, was at the time I met her still a good-looking woman with a mane of silver-gray hair, bright eyes, and a compact figure.

"I was the only one of all the Kirschners," she told me, "whom Else now and then invited to her parties. I was in fact very pretty, tolerant, and moreover a little different from other people. I'd been trained as a physical education teacher, and what good Jewish girl chooses such a repulsive profession! But compared with Else I was, of course, an innocent angel; in our family she'd been declared mad, and no one was allowed to know that I went to these parties. It seemed a little strange even to me, but I was curious and wanted to see what happened there. Darling, I can tell you, a lot happened there!"

When she recalled what she had done, a lewd smile appeared on her face, and it was as if someone had put a large, sweet-and-sour candy in her mouth. She seemed to suck on it and shift it from one cheek to the other. Unfortunately, that made her less likeable for me. "What happened there?" I asked impatiently.

"Sex," she chortled, and rolled the candy back and forth with her tongue, "sultry music, low lights, and pillows everywhere. Topless actresses served drinks and probably a few other goodies, too, and the guests, who were also pretty scantily clad, did chain dances. Now you weren't born yesterday, darling, and you know what I mean. Of course I didn't take part in that sort of thing."

Lotte's description largely coincides with Else's. In her draft libretto she describes the party at which she met Erich Schrobsdorff as follows:

> The house and garden are festively decorated, with garlands and Chinese lanterns, all the furniture has been removed, there are soft beds everywhere, and the lights are low. A wild, dancing, drinking crowd. Esther (Else), wearing trousers, is the most unbridled, the wildest. Helmut (Hans), close behind her, tries to calm her down. Esther laughs, shrieks, infects everyone with her jubilation. She kisses one acquaintance, then hurries on to the next. Then she comes to a bed where Ulrich (Erich) is lying with a girl. She looks at both of them, scrutinizes Ulrich, then moves on; a little later she returns and stands there, watching as the two kiss each other.
>
> Ulrich: "Who is that woman?"
>
> The girl: "The mistress of the house . . . come on!"
>
> She tries to pull him back and kiss him again. Ulrich, distracted, looks at Esther. She comes back, smiles seductively. Ulrich stands up, follows her into the garden.

At that point, Erich, who was twenty-eight years old, strik-

ingly good-looking and healthy as an ox, had not yet slept with
a woman. That claim was made by Alfred, Erich's younger,
loose-living brother, and I have never doubted it.

"Little Erich was not of this world," he told me merrily, "he
still moved in loftier spheres. Women chased after him like the
devil after a poor soul, but he believed they wanted to read
poetry with him or listen to his philosophical reflections. That
was all that interested him. Had Else not come along, had she
not taken him in hand and shown him what love is, he'd probably never have found out."

It was also Alfred who persuaded the innocent little Erich
to go with him to the party in the Dahlem villa. He himself
went there often, because he took part in all activities, except
for cultural ones, for which he had as little use as his older
brother did for frivolous ones. Not that Erich was a prude or
misogynist, absolutely not. There were women, aesthetic, quiet
women, who appealed to him, and there were amusements and
idiosyncrasies that he accepted in others without question,
but so far as he himself was concerned, he simply lacked the
interest and the time for them. He was a very thoughtful, long-
winded, and pedantic man, and he therefore exercised his
profession, which he did not like, with all the greater conscientiousness, and the intellectual activity that he engaged in
after work consumed all his energies.

On that evening he would rather have stayed home, but
since, partly out of excessive politeness, partly out of a fatal pli-
ability, he couldn't say no, he slowly and carefully changed his
clothes, stuck a carnation in his lapel, and followed Alfred to
his undoing.

Erich had endured many things: cultivated groups in which
people dined, made conversation, and danced in a civilized
way; elegant balls, at which the upper middle class amused
itself in a subdued way and made personal or business connections. But he had never before been to an artists' party. He

loved theater and opera and greatly admired good actors, directors, and singers; he perused with care the literary supplements of various Berlin newspapers, and was impressed by the linguistic precision and cleverness of first-class critics and essayists. But since there was no connection between his circle and theirs, he had never met an artist or a man of letters. He considered that not absolutely necessary, because he much preferred to enjoy, undisturbed, art on the stage and ideas on paper. Erich was a reserved man who did not like to venture into unfamiliar territory.

And now he stood in the midst of the turmoil of the Bohemia that he had admired from afar but that seemed alarming up close, and felt rather out of place there with his elegant suit, a monocle around his neck and a signet ring on his finger. He would have preferred a little more light and less noise, comfortable European chairs rather than crude oriental beds, noncommittal flirting rather than bacchant smooching. But he was not a party pooper, and he was also very thorough. He wanted to see all this with precision and get behind the amusements and quirks of these people. His brother had already dived into the crowd, and so he began by wandering through the rooms with an amiable smile, in order to study these goings-on, so far as he could, given the dim reddish glow. This was not easy, because someone was constantly urging him to do something and involving him in what was happening. Someone put a glass of wine into one of his hands and the whole bottle into the other; another tipsy fellow pushed him into a corner to tell him an incoherent story in a weepy voice; a young woman took the glass and bottle back out of his hands and took him off to dance in a candlelit room, while another took him away again and immediately to one of the crude oriental beds, to settle on which required considerable flexibility. Flexibility was not Erich's strong point, and neither was bacchant smooching, but courtesy forbade him to say no, so he let the girl do as she wished and landed clumsily on a pile of cushions.

The girl was pretty, but unfortunately a little forward. She took off his jacket and his vest, then threw her arms around him and began to kiss him.

Nothing like that had ever happened to Erich before. In his circles, the rules were different. Ladies waited demurely until the man took the initiative. But that had always been exactly the problem for him. He was a passive man who was repelled by the superfluous procedure of seducing a demure woman. He liked the inversion of roles. The girl, whether forward or not, had an enterprising spirit and a clear goal in mind. He had only to let himself be led.

And then suddenly this woman turned up. A remarkable figure in harem pants, with a wild mane of hair. Not his type, but attractive in a disturbing way. She passed by him and the girl, looked at them, stared shamelessly at him, moved on, came back, stopped and looked down at them, smiling, then went away again. He watched her leave.

Truly a remarkable figure and astonishingly bold. He asked the girl who this woman was, and she answered that she was the mistress of the house.

Probably it was the wine, the light, the music, the girl's kisses, the crowd frolicking around him. He was no longer in his world, he was no longer himself. He felt an enormous longing for the woman in the harem pants, a longing he found painfully upsetting. She had bewitched him.

After a while, she returned, hypnotized him with a smile. An elemental power emerged from her, a compelling will. He stood up and followed her like a sleepwalker into the garden.

In Else's draft libretto, the scene now gets more animated:

> She runs through the garden, Ulrich runs after her. At the bower he catches her, kisses her, and she kisses him back,

wildly, as if parched. Then they go back into the house and dance, looking sensually into each other's eyes. Friedel comes up to her and shaking his head reproachfully, points to Helmut, who is standing in a corner and observing the beloved. Esther shrugs her shoulders regretfully. Eva appears and tries to persuade Esther to attend to Helmut. She laughs, takes Ulrich's hand, and leads him into a darkened room. They lie down, closely entwined, on the divan and drink champagne. Helmut has followed them and peeks through the crack in the door. Friedel, who finds the unhappy man, tries to spare him the sight by pulling him away. Helmut, in impotent rage, wrenches himself free, grabs a couple of glasses that are standing around, and smashes them against the door. Ulrich and Esther sit up, shocked.

I can imagine how disturbed the bewitched Erich must have been. For the first time in his active life he'd run, kissed, danced, and lain down on a divan with a woman for a reason other than to read poems to her, and then a madman starts throwing glassware around. That's what happens when one leaves the higher spheres and enters profane territory. A very sobering experience.

He asked the woman in harem pants whether she knew this fellow who had allowed himself to be so cheeky.

Else, having recovered from her fear and overcome by the comedy of the situation, replied, laughing loudly, that he must have been a jealous man who was upset because she'd gone off to lie down on a divan with Erich. He shouldn't worry about it, she said, whoever the man was, he'd already recovered his composure.

But Erich didn't find the situation comical at all. Loud scenes and people out of control were anathema to him. People mustn't let themselves go, and especially not when an affect as primitive as jealousy was involved. Erich did not experience jealousy, and he experienced love and passion only on a higher level. He felt love for his mother, the only person in his family to whom he felt related, and passionate love, or at least some related emotion, for the creations of the human mind. One feeling sprang from the heart, the other from the head. For him, jealousy was something that took place in the lower regions, and the latter must never, ever gain the upper hand over the heart and the head.

He thanked Else for the eventful evening, and told her that unfortunately it was time for him to be going.

Else panicked. She'd fallen head over heels in love with this man, as was her way. Everything about him seemed to her noble: his face with its sharply defined features, his bearing, his way of behaving, his clothes; even on the divan, in an awkward posture, he had still remained noble. She knew only his first name, and if he left now, indignant about the ludicrous thing that had happened, disappointed in her for socializing with such men and perhaps even repulsed by the peculiar morals of the Dahlem villa, she would never see him again.

She would find it downright embarrassing, she said, if he now left with the impression that he'd gotten mixed up with a horde of savages. They were all basically civilized people, and he should stay another ten minutes and drink a glass of champagne with her in peace and friendship.

Erich remained far longer than ten minutes, because the civilized side of the group, which Else now showed him, was something he could admire. The remarkable figure in harem pants with a wild mane of hare and brazen manners who had disturbed, excited, and bewitched him, turned into Else Schwiefert, the lady of the house, a clever, witty, cultivated woman who now seduced him intellectually. Intuitively, she had recognized that Erich was a man of the nineteenth century, a Romantic and an idealist, who lived with the poets and thinkers of that period. She would reach the inner recesses of his mind and soul more surely by way of the spiral staircase of the mind than by the divan!

Thus she engaged him in a conversation about the fine arts, a subject that, to Erich's amazement, she knew better than he did. So far as the classics were concerned, she was at least as well-read as he, and she was far better acquainted with contemporary literature, theater, and music than he was. Her taste was as sure as her judgment was incorruptible and thoroughly grounded. This was a woman with feminine instinct and masculine intellectual powers, and he had never encountered this combination in the reactionary circles of the upper bourgeoisie.

No, she wasn't his type, and yet she'd succeeded in making her way into his inner sanctum and igniting a beneficent little fire there.

When Else met Erich Schrobsdorff, he was still living with his parents in Ahornallee, in Berlin's West End. The villa, which had been built in the boldest Jugendstil and was protected from the outside world by a large, artfully laid out garden, had the dimensions and appearance of a small castle.

Erich felt very comfortable there. He had his room, his library, his peace, and servants, and he wouldn't have been able to escape his father's iron grip even by moving into an apartment of his own at the other end of Berlin. Besides, the idea of escaping his father would have occurred to him as little as that of leaving his parents' home.

His father, a Prussian nobleman who was unapproachable, despotic, and heavyset, with a big head and a grim, leonine face, was the unchallenged head of the household. He had set aside the noble title of his impoverished ancestors in favor of a lucrative career, mixed with Berlin's wheeler-dealers, founded a real estate firm at the right time and, with the rapidly growing city and a highly un-aristocratic acquisitiveness, made millions. When he'd gotten that far, he married Annemarie, a girl from a good middle-class family, and had three sons with her. Annemarie was a beautiful, delicate, high-strung creature who lived out her unfulfilled Romantic yearnings on the piano and in dilettantish lyrical poems. Over the years her slender figure became matronly, her high-strung constitution became a bizarre, eccentric character, and her Romantic yearnings turned into a green and blue Biedermeier bedroom, where she indulged in the dreams that life had denied her. Only her face, as clear and delicate as that of a porcelain figurine, hardly changed at all.

The Prussian aristocrat paid his wife virtually no attention. So long as Annemarie made no trivial, wifely demands on him—and she didn't—and was a good housewife and mother—and she was—she could play the piano and scribble and live in the world of her dreams, just as he lived in the world of real estate. Their thoughts and wishes had never intersected.

Erich loved and venerated his mother, from whom he had inherited his distinguished appearance, his Romantic streak, his tendency to escape into dreams, and his enthusiasm for art. She was the member of the family to whom he felt spiritually and emotionally bound, the one who shared his emotions and interests, and had understood and supported his desire to study philosophy and literature. All that had not, however, helped him much. His father was fundamentally opposed to it. It was ridiculous and unprofitable to study the humanities, he said. Why had he finally shed his title of nobility, rolled up his sleeves, and built up a huge firm? And why had he brought three sons into the world? For the single if not sole purpose of having them devote all their intellectual powers and energy to their father's work, tripling the size of his firm, and carrying it on after his death in such a way that his first-class reputation and name remained undamaged.

Naturally, Erich had bowed to his father's will and studied

economics instead of the humanities. At a certain point the three sons were brought into the construction firm, Walter, the eldest, and Alfred, the younger, with an inherited talent for business, and Erich without it, and against his will—but all the more conscientiously.

In Erich's life, doing his duty was primary. That was how he compensated for his lack of realism, strength, and assertiveness. Since he couldn't devote himself to what he cherished and held sacred, he had to put all his sense of responsibility and conscientiousness into the dull and tedious profession to which he had been assigned. And if he couldn't keep pace with his father's dynamism and his brothers' alertness, then that had to be balanced out by a maximum of hard work and discipline.

Erich spent weekends at the office and on construction sites, and Sundays—this was also one of his duties—with his family. Only in the evening and at night could he withdraw into the ivory tower with his poets and thinkers, and concern himself with his noble world view instead of with the plans for mediocre apartment buildings.

This world view survived Hitler, the Holocaust, the Second World War, and the annihilation of six million people.

In 1948 Erich Schrobsdorff could still write to his daughter Angelika: "How much I would like to help you, too, dear Angeli, and gradually acquaint you with this real world, the only essential one, the world of absolute beauty, truth, and goodness . . . "

On the day after the party, Else received a large bouquet of select flowers from Erich Schrobsdorff, along with a little card thanking her with perfect politeness for her hospitality. She was disappointed. There was not a single red rose in the bouquet, not a single meaningful word on the card. She was even more disappointed when in the course of the day he did not call her, but then consoled herself with the thought that in his milieu it was perhaps considered inappropriate to call the very next day. He was a man of formalities, not passions. She didn't know men of this kind, and had no basis for deciding how she should react in this or that case, no guidelines as to how they were to be dealt with. She had believed that with the subdued conclusion to the evening she had established a good rapport with him and had won him over. Now she began to have doubts. Perhaps she had no rapport with him. Perhaps the eventful evening, as he called it with a trace of irony, had been nothing for him other than a one-time detour into a strange world and she only the beginning of an adventure that he didn't think it worth the trouble to end. She replayed the night in her mind: the erotic part, which had ended so inelegantly with the shattering of the glasses, and the cultivated part, which had ended with him kissing her hand and looking long and deep into her eyes. What would seem more important in his memory, the noisy truncation of a bodily relationship, or the quiet agreement to an intellectual relationship? Or had neither left a lasting impression, and had the wish to continue them not even occurred to him?

The days went by, and the more the hope of hearing from him diminished, the more desirable he seemed to her.

Else had always been attracted by the "completely different." The "completely different" had been for her the broad, free, Christian world and the people who belonged to it. Her path into this world had passed through Fritz the intellectual and Hans the sentimentalist, and even Grete the blond, straightforward bosom friend. She thought she'd achieved her goal and conquered the "completely different." Until Erich blundered into her life. Erich was a gentleman. He had the immaculate polish and integrity of a gentleman. And he had the charm of decadence, which ennobled the most everyday human behavior as patina does an ordinary object. For her, Erich ennobled the banal reality of the "completely different" and thus became a symbol of a still broader, more beautiful, noble world. Conquering that world was to become her final goal.

Erich took a good week to make up his mind. From one day to the next, he put off the decision as to whether he should see Else again or not. Had he made a spontaneous decision, it would have been positive, because the little spark she had ignited within him was still glowing. But so far as he could remember, he'd never been guilty of spontaneity, and moreover it was precisely the little spark that gave him pause. It might flare up into a small fire.

Had Else been a woman in his circle, his reflections would have been limited to a much smaller, assessable range, because he was by no means disinclined to get involved in a serious love affair with a woman suitable for him. But in Else's case everything spoke against doing so. She was not a woman with whom he could have a moderate relationship, whom he could introduce to his parents and take along to social events in his circle. Really not. Her boundless vitality fascinated and frightened him in equal degrees. Else was a volcano, always on the verge of eruption. Her thoughts and ideas seemed to be constantly seething and radiating a heat that would eventually become unbearable. He had no desire to dance on a volcano. What he was looking for was equability, balance, and stability, and Else had much to offer, but certainly not that. Her past, her present way of life, of whose vivacity he had had a taste, were murky. She had told him that she was married and had two children. Her husband must be an odd bird who didn't care what she did. Or perhaps not. Perhaps he had been the one who threw the glasses against the door. No, it was better to keep away from this loud, reckless group and to forego a love affair, even if it was not a serious one. In any case, it would founder on external circumstances, for where would their amorous trysts take place? His father would simply forbid him to carry on any "dalliance" with an unknown, disreputable woman, and Else's husband would, despite his peculiarity, certainly be grateful for that. However, there was the possibility of taking a trip with her to some quiet place with a great deal of nature and few people. He imagined a beautiful old hotel in the rustic style, big featherbeds, a green-tiled stove. A little adventure, short and painless, a long-overdue beginning that he could then put behind him.

They traveled to the saccharine landscape of the Tegernsee, to a rustic hotel with big featherbeds. An inconsolable Hans, a speechless Fritz, and a gloating Enie remained behind in the Dahlem villa. "Good things come in groups of three," she giggled, but the two men didn't giggle along with her.

Erich learned about love from Else, and, since such a favorable occasion would never recur, the story of her life as well. She had calculated correctly: with his breakthrough into the labyrinth of the senses he saw everything she had to tell him through rose-colored glasses.

To be sure, he couldn't have gotten involved in anything more complicated: a Jewess who lived under the same roof with her husband, her husband's mistress, her lover, and two children by different fathers. But what did that matter, in the end? He didn't love her, had never considered a serious relationship. A brief intermezzo, that was all. She was made for that sort of thing. A woman with ever-new, shimmering facets, never boring, never banal, never conventional. Her passion and tenderness, her trains of thought and observations, her way of laughing, of moving, of enjoying—it was all so genuine, so original, so lively, that she infected even him, the stodgy introvert, and made him discover, feel, experience things that had escaped him for twenty-eight years. There were times when he felt like a newborn, behaved like a young, light-hearted man, enjoyed life madly and wantonly. In these phases he was very close to her, was even very fond of her, feared saying farewell to her and returning to his world of absolute order and constraint.

But this feeling confused him. It did not fit into his way of seeing things. He must not fall under the influence of this woman—a Jewess who lived in absolute anarchy, just as he lived in absolute order. He had nothing at all against Jews, on the contrary, he treasured them as a cultural enrichment of Germany. He also had nothing against anarchy, so long as it remained in the private realm and did not become a public nuisance. But neither the one nor the other were compatible with his way of life and his person. He must tell himself, he must—first of all—tell her that. She must not have any illusions and believe that it would go on this way forever.

He must have told her this on their last evening, in an incredibly tactful and roundabout way, as was his custom. And she must have listened to him with a small, patient smile, and thought to herself: Ach, just go on talking, just go on talking, you big, handsome, clueless child. When the time comes you'll see how much you miss me, me, the Jewess, who has enriched your life just as my co-religionists have enriched Germany.

Erich did not leave his parents' house, but he became a regular guest at the Dahlem house. Unfortunately, I will never learn how Else brought the three men under one roof and how she divided her favors among them. Even the draft libretto does not provide any reliable information in that regard. It allows us only to presume that Hans came to terms with Erich and Erich with Hans, and Fritz with both of them. And that probably had less to do with Else's diplomatic talents than with the men themselves. One of them wanted Else all for himself, the second only a little, and the third had already long been out of the game. Had all three of them made the same exclusive claims on her, an arrangement would never have been possible, but in this way they were able get along. Although Hans felt a latent jealousy mixed with the fear of losing Else, Erich felt a certain uneasiness, and Fritz was occasionally irritable, apart from that they were all "cultivated" people who were naturally unaggressive and mutually very congenial. Erich appreciated Fritz's wide-ranging education and Hans's integrity, and Fritz and Hans were impressed by Erich's solid personality. In this way each of them benefitted from the good qualities of the others, and Else benefitted most of all. They often went out together or sat up late into the night, talking about art and literature, playing the piano, drinking a few bottles of wine that Erich had brought, eating the pea soup Enie had made, and feeling happy and attached to each other.

For me, Erich, my father, was dignity in person. I have never seen him be anything but grave, thoughtful, and absent-minded, with a quiet humor that often tempted him to make inept little jokes that amused us and him equally. I can hardly imagine an Erich who got carried away and played the role of the first or second lover. What led him to descend from the height of his ivory tower remains obscure. For Else it was clear that she was the crucial factor. In her draft libretto, this is how she described Erich and the situation into which he slipped: "He is tall, blond, and has a great deal of charm. A complicated, vacillating, tender man. Thus he will be drawn, almost involuntarily, into the chaos by Esther (Else). Only gradually realizes, to his astonishment, that he loves Esther and needs her."

Months must have passed before he realized it, and when he had, he must have been not only astonished but also scared out of his wits. This caused his carefully considered idea to collapse like a house of cards, and he found himself confronted by a situation he was utterly incapable of dealing with. The strange situation in the Dahlem villa, to which he made a not insignificant contribution, suddenly appeared to him untenable. The role he played there was unworthy of him. Why should he share, as it were, a woman with the man to whom she was married and the one whom she loved, why should he hurt people, deceive the children by pretending to be a kind uncle, disappear when the grandparents Kirschner came around, blow smoke in the faces of his own parents, who concluded from his behavior that he had finally found the right woman of his own rank, and neglect his work and reading?

In any case, this must stop. But a marriage to Else was out of the question. There were his parents, who would never, ever accept her, a Jewess, a divorcee, with two children, and there were his principles, which forbade him to marry a woman—whether a Jew or a Christian—who came from such a different milieu and whose character and temperament were opposed to his own. For him, marriage was less a matter of love than of duty, not only a lifelong bond with a woman, but also the union of two families. Seen that way, Else was the most inappropriate marriage partner possible.

So what remained? Nothing but to separate himself from her. That was the only solution, but he found it anything but easy to put it into action. The brief, noncommittal intermezzo had acquired, like an avalanche thundering down a valley, steadily increasing size and momentum, and his feelings, which had never played tricks on him, were about to become independent. He realized with alarm that in recent months he had lived more than he had reflected, indeed, one could almost say that he had lived without reflecting. It was Else who had drawn the conclusions and made the decisions in the everyday realm, and he was very comfortable with that. She decided in a minute whether they should go out to eat, to which restaurant, whether alone or all five of them, whereas he would have taken all afternoon to decide. By the end of the second act, she already knew whether a theater performance was good or just middling, and could explain why in two sentences. She could immediately point out both the weak and the strong points of a building constructed by his firm. She even kept an eye on his hair, and immediately told him when it was too long or had been cut too short.

He imagined what his life would be like without her. Days spent in the office, evenings in his library or at his circle's social events, with men of his own kind and women who were his type. A life in proportion and balance. A life without her warmth, which enveloped him like the balmy air of the first day of spring after a long, icy winter. Without her deep, full voice, her large, unveiled eyes, her liberating naturalness, which did away with his own inhibitions.

And then he recognized, as Fritz had, that for him she was like the sun, the central body in his life, bright, hot, and energy-giving. A separation from her would be a retreat into the twilight, a dim, colorless, formless twilight without beginning or end.

Erich found a compromise: they would take a long trip together to southern climes. A postponement of the inevitable end, a last, beautiful conclusion of their love affair.

Else had never traveled abroad, and all her life she had longed to do so. The idea of going off with a man she loved to foreign, southern lands she had only heard, read, and dreamed about, seeing beautiful old cities, white villages under a deep blue sky, the sea, palms, and orange trees, was so overwhelming that she didn't give even a moment's thought to Hans. She threw her arms around Erich's neck and cried for joy.

Only when she was alone did she begin to consider—not, for example, whether she should forego the trip for Hans's sake, no, no one could ask that of her, but rather how she could tell him about it. She thought she knew how he would react! He would plead with her, with that terrible desperation of his that pained and therefore angered her, not to go. He would repeat the old litany in order to persuade her that what she was thinking of doing was unfair, impulsive, self-centered, dangerous, irresponsible, unconscionable. That she should think, if not about him, then about the poor children. That she should be reasonable for once and consider what really mattered in life, and that was certainly not pleasures and adventures, but family: parents, children, a husband who was prepared to go through thick and thin with her. That he loved her as no one had ever loved her or would love her.

And she, Else, would wait with grumbling impatience until he had finished talking, and then have nothing to oppose to him. Because everything he said would be right, and her only argument, namely that she simply could not forego what was beautiful and exciting in life, would be no argument for Hans. So she would keep quiet and he, in the second phase of his impotent rage, would bring out the heavy artillery: she should understand that she was a middle-aged woman, thirty years old, and no longer young. She no longer had much time, and if she went on this way a few more years, she could count on ending up all alone. No man would be interested in woman in her thirties with two children. Not even him. Even the greatest love had to shatter when it was constantly trampled on, and he was very close to calling it off.

And then he would start talking again about Munich and his estate there and his beer brewery and the splendid life the four of them could lead there, and she would shudder inwardly. Bavaria and beer and Hans doing a mating dance around her with his red cheeks and Lederhosen. She'd rather live in Berlin without a man. But of course there would be men who were interested in her, and first of all Hans, who after all had had a daughter with her, a daughter with whom he played like crazy and whom he would never give up, even if someday he really had had enough of her, Else.

So that's how things would go, and she wished it was already over, because she could no longer bear his desperate face and the old litany and her own guilty conscience, which he knew so well how to manipulate. But what was a guilty conscience compared to the bliss that she would savor on this trip! Six weeks of Erich, sun, fascinating foreign lands—the prelude to a new, ennobled life.

That evening she told Hans what she planned to do.

The result was not at all what she had foreseen. Hans did not plead, he did not rant, he did not appeal to her conscience. He became a kind of icicle, bluish-white, rigid and cold, and said in an aloof voice that she didn't know him at all: if she went off with Erich on this trip, he would immediately leave the house and never see either her or their daughter again. It was her decision, he said, and he wanted her to make it now, right away.

The fear was like a blow to the abdomen. Else felt it spread down into her entrails, up into her breast. Her throat was so dry, and her tongue so thick that she could hardly swallow.

She'd known that there was a point at which Hans would no longer allow himself to be bent, but she hadn't expected to arrive at it so soon. It came now at a most inopportune time. But she had to decide: either Hans, the unbending oak, for the rest of her days, or Erich, the flexible conduit, for the time of the trip, at the end of which stood uncertainty. Her answer was clear: Erich, the trip, and uncertainty. She'd always chosen love, happiness, the "completely different," so why should she now choose security at the price of these treasures? No, not she! There was only this one life, with a brief youth and little doses of happiness. The future was a hypothetical concept. Planning for it was futile. Did she control her fate? Should she sacrifice a momentary, tangible happiness to a distant, unknown security, and instead of enjoying her life, shelter herself from it?

He was waiting, Hans said.

When she heard his aloof, alien voice and the words squeezed out as an ultimatum, she still felt only a little twitch in her entrails. She'd made up her mind. But nevertheless she wanted to try to make it possible for him to talk about it and to attenuate his decision.

She would go away, she said, that was final. But she asked him to think about Bettina; he could not punish her for her mother's behavior and make her unhappy.

If anyone here was making the child unhappy, he said, it was she. That she should understand that and never forget it was the only thing he still cared about. And in any case he didn't intend to talk with her about Bettina. She was her daughter and bore the name of her husband Fritz, and he hoped Erich would take care of her.

Else asked with disgust whether that was his final word.

Yes, he said, and left the room.

She did not go after him. She heard him open the door to the children's room, heard Bettina's joyful cries, put her hands over her ears with a pained grimace, and tried to think about the trip, the sun, the sea, and southern nights. But no images came, only dry sobs that hurt as if her thorax were in flames.

On the same day Hans Huber left the Dahlem villa. He left behind a letter to Fritz and Enie in which he assured them of his friendship. He left Else without a word or a glance of farewell. From the window, she watched as he went down the gravel path to the garden gate. A tall, handsome man. A stranger whom she had thought she loved, with whom she had lived for four years, with whom she had a daughter. A man who left her as a bitter enemy, never to return. She was overcome by a strangling feeling of sadness and panic. For a moment, she was tempted to throw open the window and call out his name. He couldn't leave in that cruel way the woman and daughter he loved more than anything! Without a backward look, without a word that made his departure less irrevocable. But she knew that it was hopeless and that he would come back—if at all—only if she decided for him alone. And she couldn't do that, not even for Bettina's sake. She had to live according to her own laws.

She turned away and went into the children's room. Peter lay on his stomach, drawing a picture, and Bettina was squatting next to him, watching him intently. Else sat down on a chair and looked at her children, the beautiful, small boy with blond hair and the chubby little girl with black hair. Didn't she love her children enough? Was she a bad mother?

If a mother is to be judged by her fulfillment of her duties, then she was a bad mother. But if she is evaluated by her love, then she was the best mother in the world. She loved her children with an ardent love. Wasn't that enough? Wasn't that more important than fulfilling duties?

Bettina came over to her with outstretched arms. Else took her on her lap, hugged her, kissed her little face. Hans's eyes, his nose, his mouth.

Peter looked up, with his eyebrows raised, and looked at her severely. "Uncle Hans has gone away," he said. "He said farewell to us. Too bad, isn't it?"

Else nodded

"Let me ride horsey on your knee," Bettina begged.

She bounced the whooping girl on her knee.

"If he falls in the trench," she sang, "ravens will eat the mensch . . . "

"Such nonsense," Peter said with disgust. "Ravens don't eat people."

"If he falls in the sump, the rider will go . . . "

"Bump!" Bettina shrieked.

That evening, Else told Fritz and Enie that she was going away with Erich for six weeks. The children would stay at her parents' home while she was gone, she did not yet know what lie she would have to tell them.

Fritz gave his wife a long, indulgent look and then said that it might be better to stop lying and clear the air. The castle in the air she'd built was about to collapse anyway. Hans had escaped first, he and Enie would follow. They had decided to get married. Thus he assumed that Else would agree to a divorce.

She had already seen the first stone fall from her collapsing castle in the air. This was the second. She was somewhat dazed and remained silent.

Enie, the victor who had finally wrenched the prey away from Else, began to weep out of sympathy with her friend. She must not be afraid, she sobbed, she and Fritz would always be there for her.

And what were they to tell her parents, Else asked, and what should they tell the children? First father and uncle, then neither of them. The next one already had his hand on the doorknob, Enie said to comfort her, grinning amid her tears.

The question was only whether he would turn the knob, Else said.

That depended entirely on her, Fritz declared, and in any case Erich would be a very good father and son-in-law, perhaps not quite so good as Hans, but certainly better than himself.

Else, annoyed, said that she was not amused by all that, but would not allow it to spoil the trip for her: "I'm going, and *après moi le déluge!*"

"Do you remember how it began? We were standing in the Anhalter train station, completely confused, I with a heavy heart and pangs of conscience. You were looking for the key to the trunk, then for your hat, and then for your cigarettes. Everyone was making noise and running and screaming, and we were desperately walking back and forth. Finally we sat down in the train, and as it started to move, slowly and puffing, everything dissolved in me, and I began to metamorphose. For me, traveling means beginning another life. Then I'm no longer myself, my thinking changes, my feeling changes, and when I look in the window, my face is altered. Everything is strong and clear."

That's how Else's memories of her trip begin, memories that she wrote down after their return to Berlin and that she gave to Erich for his birthday. She typed them with a violet ribbon and had them bound in a small, sunny yellow and sea-blue volume. It is a moving little book that reveals Else's essence and character very vividly:

> I slept very well at night and in the morning we were in Munich, sat happily in an extremely ugly café and ate breakfast. Then we traveled on, and every hour I said to myself a hundred times: Venice! And my heart beat so hard that I felt it everywhere, in my throat, in my stomach, in my fingertips. The train began to climb, and I realized that there, on the other side of the Brenner Pass, lay Italy, and the higher we climbed, the greater the tension grew in me. The enormous longing, nourished for years, was about to be fulfilled. I found it hard to breathe; Goethe, I thought, and then imagination and reality merged and I said not another word.

> Was it in fact bare and brown and not yet spring up there on the crest, was it really so that we were descending among blooming trees and green pastures? I almost wanted to cry. Bozen, Trento, Verona, Padua—those were the beautiful names. We changed to a small train and stood at the window. The landscape, the sky, the air—everything was different and it was as if I were in a dream. And then came Venice.

> As we walked out into the train station, I lost my com-

posure. I actually began to cry. The narrow, dark canals, the proud houses in such splendid colors—blue and brown and dark red like blood, the high, arched, noble bridges, the alleyways where laundry fluttered from one window to another. Steps led down to the water, where dark-colored gondolas were waiting. Solemnly and silently, we slipped through the canals, past magnificent buildings. The gondoliers quietly steered their boats. We stopped at the steps of a palazzo—our hotel. The room had a white marble floor, and the window looked out on a small canal, in which the water was almost black. I sat on the wide windowsill and leaned far out. There I saw the Grand Canal and beyond it the open sea.

We went to bed and, skeptically, I puffed up my pillow, because it was as hard as a stone, and the blanket was very thin. I was freezing, and because I was so cold I had to snuggle up to you, didn't I, little Erich, just to get warm. But then we couldn't sleep. Was that my fault? We had had a little argument about "reason" and "relaxation," and you were very serious and I was very sad. But it was necessary because I'd been overwhelmed by madness. This air, this city, this sky, the sea and the street life, with constant laughter and affection, had gone to my head, got into my blood. I walked through the city, and I shone so much from within that everyone looked at me and rejoiced, and I loved all Italians, all women and children, no matter how dirty they were, and I was in love with everything and everyone. How much you had to endure, you poor man, my joy in life vented itself on you.

We lay on white marble steps, right next to the water, in the radiant sunlight; we walked through the fish market and the ghetto quarter, where a horde of begging boys ran up to us, crying "Jehudi, Jehudi"; in the evening we went far out onto the sea to the *serenata*, where young men and women sang passionate songs in gondolas decorated with Chinese lanterns under the huge, nearby stars. Should one keep one's composure even there and be ashamed if one becomes sentimental? I was not ashamed. Tears ran down my face, and I prayed that it would never stop.

When we got "cultivated" and went to see the "Academia" or the churches, I longed so much for the air and the sun that all the pictures and churches meant nothing to me. You read me very earnestly the most weighty things about culture, art, and history, and were annoyed when I didn't listen to you. But I always wanted to be outside and walk through the narrow streets. Do you recall how one morning we went first to the Piazza San Marco—for matins, we said, and how every time we remained standing under the arcades and a jubilation rose up in me that was so strong that I thought I couldn't stand it without screaming or weeping or dancing. The beauty, the joy in living, the vivacity everywhere around us, was so indescribably wonderful!

From Venice they traveled to the Brijuni islands. She wrote:

At first we saw only a large hotel, a white, sunlit piazza, and many elegant people. I became a little anxious and uneasy. Here there were certainly pretensions! Venice, well Venice had been waiting for me, it approached me with open arms, whereas Brijuni was hostile. And this impression was right, but later on I didn't care, because I got used to it, and the place was after all so beautiful. However, on one occasion the aversion and resistance really overwhelmed me. They went sailing and played golf only in order to dress well and appropriately for it, it never occurred to them to walk through the splendid meadows or on the beach. They were mere shells, empty inside. You called me hasty and intolerant, and we had a serious quarrel. But it was probably the only time, and that's not so bad when people are living together. Then everything quickly becomes good again.

Once we took a sailboat to the island of Narcissus, which is tiny and full of flowers. We lay in the tall grass and were completely covered with narcissus and leaves, and I burrowed into them as deeply as I could, as if in a soft bed, and then took off my blouse and skirt and a few other articles of clothing and lay blissfully there, in the glowing sunshine. We were very crazy on that day, and I wanted to lie there forever, like a lizard. I didn't want to leave, I dug my finger deep into the earth and pressed my face into it, in order to breathe in its sweet fragrance so that I would never forget it.

From Brijuni they continued to Mostar, by way of Ragusa:

The bazaars were the most beautiful thing. The brown, bearded men with intelligent, peaceful eyes lay there motionless on their benches, smoked long pipes and drank coffee out of tiny cups that were constantly being carried across the street on a tray. Veiled women who looked like storks walked passed us. They wore long, blue capes with a hood that fell far over their faces, and a black veil over it.

We rented a car and drove through the city, saw Turkish houses that stood in courtyards hidden by walls, saw mosques with slender minarets and very large cemeteries with crooked gravestones. We drove along a little river on whose banks two women were sitting; they hastily and anxiously hid themselves from our eyes. All this was so strange and wonderful: the houses with narrow, shuttered windows that are placed so high that it's impossible to look into them, the remarkably shy women, who never feel the sun, the wind, or the sea on their skins, and who meekly put up with the men's looks and this life.

From Mostar they traveled via Sarajevo and Agram to Vienna:

The express train to Vienna was so wonderfully comfortable and sleek that I suddenly found civilization delightful again. We were awakened from the most splendid sleep shortly before our arrival in Vienna, and when I had dressed, you lazily got up, took your time getting your sponge and hairbrush, eau de cologne and hair tonic, toothpaste and hair-drying hood out of the trunk, and when you finally had everything arranged, the train came into Vienna, and you had to pack it all back up again much more rapidly than you had unpacked it. You couldn't even brush your teeth, and after that the whole day was spoiled for you. But I laughed heartily.

In Vienna we checked into the finest hotel we could find, and had a room with an anteroom and a bath. And we bathed and bathed and scrubbed all the Balkans off ourselves, and you washed my head so thoroughly that two days later it still hurt. From the hotel I was finally able to call Berlin, and the children came to the telephone and consoled me a bit regarding the end of the trip. And then we started out.

We drove in a cab to the Prater, where everyone in Vienna seemed to have gathered on that beautiful Sunday. There was an enormous hubbub, a floral pageant, and horse races, an amusement park, theater, coffee houses, all together.

In the evening we went to the Festival Hall to see
"Figaro," and the next evening we went to the Josefstadt
theater, where we saw a play by Galsworthy. We made an
excursion to the Vienna Woods and to the Kahlenberg, and
the woods were lighter and brighter green than any woods
at home. On the way back we went into an old church, in
which a service was going on, and as always in Catholic
churches, I was enchanted and ravished. Once we went to
a chic dance hall, which was in no way different from similar establishments in Berlin. Nonetheless we danced until 4
A.M. We strolled through the old city, with its flat, gray
houses, drove out to Schönbrunn, with its remarkable trees
trimmed to the point of being unrecognizable, which made
me sad because they had been so maimed, went into the
Liechtenstein gallery and stood for a long time, mesmer-
ized, before Botticelli's wonderful Madonna. But our return
lay over our experiences like a shadow that grew increasingly dark and cool. The last day came, and we watched the
trunks being carried out of the hotel room as if they were
coffins. We made the final trip together in the sleeping car,
the final trip together in a taxi. Then came our separation.
It was the best trip of my life, unclouded from beginning to
end. When I think about it, I know what happiness is.

In their outward and inward opposition, they must have
made a curious pair. Else, a whirling dervish, small and buxom,
dressed in poor taste and with an unbecoming hairdo, boister-
ously laughing and exulting, shrieking and weeping; Erich, two
heads taller than she, an immaculate figure from the tips of his
made-to-order shoes to his panama hat, moving slowly, pensively observing, and subdued both acoustically and emotionally. How did he stand those uninterrupted fireworks of
ecstatic outbreaks of feeling and enthusiasm? They must have
sometimes disconcerted him, and sometimes carried him away,

as they did in the marketplace or on the island of Narcissus. But all in all he would have welcomed a little more peace and moderation. There were probably also times when Else expressed her delight a little less tempestuously, for example in the pretentious atmosphere of Brijuni, or when Erich had informed her that one didn't fidget in church and had sometimes to be more reasonable in bed. Then she must have conjured up her civilized side and immediately won Erich back with her original observations and clever remarks. One did not escape her, this small, buxom Else, this bundle of lust for life, this spring of tenderness and warmth, this flame of clear, bright intelligence. Despite this or that reservation, on this first, long journey she must have been for Erich the revelation of true life.

Else prefaced her draft libretto with the following "Statement":

> All the characters are, despite the enormously disruptive lives they lead, decent people. They all act as if under a compulsion, and are immeasurably weak. They are pushed around and allow themselves to be driven, do not find the strength to resist, and moreover sense the excitement of this disordered, hectic life. All their relationships begin easily and harmlessly and grow over their heads. None of them is cold and calculating; they are all basically decent and honest. Ultimately unhappy and wounded by fate, they are left behind poor and empty-handed. FIASCO.

We are thus now in the phase of the fiasco that overwhelmed them after Else's return to Berlin. There was no longer a Hans, and there would never be another. Fritz and Enie had moved to Wannsee, leaving behind the divorce petition where furniture and books once stood, and lighter spots on the walls where pictures once hung. And Erich, obeying his father's telepathic call and his duty, said farewell and went back to his parents' house.

The Dahlem villa was deserted and cold, Berlin was gray and rainy. Else lay down on the bed, took two sleeping tablets, and pulled the covers over her head. She could not imagine that she would ever have the strength and the desire to get up again. She saw facing her a hydra with nine upright licking, hissing heads that grew again as soon as they were cut off.

How was she, who had never lived without the protection, support, and physical nearness of a man, to suddenly make her way alone, alone in a big, eerily empty house that had always been full of people, full of voices, sounds, activity, and hubbub? How was she to give her two fatherless children a feeling of security and protection when she herself had lost it? How was she to explain the disappearance of a father and a beloved uncle who had been taken for granted, and accustom them to the presence of a new man who, because he never stayed very long, had to arouse more confusion than trust in them? How was she to feed her children with resources that would certainly be very limited? And what was she to say to her parents? That Hans, the good friend and the son of a minister, had taken off, and that Enie, the good friend and baroness, was now living with Fritz in Wannsee and would soon be marrying him? Not to mention Erich, of whose existence the poor Kirschners had not the slightest idea. Should she perhaps introduce him as her lover, a new goy with whom she had been having an affair for the past year, and who was not planning to marry her? Who, when she really thought about it, might now even be thinking of ending their affair, offering her politely and tactfully, as was his way, friendship and possibly financial support. He was a very decent, but unfortunately very weak man, and if his parents got wind of their affair and put him under pressure, he would certainly give in.

Suddenly she doubted everything and everyone, and most of all she doubted herself.

She'd had three men, and now she had none. She'd seen life as a game, and now it was a battlefield. She'd become acquainted with battle and victory in the domain of love, enjoyment, and pleasure, not in everyday life. She was not prepared for the latter, was not equipped for it.

By running amok in the broad, free, Christian world, Else had ended up in a dead-end street, and I find it hard to understand why at this point she didn't at least try to make herself familiar with the basic concepts of everyday life and thus prove that if worst came to worst, she could take care of herself and her children.

But for her marriage was now as before a woman's destiny and fulfillment, and the man was the one who gave her status, financial security, and a task in life, not to mention a justification for her life. And if later on she also set aside the moral ideas of her generation, that did not happen as the result of a general emancipation, but rather solely in the realm of sexual freedom. Her unused talent and intelligence, her pent-up vitality and strength had apparently only one outlet, and that was the erotic and joy in life. Only in the later phase of her unsparing self-knowledge did she write in a letter to me: "Try harder, make something of yourself, I swear to you, it's worth it. Just see how I've frittered away my talent and intelligence all my life, and now I'm just sitting here. Logical!"

It's so difficult, this beginning! I still can't believe that it's beginning over again, life, everyday life, which is so hard to bear . . .

Else began with these lines the letter accompanying her memories of the trip. Instead of confronting the present and taking in hand at least one of the many problems she faced, she buried herself for a good month in the lost paradise of the trip.

Where did the time go when I could always laugh and make merry? I want to make myself hard, not surrender, just not surrender, otherwise I won't be able to stand it, I'll sink into tears, into the deepest sadness. Then everything will be black, the beauty that was will melt away, become unreal. The strength I need to be happy and beautiful will leave me, I'll fall apart, be dull, adrift, wretched. If that happens, all is lost. I have to find support, because I'm like a child who has to work for the first time and stands there wobbling. This little book should help me: I flee to it when I feel in danger of being overwhelmed by everyday life, the pressure, dark thoughts . . .

She went to her parents' home to pick up Peter and Bettina. Her happiness on seeing her children again, on feeling again, was so great that it temporarily dissipated her dark thoughts. Children and old people, she said to herself, live in their own world. The former quickly get over changes, the latter no longer really perceive them. She did not need to give her parents any profound explanation.

They asked whether it had been beautiful at the home of her friend in Italy.

Heavenly, Else replied.

She was deeply tanned and seemed to be in full bloom. That was enough to prevent Minna and Daniel from having doubts about either the visit to her friend or their daughter's welfare.

The children were in excellent physical and psychological condition and wanted only to know if their mother had brought them something.

Well, that was easy!

Else took the children back to the Dahlem villa with her. For a few hours, everything went well. The children were busy rediscovering their toys, the garden, and the maid, Frieda. But when evening came, Bettina asked where Papa Fritz and Uncle Hans were, and Peter said, shrugging his shoulders, "She really doesn't understand anything."

The four-year-old Bettina, a thoroughly trusting child, did in fact not understand anything, and when her mother explained that the two papas had gone on a long trip, she calmly accepted this and asked no further questions. It was different with Peter, who was now nine years old.

When I look at a photo of him taken in that year, I can see that it was hard to fob him off with lies or half-truths, and I can imagine that in his case Else didn't even try. In the photo he's wearing a black Russian tunic with a little stand-up collar and a wide leather belt, and has the face of a beautiful child with the expression of an intelligent adult. There is the prominent forehead with the arrogantly raised eyebrows, the alert eyes that nothing escapes, and the deeply indented corners of his mouth that express stubbornness and skepticism. There is nothing accidental in this face, nothing vague. The boy not only sees, hears, and feels; he thinks, he wants to know, he wants to figure things out. I believe he was the only one of us children who saw, understood, loved, and accepted our mother as she was.

When Else had finished writing her notes about the trip, her feeling that she was pregnant became almost a certainty. Nonetheless, she couldn't believe it. The doctors had told her, after she had had a complicated gynecological infection, that she would have forego having any more children. She was very upset about this, because her resolution to have a child with every man whom she loved was still in force and had flared up again with her passion for Erich.

"On the trip to Italy with your father I prayed for a child in every church we visited," she told me in her religious phase, "and my prayers were heard."

So in churches she must not have simply fidgeted and

wished she were outside again, but also said a little but unusually effective prayer. Even her doctor, to whom she finally went, regarded her pregnancy as a miracle. Else did too, naturally.

A child by Erich, a product of the blissful trip, a gift from heaven, the finger of God!

She must have thought in such categories and completely forgotten that the circumstances under which the poor little thing was carried and born were again highly unfavorable, and the problems, of which there had already been more than enough in her earlier pregnancies, were to increase several times over. Or perhaps she believed that God would now not merely touch her with his finger but hold his whole hand over her and the growing child.

Erich, in his extreme decency, could now no longer slip away from her. His father, the Prussian aristocrat, would reject the unsound Jewess, but the Kirschners had already done that in the case of Fritz, the unsound goy. Peter had broken through her parents' narrow-mindedness and intolerance, and the new little miracle would do the same for Erich's parents.

The pregnancy gave Else a tremendous lift. From one day to the next, her despondency turned into a need to be active. She no longer feared anything, not Erich's indecisiveness, not his parents' hostility, not her own parents' exasperation, not divorce, not Peter's outrage when he had to recognize that it was once again not a black-and-white puppy, not the sympathetic or uncomprehending looks of her acquaintances and friends, not rain or storm.

It was Erich who first learned about the gift from heaven, and I hardly dare imagine his intense, if also well-behaved horror. He was already incapable of resolving the Else problem, and now there was the problem of Else with child!

So he must have grappled with his thoughts at great length, evading the only two alternatives—marriage, which was for him out of the question, or abortion, which he, a simple man and a devout Christian, could never, ever countenance. And she must have thought: Ach, just go on talking, just go on talking, you big, handsome, clueless child, you'll see how this half-Jewish child will enrich your life.

So he must have postponed the decision to a remote future and left his parents in ignorance. And she must have pressed ahead and made a partial confession to her parents. They were not, of course, told about the interlude with Hans, and so Fritz bore all the blame. They never wanted to see again a man who had first seduced their daughter and carried her off, and then committed adultery and left her and his children for a Christian baroness. Thereby avoiding any reference to the other one, that scoundrel who had brought this disgrace on their daughter.

Erich was thus introduced to the Kirschners, and when he entered the apartment with an amiable smile and a bouquet of exquisite flowers, shook Daniel's hand, and kissed Minna's, they could not conceal the fact that they were impressed. Their indignation yielded to appreciation, the brusque greeting that they had intended to give him yielded to a soft "very pleased to meet you," their dismissive expressions to an awkward smile. Their world-order was overturned. Before them stood a gentleman and not a scoundrel; he was a goy, true, but one with a lot of class. How should they reconcile that with the disgrace he'd brought upon their daughter?

Erich was invited to come into the living room and served coffee and pastries. They talked about real estate, which greatly interested Daniel, and about Goethe, Minna's and Erich's favorite poet. About the disgrace not a word was said.

Only after Erich had left did Daniel and Minna remember the disgrace and take their daughter to task: after all the messes she'd made in her life—a good-for-nothing husband, a broken marriage, two fatherless children—was she really thinking of bringing yet another illegitimate child into the world? Why, in God's name, had she and Erich not long since gotten married?

She was not to blame for that, Else replied, but mainly Erich's father, who would not put up with a marriage to a Jewess, and especially a divorced Jewess with two children.

That was the last straw, the Kirschners said, enraged, it was simply intolerable! Just because she had another faith, wasn't she putting up with this brute in her house? What did it matter that she was a Jewess? Germany was her country, German was her language, her culture was German, her family was German, her education was German!

How about Fritz, Else asked, he also had *only* another faith, and otherwise was German, German, German, German. Why had it mattered to them that he was a Christian, so much that for a year they forbade him to enter their house?

That was entirely different, Minna said, and Daniel added, encouragingly, that these were trifles, and that everything would work out in the end. Her Erich was a splendid man and an honorable person, you could see that at first sight. Little Else mustn't worry.

But she did worry. Her initial euphoria had evaporated, and she had to admit to herself that the consequences of the miracle were not as brilliant as they had at first seemed. Erich had even gone so far as to tell his father about their liaison, but after the latter had cross-examined him regarding her personal particulars, he had declared that he could not accept his son's association with such a woman and therefore expected him to behave accordingly. Erich, vacillating between his father's demand that he break off their relationship and Else's demand that the relationship be given more substance, behaved cautiously. He accommodated both old Schrobsdorff and Else, acting like a good son to the former and a reliable companion to the latter, and left the decision to a *deus ex machina*.

Else's initial confidence, her urge to act, and her gaiety gave way to a great weariness. She, who had enjoyed her earlier pregnancies, began to suffer under the psychic and physical pressure. She felt alone in the big house, in which parties and social gatherings no longer took place, acquaintances who wanted to amuse themselves stayed away, and her few faithful friends depressed her more than they encouraged her with their well-intentioned but useless advice.

Even the children, who were used to a turbulent household, the presence of two men, and a mother who was always lively, began to notice the joyless atmosphere. Erich, who appeared only in the evening and either went out with Else or spent a few quiet hours with her, was a poor substitute. Although he often brought the children gifts and was kind and patient with them, took Bettina in his arms, and stroked Peter's head, he was and remained a guest, from whom little more could be expected or demanded than from any uncle who happened to come for a visit. That was enough for Bettina, who enjoyed being with him and was trusting and affectionate. In contrast, Peter treated him with scarcely concealed disapprobation. To herself, Else explained his attitude as jealous, a normal reaction that any growing boy might have to his mother's lover, and was not further concerned about it. Once Peter got used to Erich, integrated him into his life and had realized that he, the son, would retain her full and complete love, his attitude would certainly change.

As far as her children were concerned, she was a poor psychologist. To be sure, Peter was jealous of the interloper who played such a large role in the life of his beloved mother, but that alone was not the problem. It was Erich's nature, which he found alien and unpleasant; his reserve and methodical way of doing and saying everything, his lack of spontaneity and exuberance—two characteristics that he experienced in himself and in his family and that were for him expressed in passion and abandon, the full, wild life in which there were no boundaries and no calculation. At that time he already had a completely consistent little personality, incorruptible and uncompromising. Erich was and remained for him Uncle Schrobsdorff, the stranger, whose quiet kindness and generosity were for him no more than tepid compensations for his lack of true love and total devotion.

At this time, the distraught Else most often sought out Fritz and Enie. She had complete confidence only in them, whom she knew from the ground up, and with whom she didn't need to pretend or conceal anything. There, in the comfortable little house with the overgrown garden, she felt happy and secure, there she could express herself, weep, complain, and sometimes even laugh with Enie, just as they had earlier laughed themselves out of bad situations. The rural Wannsee house soon became a refuge for Erich as well, and his attachment to Fritz and Enie deepened into a lifelong friendship. The two men, who shared an aesthetic worldview and the need to be left in peace, took long walks along the lake or retired for an hour or two to Fritz's library, in order to devote themselves to philosophical reflections. The two women, who were alike in temperament and elementalness, shared their love for a clear, simple life about which their men understood next to nothing.

Enie didn't give useless advice, and she didn't pay attention to every word. She said what she thought, straight out, often bluntly, and Else preferred that to the cautious, verbal beating around the bush in which she often felt like a doomed person in the hands of bumbling doctors.

She shouldn't complain now, her friend told her, she had known exactly what she was doing, and one really couldn't say that about Erich. He'd never known and never would. He was saddled with things and then dutifully carried them further. A man as soft as butter. For him, all life was a matter of "in for a penny, in for a pound."

When Else's pregnancy became clearly visible, Erich suggested that they leave Berlin. Here, where they would inevitably meet people they knew, she might encounter intolerance, hatefulness, and abuse, and he wanted to spare her that. She was not currently capable, either psychologically or physically, of calmly ignoring such annoyances. A warmer, more beautiful, more harmonious place where she knew no one, a nice, comfortable hotel, in which she could relax and rest, would do her a great deal of good. He'd thought of Lugano . . .

Else began to laugh, a pathetic bitter laughter. She thanked him very much for his care and concern, she said, but for her part she would prefer other people's hatefulness and being near him to harmonious Lugano and being far away from him. But this was not about her.

This was the hour of truth, which was to be repeated twelve years later under fatal circumstances. Else, who could become a danger, was sent away. Gently, cautiously, and at Erich's expense. To a beautiful, warm place, in a nice, comfortable hotel, where she knew no one and the stain that threatened to put them all in an uncomfortable position could be covered up.

Else, despondent and insecure, did not resist. She took Peter to her parents, and traveled with little Bettina to Lugano.

Erich's behavior had enormously disappointed her. This man had neither backbone nor natural instincts. The child she was bearing, his child, was for him nothing but an awkward accident that had to be concealed. His absurd fear of his father was accompanied by a certain repulsion for her unaesthetic belly, and he was embarrassed to be seen with her in public. Oh, yes, she knew her Erich, his idiosyncrasies and eccentricities, which had always amused her so much. But now they were no longer amusing, they were even profoundly sad and unforgiveable. Instead of standing by her and his child at a time when she needed him more than anything he sent her into exile, and instead of giving her love and support he gave her money and good words. And the worst of it was that he saw his own behavior as unobjectionable and was not tormented by a guilty conscience. He actually believed that he could offer her nothing better than a peaceful stay in a pleasant place, in a comfortable hotel. What else could a pregnant woman who consisted of nothing more than a belly want? For Erich, women, with their obscure surges of emotion and peculiar bodily sensations, were now as before incomprehensible beings. He knew his mother, but she stood above the category of general femininity afflicted with a womb, and her surges of emotion concerned primarily art. And so far as Else was concerned, as a woman she was so different from the rest that she was outside the norm and had nothing in common with other members of her sex. How should poor Erich know that every woman, even the one who stood above general femininity, needs not only financial but also moral support, not only a sense of duty, but also tenderness? Erich, with one foot in the male world of the wheeler-dealers and the other in that of poets and thinkers, couldn't know that, and obviously he couldn't feel it, either.

For Else, that was the sore point. Living entirely out of feeling, whether or not she wounded others, she suffered from Erich's rationalism, his lack of intuition, his inability to give her what she called animal warmth. And although she continued to try—right up to the end of her life—to put his great human advantages over his innate weaknesses, not to blame him for them, indeed often to assume herself the blame for his behavior, she never succeeded in repressing a profound resentment against him. Over the years, it decreased, with the shift from love to friendship and finally with the political events that forced her to become completely independent of Erich, but at that time, when her love and the expectations and demands associated with it were still alive, she was in serious discord with Erich and with herself.

Her letters to Fritz and Enie vacillated between resentment, insight, resignation, and delicious self-irony:

Today it has been a week since I left Berlin. Despite the sleeping car, the trip was so arduous—I sat with poor Tina in the train for twenty-two hours—that to tell the truth I don't know how I can go on or even come back. I'm totally exhausted. The first impression of Lugano was so beautiful, however, that I became very cheerful and forgot all my fears. Gentle, glittering lakes, huge mountains, a radiant blue sky, hot sun. Unfortunately, shortly thereafter mist hid both the lake and the mountains, and then it began to rain, at first a drizzle, then a downpour, and that's how it has stayed. God knows I don't consider this a pleasure trip. It's just that for an already gray mood a gray sky is not exactly the best thing. I've absolutely had enough of the South, can't stand the people. But maybe that's just because my other trip to the South was so beautiful and I was then so happy. At the expense of others. You reap what you sow, my mother used to say, and she was right!

This is just a short report on the outward circumstances, about my inner state I say nothing. It has already been discussed far too much, especially by Erich, who thinks he can replace things by clever words. Fallacy! We've seen what has come from talking, but we don't know what will happen now . . .

Else felt abandoned by God and the world, and when Fritz and Enie incautiously wrote that Erich was apparently leading a busy life in Berlin, she exploded:

That so much is going on around Erich did not exactly enchant me. If things go on that way I'll probably never hear from him again. He abruptly calls or sends me money, but my requests that he write to me fall on deaf ears. And why should he write me? During the day he has business to transact, and in the evening he has social events, and moreover he's sluggish. It takes him twenty-four hours to write a letter and a year to make a decision. So he can't scribble a few lines or act spontaneously out of feeling now and then. Every word has to be profound and beautiful, every action weighed, turned over, and examined a hundred times. And I see the result—neither letters nor actions. I am resigned; the man can no longer be changed. He's been living with his parents for thirty years and dances to the tune of his inhuman father. He has never dared to do what he really wanted, whether it was private or professional, and he never will. He's good, but weak. Don't reproach him, he'll be on the verge of a nervous breakdown. Well, so am I. I go from one state to the other, I'm excited, offended, furious, impatient, desperate. Your advice, Pitt, is good, but unfortunately cannot be put into action. How should I do that: live like a tortoise? My shell grows so slowly, and besides, I'm not the kind of person or animal that could live in one. What can you still get out of life, if you no longer let anything touch you? But for a few months I might nonetheless like to have a shell.

Instead of a shell she got an increasingly thin skin, and her nervous condition and difficulties sleeping got steadily worse. Finally she went to a doctor who, as she wrote, kept fiddling around with her and was amazed that his medicines didn't help.

Do you think I sleep? I don't sleep at all any more. Never. I read incessantly, and pure crap. Here there is a lending library that has taken as its task to spoil people's taste even further. Yesterday I dove into a novel in which there were a great many serving maids, and they all had a child, and 50 percent of them died in childbirth. Should I take that as a hint? And then there are the crossword puzzles. If I discover one in a magazine, I jump on it. Recently I bought myself a whole book of puzzles, but as soon as I opened it I no longer felt like doing them. I think the attraction of figuring out the puzzle lies in its rarity. Where does attraction not lie in rarity? So after the fiasco with the puzzle book I bought myself a needlework project. I did my last one when I was seven years old, and it turned out better than the one I'm working on now. But if mother could see me with a needle and thread, she'd sigh and think that I've finally managed to return to my true vocation.

The best part of my days is bathing. I lie in the tub for hours and it seems to me that I look like a jellyfish in my shape, color, and utility.

The hotel is still full of guests—unsophisticated people whom I wouldn't touch with fire-tongs. 'Fine' ladies, who stay here for months, spend a fortune for it, and rest—from what, I can't imagine. They sit mainly in the lobby, chat genteelly, and consider everyone who does not belong to their circle suspicious. Especially if she is pregnant and a husband who would justify her condition never appears.

Today is Sunday, everything is gray and hazy. I wonder whether I will ever have another beautiful Sunday. I used to not like Sundays, but now, when I think back on them, they seem delicious to me. That's how it is with everything . . .

It was now early December, and in Lugano things were becoming increasingly uncomfortable. Else's mood declined with the barometer and Erich's failure to write or act. The only things that still delighted her were little Bettina, who found everything beautiful and enchanted everyone with her amiability and contentedness, and Enie's letters:

"You can't imagine," she wrote to her friend, "how starved I am for news from Berlin, and no one conveys it as wittily and maligns it as wickedly as you do. And there's no one I can really jaw with except for you and Pitt. Most people adopt a peculiar tone, a kind of unspontaneous epistolary German, which is moreover burdened by uncertainty as to how they should speak with me now: cheerfully, optimistically, and 'after all, it's not so bad,' or admonishingly, edifyingly, 'just don't play your last card wrong,' or both together, so that I have only to choose between not so bad and my last card. You and I simply speak the same language, and I can tell you how I really feel.

"Unfortunately, I can't believe what you tell me about Erich. How can he not curse me for all the problems, troubles, and costs I have caused him and am still causing him? He had no idea what lay ahead of him, as unworldly and eccentric as he is. Moreover, he didn't want it, and acquiesced only because of his decency.

"No, we won't spend Christmas together. He'd like to come, but he doesn't dare because of his parents. It would be the first Christmas he ever spent without them, and if it also came out that he was spending it with the Jewess, the Schrobsdorff family's Prussian honor would be lost. I haven't any idea when we'll see each other, and to tell the truth, I can't stand any more! Maybe I'm being unfair to myself, things could be much better, or they could get even worse. But whether better or worse, things will never be as they once were. We've destroyed everything!"

As Christmas approached and people were getting ready to

leave the hotel, Else could no longer bear it in Lugano. She wrote to Enie:

> "Here it's dull as ditchwater, everyone has gone away. Rain. An old goat is running around pumping everyone for information, a charming young widow who has already lost two husbands is wasting away, an elegant French married couple with a car complains about the food. In the evening, I used to gossip with an aristocratic pan-German woman landowner, a seriously ill man whose wife ran away precisely here, and a jolly but stupid Swiss woman. That was my circle!
>
> "Yesterday Wilhelm Herzog called me and said I should finally come to Davos. I would love to do that and would immediately set out if I were not afraid for Tina. Probably silly, because Davos is a winter health resort like any other. I've always wanted to go high up in the mountains in winter. All that snow, the clear air, everything so white and pure—it must be splendid. My doctor also thinks nothing would happen, the journey is short, the delivery won't take place for a month, but he thinks it would be so depressing there. Nonsense! It's not sick people who depress me, it's dumb ones. I need people, not 'fine' people, I need conversations, not medicines."

So a month before the delivery, which was to take place in Berlin, Else traveled to Davos to see Wilhelm Herzog, a good friend and then a well-known writer. From there she wrote another short, hasty letter to Fritz:

> "Pitt, relieve me of at least one concern and finally spend some time with little Peter. You neglect him in a way that you will someday be reproached for. He's already ten, and although my parents give him the best of care, he may

sometimes still miss his father. Who will celebrate Christmas with him? My parents will certainly not celebrate it, not even for his sake. And what about Tina? The poor little thing is looking forward so much to Christmas, and asks every day when we're going back to Berlin. Ach, enough!"

On the morning of December 24 Else started back to Berlin. She had intentionally planned it that way, because she couldn't bear the thought of the lonely Christmas Eve without Erich, in a foreign place and in the company of sad and bitter thoughts. The less importance she attributed to the day, the less festively she spent it, the better. However, she intended to interrupt her trip in Freiburg and improvise a little Christmas celebration for Bettina in a hotel where she had reserved a room. But one does not pray for the impossible in Catholic churches and then get what one asks for with impunity. To the child it seemed a good idea to further strengthen her mother's belief in miracles by coming into the world prematurely, on Christmas Eve. She surely didn't know to what a burden she was subjecting herself by doing so.

Else, who had just lighted the candles on the hastily purchased tiny Christmas tree, blew them out again, but the always charming and contented Bettina thought that was going too far, and began to cry.

"Just imagine," her mother consoled her, "now you're going to get the most wonderful Christmas gift that a little girl could ask for, a little brother or sister, a real Christ child."

The Christ child, a girl, was born with a caul that lay on her sparsely-haired head like a handkerchief. Another sign of good luck! It was almost too much of a good thing. At that moment Else found the right name for the symbol-laden child: Angelika.

Erich, who was informed of his daughter's birth, went to

Freiburg the following day. He was not what might be called a proud, happy father. All the more because the child was a girl. That was all he needed! He'd hoped that if he had to become the father of a child, it would at least be a son. Sons had more to offer, he thought. The only thing this girl had to offer was that she had managed to be born on Christmas Eve. Perhaps there was at least some deeper meaning in that.

He was very upset. There was not only the first encounter with his daughter, for whom he would be, for better or for worse, responsible for the rest of his life, but also the reunion with Else, whose irrational moods, from crying fits to outbursts of rage, still haunted and depressed him.

The separation, which she seemed to hold against him, and the birth, which was said to unleash unpredictable processes in a woman's body and mind, might have further aggravated her condition.

He found a new Else: beautiful and pale, with big doe-like eyes, quiet and turned inward on herself, with a gentle smile. Erich hardly dared move. He approached on tiptoe, silent, smiling, and with the fervent thought: dear God, let her always be so pale and inward!

She lifted the newborn up as if she were a winner's trophy of pure gold: "Angelika," she said softly and reverently.

Erich looked at the maggot-like creature with his characteristic politeness, but the longer he looked at it, the more concerned he became. He'd never seen a newborn up close, and for the life of him couldn't imagine that it would become human. "Do you think the child is normal?" he finally asked awkwardly.

Else began to laugh. Now that she held in her arms her daughter, with whom her strength, happiness, and confidence had returned, she found Erich's unworldliness amusing again. She declared that this was not only a normal but a perfect, a wonderful child. Seventeen years later, when he went dancing with her for the first time, he would be the proudest father in God's wide world.

Now Erich had to laugh. He never laughed heartily out loud, but rather to himself, deeply, slowly, and in rounded tones.

He asked whether between now and the time she was seventeen something might be done with her, or whether that was too much to ask of a girl.

In two years at the most, Else said, he would be head over heels in love with her and do far too much with her.

Aha, Erich said with a skeptical look at the ugly infant and gave another of his deep laughs.

I've been told that I was an unusual baby. I never screamed, but instead angrily scratched my face. My mother, who was supported out of love by the Kirschner grandparents, panicked. The three of them took me to a doctor. He examined me and found that I was not a deaf-mute, as they had feared, but a very healthy child in every respect. He recommended that they put mittens on my hands and be happy that I didn't scream. But the mittens annoyed me so much that I screamed. Everyone was greatly relieved: thank God, an entirely normal child!

The mittens were taken off, and I immediately fell silent and resumed my earlier activity.

Since the age of psychology had not yet dawned, no further thought was given to my behavior until the next peculiarity appeared. At some point I stopped scratching, the red streaks healed up, and I became a plump, blond, pretty baby.

My memory reaches back to my second year of life. It consists not of coherent sequences but of schematic images that can, however, suddenly become so insistent on some insignificant detail that I'm not sure whether they come to me from my memory or from something I was told.

At that time we lived in Wannsee, on Lindenstraße, a steep street at whose highest point our house stood. I see an unusually large, asymmetrical room with a parquet floor. Also a black, open piano and a long, upholstered bench in front of the French doors leading to the terrace. A stairway connects this room with the upper floor, where the children's room Bettina and I shared was located. Its walls are painted with large figures; I no longer recall what they represented, I have a clear memory only of the colors: light blue, yellow, and orange.

The garden is large and goes downhill along with the street. There are many trees in it, and the grass is thick and high. The berry vines are in the back part of the garden, in a narrow strip that connects with the back side of the house. I see the terrace clearly, and never without my grandparents, the petite, black-clad Minna, with her small, dark face and iron-gray hair, and the short, round-bellied Daniel with his pink, bald head and the wart under the left corner of his mouth. They are sitting at a round table under a parasol which—though I might have added this detail—has the shape and colors of a mushroom. Still today, parasols are for me the symbol of security, because they are inseparable from my grandparents. Grandma and Grandpa Kirschner appear in my memories even before my mother, and that may be because the phase of my first conscious awareness took place while she was away. I learned later that she was then on a long trip with my father, and my grandparents were living with Bettina and me in Wannsee.

Thus they were the first people I consciously loved and who gave me, with their consistent kindness, patience, and tenderness, the feeling of unconditional security, a feeling I was never to have with my mother. I see them not only at the round table on the terrace, urging me to eat with jokes, songs, and little games, I also see them on walks with Bettina, me, and Linda, our huge Newfoundland, clinging to whose thick, black fur I made my first attempts to walk. My sister and I walked on ahead, and Linda, ever ready to save us, followed close on our heels, while Grandma called in a voice that I can still hear: "Halt, halt, halt, halt . . ." It is a clear, ringing voice that rises one note higher with each "halt." In this first memory series, my mother finally appears: a straw hat with an enormous brim, a large, laughing, dark brown face with strong white teeth and wide-open, phosphorescent eyes. A wild, strange, frightening face that I'd never seen before. I know—or someone told me— that I was sitting on a high piece of furniture and my grand-mother was dressing me. The face came nearer, becoming ever larger, ever more frightening, and I began to cry, clung to my grandmother, and hid in her protective arms.

And my father? He appears neither in the first, schematic memory images nor in the later, more exact ones. And yet I've been told that he was often with us in Wannsee and followed with increasing wonderment and attention—though from a certain distance—my development from a maggot-like crea-ture to a cute little child.

I don't see my brother Peter, either, but that may be because at that time he was in a boarding school and seldom visited us. Thus the two men whom I have most admired only come into focus in my fourth year of life. Up to that point the women who mothered, coddled, and pampered me played a more important role. Elisabeth and Gertrude are clear on the screen of my earliest memories.

They're coming up the gravel path to the house, Elisabeth, Valkyrie-like in stature, with fair, delicate features, a pink sum-mer dress, and a small white hat; Gertrude, also in a light dress, but without a hat. I'm playing with Bettina in the garden, and she tells me that these are the two maids, who have come to introduce themselves to our mother.

Gertrude, the chambermaid, and Elisabeth, the cook, became for me indispensable members of the family. I see myself in the bathtub, and over me is Gertrude's good-natured face. She is washing me gently with a big, soft sponge, and singing "All my little duckies swimming on the lake."

I see Bettina and myself on Elisabeth's ample lap. She has put one arm around my sister, the other around me, and is telling us exciting stories. In the morning, when I'm still lying in bed, I hear the two maids bustling about the bedrooms and the kitchen, hear their steps, their songs, smell floor polish and freshly brewed coffee—and for me that is also security.

My mother then appears more and more clearly and soon becomes the central figure in my life. Her face pushes all others into the background, becomes the most beautiful, most beloved face in my little world. In my memory it looks like a dark sun, her voice sounds like black silk, her body feels like puffy summer clouds, and she smells like damp earth.

She calls me her little spider monkey, because I'm constantly seeking to be near her, hanging on her neck, her hand, her skirt, literally creeping into her. She hugs me to her belly, her breast, takes me in her arms, her lap, showers me with ever-new endearments, silly and gentle, tempestuous and playful. I see the tall fir forest through which my mother is walking to pick up Bettina at school, the lake where we play together, with its sailboats and water birds, the gray, massive car in which we do our shopping; and I see people coming into and going out of our house, many people, but not one of their faces has remained in my memory. They talk, laugh, play the gramophone, lie in the sun, eat, smoke, drink, and behave like silly children with each other. They smile at me, grab at me, try to put me on their knees. I am a serious, reserved, shy child, easily frightened, easily disgusted. I don't like people, whether adults or children. I'm afraid of them. But I like animals. No animal frightens me, no matter how big it is, and no animal disgusts me, no matter how dirty it is. I'm crazy about fur, whether it is coarse and dark, like that of our Newfoundland, Linda, or downy soft and white, like that of my Angora rabbit,

Hoppelchen. I feel his fur under my hand, on my cheek. I see us walking through the big, asymmetrical room, I on tiptoe in ballet slippers, Hoppelchen a few short jumps behind me. For weeks, I walk through the house only on tiptoe. My toes hurt, even though they've been padded with cotton wool, and sometimes even bleed. But I find it exciting to walk differently from ordinary people. How did I get ballet slippers? I no longer know. I wanted them and I got them, just as I got everything I wanted. I grew up with a great deal of love and fulfilled wishes in a wonderful, protected pen. I hardly came in contact with the outside world and its inhabitants, and when it was absolutely necessary for me to do so, then only when holding my mother's hand.

I still remember very well the terrible incident at the hairdresser's. I'm sitting on a high chair under a white mantle, and the hairdresser, a friendly man, is cutting my hair. My mother lets go of my hand and says she's going for just a minute to the grocery next door to buy something. She's gone before I can protest. I see myself in the mirror, alone among strangers in a little room. And then suddenly I can no longer breathe, I gasp for breath, turn pale and am seized by panic. The hairdresser runs out of his shop and gets my mother. As soon as she is at my side the feeling that I'm going to suffocate subsides.

"I'm afraid we're not going to have an easy time of it with her," my mother says, "she's a complicated child."

That was a good time for my mother, perhaps the best of her life. The zone of nerve-wracking turbulence that had hurled her from one love, lie, complication, and uncertainty to the next lay behind her. She saw her future the way one glimpses a landscape on a radiant, beautiful day from the window of a descending airplane: an enchanting, perfectly cut-out pattern of geometrical forms and bright colors, all orderly and neatly arranged, no blurred lines, no confusion, no malformation. On this piece of earth, which promised so much beauty, brilliance, and happiness, she was about to land.

Erich had still not married her, but now it was only a question of time. With Angelika, in whom he had discovered his earnestness and, moreover, his mother's nose, Else had become certain of him and could wait in peace.

The more complicated his daughter became, the greater his interest in her, and what he had earlier done only out of politeness and a sense of duty, he now did out of a slowly but steadily growing need. And thus he became more decisive, firmer, and more open. And Else, who during her pregnancy had feared that their relationship would collapse, realized that a new, wonderful change had occurred. She now no longer loved him with the simple, wild passion that had made him nervous, and he no longer felt her to be a foreign body in his life. They felt themselves deeply bound together by their daughter, and each of them took the other's disadvantages lightly and enjoyed the advantages: she enjoyed Erich's integrity, his reliability, and his financial generosity, and he enjoyed Else's intellectual and emotional vitality, with which she attracted flocks of people and became the center of a constantly growing circle. People were allowed to join this circle only on the condition that they were tolerant, intelligent or at least amusing, artists or at least connoisseurs, literary or at least knowledgeable about literature, good-for-nothings but at least talented. Erich, who had never had access to people like that, felt stimulated and enriched, and spent more and more time in Lindenstraße.

Else was more serene than she'd ever been in her life or ever was again. She was leading the kind of life that corresponded to her temperament: without everyday obligations and routine, independent and yet financially secure. She had everything that seemed to her important or indispensable: her children, a first-class man, a large, interesting circle of friends, a beautiful house in a rural environment that was also close to the city; she had seclusion and nature, when she felt like it, society and bustling activity when she wanted it, and travel abroad with Erich, trips to Hiddensee with friends, great admirers and small, harmless flirtations.

She was 35 years old, in perfect health, and exotically beautiful. She had everything—everything except marriage. And although she had shaken off all the conventions and constraints of bourgeois society, for her marriage remained the culmination of a woman's life.

I've been told that my mother brought me into the Schrobsdorffs' house like a trophy. I must have been about three years old and have no memory of our victorious entrance, but I don't find it hard to imagine.

My mother in a simple but elegant suit, with kid gloves and a soft felt hat, and I in a dark blue Hamburg coat with a white piqué collar, with a fresh haircut and a small, dark blue bowler hat on my head. I sat on my mother's right arm, anxious, bewildered, and clutching a stuffed animal. We walked up the white marble stairs, and my mother, knowing that we were being watched through a crack in the heavy, dark front door, held her head very high and smiled with a trace of irony.

On the porch in front of the high, arched double door, she said to me: "You needn't be afraid, sweetheart, we're visiting your grandparents Schrobsdorff, and they are very eager to meet you." Then she pulled on the bronze knob.

A maid in a black dress, white lace apron, and cap opened the door for us, saying "Good day, gracious lady," and helped my mother take off my coat. The anteroom was paneled in dark wood, and the milk-glass lamps were in the shape of swans. My mother took me in her arms again, smoothed out my hair and her turquoise-colored silk dress that was smocked over the breast, waited until the maid had opened the door, and then stepped aside. The room in front of us was immensely large, as high as a church and gloomy. Light came only through the windows of the surrounding rooms and from a pair of colored glass lamps that glowed dimly. On the floor was a big Persian carpet in muted colors, and around the fireplace stood a few heavy armchairs and a low, oval table with gilt bowlegs.

My mother clutched me closer to her and went up to a group of people who were standing there as motionless as statues on a monument. At the same time a woman emerged from the petrified mass and came toward us with outstretched arms, making jubilant sounds. She was tall and massive, and wore a long, large-flowered gown, out of which rose a small head with a marvelously beautiful porcelain face and a powder-puff of silvery hair.

"Welcome, Else," she called out, "Angelika, my dear child . . . "

She was already within reach, and the group of people came back to life and started moving toward us.

This was too much for me. According to what I've been told, I said: "I wish they were all animals!" and shuddering hid my face in my mother's bosom.

For a moment there was a dead silence that was broken by a grim laugh coming from an armchair before the hearth, followed by a gray-maned lion's head. As if by command, the whole group broke into laughter. "Show me the child," the Prussian aristocrat said, "seems to be a remarkable little thing."

She walked up to the armchair, and the group arranged itself in a half-circle around us. I cautiously gave my new grandfather a long, searching look, and then looked at the rest of the family: the bullet-headed Uncle Walter with his small, pinched features and cold eyes, the mischievous Uncle Alfred, with his thick blond hair and fleshy face; a few stiff gentlemen and genteel ladies who were close relations of the Schrobsdorff house.

"So, so," my grandfather said, "a cute little girl," and held out his hand to my mother.

That was the signal that required all the stiff gentlemen and genteel ladies to shake hands with her as well. We were accepted, we were members of the family, and Annemarie, my new grandmother, hugged us ecstatically to her prow-like, large-flowered bosom.

Erich married Else in 1930, shortly after this successful debut in the Schrobsdorff house, and three years before Hitler took power. She now had a husband, he had a legal wife and daughter, Angelika had a legitimate father, Bettina and Peter had an irreproachable stepfather, Minna and Daniel had an amiable son-in-law, Annemarie and Alfred Sr. had their first daughter-in-law and their first grandchild. Each had what he wanted and needed except for Erich's father, who did not exactly need a Jewish daughter-in-law, and Else's son, who did not under any circumstances want a stepfather, of any kind whatever. But that didn't matter. The main thing was that order prevail, and it prevailed now and was to be still more firmly established.

Daniel, whose wholesale business had gone bankrupt in the crash of 1929, and Minna, who no longer embroidered tablecloths for her own amusement but rather to earn a little money on the side, were invited for coffee at the home of the Schrobsdorffs, who noted with relief that both of them, while not precisely of the same social standing, were yet good, honorable people whose principles, so far as family and duties were concerned, coincided with their own. They spoke to each other as businessman to businessman, as mother to mother, and formed a relationship that was not without affection on the part of the women and not without respect on the part of the men. Invitations were repeated at regular intervals and even included the Christmas celebration, an honor that the Kirschners, despite the discomfort it caused them, dared not refuse.

Else left Wannsee and moved with Erich and their daughters to an elegant house in Berlin-Grunewald. Elisabeth and

Gertrude accompanied them. Linda, who was too big, and Hoppelchen, who was not house-trained, were replaced by an Irish Setter and two grayish-blue Persian cats. They made a decorative trio. Peter, who was now fourteen, handsome, smart, lazy, and frivolous, infatuated with his mother and hostile to his father-in-law, attended Salem, the most exclusive boarding school in Germany. Bettina, nine, who remained a contented little girl, lived with her new Papa, the only one in her life who was to become a real father to her. Angelika still clung like a spider monkey to her mother, but soon discovered her father and became attached to him with a shy, reverential passion.

Else had become Frau Dr. Schrobsdorff, a lady with all that accompanied that title, but without its affectations. Her wardrobe was filled with silk underwear, dresses for every season and occasion, coats made of cloth and fur, shoes and sandals with high heels, and hats with broad brims, feathers, and veils. Her hair was cut in the latest style, she wore lipstick, and painted her fingernails red. She had become as slim as her stocky body structure allowed, and as fashionable as her interests allowed. But she never had the kind of figure or polished elegance that impressed people. There was always a curl that could not be tamed, cracked nail polish, a run in her stocking. Basically, she cared little about fashion and cosmetics and not at all about jewelry.

In the same year came the premiere of Fritz Schwiefert's *Margherite and her Three Uncles*, the comedy that he based on Else and the time he spent in the Dahlem villa. They went to the premiere together, the two, big, esoteric men and the two petite, earthy women. They watched pass before their eyes once again that part of their past out of which emerged two marriages, two children, and a Nazi, and that ended, on the stage as in life, with an "All's well that ends well." Or so they thought.

The play was a huge success, and Fritz became famous and wealthy. He retired to a magnificent estate called Am Kleinen Wannsee. Enie was expecting a child, and with her pregnancy, her husband's success, and the comforts of an affluent lifestyle she'd become happy and therefore calmer.

That was the situation in 1930. Order and clarity prevailed.

Else had trod a long, dangerous path out of the textile-making Jewish milieu into the Prussian upper class, from the little bourgeois girl to a lady of the great world. She had followed the golden thread of her dreams, and she had reached her goal. There was no longer any "completely different." She had become part of it, she was integrated into it, body and soul.

The house in Hubertusallee, in Grunewald, was a two-story villa, not counting the basement, where the doorman and his wife, Herr and Frau Höhne lived. It was white, and I think ivy-covered. The windows were high and narrow, and on the front, right in the middle of the façade, a balcony bulged out from it. There was only a small front garden with a hedge that concealed the fence. The entrance was on the left side.

In the morning, the horse-drawn carriage stopped in front of the house, and I ran down to give the two feisty brown horses sugar cubes. My mother stood at the window to keep an eye on me. She was constantly afraid that something might happen to me, just as I was constantly afraid that something might happen to her.

I still recall the layout of the house very clearly, the size and shape of the rooms, the beautiful old furniture, the Persian and velvet carpets, the many pictures, chandeliers, pleated curtains and long, ample drapes of heavy fabric. On the lower floor was the entrance hall, roomy and more than two stories high, on one side of which, closest to the street, was the very large living room, the dining room, and my mother's bedroom and dressing room, and on the other side, my father's bedroom, his library, and the kitchen. A stairway with a massive wooden banister and a dark green runner led from the entrance hall to the upper floor, where the bedrooms for Bettina and me, Peter, and the maids were located.

For me, crystal clear memories are bound up with each of these rooms: the children's room full of colorful toys, in which Bettina and I waged pillow fights from one bed to the other, my father read to us before we went to sleep, and then joined us in saying the Lord's Prayer, sometimes in Latin, sometimes in German; Peter's room, with the big canopy bed, which he lived in for only a year and in which my sister and I so much liked to sit on the windowsill in the winter, shelling peanuts and eating them, chatting and looking out into the snow flurries. There we also organized little parties, cooked inedible things on our doll stove, and invited our father to join us. I still see him sitting on the floor, in an uncomfortable posture, holding a tiny plate in his hand, and I could swear that at his first bite he uttered his famous "Oh là là!" And I see the brightly lit entry hall from the top step of the stairway, on which Bettina and I, feverish with excitement, huddled to watch the guests enter: ladies in evening dresses, gentlemen in tuxedos. Oh, the glitter and the mystery that radiated from these beautiful women and courtly men, the fragrance, a mixture of perfume and Turkish tobacco, that rose up to us, the wealth of voices and laughter, the dance music played by a small orchestra: "It can happen only once, it will never return, it's too beautiful to be true . . . "

Damned memories, crystal-clear and uncanny. Why hasn't the filmstrip in my head broken or even faded? Why do I still see the brocade armchair in which my mother often sat reading in the morning, the little secretary at which she wrote letters, the piano that stood between the window and the door to the balcony? Why haven't I forgotten the seating arrangement at the round dining table—my father on my left, my mother on my right, and Bettina opposite me—the high, narrow backs of the chairs, the gold and black borders of the plates, the silver napkin rings on which our names were engraved? Why am I still overcome with a sense of being lost when I think about my mother's bedroom—the white varnish, the light gray velvet carpet, the reddish half-light that shimmered through the Bordeaux-colored curtains, a carafe of water and a pillbox on the night table. And she so little in the huge bed, the duvet pulled up to the tip of her nose, her almost lashless eyes with the high eyelids clamped shut. She was so far away from me in her numbed sleep, from which she reawakened to life only slowly and with difficulty.

I don't recall having ever seen my father in her bedroom, and I saw her in his only when I was allowed to lie in it during the day because I was sick. He had a marvelous bed, similar to my brother's, with a canopy of dark wood and a gold-brocaded dark blue curtain that could be closed. Where I saw my father most often was in his shrine, the library. This was an awe-inspiring room that suited him well. All four walls were covered with books from floor to ceiling, and they gave me a feeling of deep peace. I was allowed to go into the library only when my father was there, and had to be very calm and quiet. We sat next to each other on the dark blue silk-covered sofa, he with an open book, I with my hands folded in my lap. Sometimes he put his arm around me and kissed me on the cheek or the hair. He talked with me, seriously, as if with an adult, or he read to me out of one of the books. I did not understand much, but it was thrillingly beautiful. Basically, everything he did and said was thrillingly beautiful. I never saw him when he wasn't perfectly dressed from head to foot, with a monocle around his neck, a pearl tie-pin, his signet ring on his finger, and his full, dark blond hair, which swept back from his forehead in deep waves, carefully combed and wonderfully fragrant with eau de cologne.

Yes, he was wonderful, my father, and so different from all

others. I couldn't love him the way I loved my mother, with that wild spider-monkey love, or feel as deeply and warmly secure as I did with my grandparents Kirschner, or cry about something and beg as I did with Gertrude. My father could only be adored from a certain distance. I did that, and so did everyone who knew him.

I never saw anyone say a loud or disrespectful word to him, not even my mother, who at that time often screamed and stormed. Not Elisabeth, either, who had in the meantime become the highest authority in our household, and regulated us all, including even my father, but only very quietly and assertively, and never with a trace of impoliteness. I once heard her say to him: "Herr Dr. Schrobsdorff, you won't be doing Angelika any favor if you fulfill her every wish. A child must know where the limits are. So don't bring a second dog into the house!"

I'd wanted a dog that belonged to me alone, but in fact I didn't get it. Elisabeth was the only person who knew how I was to be handled, and had my parents not constantly undermined her educational methods, I would probably have been a less complicated child.

Elisabeth came from Stralsund, where her father kept a store that sold imported products and her mother had taught her the art of hearty Pomeranian cooking, for which we all paid the price. When she came to us, she might have been in her late twenties, a young woman, but unusually mature and clear-sighted.

"Now, don't you give me any trouble," she used to say to me, "and eat up that half-slice of bread! Why can't you ever act normal? Just look at your sister!"

She loved me, there was no doubt of that, but she loved Bettina more, as I now guess, out of a deep sense of justice— Bettina the normal child, who certainly did not know but instinctively felt that she did not enjoy the privileges that her older brother and her younger sister did, and took it for granted that she couldn't make the same claims.

Nothing remained hidden from Elisabeth. She had second sight, which allowed her to see through each and every one of us, and she foresaw everything that was brewing.

Even then, in the house on Hubertusallee, when order finally prevailed and we lacked for nothing.

The move from rural Wannsee into the city, to a house without a garden, from a footloose life to a regulated married life, did not suit Else. The days, weeks, months went by with a sameness that made her restless instead of peaceful. At eight in the morning, Bettina left for school and Erich for his office. At 1 P.M. they returned, and we ate lunch together. Afterward, the children went to play in their room, while Erich withdrew for an hour to his library. At three he returned to his office, and the little girls went for a walk with Else or with Gertrude. Between seven and eight, Erich returned home, fussed about a long time freshening up, read the children a fairy tale, said the Lord's Prayer with them, and then joined Else in the living room, where she sat alone or with friends. She usually had something planned for the evening, and Erich accompanied her without protest to cultural events, restaurants, and parties, was a charming host or an amiable guest. But she noticed that he was tired and in many cases would have preferred to stay quietly at home.

On Tuesdays and Fridays, she took her daughters to their grandparents Kirschner in the early afternoon, and felt obliged to stay there half an hour. On Sundays they had decided—Erich, Bettina, Angelika, and she—to arrive at the Schrobsdorffs' house at one o'clock sharp. The midday meal they ate—with heavy dishes and conventional conversations, the subsequent hour of rest, the walk in the Grunewald, and the return for coffee, pastries, and whipped cream, were a family tradition that could not be violated under any circumstances.

Their life had been a chaos, a steep up-and-down of passionate feelings that sometimes succeeded in keeping her in suspense and sometimes not. Now it was order and routine, a tepid, still water without depths, without turmoil, without cliffs. She did not encounter the currents of the open sea or unexplored shores; instead, she turned sluggishly round in a circle, inch by inch. Naturally, she had her friends and acquaintances, small, harmless flirtations, and great admirers who had followed her from Lindenstraße to Hubertusallee, but now these relationships and gatherings were also subject to certain constraints—concern about Erich, and etiquette, which was important to him. In Wannsee, people had eaten and slept, made music or noise, romped in the garden or lain in the sun, whenever they felt like it. Male and female friends had come and gone at the most impossible times, spent the night at their home, organized impromptu picnics and parties. They'd gone swimming in the moonlight and sledding in the snow. They'd been silly, childish, and crazy, but even Erich had had fun, been a friend and a lover, and sometimes even a little boy. Now he, a son who had lived exclusively in his parents' house until the age of thirty-two, was suddenly a husband and a father, responsible for a family of four, the head of a lavish household. And since he took nothing lightly and found nothing easy, to fulfill his family duties he needed an abundance of time and strength, and perhaps as much willpower as his work required.

Else was aware of all this, was grateful to Erich, and sometimes felt sympathy for him, loved him with that new, passionate love, and continued to feel deeply bound to him. But she wasn't a woman who could fool herself and convince herself, with the help of self-deception, of a contentedness that she simply did not feel. She'd achieved precisely what she'd wanted and intended to achieve. She didn't regret anything, oh, no, nothing at all, and she rejoiced in many things that this new life of hers offered, knew very well that for a woman with her impracticable upbringing and a taste for comfort, she had hit the jackpot, but that didn't alter the feeling of listlessness and emptiness that tortured her more and more frequently and persistently.

The insomnia that had been since her youth a symptom of inner unrest and tension began to torment her again, and as a result of the barbiturates she took every night, waking up in the morning was difficult and accompanied by headaches and drowsiness. Only when Elisabeth had brought her a pot of strong coffee and she had drunk a few cups of it did she come around.

"Frau Schrobsdorff," Elisabeth warned her from time to time, "You're doing yourself in with this stuff."

"If I don't take it and don't sleep at night, I'm even more done in," Else replied querulously.

She was furious with herself. Precisely she, such a healthy, physically robust person had to be plagued by a disorder for which there was no cure. Her nerves became increasingly fragile and the outbursts of rage to which she had always been inclined became fits of anger. She was now made furious by little things such as Angelika's complicatedness, Bettina's sluggishness, or Peter's laziness, to which the director of the boarding school had repeatedly drawn her attention, asking her to talk some sense into her extraordinarily talented but inattentive son.

She bellowed at her daughters and ran out of the room before they even knew what it was about; she called up her son, bellowed at him as well, and hung up before he could say a word. She immediately regretted doing so and ran back into the room and showered her daughters with endearments; called her son again and overflowed with love. Every time she swore anew never to scream again. What could the poor children do? They were not to blame for her labile nerves. So let them be a little complicated, sluggish, or lazy. The main thing was that they were happy.

I feared my mother's accesses of rage more than the witch in "Hansel and Gretel." These were moments of fear and terror that I already knew more than enough about. In a picture of me painted in these years by the artist Jäckel, a friend of my parents', I look like a Käthe Kruse doll looking out at the world full of suspicion and rejection. My sister still maintains that I was a dreadful child: silent and malicious. In one of his last letters, my brother wrote: "At that time she was already a headstrong and self-assured little person, a future Lucrezia Borgia . . ." The statements made by my siblings almost coincide, except that Peter, who had not had to put up with me as Bettina had, saw things somewhat more positively.

When I was five, my parents considered me a highly talented child, because I could already read and write poetry as well. The first poem I said to my resigned sister went this way:

> I'm already awake
> the sky is dark, the stars glitter
> what am I doing here on Earth?
> I have no husband, I have no child
> what am I doing here on Earth?
> I'd rather be in heaven's tent."

Bettina said only: "You're completely crazy," but my parents were shocked, perhaps more by the content than by the lyricism. As always, for them I was a great talent, though this does not, in my opinion, emerge very clearly in the following poems. They do not deal with problems as urgent as my lack of a husband and child, but instead praise, in emotional terms, nature and Christmastime. In approach, they resemble those of my grandmother Schrobsdorff, from whom my nose was not my only inheritance. It must have been she who inspired me to write them, with her blue and green Biedermeyer bedroom and the grotto in the garden. That was where she wrote her poems, and there she read them to me, but fortunately not only her own. These were splendid rooms, stylish right down to the spittoons and bellpulls, gems in the generally spectacular house that made up for the tortuous meals. I liked to sit at the magnificently set table, but instead of eating, I intently observed the Schrobsdorff tribe: the grandfather, who presided at the head of the table and to whom my relation consisted in curtseying before him and then offering my forehead for a fleeting kiss; my grandmother in one of her large-flowered gowns that she had made by amateurish seamstresses, so that these poor creatures could also earn a little money; Uncle Walter with his pinched face, whom I regarded with disdain and whose smile, which looked like he was biting into a lemon, I never returned; his wife Leonie, whom he had recently married, an extravagant figure who couldn't have sprung from the pure German race and who two years later died from an ectopic pregnancy; Uncle Alfred, the black sheep of the family, who charmed me with his jokes, tomfooleries, and funny faces; and also this or that relation who was fed at the table of the rich and always behaved with quiet humility.

I sat between my mother and my father, who put little bites of venison or hare, pheasant or partridge on my plate and from time to time pleaded with me to put them in my mouth. I was a child who considered eating to be as superfluous as washing her neck and ears, and who easily became sick at the sight of food of any kind whatever. But when the meal was finally over and the adults, at least a couple of pounds heavier, had stretched out in various bedrooms for a little nap, what Bettina and I considered the most exciting part of the day began.

Sometimes we were allowed to play ghosts with Helga Lange, the chauffeur's daughter, on the top floor, where the rooms were no longer used and the pieces of furniture, covered with white sheets, were like uncanny figures, or play leapfrog on the paved courtyard in front of Helga's parents' tower-like home.

Sometimes I preferred to remain alone and daydream for a while among the exotic plants in the conservatory, or on the polar bear rug in the music room, whose realistic head with its wide-open mouth and red tongue fascinated me. It often happened that my grandmother forewent her nap in order to devote herself to me. If she didn't read me poems, she played the piano, with perfection and great feeling.

I sat alongside her on the upholstered piano bench, while her dogs, Strolchi, an aged dachshund who was coming apart at the seams, and Pucki, an ill-tempered Pinscher, both perfumed and bedecked with large silk ribbons, listened to her just as reverently as I did. Yes, those were wonderful times, and even the obligatory walk in the Grunewald pleased me. We went there in a convoy, I with my grandparents in an enormous black car driven by the liveried Herr Lange, who was separated from his passengers by a sheet of glass and communicated with them through a speaking tube. We walked in two groups, one male, which talked about real estate, and one female, which discussed current events. Because of my marked aversion to tortes and whipped cream, I was spared the subsequent coffee hour.

Such were Sundays at the home of my grandparents Schrobsdorff, whose strict ritual forced me to adopt a behavior that sometimes became a burden, despite all the pleasure. In the house in Ahornallee I never felt so free, so happy, and so warm as I did in my grandparents Kirschners' apartment. I loved them with an elemental, serene love not mixed with fear, as was the painful love I felt for my mother, and the reverent love I felt for my father. It was a love that made me happy and freed me from the anxiety that constantly lurked in me. There was nothing more calming than to sit in the penumbral living room, with Grandmother on the little platform at her sewing table, Grandfather in his armchair under the floor lamp with a green shade; nothing more amusing than Grandfather's round belly, his pink, bald head, and the wart under the left corner of his mouth, which he claimed was a doorbell button, and said "kling-a-ling!" whenever I pushed on it; and nothing more familiar than my grandmother's black clothes, the medallion on her high collar, and her clouded face, out of which the sun broke forth on me with every glance. For them I was not the complicated child, the strange little girl, the great talent; for them I was simply a child, a beloved child, who had to be treated calmly and with care.

When I was five, I was sent to the private school that was directly across the street from our house. This was a major mistake on my parents' part and should probably be attributed to my ability to read and write poetry. The school was the first place where I had to remain alone for hours in a strange environment and among unfamiliar children.

I had always avoided contact with children my own age and could not be convinced to take part in the children's parties to which I was invited. For me, children were even scarier than adults, because they were uncontrolled, and the racket they made, the games they played in groups, and the ways they related to their coevals were often based on a cruelty that was instinctively communicated to me. And now I was suddenly confined in a room with five of these little poltergeists, and saw them as my enemies to boot, with the result that I fearfully and distrustfully isolated myself from them. I got along no better with the teacher, for with words I could not write and mathematical problems I could not solve she put me in a terrible quandary and made my fellow pupils laugh scornfully. School became a torture for me, and I became the victim of indefinable but in no way simulated conditions. My parents didn't know what to do, and tried to balance the vexation of learning with the joy of dancing. So I was given tights and a little skirt of light blue satin and began taking ballet lessons. Now that was something completely different! My mother was allowed to stay during the lesson, the teacher, slender and agile in her black leotard, impressed me, and I almost liked the little girls, who were all just as light blue and willing as I was. I danced with enthusiasm and strove to become a prima ballerina as soon as possible.

As for my choice of profession, I had no worries at all. For me it was clear that I would become not only a prima ballerina but also a poet and a landowner. The first and second professions would not be difficult to manage, because I was already on the right path and had already had successes. But for the realization of the third I was largely dependent on my father. He was the one who had a great deal of money, and would have to buy me what I needed to be a landowner.

I told him my plan, and he listened to me very seriously and then said: "Oh là là." This was the prelude to a long thought process during which he walked up and down the room, mumbling to himself. I waited quietly and patiently. When he stopped and said, looking up at the ceiling: "All right . . . good . . . finished . . . done," I knew that the time had come. He smiled at me and asked if I was thinking of an estate. Since I had exact ideas, I could immediately tell him: a manor house, horse-stalls, many, many animals, and a huge garden with fields, meadows, and forests.

He asked whether for starters a normal farmhouse, two stalls, a couple of animals and a big, beautiful garden with flowers and fruit trees would do.

I thought about it, decided that that was enough to start with, and nodded.

Good, he said. We can do that.

That weekend we drove out to a small village on a big lake near the frontier of Brandenburg. It was about 30 miles from Berlin and was called Pätz. I learned that part of the village, a great deal of land, and a brickworks belonged to the Schrobsdorffs.

"What about the lake," I asked, "does it belong to us too?"

"Humility is not exactly your strength," my father said, and laughed to himself. "No, the lake does not belong to us, but that house over there does. Would you like to have it?"

I stared at the house, a large, beautiful house built for people. Up to that point I had always been given only dollhouses. "Can I really have it?" I whispered.

"Yes," my father said, "from now on it belongs to you, your mother, and your sister."

"Of course," I said, disappointed. "To them too."

And so Pätz came into our lives.

Pätz was the turning point in Else's life. It restored her freedom, the unrestricted existence without constraints or routine, her sleep, bubbling vitality, and radiant, deeply tanned face. Never was her appeal for people stronger, her success with men greater, than in the period between 1932 and 1935. And never had she made such uninhibited use of them.

It would have been easier for me and more effective for the story if I could claim that she had sensed the coming catastrophe and thrown herself into life before she had to let it go. As if she were living, so to speak, her swan song. But that's not how it was, at least not at the beginning, in 1932; later on, perhaps, when despite all her desperate attempts to blend in and deceive herself to the point of unconsciousness, she still repeatedly had moments of ineluctable clear-sightedness which, like phantom pains, continued to produce their effects during the long stretches of mental derangement. It may be that she was acting on the basis of feeling: in any case, it doesn't matter, and now I do what I can with what there is. In a letter written in 1943, in which she warned me that I would lose my father if I were not "more reasonable," she wrote: "You might not notice it, and your papa might not show it, but inwardly something in him would break. And once that happens, there will be nothing, nothing at all, that can be done. Then you'll have lost him. Forever. Believe me, I know this very well, because I also lost him by being unreasonable, selfish, and addicted to pleasure. I didn't ask what was good for Papa, I asked only what was good and easy for me. He worked, and I amused myself. He never said anything, but inside he was bitterly disappointed, and he didn't love me as much as he earlier had. Papa worships duty, goodness, and propriety . . ."

So that was the balance sheet Else had drawn up for those four years, and she never got over it.

It's pointless to ask what came over her at that time. Asked, she herself would probably have shrugged and answered: "Madness." She was anything but a clear-minded person who reflected on her actions and took responsibility for them. That came only later on, after the breakdown, and it was accompanied by an unsparing self-knowledge. But up to that point, despite her high intelligence, experience, and sporadic insight, she lived only on the basis of a jumble of feelings and drives and allowed herself to be led, as she wrote in an early letter to Fritz Schwiefert, not by reason but by her feelings.

Pätz, a little nook in the middle of nowhere in which one could throw off civilization and devote oneself to unrestrained joy in nature and the senses, was the triggering element. It was a mixture of Dahlem and Wannsee, but with the decisive difference that Else's relationships with men in Dahlem had been motivated by love, and in Wannsee had remained platonic. Now they were neither. She became infatuated, of course, with this one and that one, but it also worked without feelings, and perhaps even better.

Pätz became an El Dorado for many people. Friends brought acquaintances along and acquaintances brought their friends, women brought their secret lovers and men their newest mistresses, parents brought their children and children their playmates. They lay in the sun, swam in the lake, played bocce and croquet, amused themselves in harmless and harmful ways, found each other, separated, became infatuated, deceived one another, quarreled and reconciled.

It was certainly not a banal, boring group. Many of the men were famous or became famous, many of the women were beautiful or attractive in one way or another. They were all original to the point of being exceptions that had to be tolerated for some reason. They were not interested in politics or only at the eleventh hour. Money played no role so long as one had enough to live on and friends who gave parties and had country houses. They were not materialistic, and neither were they idealistic. They were liberal, and got involved only when it was a matter of "higher values": art and culture, literature and the humanities. Their motto was "Let's go, we're going to live!"

Ellen Gallweit was part of Else's immediate entourage. She was the daughter of her former sister-in-law Luzie and Walter Slezak, the son of the two-hundred-pound opera singer Leo Slezak. Ellen had developed into a twenty-year-old femme fatale who had grown very tall and beautiful, bleached her hair platinum blond, was tanned nut-brown all over, dressed provocatively, attracted astonished attention wherever she went and fascination wherever she lay. There was a legend, which persisted until the death of the last of her lovers that I know about, that Ellen had a natural talent in matters of love, was eager to learn new kinds of sex play, and was prepared to do anything with joy. She was, moreover, a good-hearted, always amusing person who was inclined to exhibitionistic displays, a talented draftswoman, and, thanks to her childishness, a wonderful playmate for children of all ages.

Walter Slezak, then a pretty blond good-for-nothing in his early twenties (when I saw him again in the 1960s, he had turned into a monster with his father's weight), had the same merits in love as Ellen did, was always amusing and full of extravagant ideas that were then, with the help of others present, suffused with life. He raced on the Avus track and is said to have made Mercedes racecars famous.

Thus it was these two very young experts in gaiety and sex who attached themselves to Else more than any of the others, and with whom she "engaged in indiscretions" as she put it. She was certainly not the only one who did. Pätz was the El Dorado of indiscretions.

Peter also took part in the pleasures when he was on holiday. He was then going through puberty, a phase in which young men are generally unpalatable both inwardly and outwardly. Not Peter. He was beauty and charm in person and was initiated into the art of love by Ellen and into the art of driving by Walter Slezak.

His unusually strong relationship with his mother must have been decisively shaped during these years, in which it was transformed from the creatural love of a child into the reflective love of a young man. At that time it was far less Else the mother that he came to know than Else the woman.

In 1940, when they had already been living apart for two years, he in Greece, she in Bulgaria, he admitted to her in a letter:

"And so far as love is concerned, tell me, do you really know how much I love you? No, of course you don't, because I love you more than sons love their mothers, because I love you not only as a mother but also as . . . how shall I put this? . . . as, well, as a woman, yes, as a woman, I can't express it any other way."

Else, so much and so strongly loved—what was her secret? I, who also loved her so much, don't know. I believe that no one who fell for her knew. I see her before me in the wide beach pants that people then wore and a wrinkly blouse: a little bit of a belly, round shoulders and arms, a short neck and on it the beautiful head with its noble nose, the dark, sunlike eyes and the delicately curved mouth. She's laughing, she has the happiness that she needs so much, she isn't missing out on anything.

Her nickname "Schnuff" dates from this time. I don't know who gave it to her or for what reason, but from then until her death she was always called Schnuff by her friends. Even Erich called her that, whereas she gave him the nickname "Goody." Its origin is easy to discern.

Schnuff, who engaged in indiscretions, and Goody, who worshipped duty, goodness, and propriety. They were an ill-matched pair who were to get caught in the machinery of the Third Reich.

But at the time they couldn't know that.

For me, Pätz was a white house with blue shutters and a red tile roof. It was a green tiled stove, wooden floors, duvets, and washbasins made of thick porcelain with floral designs. It was a huge garden with apple, pear, and plum trees, with raspberries, gooseberries, and currant bushes, with marigolds, asters, dahlias, with butterflies, bees, and large-eyed grasshoppers, with gorse and elderberry bushes, with herb and vegetable beds, with trees that one could climb to sit invisible on the thickly leaved branches, with a swing, on which one could fly up into the sky, with a cesspool, around which we made a wide detour, and a spring, from which water was pumped; it was the rippled blue lake, the rolling gray lake, the silvery lake flat as a mirror, with sharp, long reeds and velvety brown cattails, with fish that glittered under the surface of the water, with a narrow pier made of unplaned wood and a green-painted rowboat; it was the Schwankes' square-built house, with the ugly-but-comfortable dwelling and the steaming stalls, the fenced-in courtyard and the dung-heap, the hens and the handsome, aggressive cock, the goats and pigs and later the ponies; it was the broad, good-hearted Emma and the dry, taciturn Otto Schwanke, who took care of the house and the garden and let me awkwardly help them; it was the Lieske Inn, across the street, from which beer and apple juice were brought, and, a little farther on, the Riesenbarg butcher shop, in which there was good, homemade sausage; it was the obedient neighbor children Carla and Vera von Güstrow, with their governess and huge, gray Great Dane; it was eels with green sauce and pickle salad, and berries with cream; it was heat and milky, overcast mornings and rain that beat against the windowpanes, and long, blue twilights and scary storms and moonlit nights when you could see the elves dancing.

Pätz was the romance with my brother who, lying in the sun, wanted me to tickle him with a blade of grass—up and down his smooth, narrow back, his neck, shoulders, long legs . . . , and next to us the gramophone with the latest American records, to which he hummed and sang and kept time by hitting the earth with his hand, then suddenly jumped up and took me in his arms and danced with me, whirled me around in circles, threw me into the air, caught me, kissed me; it was games with Ellen, games that she had invented and that were insanely comical: disguised or dressed up as ghosts, frightening other people in the house, or running naked out through the garden to the lake, or competing to see, for instance, who—she, Bettina, or I—could burp the loudest; it was also the discovery of the female body, which, standing stark naked in front of the mirror, she demonstrated to my sister and me and explained from head to toe. It was the first little-girl crushes on beautiful older women, such as the delicate, blond Ibi Wendtausen, and the blooming, dark Ilse Hirsch, whose little husband with a bald head and highly polished

lenses in his glasses was our pediatrician, the only one who succeeded, with jokes and calm logic, in curing my indefinable illnesses; it was the encounter with death in the form of a slaughtered kid, a stiff body that I examined for a long time with
intense curiosity, and a drunken woman who was pulled out of
the lake not far from our house, an event that I certainly did
not want to miss and rushed out to have a closer look of the
water-corpse; it was my acquaintance with Ilya, a demonic-
looking, tousle-headed White Russian who constantly ran after
my mother; with Herr Gypkins, a striking man who drove a
sports car, dressed in loud clothes, had bright blue eyes and a
head of silver hair—a repulsive man whom my mother treated
oddly, differently from the way she treated everyone else, and
with whom I never shook hands, never, no matter what he did
to get me to do so.

Pätz was the first depressing awareness that men and
women had another side in addition to the one they showed
me, a sinister, incomprehensible side that suddenly flashed out
in a gesture, a laugh, a word, or look that they exchanged with
each other, lurid and dreadful, like lightning bolts in a blue-
black sky, from which I hid under the duvet.

And it was the childish, innocent happiness that was put
into the cradle with me when I was born on Christmas Eve
with a caul over my head.

In 1932, Else was still being discreet and Erich had no idea
what was going on. The blissful life entirely devoted to nature
and the senses was being played out in Pätz, and was cleaned
up when Erich spent the weekend there. In Hubertusallee,
order and routine still prevailed. Angelika and Bettina went to
school, and on Tuesdays and Fridays they were delivered to the
grandparents Kirschner. Erich spent his days at the office and
joined Else and her entertainment program in the evenings.
Elisabeth saw to it that the household ran smoothly and

Gertrude took care of the children. Once a week the washer-woman came, and once a month the tiny, hunchbacked seam-stress who made the children's clothes. On Sundays they still went to eat the midday meal at the home of the grandparents Schrobsdorff.

Else's favorite friend during this time was Ilse, who was one year younger and our pediatrician's wife. The basis for this friendship was their shared love for life, exultation, hub-bub, and gaiety, their confidential revelations regarding their respective flirtations, and hours-long "gabs," as they them-selves called them. It was an intimate relationship without depths. Even as the hour of truth approached, when Ilse became a convinced Zionist and insisted that she and her fam-ily emigrate to Palestine and Else, under pressure from her son, occasionally had to take her head out of the sand, no really serious conversation seems to have taken place between them.

Ilse, who is now 83 years old, beautiful, charming, and has remained basically young and positive, lives in Jerusalem and rightly calls herself my vice-mother, still has the notebook in which she recorded all the parties that she gave, partly with her husband, partly with Else in Hubertusallee.

It seems to me remarkable when I see listed, for example under the date May 30, 1933, the dishes and drinks that were served on that evening—strawberry or peach punch, cold roast veal or hot sausages—and eerie, when I read the names of the guests invited, all of them long since dead, many of whom I knew personally or through countless anecdotes: the smug Gypkins, who became famous for his invention of a sweet known as "Sarotti-Moors"; the trio of painters Fritsch, Röhricht, and Heini Heuser, by whom we were painted in turn; the enormous Wendtausen, who with his enchanting wife Ibi emigrated to England and there became the German news announcer at BBC; the comical, little Friedel Strindberg, who was said to be Wedekind's son; the physician Fritz Rotbart, whom I loved and who went to America, and his girlfriend Sonja, whose sculptured beauty and plantlike passivity fascinated me; my uncle Alfred, the second son of the Schrobsdorff household, who married a Jewess, Ali Gito, a romantically gloomy young woman who leaned on the piano and sang "Love comes, love goes . . . "; the actress Hilde Körber, with her husband, Veit Harlan, who later made the most evil propaganda films for the Third Reich.

"You can't imagine," Ilse says, "how gay we were then."

But I can imagine it, and why shouldn't they have been gay? They were young people, cocky, assertive, self-centered, in love with life, in love with love. They'd been through the First World War, the Kaiser's abdication, the troubles and woes of the Weimar Republic, inflation, unemployment, the stock market crash. They'd lurched from one horror to another, and yet the pimple that had to show up on the day of a first rendezvous with a desired man was more important to them than, for example, one of the SA's terrorist acts.

Political catastrophes washed over them and passed on. If one worried about everything, one would be old at thirty. One was at the mercy of these things, whether one complained or amused oneself—so it would be better to amuse oneself!

"I can still see them dancing," Ilse said, "Erich, the good fellow, with Josepha, Peter with Ibi, Schnuff with Gypkins . . . 'It can happen only once, it will never return . . . ' that was the great hit at that time, and we all sang along. You can't imagine how crazy we were!"

But I can imagine it, and why shouldn't they have been crazy? Life was beautiful, love was beautiful, they themselves were beautiful, and most beautiful of all on those nights that never returned.

"And then, when all the guests had left," Ilse said, "Schnuff and I sat down together and let the party fade away. Sometimes the sun was already coming up, but of course we still had to have a thorough chat about everyone who had been there."

Then Else and Ilse sat in the large room with the furniture pushed up against the walls, the empty glasses, the plates covered with uneaten food, the overflowing ashtrays, and let the party fade away. Only one lamp was still burning, and they had slipped off their high-heeled shoes and stretched out on the couch or in cuddled together in chairs. Else smoked a last cigarette, ate a last little torte; they giggled, whispered, confided in each other—Else that a man had kissed her, Ilse that another had invited her to tea.

Yes, that happened only once.

In spring, 1932, Else and Erich traveled to Palma. From there Else wrote her friend a long account of her trip:

> Dear Ilse, just now I walked out of the bedroom into the little living room, and from there onto the balcony, and now the whole deep blue (no poetic exaggeration, it is really deep blue!) sea lies before me, and over me there's a sky that's just as deep blue, with a beaming sun. On the balcony, as I said, sits your friend Schnuff, in her nightgown; she's already tanned and writing while Goody sleeps (I'd like to have his sleep!).
>
> Should I tell you about our trip? It was not unamusing—sometimes like a movie, sometimes like a nightmare: car, train, car, airplane, car, ship, car, Palma, all in all, forty hours. In Stuttgart we got into the airplane, and five hours later we got out in Marseilles.
>
> Remarkable! Especially since flying wasn't made for me. More plainly: it's horrible. The plane bounces over a field, stops, roars forward, stops, makes a noise like ten DKWs[1]

---

[1] DKW (Deutsche Kraftfahrzeug Werk) was a brand of large automobiles and racecars. [Trans.]

and flies. Under you, nothing but clouds. Everything gray-ish-white. As a precaution, I'd already taken a lot of pills, and as far as Geneva it was all right. But after Geneva I got sick as a dog, whether from flying or from the pills, I don't know. The thing swayed around as if it were drunk, and I felt exactly the same way. My Goody was also beside himself, constantly waked me in order to point out invisible beauties, found me lacking in interest and didn't understand why I always immediately went back to sleep. Typical Erich!

From the airplane we then got on a ship, going from the frying pan into the fire. This could no longer be called mere pitching and tossing. All the passengers rapidly fled to their cabins, and I alone sat cheerfully in the dining hall, ate, drank, smoked, and then slept better than I have for years. I'm a water person, not an air person.

So, now comes the best part: since we'd flown as far as Marseille, my wardrobe trunk with all my things was sent on by train. Do you think it arrived? It didn't. And do you understand what that meant? I sat there in my traveling clothes, with no underwear, no dresses, no shoes, nothing. Everyone in white and I everyday in the same boring, much too warm suit. In the evening we had to eat in our room, because evening clothes were obligatory for dinner. Ilse, I was screaming in desperation. My Goody suffered and quietly put up with me, and we gradually bought a few things, all of the most mediocre quality, because here there is nothing decent. And then when I was correctly, though badly, dressed, the trunk arrived . . .

Palma is not very beautiful, too big and dusty, but in the evening, when there is a procession through the streets, it is very pretty. The whole city full of people and music. Your husband Walter would love it here. There are pretty girls with black eyes and a thick, long braid down their backs.

And delightful children, but no prams. The mothers carry the tiniest little creatures around with them in their arms, and some of them already look a little faded. As for the hotel, it is first of all luxurious, and secondly rather dull. Full of Englishmen, and you can hardly believe what that country produces in the way of ugly women.

The day before yesterday we swam for the first time. One goes down from the hotel in a swimming suit, sits on the rocks, and suns oneself. The sea is splendid, fairly warm, and completely calm. When I have water and sun, I don't need anything more to be happy . . .

A few lines from Erich follow:

Dear Hirsch family, I see by the number of pages that my wife has already given you a full report. It will be somewhat confused and one-sided, as always, but I don't have to read it. With noble, masculine reserve I have put up with her whining until the trunk—as I had predicted from the outset—arrived. Then began my second trial: clothes everywhere, shoes, ribbons, hats, on all the tables, on MY bed, and where not? This gets steadily worse with age. Where it is leading, I see every day in the old Englishwomen: ninety years old, light green dress (mermaid), little facial moles, a glittering shawl, a headband. So if one sets aside the aforementioned femininity and a few other unaesthetic things such as sticky knives (only a little on the handle), then it is very beautiful and relaxing . . .

This was the last trip Else and Erich were to take together.

In the summer of the same year I took my first trip with my parents and sister. We drove by car to Wasserburg on the Lake of Constance. My father and mother took turns driving. He was a bad, absentminded driver, and she was a bad, nervous one. She screamed, "For God's sake, dear, watch the road!" And he replied, "Schnuff, please don't get so jittery."

In Wasserburg we stayed in a hotel right on the lake. We took our meals on a long, roofed veranda. Almost every noon, we were served whitefish with an incredible number of bones. My mother dissected them with great care, and my father gave me a good talking to, but I wouldn't touch them. Naturally, a bone that I would choke on always remained somewhere.

"A complicated child," my mother sighed, and my father said, "Oh là là!"

Diagonally across from us sat a couple, the man with his back to me, and the lady, who was still quite young and pretty, facing me. I noticed that they were watching me, and they smiled when I gave them a quick, secret glance. Their smiles led me to put a grim look on my face, and them to laugh quietly to themselves. The whole scene was repeated every day, and became a *circulus vitiosus*: the more fiercely I looked at them, the more they laughed. Then one day they came into the dining hall with a large object hidden under a cloth. They came up to us, greeted my parents, put the object on the table in front of me and raised the cloth. I was looking down at a miniature landscape, with meadows made of moss and forests made of little twigs, and rivers and a lake of blue glass. It was a real work of art, the most beautiful I'd ever seen.

"I made this for you," the lady said, "do you like it?"

I looked up at her, and for the first time she remained serious, while I smiled.

The next day they didn't come to lunch. They'd left, and I was sad.

We stayed ten days, but apart from the rocks, the lady, and the miniature landscape I remember only the mice, a considerable number of field mice and jumping mice that Bettina and I fed bread and cheese crumbs in the barn next to the hotel, and Peter, who came one day from the nearby boarding school. He was sixteen, ten years older than I, and in my eyes he was a grown man. He was wearing long trousers and a golden chain around his neck with a heart-shaped pendant, on which three words were engraved. When he took me in his arms, I tried to read them, but they were in a foreign language.

Peter explained to me that the heart was a gift from Ellen, the language was English, and the words were "Everybody loves you." He told me that I should repeat them after him, because it was high time that I learned to say such an important sentence in English as well. I said: "Everybody loves you."

Else wrote to her friend Ilse, who was vacationing in Denmark, about our trip back to Berlin:

Wasserburg lies behind us. We are driving back to Berlin in over 100-degree heat, and stayed one day in Würzburg, where everything we saw was baroque. So much baroque! But very beautiful. When we got to Oberhof, our car, which up to that point had been exemplary (only one flat tire the whole time!), broke down and no longer showed any trace of ambition. That was the day before yesterday. After spending a while vainly trying to get it started, to our astonishment yellow flames flared up. The carburetor was on fire, and Erich said bemusedly, 'A miracle the car didn't blow up and take all of us with it!'

So we waited in Oberhof until the car was repaired, and then drove in the 120-degree heat to Berlin. That is a slight exaggeration, but the sun really didn't want to go down. The good old sun, if only we had it today! We arrived in Berlin on Thursday; on Friday the children and I jumped, in 140-degree heat, into the Halensee swimming pool, where Angeli's little dress and my cap were stolen (better than the other way around!), and by five in the afternoon we were sitting, trying to escape the heat, in the train to Königswusterhausen and then on to Pätz. We and the Fritsches—all three of the Fritsches. When we got there, it was already getting overcast and cool. The blessed land! I was not at all curious about Berlin, and I prefer Pätz under overcast skies to Berlin in the sunshine.

Here there is currently a dreadful amount of noise. Schniefke Fritsch (eight years old and terribly fat) is bellowing. Tina is whimpering, Angeli is crying, Ellen is playing solitaire, Herr Fritsch is trying to calm everyone down, Olli, the terrier, is romping with Heidi, the Spitz, and Frau Fritsch is reading scores and singing them. The house is shaking so much that a washbasin full of water has just fallen off the wash-table on the upper floor. The room is swimming, Frau Schwanke is mopping up, Gertrude is shaking her head. Tomorrow Heinz Riefenstahl is coming, and also a bocce set, which we quickly bought in Berlin. The peaceful life in the country . . .

The year 1933 brought three events: Adolf Hitler became chancellor of the Reich, Peter moved into the house in Hubertusallee, and Bettina and Angelika were taken out of school. None of these events had anything to do with the others.

Erich and Else were upset, beside themselves, about the first event. How was it possible that a crazed upstart whom none of them had taken seriously could take power with his band of terrorists and criminals?

As for the second event, Else had decided to keep a tight rein on Peter, who had skipped the last class and now had to prepare for the Abitur examination in the public schools, and to see to it that he studied hard and in a disciplined way.

Regarding the third event, they had come to an agreement that a tutor was the best solution, because if they put the girls in school they would not be able to spend long periods in Pätz, and in any case Angelika seemed to be hopeless as a pupil. Unfortunately, so did Bettina.

Peter took possession of the room with the canopy bed. He set up his gramophone, replaced a gold-framed still life with a female nude by Toulouse-Lautrec, took out of trunks and bags clothing, books, notebooks, and a huge number of odds and ends he had collected or been given, and left it all lying where it had fallen. His mother, after casting a despairing look on the chaos, said that it was a good start, and sent Gertrude to put things in order.

Angelika and Bettina were introduced to the new tutor, Fräulein Meinhardt. She was young and chubby, with a round face, a great deal of hair, and very little authority. The children giggled, and she giggled with them. Else gave her a list of the subjects in which her daughters were weak and those in which they were strong. The list came out unequal: Bettina was good in drawing and singing, and Angelika in reading and gymnastics, and they were poor in everything else. Fräulein Meinhardt seemed somewhat shocked, but then got hold of herself and said airily that she would work on that.

On April 1 the new rulers' boycott went into effect.

SA and SS men rolled through the city, posted themselves in front of the homes of Jewish academics and in front of department stores and shops owned by Jews, daubed filthy words on display windows, cursed and attacked those who dared to enter the businesses and those in the streets and on public transportation whom they identified as Jews because they had a large nose or curly hair. In the evening they continued their raids in cinemas, cabarets, theaters, and night clubs, and with their fists and boots established order in that degenerate, decadent, Judaized sink of vices, Berlin.

It was not an April Fool's joke.

Else called her parents and urged them not to leave the building.

Erich called the Hirsches and told them, according to Ilse, "Come here immediately with your son, and bring as many Jewish children with you as you can."

They came even if only with their own child.

It was a sad evening in the living room in front of the fire, perhaps the first sad one that the merry Ilse, the witty Walter, the lively Else, and the amiable Erich had ever spent together. Else sat in an armchair, somewhat slumped, her eyes wide open and fixed. Erich paced up and down the room, mumbling to himself, stopped, looked up at the ceiling, then resumed his pacing.

"Goody," Else asked, "do you understand this?"

He looked at her absentmindedly; his thought process was not yet concluded. Only two or three minutes later did he say: "I shall take care to refuse to understand this, too. One must not yield to the mob's repulsive ways of thinking. But you can be sure that what they allowed themselves to do today, they will not do a second time. They have slit their own throats. Hitler, that criminal shop-boy with a greasy forelock, is as good as dead. Germans won't go along with that."

"Germans elected that criminal shop-boy," Walter Hirsch said.

"The scum elected him, or do you really think the whole people, the intellectual Germany we rightly love, suddenly stands firmly behind a mentally ill criminal?"

No, Else said, she didn't really believe that. The whole thing was probably only a big fuss.

The fuss was over the next day. The SA and the SS had disappeared from the streets, the filthy words had been removed from the display windows, Jewish department stores and shops were full of customers, Jewish restaurants and cinemas were full of people. Well, then! Else, Erich, and their group of friends agreed that such outrageous incidents would never happen again. The guy had seen that he was on the wrong track. If he tried anything like that again, he was gone!

Two days later, Else, her daughter, Fräulein Meinhardt, Gertrude, and Ellen set out for Pätz; Peter and Erich were left under Elisabeth's care in Berlin.

I hope for once it goes well, Else thought, and asked Peter for the nth time to study hard and have consideration for Erich.

He embraced her, spun her around in a circle, kissed her, and promised to behave impeccably.

Erich devoted himself again to his duties and, with even greater fervor than before, to his books. In them he found proof of the view that the German people was a people of the intellect and of humanism. Every evening, he also read for half an hour one of the newspapers that had piled up in a corner of the library. He simply couldn't give more time and attention to these readings, but he also couldn't bring himself to throw away the old numbers without touching them, reading only the newest ones. Thus it happened that in April 1933 he was reading a paper from June 1932 and calmed, fell asleep over it.

Peter spent his days sleeping, reading poetry, and listening to the gramophone. When dark fell, he left the house and let Walter Slezak introduce him to Berlin nightlife. That was how he met Sergette von Cjeka Cajado, the sixteen-year-old daughter of a Polish woman and a Portuguese aristocrat, a very pretty, wild creature with whom he fell head over heels in love.

Elisabeth sat in the kitchen, drank strong, black coffee, smoked cigarettes, and looked into a gloomy future with her second sight.

"This will all end very badly," she murmured, referring to both the German people and the Schrobsdorff family.

My first encounter with the Third Reich took place on the day of its glorious establishment. When early in the morning I walked into the living room to read a book in my mother's brocaded armchair, I saw Elisabeth raising a flag on the balcony. I found that enormously fascinating, and ran out to her.

"Get yourself back inside," she said grumpily. "It's cold out here."

But I was not about to do that, because the view before me was much too exciting. Every house around ours was flying a flag, and a flag that I had never seen before, at least so far as I was aware. It was a red flag with a black sign in the middle.

"Why are flags flying everywhere today?" I asked Elisabeth.

"Because today we have a new leader, and his name is Heil Hitler."

"Heil? There is no such forename."

"You'll be surprised what all there is."

She shook out the flag and stuck it in the holder. I saw that it was a black-and-white-and-red flag.[2]

"You've got the wrong flag," I said. "Look, the others are all much prettier."

"Those are shit-flags."

"What?" I asked, shocked, because I'd never heard such a word come out of her or anyone else's mouth.

"Come on," she suddenly said very gently, putting her arm around me and leading me back inside. "What I said is a secret between us, and you mustn't tell anyone, because otherwise I can never have another secret with you. Do you swear it?"

I swore and was very proud to have a secret with Elisabeth.

But the interesting flag whose prefix I was not allowed to mention to anyone, did not leave me in peace. Again and again I went to the window, looked out, and wished our balcony could also be decorated so beautifully. When my mother got up, I showed her the splendid sight of the buildings flying flags.

"Wonderful," she said, without a trace of enthusiasm.

"Ours isn't pretty at all," I complained, "I want another one like that."

---

[2] The German imperial flag in use until 1918 and used by the Weimar Republic foreign services until 1933.

"We don't have another."

"We could buy one."

"Please, Angeli, leave me alone."

I whined all morning, and at some point my mother lost her temper and yelled at me. I began to cry and she to feel badly, and then we both went into the city to buy the flag I wanted so much.

"A very little one," my mother said, "I don't have any more money."

I was satisfied with a very little one, and as we came back out onto the street with it, I began to wave it proudly back and forth.

My mother hailed a taxi, and the driver glanced at the little flag and said skeptically, "We'll see what good will come of that."

As soon as I came into the house, I ran to Elisabeth in the kitchen. She stared silently at me and the new acquisition in my hand, and then went to my mother and said: "You know, Frau Schrobsdorff, I think that is going too far. Are you going to buy Angelika a party badge too?"

Nobody wanted to put the flag on the balcony, not even Gertrude. Only when my brother got up around noon, did he do me the favor. My mother and Elisabeth watched in silence.

"Let the kid have the thing," he said, "she has no idea what it is."

When my father came home I immediately took him to the balcony and showed him the new flag.

"Oh là là," he said. "Where did that come from?"

I told him that my mother had bought it for me.

"Schnuff," he called into the room, "do we have to have this?"

I thought they were all behaving very strangely and saying things that were completely incomprehensible. When I went to the balcony the next morning in order to look at my brand new little flag, it was gone.

"It must have been the wind," Elisabeth said, "now drink your cocoa."

It was a very tumultuous year. Not because of Hitler, who could be more or less ignored, thanks to an ivory tower and a refuge in Pätz, but because of the anxieties and misadventures within the family, which could not be ignored. If you heard Hitler on the radio, you could shut it off, and if you saw his followers, alone or marching in unison, you could look the other way, if you read a disturbing headline in the newspaper you could put it down. But something had to be done about Peter's escapades, Erich's stomach pains, and Angelika's bladder infection.

Else left the undisturbed Pätz and went back to Berlin.

Her unexpected arrival resulted in a painful revelation. She found Peter, not at his desk, where he belonged at eleven o'clock, but with Sergette in the canopy bed.

But it wasn't Sergette who upset her, nor was it the sight of the two adolescents in bed together, it was Peter's neglect of his duty, the imprudence and selfishness with which he took each day as it came, qualities that she recognized all too well in herself. What would happen to the boy if he started down that path when he was barely seventeen, if he squandered his talents, which were so much greater than her own, if he always only took, never gave, and snubbed her and Goody, who did everything for him, with a charming smile?

She stood in the doorway, stared at the entwined pair, and tried to control her rage. But as always, she failed.

"Do what you like, Peter," she screamed, "go ahead and destroy your life, but don't expect any more help from Erich and me."

She turned on her heel and slammed the door behind her.

That was the prelude to an unsavory period in the life of the family. The doctor had found an incipient stomach ulcer in Erich, a problem that then required a long and exceptionally unpleasant treatment. His face and body grew smaller, the two wrinkles that ran from the wings of his nose to the corners of his mouth grew deeper, his gaze still more distracted, and his appearance thus became even nobler. Although he felt limp and often wretched, he remained amiable and patient, fulfilled his duties with undiminished thoroughness, and neither spent less time at his office nor stopped reading the children fairy tales in the evening and saying the "Lord's Prayer" with them. However, with increasing frequency he now let Else go out alone or made his excuses to her guests and withdrew more and more to his library.

Angelika, whose bladder infection could at that time be cured only by rest, warmth, and liters of cranberry-leaf tea, had to remain in bed for six weeks, a situation that she discovered had certain advantages. She was allowed to lie all day in her father's canopy bed, did not have to take part in Fräulein Meinhardt's silly lessons, was often visited by her grandparents Kirschner, who read to her by turns, and by Ellen, who played Parcheesi with her, by Sergette, who did magic tricks for her, by the doctor, Uncle Hirsch, who treated her with a light hand and much humor, and when she demanded caviar for lunch she got it. The poor child ate next to nothing, was only skin and bones, and if she now had an appetite for caviar, then that was better than nothing. Angelika was and remained a complicated child, but still simpler than Peter, with whom Else could do nothing at all.

He drove her crazy and soon thereafter wound her around his little finger, worked for twenty-four hours and then disappeared for two days, wouldn't listen to Erich, gave him cheeky answers, declared that he would never bother him again, and shortly afterward asked him for money, quarreled with Sergette and lavishly celebrated their reconciliation in a hotel, restaurant, or bar and made debts, brought his grandparents Kirschner extravagant gifts and at the same time pumped them for money, went to Wannsee to see his father, fought with him, swore he would never see him again, and spent the next weekend at his house with Sergette, disappeared one evening, without a driver's license, in Erich's car, drove it into the ground out of negligence, emerged from it like the phoenix from his ashes and declared dejectedly that from now on he wanted only to study. The phase of contrition lasted almost a week, and then it started all over again.

Else screamed, stormed, threatened, pleaded, and wrote him letters that were, in contrast to her verbal outbreaks, full of insight and prudence, love and generosity, tolerance and unconditional honesty.

It was an endless drama of quarrels and armistices, noisy scenes and fervent reconciliations, that was staged in the house in Hubertusallee.

"Just look," Peter wrote to his mother in 1940, "where we are closest—it's in our wild unreasonableness and impulsiveness."

Else would have much preferred her son not to have inherited her wild unreasonableness and impulsiveness. Because it was these qualities that ruled her life, for better or for worse, made her guilty and others unhappy. She was anything but proud of this, and feared for her son, who was well on his way to repeating her mistakes. But she would be as little able to protect him from them as she had herself.

Else experienced periods of severe despondency, in which she suffered from her own shortcomings, her fear for her children, and the depressing feeling of a steadily increasing estrangement from her husband. But the periods of wild unreasonableness and impulsiveness outweighed them by far.

One day my father lost his temper. He'd never lost his temper before, and he never lost it again. It was only a brief outbreak, but for me it was a dreadful and incomprehensible event, rather as if a storm had suddenly appeared out of a clear sky and ripped off the roof over our heads.

It was a few weeks after my illness, during lunch. We were sitting at the round table, my father to my right, my mother to my left, and Bettina opposite me. Peter's room was above the dining room, and when he got up about noon and started studying, he always listened to his American jazz records and tapped his foot in rhythm. Thus we heard the tapping and the jingling of the crystal chandelier that hung over the table. And, in particularly loud passages, also the music. On that day he was listening to a song that Peter and I preferred to all others: "San Francisco, open your golden gates . . . " He had taught me the lyrics, and we had often sung them together. My father had mashed potatoes on his plate, without gravy, and also some piece of lean meat. Elisabeth was very careful to see that he adhered to his diet, and always prepared the same dishes. It must have been after a major quarrel with my mother, because Peter had already been studying for a week, for a week we had been hearing foot-tapping and jingling, and my father was eating mashed potatoes.

Then it suddenly happened: he left his fork sticking in the mashed potatoes, jumped up from his chair, threw his crumpled napkin on the table, and said in a loud, hostile voice: "I've finally had enough of all this!" Then he turned on his heel and left the room.

All three of us were petrified with fear. My mother and Bettina had paled and I must have too. What was wrong with my father? What had he meant by the words "all this"? Had he said "of it," then it could have been the mashed potatoes or the foot-tapping or both that he had had enough of. But "of all this" might include me and my mother.

I looked at her. Her face was no longer petrified, but instead distraught and very sad. Bettina, who never wept in the presence of others, left the room. I asked whether my father had finally had enough of me, too.

Of course not, she said, my father loved me more than anyone in the world. But he was having a very hard time with his stomach pain and his heavy workload. He didn't allow himself any rest, and when you do that, such things sometimes happen.

In the evening my father came into the children's room. He was, as always, pensive and amiable, read to us, in his felicitous way, a fairy tale, and said the "Pater noster" with us in Latin. But his good-night kiss was different—such as I had not seen for a long time nor would see again for a long time.

In 1934 the president of the Reich, von Hindenburg, died, and Hitler made himself, as "Fuehrer" and chancellor of the Reich, the head of state.

Thus he was now firmly in the saddle, but he seemed to have become reasonable. To be sure, Germany was now a dictatorship in which there was only one party, the National Socialist Party. And a few disagreeable ordinances had been issued: non-Aryan officials, except for war veterans, had to "retire"; new appointments of non-Aryans in schools and universities had to be restricted, and German citizenship might be withdrawn from "undesirables." But no new riots had occurred, and the more than 500,000 Jews who then lived in the Third Reich saw no urgent reason to leave Germany.

In that year Erich gave Else a red automobile and Angelika a pony. The car was so big and heavy that Else couldn't turn it, and the pony was so lazy that Angelika couldn't make it run. This made a great contribution to the general cheerfulness.

Peter had taken his Abitur exam lightly and passed it with a high score, and this won him Erich's favor in the form of a check for a large sum. However, this was followed by a warning not to rest on his laurels, but instead to start thinking about a profession. Peter heartily thanked him for both the check and the tip about thinking about a profession and left for Italy with Sergette.

Nothing had changed in Else's lifestyle. She and her friends went on living their life of pleasure, and the subject of Adolf

Hitler was mentioned, if at all, only in a tongue-in-cheek, trivializing, or disgusted way. They could not be expected to take seriously this clown with his shrieking, staccato speeches, his obsession with Aryans, and his exaggerated plans for the future. Where were they, then? They were in Germany, after all, a highly civilized, highly-cultivated country!

Only Ilse Hirsch, Else's close friend who had belonged to a Zionist group for years and had been influenced by its warnings and appeals, firmly maintained that it was time to leave Germany and emigrate to Palestine.

Else laughed. Hitler was a godsend for the Zionists, she said, spreading panic so that Palestine would fill up with Jews. That was just as exaggerated as his plans for the future. Of all people, must it be she, Ilse, who had both feet firmly planted on the ground, who allowed such screwy nonsense to be put into her head. She should just shut up about it. Germany was still her country, Berlin her city.

Still, Ilse said, but maybe not for much longer.

Well, then, when "still" was over, she should go plant potatoes or whatever in Palestine, but in the meantime enjoy her life here.

They both enjoyed it.

In a letter Else wrote to her friend, who was apparently on a trip:

> Yesterday Alfred, Anja, Nelly Dreifuß, Herr Schönborn, Heini, and Josepha were at my house. Alfred made us nervous, as usual, with his film camera; Josepha was charming, because she'd hardly opened her mouth before some nonsense came out; Herr Schönborn had just returned from New York, and is my current relationship—so that you know, in case someone tells you when you get back. Erich left on a trip Wednesday and won't be back until Monday, and I'm constantly going out to dance and dine with Herr

Schönborn. And with others, too. I have the car, after all, and see various men from morning to evening: Strindberg, Walter, Heini, and Heinz Riefenstahl—the latter being incredibly decorative. I can hardly fit everything into the days Erich is gone. Yesterday I picked up your little boy, who had gotten completely lonely—no one was taking care of him. We—Tina, Angeli, and your son, Tommy, went for drives in the car, walked, bought Easter eggs, and finally ran into an army of Nazis with music and flags—thousands of Nazis! We stood on the curb, and while Angeli emphatically stepped forward, raised her arm, and shouted "Heil!", Tommy stepped back several paces, looked at Angeli with fascination, raised his arm (the wrong one) and whispered "Heil." Whereupon he blushed with shame. Erich, to whom I told this story, said he was a very smart boy.

In 1934 we celebrated Christmas with Grandma and Grandpa Kirschner both at our home in Hubertusallee and at the home of my grandparents Schrobsdorff. It was the last time, and its omission was probably the only thing in the following sequence of great, oppressive events that my good Kirschner grandparents did not regret.

On December 24 we always had a combined program. In the morning we had my birthday celebration, followed by breakfast, champagne (a few drops of which I was also sometimes allowed to have), and of course many presents. I played with my presents until around 4 P.M., when my grandparents Kirschner arrived, and the next handing-out of presents was prepared by my parents. So that we did not see these preparations, we all had to go into the children's room and wait there behind closed doors. I was so excited that Grandma kept putting her hand on my forehead and sighing: "This is all too much for the child. She'll get sick on us again."

But Grandpa smiled and said: "Nobody gets sick from joy,

isn't that right, my little angel?" And then he asked me the question that never failed to be asked on my birthday: "Is it nice, having a birthday?"

Since my father placed every gift with the greatest sense of order and aesthetics, and had to keep going up to the Christmas tree to straighten up a candle, to move a nativity figurine a centimeter forward or backward, this took intolerably long, and would have taken much longer still if my exasperated mother hadn't cut the process short by throwing open the door and calling us in. Then we all came out of our rooms and rushed down the stairs, Elisabeth and Gertrude in dark dresses, Peter still quickly knotting his tie.

My mother sat at the piano and played "O come, little children . . . ", my father was just lighting the last of the candles, and Grandpa, who was still terrified by the sight of the colorful, glittering Christmas tree decked with many burning candles, said: "Dear Fräulein Gertrude, could you please bring a pail of water?"

Only when the full pail stood next to the tree and he had gauged the risk of every candle did he calm down somewhat, and my mother began to hum "Silent night, holy night." We all sang along, except for my grandparents, who couldn't bring themselves to sing "Christ the Savior is here . . . ", and my father, who couldn't sing a note and so just muttered to himself.

Once we had somewhat laboriously made our way through the song, my father read us a passage from the New Testament about the birth of Jesus: "And the angel said unto them, Fear not: for, behold, I bring you good tidings of great joy, which shall be to all people. For unto you is born this day in the city of David a Savior, which is Christ the Lord."

Then the presents were handed out, and there were many of them and they pleased everyone. But I hardly had time to play with the new load of presents, because we had to be at my grandparents Schrobsdorffs' house at seven o'clock. And now the whole of Christmas descended upon us. I've never again seen such expense and luxury as in the Schrobsdorffs' home. One had to give the Prussian aristocrat this much: he wasn't miserly, and he knew how to show it.

The table bearing presents for about twenty-five participants in the celebration reached from one wall to the other of the huge hall; the big, sparkling star that topped the silver fir, the most perfect specimen of its species, touched the six-meter-high ceiling and was decorated with silver balls, tinsel, and countless candles. The table set with crystal and silver was almost as long as the table with the presents and as glittering as the Christmas tree.

And we were all gathered together in harmony and good feeling: the maids with particularly pretty lace aprons, the gardener and the chauffeur Lange with his wife and daughter in their Sunday clothes that looked as if they were a size too small, a couple of relatives down on their luck who kept decently in the background, and the house's three sons: Erich with his Jewish wife and his Jewish parents-in-law, Alfred with his Jewish wife and his Jewish mother-in-law, Walter with his Jewish fiancée Ulli.

I don't know who, in the far-reaching Schrobsdorff family, even knew or guessed that the house of its head was contaminated by Jews, and I am fairly sure that the grandparents were not even aware of the ancestry of their second and third daughters-in-law. Anja had been able to erase all traces of her descent, because her mother drowned at the appropriate time in the lake at Pätz, and in Ulli's case, investigations had prudently been abandoned in view of the fact that her husband was a party member and a high-ranking officer. In any case, I learned the women's dirty little secret only long after the war was over, and at that point they were already dead.

But in 1934 harmony and good feeling still prevailed, as I have said, and little, plump Else, stocky Anja, and sleek Ulli—

each one darker than the next—sang Christmas carols, accompanied on the piano by their mother-in-law.

Oh, it was wonderful—the splendor and magnificence and ceremony, the festively dressed, reverent people, the fragrance of beeswax and *pfefferkuchen*, the sublime Christmas songs. I stood next to Grandpa Kirschner and held his hand, because I knew that he saw us all about to go up in flames. In this overpowering atmosphere he didn't dare ask for a pail of water, and also probably had to admit to himself that given the size of the tree, it wouldn't have done much good. So he stood there bravely, smiling his enchanting smile, though it was somewhat pained, and probably thinking about his first mistake, Else's little disheveled Christmas tree, which he had hidden in the broom closet when his father Aaron appeared. And Grandma Kirschner, who had become even smaller, with her face even more deeply furrowed by melancholy and skepticism, stared, in a solemn and detached manner, straight in front of her. What was she thinking about? About her dead son, with whom her life would have gone differently, whom she would have loved, honored, and supported as a good Jewish son for whom there was nothing more important than his mother, the family, and the close bond among those who share the same blood and the same belief? Was she thinking about her daughter, who had long since left her parents in mind and heart, who, although she was in the same city, lived in another world, and who saw her mother only as a burden? Was she thinking about her grandchildren, about the girls who didn't even know her origin, who were growing up in an illusory world in which there was everything except a firm foothold?

Oh, I was happy on that December 24, on which there were three distributions of gifts and splendor and magnificence and ceremony. And parents and grandparents and siblings. And harmony and good feeling.

In 1935 the Fuehrer reintroduced compulsory military service. Only German citizens and those of "congeneric" blood
could become "citizens of the Reich." The sale of Jewish newspapers was forbidden. Marriages between Jews and citizens of
German blood were forbidden. Jews under the age of forty-
five were forbidden to work as domestic servants. All Jewish
officials were "furloughed."

In June of that year Else wrote to her friend Ilse:

We had a lovely Pentecost, we were with Alfred, Anja,
Jäckel and Brigitte in Pätz, and either played bocce or
broiled ourselves in the sun. I am very tanned. Goody is
going to Frankfurt today, and since you're already there,
you can meet. He has one darling after another—who
would have expected that of him! Last week it was blond
little Irene, this week it's the brunette Gaby Oppenheim.
You'll have to hurry up if you want to get your share.
Yesterday I was in a café with your husband Walter, Heini
Heuser, and Narzissa. I invited them all for supper tomorrow, Sunday, along with Margerita and Wendtausen. There
are eggs with anchovies, chicken with sweet peas and straw-
berries. What a shame that you aren't here. Walter is looking forward to emigrating to Palestine—well, and you are
too. Tried again to convince me to emigrate as well, but he
should just give up on that. I have a hard time seeing you in
the lauded land; it would be simply unbelievable—Berlin
without you, you without Berlin.

For Tina's birthday we had a large children's party.
Alfred and Ellen were also there and they outdid any of the
children in infantile behavior. Alfred played peek-a-boo
with Ellen and grabbed her breasts so often that even innocent little Tina noticed it. When a little girl playing a guess-
ing game had to describe the meaning of the word
"feather," she said: "It's little and long." After a pause, she

added: "And comes from birds." At that, Alfred and Ellen became unbearable. They shrieked and laughed madly, and I finally had to throw them out. So that's the latest news from Berlin. Interesting, no? Come back soon—I miss your antics.

There are times when I have doubts about my mother's mind and those of her friends. Did she, did they really have so little political knowledge and conscience that they calmly went on playing their way through a dictatorship in which they, who were not of German or congeneric blood, were slowly but surely losing their human rights? Of course, my mother also wrote other letters to other people or had other conversations with them, and her friends certainly did not play only bocce and peek-a-boo. It can be assumed that they experienced times of dread and horror, but unfortunately they considered it superfluous, imprudent, or futile to draw the consequences. The only ones in this group who did were Walter and Ilse Hirsch, but to judge by the tone of my mother's letter, she seems not to have taken them seriously in any way. "I have a hard time seeing the two of you in the lauded land, either; it would be simply unbelievable—Berlin without you, you without Berlin."

But how could my father reconcile his humanism and my mother her honesty with what was going on in Germany? They must have locked their principles away in a secret compartment and believed that they could take them out again once the horror was past. The horror, which became steadily more horrific, and required them to lock up more and more in their secret compartment, hoping that it would remain intact there.

I don't know what was going on in them, I know it less and less as the story goes on, and I fear that they themselves didn't know.

In the spring of this year Peter left the house in Hubertusallee and moved into a tiny garret apartment in immediate proximity to the Kurfürstendamm.

The relationship between him and Uncle Schrobsdorff, as he continued to call him, which had seemed to improve after his brilliant performance on the Abitur examination and the generous check, had soon thereafter reached a low point. Peter bore Erich's obsession with duty as badly as Erich bore Peter's neglect of duty. Erich declared that it was incomprehensible that a young, healthy man could party day and night instead of envisaging a profession, course of study, or at least a useful activity. Peter declared that it was an impertinence to expect him to already be preparing, at the age of seventeen, for his life's work. Should he, out of love for his Uncle Schrobsdorff, become a real estate broker or a philosopher, or, to play it safe, a government official? He had no idea, he said, what he wanted to do with his life, and he knew himself well enough to know that he wouldn't have one in the foreseeable future. The only thing he knew was that he wouldn't remain in this lousy country if things went on as they were. He'd leave it to people with a sense of duty and responsibility.

That summer Ellen was engaged to Jack Blackwood, an English correspondent who said very little and drank a great deal; Ilse Hirsch went to Palestine for four weeks to find out about living conditions there; Anja, Alfred's Jewish wife, gave birth to twin boys, and her husband built her a large manor house in Pätz.

In the fall of the same year, Else and Erich separated.

This was not in itself surprising. It was a bad marriage, and under normal circumstances the decision to separate would have been reasonable. But the circumstances were unfortunately not normal, and the moment at which they separated makes the separation itself questionable, even if one reconstructs the love and marriage relationship between the two and concludes that it was doomed to fail from the outset, and was based only on Else's self-assertiveness and Erich's sense of responsibility.

Else had never deceived herself regarding this point, and unmistakably refers to it in various letters. For example, in one she wrote to Enie during her third pregnancy: "He really didn't realize what he was getting into, unworldly and eccentric as he is. Moreover, he didn't want it at all, and acquiesced only because of his decency . . . "

Else was thus well aware of her guilt and Erich's innocence, but does the marriage that Else initially forced on him and then wrecked justify Erich's decision to separate from her in 1935? Was he really so unworldly and eccentric that he saw the political situation as no impediment and the clear signs provided by the Jewish pogroms as simply specters that were not reasons for serious concern? Or were there in fact considerations urged by his family to which he had to yield by initiating a separation that would have happened anyway, even without Hitler? And Else? How did she react to that?

I'm quite sure that she didn't connect Erich's decision with current political events, because his integrity, his unconditional reliability and solidarity were for her beyond doubt. Furthermore, she continued to be convinced that the conditions in Germany, no matter how revolting, represented no genuine danger, and certainly not for her, who had moved so far away from Judaism that only the entry on her birth certificate identified her as a Jew. Thus Erich's desire to separate was for her a purely personal and in no way surprising one, and I can even imagine that the idea of being completely independent and no longer needing to consider others was not unwelcome to her. So long as she didn't get divorced—and there was no question of that—her life would go on as before, without any great changes. She had already long since gone her own way, and spent more time in Pätz with her friends than with Erich.

Her plan was to move to Wannsee, to a place that she loved

and that offered her and her children what they missed in Berlin: nature, water, a garden. From this point of view it would be easy to explain their move to Angelika and Bettina, and not upset them.

Erich would visit them every weekend and their relationship would be much less tense and forced than it had recently been when they were under the same roof. They would remain good friends or perhaps even become better friends.

So they separated in the winter of 1935, on the best of terms.

We moved to Wannsee, to a street called Am Birkenhügel, which really was on a hill with many birch trees, whose white, black-flecked trunks and light green leaves I liked very much. The house was smaller than any we had lived in up to that point, but wonderfully pretty. It had a large, beautiful garden, and I had my own room with wood-paneled walls. I was somewhat confused by the change, but not really sad. My mother had explained to me that it was better for children to live outside the city, and that basically I now had three houses: one in Wannsee, one in Berlin, and one in Pätz. That made sense to me, and I found it exciting to have three houses. Naturally, I sometimes missed my father, in the evening, for example, when he used to read fairy tales to Bettina and me, or on Sunday morning, when everyone else was still in bed and the two of us ate breakfast alone. I also missed the quiet, reverent hours in the library. But I really hadn't seen him much, and he had promised me that he would come to Wannsee every Sunday, take me to Berlin now and then, and spend part of the holidays with us in Pätz. And he did it, too.

In addition, he had given me a dog, an Irish terrier, that belonged to me alone. His name was Flash, and he had a short, reddish-blond coat and a mustache that had to be brushed every morning. When he was particularly happy or embarrassed, he grinned. No, I'm not exaggerating: he drew his upper lip back, showed all his teeth, turned, spun around, and writhed like a person dying of laughter.

My mother bought me still another parakeet, a green one, which despite all my efforts refused to learn to say a single word, but did screech prodigiously and often sat on my shoulder.

Elisabeth had stayed with my father in Hubertusallee, and Gertrude, after the death of her mother, had gone home to her father and younger siblings to run the household for them. We had a maid about whom I no longer recall anything except that she was a Catholic and went to church every Sunday. That seems to have been for me the only remarkable thing about her. Perhaps because I had still never been in a church, except as a tourist. I had received my religious knowledge exclusively from my father, and that was more than sufficient. I knew that Jesus was a Jew and that the Jews were a people who had lived in Palestine a long time ago. He had told or read me many stories about Jesus. They had always been very impressive, and he'd explained their ethical meaning, as he called it. Being a Christian, he told me, didn't mean running off to church every Sunday, but instead behaving like Jesus: decently, kindly, justly, honestly. That was all that mattered in life, and it did not depend on any religion, but rather only on oneself. When I was a little older, he said, he would read me the Sermon on the Mount and we would listen to the St. Matthew Passion, which contained everything he considered important about being a human being.

We didn't live long at Am Birkenhügel, about six months, and that time left no strong impressions on me. I can't remember a single guest, only two nocturnal visitors who, even though they entered the house silently and stealthily, awakened and disturbed me. My room was next to the living room, and since I always slept with my door half-open, I heard exactly what they were saying.

One of these visitors was Peter, who was asking our mother, in a low but terribly pressing voice, for money. Sergette, he said, was presently with her mother in Warsaw and had become ill there. He absolutely had to go to her. Our mother replied that she didn't have the money for this trip and couldn't ask my father for it. The situation had changed since she was living with us in Wannsee and as a result he had twice as many expenditures. He was already paying an arm and a leg, and she simply wouldn't think of asking him to shell out still more money for a completely unnecessary trip to Poland. Peter said nothing more and left the house, obviously furious, without even saying good-bye to her. As I later learned, he traveled to Warsaw in a cattle truck.

The second secret visitor was Gypkins, whose deep sonorous voice I immediately recognized. He said that he'd decided to emigrate to America as soon as he could, and had come to say farewell. There was a long pause, and then my mother asked if he'd gone crazy; as an Aryan—it was the first time I heard that word, and I didn't understand it—he had really no reason to leave Germany. Gypkins replied that as an Aryan he had every reason to leave a country in which that ridiculous word was hung on him like a medal. And she would do well to do the same, he said, because Germany was well on its way to becoming a cesspool.

I'm sure that this conversation stuck in my memory because in it the unknown word "Aryan" and the cesspool I knew from Pätz came up. At the time, of course, I didn't understand the meaning and the connections, and also wouldn't have dared ask my mother about them, because I didn't want her to know that I'd been eavesdropping instead of sleeping.

During the time we lived at Am Birkenhügel, Bettina and I were no longer taught by Fräulein Meinhardt. I didn't go to school, either. We spent the whole summer and part of the fall in Pätz, and that was wonderful. There things had remained just the same, many people who were coming and going, were always amusing, and got up to mischief. I had my pony and also a little cart in which I could drive about, and my little Irish terrier, Flash, whom I often made laugh, and my swing, on which I flew up into the sky, and my tree, which I climbed in order to write poetry. My father also came, stayed a whole week, took me to the brickworks and Uncle Alfred's new house, on long walks, and on boat rides.

We spent Christmas and New Year's in Hubertusallee. There were, as always, three distributions of presents and a great deal of splendor, magnificence, and ceremony at the elder Schrobsdorffs' home. But Grandma and Grandpa Kirschner and Peter were not there.

On New Year's Eve my parents went out, my father in a tuxedo, my mother in a long evening dress of bottle-green taffeta. They looked very elegant. Bettina and I remained at home with Elisabeth and celebrated with paper streamers, joke items, and fortune-telling. Elisabeth drank schnapps and was very happy, and then suddenly terribly sad. She put us to bed and told us once again the story of Rumpelstiltskin. We all liked it very much, especially the part where he dances and stamps his foot and sings: "For no one knows my little game / That Rumpelstiltskin is my name!"

In March 1936 Jews were deprived of the right to vote for members of the Reichstag. This was the only anti-Jewish law made that year, because in August the Olympic Games took place in Berlin, and in view of that it was considered advisable not to annoy world public opinion.

Else moved with her daughters from Birkenhügel to Hohenzollernstraße, into a large, centrally located building only a few minutes away from schools, bus stops, and shops. With Erich, she had decided to send the children to the Wannsee school. It would do the unworldly, spoiled Angelika good to finally be with children her own age for a change, and to lead a completely normal life. This completely normal life was thus supposed to begin in the year 1936.

Bettina, who was now fourteen, was not happy about our parents' strange idea, but accepted it without protest. Not Angelika. She put up resistance that would have been suitable had a crime against her been planned. Else, who was probably well aware that her behavior arose not from a lack of proper upbringing but from fear, suffered but remained firm. It was high time she and her children learned to know not only the easy, pleasant side of life, but also the one that required seriousness and discipline. Otherwise they would come to nothing.

Else was now thirty-four, and thus at an age when women begin to form certain ideas about the future. Since she had lived in Wannsee, her need for jubilation, hubbub, and gaiety had diminished. She now often saw Fritz and Enie again, drove into the city with them, where they met Erich and thus spent an evening together as they used to do, went to the theater, dined in a restaurant, or retired to Hubertusallee, where they carried on long conversations in front of the fireplace and Fritz played the piano.

It was these evenings that now gave her the most, along with these two men whom she had so passionately loved and with whom she would remain most deeply connected, as she now knew, until the end of her life: Fritz, the first who opened the door to the beautiful, broad, Christian world for her. Erich, the last, who was to close it behind her. And Enie, her enemy and then her friend, whom she had known for twenty years and who had experienced with her every phase of her development from a little Jewish girl who believed in marriage to the mature woman who had swept away all conventions and scruples. Who was closer to her than these three people, whom she had attracted with her warmth, joy in life, and lack of scruples?

They often spoke with pleasure about the past, which, transfigured by distance, seemed so fulfilled and wonderful.

They had lived, loved, suffered, but the suffering, precisely the suffering, had been for her the quintessence of her youth, a productive suffering from which a new feeling, a new strength, a new beginning had emerged. Would it ever come again, would they later on, when they sat together in front of the fire again, be able to speak about the next twenty years with the same humor, the same wistful melancholy?

Hitler, the Nazis and their loathsome politics were very distant from this idyll. They were in fundamental agreement that this was a gang of criminals, a disgrace for intellectual Germany, a corruption of all human values, a temporary hard time that they had to endure by gritting their teeth, holding their noses, and averting their faces. It could not last long, because if the opponents of the Nazis within their own people did not succeed in getting rid of this tyrant, then the rest of the world would take care of him. And until that time Erich and Fritz had their ivory towers in which they cultivated their intellects and souls, and Else and Enie had their gardens, in which they enjoyed nature. Naturally, there were incidents in which reality could not be ignored and the filth hit them between the eyes, like the party badge on Walter Schrobsdorff's lapel, with which he appeared one Sunday at lunch and thus immediately prompted Angelika to ask what kind of brooch he was wearing; or the occasions provided them with a moment of piercing doubt and vague apprehension, such as the emigration of the Hirsches, for whom Erich and Else threw a farewell party in Hubertusallee.

Yes, the unthinkable had happened, and Else's beautiful, radiant friend Ilse, with whom she had fooled about and laughed so much, her witty friend Walter, with whom she had amused herself so much, went to Palestine. And with them went part of her beloved Berlin, irreplaceably, irrevocably.

They had all come, everyone except Gypkins, who had already left Germany. They drank, more than usual, danced, more frantically than usual, but the light, gay mood of the earlier parties refused to resurface. It was not just the sadness about the loss of their friends, it was the worrisome question: were their fears justified? Could one no longer live in Germany? Were they all in danger?

At midnight, Erich gave a little farewell speech. He often gave speeches, willingly and well, chose thoughtfully beautiful, rounded words, spiced them with gentle humor and a touch of pathos. But this little speech contained a large dose of pathos and no humor. Ilse, who often described this farewell party to me, now remembers only the thrust of the speech, and it was, she says, very beautiful, but somewhat sentimental.

But then something very funny happened, about which she still laughs: "When he had finished," she told me, "there was a gloomy silence, and we were all terribly sad, and then Fritz Rotbart, in order to improve the mood, suddenly said: 'So now we'll all throw our glasses against the wall!' And your father, who was still immersed in his speech, woke up and shouted: 'No, no, no, please don't!' It turned out that they were very valuable champagne glasses. I tell you, Angeli, it was too funny!"

Ilse and Walter Hirsch left Berlin with their two sons in April 1936 in a train carrying Jewish emigrants that left from the Anhalter Bahnhof. There were hundreds and hundreds of them huddled on the platform and at the train's windows, all of them leaving behind what they had built, what they had loved. And suddenly a man appeared amid this teeming mass, blond, elegant, and taller by a head than all the rest.

"I was so surprised to see your father," Ilse said, "and somehow it was also a little embarrassing for me, because it was immediately obvious that he wasn't one of us, I mean that he wasn't a Jew. But naturally I was also happy and waved to him. He made his way over to us, and when he stood in front of us and the thought came to me that we might be seeing him for the last time, I was quite miserable."

He gave her two books as a farewell gift, and they are still in her library. One is called, appropriately enough, *Our Germany*, and the other *Berlin*. And the dedication in it reads: "Dear Ilse, in case over the years your memory of Berlin evaporates, leaf through this book, and perhaps you will think of us—which couldn't hurt. Until we meet again soon. Most sincerely, your Erich."

"Yes," Ilse said, "that was your father. He lived in another world."

So I went to the Wannsee school, and compared with it the private school in Hubertusallee was a paradise. The schoolmistress, who taught us almost all subjects, was a dragon who was out to get me, the rich, pampered loner. The children, although they were all younger, were much bigger and more robust than I, wore ugly clothes, and had coarse faces and braids. There were bosom friends who always went arm in arm, put their heads together, giggled and whispered, and cliques that concocted dirty tricks and behaved boorishly. During recess, I stood alone in the farthest corner of the schoolyard and hoped that no one would notice me, because the cliques were threatening and the bosom friends were as poisonous as old maids. But they gave me at most a malicious look or a sneering word.

It often happened that I vomited in the morning, and then I didn't have to go to school. However, it had the disadvantage that I got on even worse than usual with my homework and when I gave a wrong answer or none at all the dragon gave me a dreadful rap on the wrist and sent me to stand in the corner. My life had become one long torment, and I envied my sister, in whose right eye Dr. Rotbart, who now was our doctor instead of Uncle Hirsch, had discovered a tubercular infection. That meant that after one month she could no longer go to school, had to remain at home, and henceforth could only lie in bed and eat.

Probably I would have also been taken out of school again because of my vomiting, but before that could happen Karin came into my life.

I see her walk into the classroom at the dragon's side: a girl still bigger, more robust, and wearing even uglier clothes than the others, her light-skinned, blue-eyed face a little coarser, her braid still thicker and longer, but for all that made of pure gold.

"This is your new classmate, Karin Schröder," the dragon said, and led her to my desk, the only one that still had an empty seat. Karin nodded to me, sat down, unpacked her school supplies, and then folded her arms over her breast, awaiting further orders. I realized that I had sitting next to me a person who had never known fear.

That day we were taking a test on arithmetic, and after I had looked at the sheet I knew that I wouldn't be able to solve a single one of the problems. Next to me sat Karin, who carried out her calculations with ape-like swiftness and wrote down the results in her examination booklet. When she had finished, long before the end of the time allowed, she cast a glance on my paper, saw that I had done nothing, and pushed her examination booklet a little closer to me. I was so flabbergasted that I didn't react at all, and continued to stare in front of me. She gave me a kick under the desk and pushed the booklet still closer. That was the moment at which we became inseparable friends and my torment, whether in the classroom or in the schoolyard, came to an end.

Karin was not only my friend—true as gold, hard as steel—she was also my bodyguard and disciple. She paid none of the other girls any attention, and if one of them looked at me crooked, Karin had only to take a step toward her to put her to flight. The others envied me Karin and her unshakeable friendship. They knew who she was: a first-class athlete, an ace in dodgeball, and the leader of her League of German Girls group.

That did not impress me at all. I cared nothing for sports,

found dodgeball disgusting, and was not interested in the role of a League of German Girls leader.

When Karin made her first visit to our house, she appeared in her uniform. It was probably her best outfit, or else she wanted to impress my mother, or it may be that she had just come from some knitting, singing, or athletic event. In any case, she stood in full regalia in front of our door—navy blue skirt, white blouse, black scarf with a leather clasp, and somewhere the swastika, I no longer know where—the prototype of the strapping Hitler girl.

My mother was speechless for a moment. She looked from Karin to me and back again, and I said proudly, "This is Karin, my new friend."

"Wonderful," my mother said, and shook the girl's hand. Karin curtsied. She had been very well and very strictly brought up by her parents, who reminded me of our doorman and his wife in Hubertusallee, Herr and Frau Höhne. She always said please and thank you and *guten Appetit* and *Heil Hitler*—but the latter not in our home, because she knew that I found it silly. She once asked me why I wasn't in the League of German Girls, and I answered, in good conscience, that the one and only reason was that I had no interest in anything so stupid. Karin accepted both this explanation and my lack of interest without further question. She accepted everything I said, did, didn't do, demanded. Thus for hours we took turns reading fairy tales, stories, and whole books out loud. We listened to the same gramophone records, from popular hits to opera arias. And then for my mother's birthday I learned a ballet routine with her. Karin danced like an elephant in a china shop, but she did so sedulously and with pleasure, and thereby earned great applause from the very disciplined audience, which managed to remain serious. In turn, I became a good pupil, thanks to my friend, copied error-free tests off her, and always gave the right answers, which she whispered to me.

Karin's devotion, which verged on slavery, gave me a feeling of security and responsibility. Since she came from a poor background, it was my duty to see to it that she lacked for nothing and that she came to know the beautiful side of life and shared it with me. Karin came along when we went to Berlin, took an excursion to the Spree forest, or spent holidays in Pätz. She had to ride the pony and drive the little cart, and swing with me—she standing on the seat, I sitting. We built huts in the garden, in which we stayed alone, and climbed my tree, though without writing poetry, because I couldn't teach Karin that. I, who had always put the highest value on what belonged to "me alone," was now happy when Karin shared it. I shared my animals and my books with her, my toys and clothes; and when I was given a pair of roller skates, I gave Karin the left one, and we skated together, each of us on one skate.

Karin, the big, strapping Hitler Girl, made me a new, happy child, and I, the complicated crossbreed, made her one, too.

In the course of 1937 the number of Jewish children in German schools was still further restricted. Jews were given passports for travel abroad only in exceptional cases.

When this law was issued, Else felt for the first time really queasy, as if she had fallen into a trap and it was about to snap shut. Not that this regulation was applicable to her—she was still married to a citizen of the German Reich and had a child with him. But there were her parents, relatives, and friends who did fall under this law. Now she finally asked herself: what new, monstrous steps would the Nazis take? When would they be stopped?

Erich was just as upset as she was, and said that they had to think about taking certain precautions in this situation. Not that she and the children were in danger, or her parents, the old people, but no harm had ever come from considering what would have to be done, if . . .

Else spoke straightforwardly with her parents—also for the first time—about the situation, but met only with resignation—cheerful on the part of her father, sad on that of her mother.

"Anyway, so far as we're concerned, it's no worse," Minna said.

"We're no longer considering taking a trip around the world," Daniel smiled.

"Yes, but the young people," Minna sighed, "I'm really anxious and afraid for them. The Zionists among us are, luckily, already in Palestine—Paula, Bruno, and the children, Lotte and her husband, Emanuel and his wife and sons. By my God, over there with the Arabs it won't be any better. And anyway, one can't escape one's fate."

"Don't worry about us, Else," Daniel said soothingly, "things are never as bad as they seem, and they'll soon calm down again."

However, their son Peter was of a different opinion. Things would certainly not calm down, he said, and they would do well not to allow themselves to be calmed.

That was all Else needed! What she was looking for was a confirmation that the Nazis were still not to be taken so seriously, and not a warning that they couldn't be taken seriously enough.

Irritated, she asked him why he always had to exaggerate so much, in every domain. Couldn't he finally grow up and become a little more levelheaded? He should think about his own life rather than about Herr Hitler and his cohorts. All this was only his way of avoiding making personal decisions. If he really wanted to help her and spare her concern and worry, then he certainly wouldn't do it with gloomy political predictions but rather by giving his life a direction and a content.

He hadn't realized, Peter replied, that she was so easily influenced in her opinions and analyses. Her image of him was probably based on Uncle Schrobsdorff's crap, and what she thought of Germans was too. He was a lazy, superficial scatterbrain, and the Germans were a people of poets and thinkers that was tempted by the devil from time to time, like all great spirits, but would obviously find its way back to itself and to its traditions. If one of the two of them was irresponsible or completely confused here, it was Erich, not he. He considered Erich a man who was too weak to withstand massive pressure, and too out of touch with reality to see what was really going on around him. She mustn't count on Erich in these two areas.

So she should count on him, maybe? Else asked ironically.

He couldn't swear to that, but he was in any case always prepared to advise her and give her moral support.

Oh, this son, this madman, this dreamer! As if he knew which side was up! Yes, Erich was weak, out of touch with reality, and still under the influence of his family, which had never trusted her. And yet he was the only one on whom she could completely and utterly rely. He would never act against his conscience or his ethical principles.

It was shortly after this confrontation with her son that Else, during the traditional Sunday dinner at the Schrobsdorffs' house, discovered the party badge on the imposing, large-flowered bosom of her mother-in-law. She couldn't believe her eyes, but no matter how often she looked away and then back again, there it was, the swastika, and Annemarie, who was apparently unaware of the affront, behaved just as naturally and effusively as ever.

Erich stubbornly refused to notice the badge, and it was Alfred who took Else aside after the meal, when the family had retired for an hour's rest, and said he had to speak to her. They went into the conservatory, and Alfred shut the door behind them. "So now your mother has joined the Nazis," Else said.

"She had to, she had to," Alfred chuckled, "my old man can't join the party because he's a Freemason, and so she had to go for it. Somebody has to do it, don't they, because otherwise the business will be harmed. Pure opportunism! My father has no use for proletarians, and all my mother knows is that the guy's name is Hitler and that you say 'Heil' to him."

He shook with laughter.

"I don't find that so terribly funny."

"If only everything were as funny as that is," Alfred said, suddenly turning serious, "then we could confidently laugh ourselves to death, but unfortunately it's not. The situation is becoming downright dicey. What am I to do with my mother-in-law? I like the old lady, she's a quiet, elegant person, but what should I do with her now? Anja is making life hell for me, she does that anyway for everything and nothing, but especially on this point. She wants to get her mother out, but first of all she can't get a passport anymore, and secondly, I can't just dump her any old place and say, now see how you can get along. Abominable situation! Tell me, what are you going to do with your parents?"

"Nothing at all," Else said dryly, because for her this was now really going too far. Alfred had never been someone to take seriously, but now he had cracked up completely.

"Nothing at all," Alfred repeated. "I see."

"Can you perhaps give me a reason why I should 'do' something with them?"

"To keep the Nazis from doing something with them."

"Please, Alfred, they are old people, they were born German citizens and they've never done anything wrong either politically or privately. So please don't act crazy."

"I'm not acting crazy, Schnuff, it's our grandiose ruler who's acting crazy. It's not a question of guilt or innocence, old or young, German or Chinese citizenship, but of race. I was aware that my brother Erich lived on the moon, but I didn't know that you've moved there now too. You and Anja are protected by marriage to us, and the children we share are, too. Ulli in any case. Her husband is a party member, and her parents have disappeared, I don't know where. But people who are not married to "Aryan citizens of the Reich" are in for it, believe me! And many of those who were against the Nazis— now I'm talking about Aryans—are also going to start toppling, because though they won't be affected directly, their jobs and assets and families and God knows what else will. So come down from your moon and wake up a bit!"

That evening Else told Goody about the conversation. Unfortunately, Erich said, he's not entirely wrong. Of course, a lot of it was exaggerated speculation, and of course old, retired people were not going to suffer, but the undercurrent . . . well, yes, he was himself very worried and would advise every young, unprotected Jew to leave the country until this plague was over.

Else was silent. She didn't want to hear any more. With every conversation a piece of ground was cut from under her feet. Even if she couldn't take Peter's drivel and Alfred's exaggerations so seriously, she couldn't ignore a spark of truth in them. And through Erich's careful words this spark had become a blaze. If Goody said that Alfred was unfortunately not entirely wrong, and he would advise every young, unprotected Jew to leave the country, then that was a warning that had the greatest weight. Else went to see Enie, the only one who spoke her language, told her what Peter, Alfred, and Erich had said, and asked her what she thought of it.

Peter was eighteen and still wet behind the ears, she said, but so far as the Schrobsdorffs and indeed the whole family were concerned, that scared the hell out of her. But it didn't surprise her a bit. The old monster would sacrifice anyone, including his sons, to the business; Walter was just like his father, but devious and malicious to boot; Alfred was good-hearted, but had no backbone at all, and the old lady, well, you could forget her. The only one in the family who had any character was Erich, but character had never triumphed over unscrupulousness. She really couldn't tell her how the family would react if the Nazis were to hold a pistol to their heads. She was not worried about Anja, she was still worse than the Schrobsdorffs, or about Ulli, whom Walter had long since put out of danger, but she, Else, was exposed to it and was more-over separated from Erich. Couldn't they live under one roof again?

No, Else said, she couldn't ask that of Goody after all she'd already done to him.

Under normal circumstances, guilt feelings and magnanim-ity are very admirable, Enie replied, but probably not appro-priate in this critical situation.

Now the ground beneath Else's feet had been completely cut away, and she felt as if she were on the high seas. Dizziness and nausea alternated with resignation and indifference. Berlin began to sicken her. It was gasping in the Nazis' stranglehold, and a new, Teutonic Berlin full of flags and parades, uniforms and genuine German clothing, Schillerian dramas and Wagnerian bluster, raised arms and clicked heels was being born. No, it was no longer her Berlin out of which she was being uprooted, out of which more and more familiar faces that she had honored from afar as artists and had loved inti-mately as friends were disappearing. She wanted to get out of this city in which she had been born, with which she had grown up, in which she had come to know life, love, and hap-piness, and that was now becoming a hostile stranger to her.

She decided to go for an extended stay in Pätz, where she would encounter no swastikas and no boots, no beaming, fanatical looks, and no terrified Jewish faces.

Dr. Gerhard Richter came into the house; he was a Ger-manist, in his middle thirties, with first-class references and regular features, an irreproachable character and a fabulous figure. He wore his dark blond hair slicked back and glasses with narrow gold rims over his brown, earnest eyes. He was the perfect example of a tutor, and with him and her daughters Else went to Pätz.

I liked Dr. Richter very much. I liked most men, trusted them far more than women, and considered them smarter. That I was right about that became immediately evident in our lessons. Fräulein Meinhardt had giggled and been unable to explain anything to us; Dr. Richter never giggled and explained everything with what he called logic. With this logic he could also clear away many of my fears. He liked me as much as I liked him, but he never danced to my piping. He remained serious and determined. He was an absolutely serious and determined man. Also in the way he dealt with my mother.

"Frau Schrobsdorff," he often said, "please, let me do that. Angelika knows exactly what is wrong and what is right."

And to me he said: "Angelika, you're an intelligent girl, and it becomes you very ill when you behave like a little child."

Then I felt foolish and was embarrassed. He taught me thoroughly in the subjects in which I showed interest, had me write many essays, and spared himself and me the trouble of studying mathematics.

"There's simply no point to it, Herr Dr. Schrobsdorff," I heard him tell my father once, and my father replied: "Then let's just leave it."

My father also thought a great deal of Dr. Richter, and even let him teach me about religion. Thus I also learned, when I was already rather advanced, that my mother was a Jewess, like Jesus. Naturally, I didn't believe him. There had been Jews many centuries ago but for a long time they had no longer existed. Dr. Richter's revelation must have been one of his rare attempts to make a joke, and I laughed loudly.

Fewer people came to Pätz than before, and that pleased me. My friend Karin spent the Easter and summer holidays with us, Ellen came with her fiancé, Uncle Jack, the painter

Heini Heuser with his daughter Narzissa, Uncle Alfred with Aunt Anja, the twins, the nursemaid, and their newborn baby, Marianne, and Peter with his new girlfriend Liena.

Liena, who was seventeen, had a somewhat chubby figure and an exotic face in which everything was big, gloomy, and beautiful, and she excited me very much. She had the eyes of a cat, only they were black and also edged in black, and she wore violet-colored lipstick on her very full lips. As the daughter of the famous Russian ballet-dancing couple Victor and Tatiana Gsovsky, who had opened a ballet school in Berlin, she danced as well, of course, and that, along with her somber inapproachability, made her irresistible for me. Peter was crazy about her, and although I considered it impossible that Liena could be crazy about him, or about anyone, in the garden one evening I heard her say to him: "I love you, I love you, I love you . . . " I wished very much that she would also say that to me sometime, but that wish remained unfulfilled.

On the other hand, I was allowed to tickle Peter with a blade of grass, as always, and sometimes he took me piggyback and galloped around in a circle with me. I loved him at least as much as Liena.

Yes, that was a wonderful time. My pony Mucki had had a foal, whom we called Shetty. It was the most loveable creature I'd ever seen, no bigger than a German Shepherd, and still covered with long, sand-colored hair. I lay down next to it in the straw, my arms around its neck, my face pressed to its incredibly soft nostrils.

That year my father bought a horse, a real one, whose name was Evergreen. He was reddish-brown, had a black mane, a white tail, and a heart-shaped patch on his forehead. My mother, who had at some point taken a few riding lessons, suddenly wanted to ride. She had become very athletic, and I believe she owed that to the equally athletic Dr. Richter. For example, to my alarm she swam at his side all the way across

Lake Pätz, at least two miles, and back. I was beside myself with anxiety about her, but Dr. Richter insisted that nothing could happen to her because she was such an outstanding swimmer and because he was a certified lifeguard. As I said, I trusted him, but still sat on the pier with the telescope until they had swum to the other side and back again.

And then they began to ride. First only in the garden, on the longe held by Dr. Richter, and always in a circle. But the horse had the peculiarity of stumbling over everything and nothing. Dr. Richter trained it for hours, but it went on stumbling. My mother said there was nothing to be done, and began riding out early in the morning. She was always back for breakfast and told us how lovely it was to ride through the forest, and how often Evergreen stumbled. One morning she didn't come back. We waited, I wailing, for an hour, and then Dr. Richter organized a search party. He, Emma and Otto Schwanke, Gertrude and I were to comb the forest in various directions. Since word immediately got around that Frau Dr. Schrobsdorff and Evergreen had disappeared, the whole village soon took part in the search. At some point we found Evergreen, cheerfully eating grass, and about quarter of a mile farther on, my mother, in her undershirt, her blouse tied around her broken thigh, crawling through the forest on all fours. Evergreen, she reported, had stumbled, fallen with her, and unluckily landed on her legs.

I have especially happy memories of the following weeks in Pätz. With her leg in a cast, my mother couldn't move about and was within reach from morning until evening, from evening until morning. My sister, who because of her tuberculosis still had to stay in bed and eat, and thus had become very fat, could no longer run around after me and annoy me, and so I could run around all the more. Out of revenge she told me one day that I would become an old maid, because girls who wrote poetry always did. With great regret, I immediately stopped writing poetry. But there was enough distraction.

There was Ellen, who still hid her bottles from her fiancé, and Jack, who looked for them like Easter eggs; there was Liena, who sat, beautiful and gloomy, in the shadow of a tree and was unapproachable, and Peter, who lay at her feet and read to her; there were Alfred and Anja, who argued noisily, and the wonderfully pretty twins, one of them light-skinned, the other dark-skinned, who sat or stood around silent and motionless, wherever they had been put; there was Heini Heuser, who painted a picture of our house, and Dr. Rotbart, our doctor, with whom I was infatuated and therefore did everything I could to distract his attention away from his patient Bettina and focus it on me; there was Karin, with whom I was allowed to clean out the horse-stalls, and the foal Shetty, who visited my mother in the living room on rainy days; there were the Schwankes, who let me feed bran to the goats, which I did so generously that their bellies swelled up like captive balloons; there was Dr. Richter, who carried my mother in his arms from one room to another, did gymnastics with Peter and Ellen, and trained Evergreen; and finally there was Grandfather Schrobsdorff, who had had a stroke and was somewhat crippled on his left side and was recuperating in Uncle Alfred's house. I often went to see him, certainly not out of sympathy, but rather out of curiosity. When I had curt-sied before him, I sat down opposite him and didn't take my eyes off him. He had not become in any way more approach-able, and my grandmother considered that a good sign. She was constantly scurrying around him and making him very nervous.

"Angelika," he used to growl, "the worst thing about being ill is that you have a harder time getting your family to leave you alone. Remember that."

I don't know what led Else to go in the fall with Dr. Richter and her daughters to spend six months in French Switzerland, in the village of Crans-sur-Sierre. It may be that this stay was a trial balloon launched to find out whether, in the event that worst came to worst, Else and the children could escape to Switzerland and live there for a lengthy period of time. If that was the case, Else must have at least toyed with the idea of leaving Germany. But then it must have turned out that it was impossible to emigrate to Switzerland because of the regulations there.

However, it might have been something else altogether, and the reason much simpler in nature. Else, who in the seclusion of Pätz had led an easygoing life handicapped only by her broken leg, feared returning to Wannsee. Although Wannsee was not in the middle of Berlin, it nonetheless lay within the dangerous area where one might be exposed to the Nazi bacillus and bad news and incidents. They had all felt so good in the freedom and purity that only nature can provide and under the discreet protection of Dr. Richter, who had become a friend for the children and a lover for Else. Should they now return to Hohenzollernstraße, where they had no protection, and put the children in school and her in a poisoned atmosphere?

Why should she subject herself to this anxiety, why should she expose Bettina, who was cured but still weak, and the complicated Angelika to possibly damaging influences? She must have discussed the matter with Erich and found that he agreed with her. Doubts and fears had taken up residence in him as well, and tormented him even in his library. It would have been almost impossible for him to avoid seeing the collapse of his Germany or to ignore the increasing number of party badges on the lapels of apparently decent people, the laudatory remarks about the rise of the Third Reich, its economic achievements, and the new, beneficial order in the country and the people. It was becoming increasingly difficult for him to escape his family's leading questions and recommendations and to avoid quarrels with his brother Walter, who had flatly advised him to divorce Else. Yes, a lengthy stay for Else in some absolutely peaceful and safe country would be a relief for all concerned.

Else preferred French Switzerland, which offered her the language and the cuisine that she loved so much. A small, idyllic place, high in the mountains, with lots of fresh snow and radiant blue skies. How much good that would do them, helping Bettina convalesce, improving Angelika's appetite, and giving her a general sense of well-being.

Dr. Richter was sent to Switzerland to find this cure-all place, and he found it in Crans-sur-Sierre, a picture-perfect village nestled in a coomb at the foot of gigantic mountains. He rented a chalet that was located outside the village, at the end of the world, and accessible only by horse-drawn sleigh or on skis. It consisted of a ground floor and two stories, was constructed of dark wood, and simply but comfortably furnished. He hired a maid, whose name was Eugénie and who cooked French-style, and procured two sleds and four pairs of skis in various sizes. Then he telegraphed Else to tell her that everything was ready for her and the children to arrive.

They got there in early October. The first snow had already fallen, and the children rejoiced in the fairy-tale landscape. Else stretched out her arms, threw her head back and rejoiced with them. They had landed in a new, glittering world of illusion.

I still have a photo of my mother taken in Crans-sur-Sierre. She's wearing a Basque beret, a pullover from which a bit of white collar peeks, a pair of black ski pants with a white belt and white, calf-high leggings. She's leaning on the cast iron railing of the stairway that led to the house, and behind her there's a bit of fir forest and a great deal of snow. She is looking down at the person who took the picture, and on her deeply tanned face there is a smile that is about to turn into a laugh. I often saw this smile on the verge of laughter when she was looking at Dr. Richter. With his seriousness, he made her want to laugh. Even I, as a child, understood that she liked to make fun of him and then he sulked for hours, did not speak, gave only very curt answers, and showed himself even more serious than usual. Bettina and I found this very funny and called him an offended liverwurst.

"Frau Schrobsdorff," he used to say, "if it amuses you to undermine my authority, please feel free."

My mother and the imbalance must have often caused him pain. A young man who was, so to speak, in her service, awkward and hopelessly in love with her, and she, a woman of the world, shimmering, experienced, and using him as a lover. Although there was also a serious side to their relationship. I think she spoke with him more often and more openly about her fears, humiliation, and perplexity than with others. I also think it was he who tried to persuade her to tell her daughters the truth and thus to forestall what might still come. That is the only way to explain why at that time, there in Switzerland, he unsuccessfully tried to explain, using the example of Jesus— the only Jew I knew about from hearsay—that my mother was a Jew.

My mother continued her athletic activities in Crans-sur-Sierre, and Bettina and I had to participate in them. Dr. Richter seemed to be proficient in every kind of sport. In the morning we did gymnastics, under his direction, on the glassed-in veranda, and after breakfast he gave us skiing lessons. I could have done without both of these and spent the whole day playing in the brook. This brook ran along the edge of the forest near our house, and Bettina and I, wearing high rubber boots, broke through the ice and floated homemade rafts on the stretches we had freed up. During these cold, wet, but fascinating games I caught a second bladder infection that was considerably worse than the first one and could not be healed with cranberry-leaf tea. Once a week, I had to go to a hospital located in Montana, a little town that was about five miles away and could be reached only by horse-drawn sleigh. There my bladder was irrigated, a highly painful procedure that justified my howls and screams. My mother, who could not bear my pain, fled the room as soon as the doctor approached me. It was Dr. Richter who held me in his arms with gentle force, stroked my hair, and quietly encouraged me.

When the treatment was over, I was wrapped in blankets and laid in the sleigh, my head in my mother's lap and my legs on Dr. Richter's knees. And the torture I had endured was worth it for this return trip, which I could enjoy without fear. I lay blissfully there, listened to the bells ringing on the horses' necks, the rustling of the forest through which we were passing, and the hissing of the runners on the hard snow. I looked into the landscape deep in snow, with its undulating, glittering surfaces, the huge mountains, whose highest peaks turned red at sunset, the endless sky, sometimes blindingly blue, sometimes, higher up, pearl gray and touching the crowns of the trees, sometimes atomizing into billions of swirling snowflakes. Cuddled close to my mother, I could have glided on forever through this landscape, in which there were fairies and snowkings, elves and ice princesses.

On December 23, my father arrived and brought with him two large trunks full of gifts. It was a different, more improvised, less pompous Christmas and birthday celebration, but I found it particularly beautiful.

Dr. Richter took Bettina and me skiing in the forest in order, after a long inspection, to fell a tree and bring it home on two sleds tied together. We all decorated it and were very merry and relaxed. The grown-ups drank red wine and laughed as I had seldom heard my father and Dr. Richter laugh. My mother looked like the beautiful Indian woman in my book whom the Whites had taken prisoner.

On the morning of Christmas Eve we celebrated my birthday, as always, and then I went on a long sleigh ride with my father. He talked about Jesus, whom he jokingly called my brother, because we were born on the same day, and I wanted to hear for the umpteenth time how he had been nailed to the Cross. My father told the story, slowly, with a dreamy look in his eyes, and then he finally came to the part where my whole body got goose-bumps: "Now from the sixth hour there was darkness over all the land unto the ninth hour. And about the ninth hour Jesus cried with a loud voice, saying, My God, my God, why hast thou forsaken me?"

"Do you think," I asked after a long pause, "that God will also forsake me someday?"

"No," my father said, "he didn't forsake Jesus and he won't forsake you, either. Jesus just believed that in a moment of doubt and pain, and you may also someday have moments of doubt and pain in which you believe it. But remember then what I'm telling you now: he'll never forsake you!"

My father stayed with us until December 30. He played with Bettina and me, read to us, prayed with us, carried on long conversations with my mother and Dr. Ritter after we'd gone to bed, but none of us ever succeeded in persuading him to go skiing. He said that sports and eating vegetables—which Dr. Richter also considered very important—were unnatural inventions.

He had hardly departed before Peter descended on us like a storm, built huge snowmen with Bettina and me, organized wild snowball fights, learned French cooking from the charmed Eugénie and gymnastic exercises from Dr. Richter, and immediately declared that although he'd never been on skis, he was a born skier.

I will never forget our first ski tour together, on which we climbed in single file, with Dr. Richter in the lead, a high hill suitable for training. But only one side of the hill was suitable, because the other side was closed off with a barbed-wire fence, presumably marking the boundary of a grazing area. Hardly had we reached the top and Dr. Richter was beginning to warn us, when Peter started down the other side of the hill, crying "Now we'll see!" and raced straight toward the fence. My mother who saw her son in danger, and I, who saw my mother in danger, rushed screaming after him. Dr. Richter shot past us and bellowed "Fall down!" Fortunately all three of us obeyed his order and fell. Above, on the crest, frozen into a pillar of salt, stood Bettina. Her reactions were always a little delayed, but all the stronger. Thus she so abruptly started down the hill that she immediately fell and rolled halfway down. Dr. Richter, the only one who was standing up, stuck his pole in the snow, held his head with both hands, and shouted: "As I look around on this noble assembly, what a glorious sight makes my heart glow!"

For me, New Year's Eve was just as unforgettable as this unfortunate ski outing. After the meal, we drove in the sleigh to Montana and there went to a nightclub, the first I'd ever been in. I see it now: a rectangular dance floor of black marble; here and there conversation areas separated by low wooden walls along which stand upholstered benches with many cushions, round tables that also have black marble tops and little lamps with red shades. On a podium, a four-man orchestra. Waiter in a tailcoat, gentlemen and ladies in evening dress.

And I live it again, this exciting moment, in which the light was reduced to a dim red glow and the orchestra began to play a passionate tango. I see Peter stand up, put his right hand on his heart, and make a deep bow to our mother, and she, smiling, rise and go with him onto the dance floor. I see them dancing, Peter tall, slender, in a dark suit, she small, delicate, in a long, black silk dress. I was so proud of the marvelously handsome couple that my mother and my brother made, so happy. We drank champagne, we laughed and kissed each other, we loved each other very much. And then we drove home in the sleigh through the blue and silver starry night, Peter on the box next to the driver, my mother, Bettina and I under a thick blanket on the rear seat, and Dr Richter opposite us on the jump seat.

Peter cracked the whip and sang the hit song: "When will you be with me again," and my mother put her arm around Bettina and me, hugged our heads to her breast, and said: "Now we're going straight up to heaven."

That was the last time she had all three of her children around her.

On March 13, 1938, German troops marched into Austria. Among the regulations issued in that year were:

Jews must declare their assets.

Jews are forbidden to engage in certain professions.

By January 1, 1939, Jews must carry identity cards at all times.

Starting on September 30, 1938, Jewish doctors will be considered only "health workers."

All Jewish street names must be eliminated.

Starting January 1, 1939, Jews may use only Jewish forenames. If they use German names, they must add to them the names "Israel" or "Sara," respectively.

Jews as a whole will be required to pay reparations of one billion Reichsmarks.

Jews must immediately repair all damage done by the pogrom—the so-called *Reichskristallnacht*" at their own cost.

Jews may no longer operate any shops or craft businesses.

Jews may no longer attend any theaters, movie houses, concerts, or exhibitions.

All Jewish businesses are dissolved.

Starting immediately, Jews may no longer move about at certain times and in certain places.

Jews' driver's licenses and registration papers for motor vehicles are canceled.

Jews must sell their businesses, and hand over their securities and jewelry.

Jews may no longer attend any university.

Else returned with her daughters to Hohenzollernstraße at the end of March, that is, after the annexation of Austria.

The first regulation of that year, the one concerning the declaration of assets, was issued at the end of April. Else still did not consider this regulation a reason to change her life. And Erich seemed willing to accept her behavior. There was apparently no one who could put an end to the madness.

For me, the year 1938 is one of the most inexplicable and tragic-absurd. The fruits of five years of credulity bordering on mental derangement were now ripe.

Unfortunately, Else and Erich were not an isolated case. Hundreds of thousands of people fell victim to their error of judgment. But roots, as in Else's case, and worldview, as in Erich's, can be extirpated only by taking part of the heart with them, and who wants to have part of his heart ripped out and know that the wound will never heal? Only when the whole heart is at risk and the drive for self-preservation comes into play does one prefer to allow oneself to be mutilated.

Today, I understand this better than ever, and can nonetheless not fathom it. It is Erich's passivity, Else's refusal to accept the truth, the complete confusion of these two in no way limited, uneducated, or indigent people—that remains inconceivable to me.

"We no longer knew what to do, Erich and I," Else writes in a letter to her friend Ilse Hirsch in Palestine, and this not-knowing expresses itself in their case as a frantic urge to do simply preposterous things that in some cases led them even deeper into disaster.

Now, when it would really have been appropriate to have Bettina and Angelika taught at home, they were sent back to school, this time to a superior girls' school in Nikolassee, twenty minutes' bus ride from Wannsee. In addition, they went into the city twice a week, because Bettina absolutely had to attend an art school there and Angelika had to attend Victor and Tatiana Gsovsky's ballet school. Sometimes they looked in afterward at the home of my Kirschner grandparents, to whom Else had given a parakeet to cheer them up. They had named it Pipa, treated it with great care, and were delighted when he flew around the room, shrieking dreadfully, landed on Daniel's bald head or Minna's shoulder, tore up a newspaper, pecked seeds out of their hands, and, wonder of wonders, said his own name—his first and last utterance.

"He brings life into the house," Daniel said and told us about the wild hunt that took place every evening when the parakeet was supposed to go back in his cage and wouldn't allow himself to be caught.

Wasn't a part of Else's heart already ripped out on seeing her disenfranchised, defenseless parents? The most loving parents and grandparents in the world, who now owed their happiness to a bird and who had themselves become birds, outlawed birds, terrified, wounded little birds who hardly dared to go out on the street and vegetated, like their parakeet, in a cage, out of which they could be taken and have their necks wrung.

Of course, at that time Else didn't consider it possible that their necks might be wrung, but wasn't what was already being done to them bad enough? She could bear her parents' psychological pain no more than the physical pain of her children. She ran away from their misery, just as I ran away, years later, from hers.

"You reap what you sow," she used to say. She said it increasingly often in the last ten years of her life, and with a certain satisfaction, because she saw in each blow that struck her only another justified punishment.

And so in this year 1938 she ran away not only from her parents, but also from herself. That was the worst. She ran like a hunted hare, zigzagging, futilely, helplessly, and was on the lookout for every hollow, every hole, every bush in which she could hide from those who were hunting her and from herself. And she got more and more lost.

The systematic persecution of the Jews began in June 1938, and up to that point a "normal" life still prevailed in Hohenzollernstraße.

Erich, who had moved out of the house in Hubertusallee into an apartment on Johannaplatz, came every weekend. His ulcer had healed, but he was exhausted and disturbed. Twice he fell asleep while driving to Wannsee and collided, fortunately at low speed, with a tree. His confidence in intellectual Germany's victory over the mob had been undermined by painful doubts.

Five years had passed since the criminal shop-boy had taken power, and nothing had happened. Erich confronted the collapse of his world with quiet desperation. In addition, he was seriously worried about Else, who lacked the strength his belief gave him and the serenity his humanistic ideas gave him. She had no inner sanctum into which she could withdraw, and only with that could one succeed in surviving this terrible time with dignity. How should he show her the right, the only path that led out of the labyrinth of dark fears? And likewise Angelika, who according to the Nuremberg Laws fell into the category of first-degree crossbreeds, and who, according to Dr. Rotbart, suffered from psychological disturbances—nightmares, shortness of breath, claustrophobia— how could he protect his beloved daughter from horrifying discoveries?

They continued to go to the Schrobsdorffs' villa for Sunday dinner. There they often saw Dora Taslakova, a Bulgarian physician who had treated the old man when he had his stroke and of whom my grandparents thought the world.

She was a resolute, unmarried woman, a capable, conscientious doctor, and moreover one of the few to whom my despotic grandfather would listen.

Because of Erich's party-line brother Walter, who insisted on political clarity in the family, and because of Alfred and Anja's constant quarrels—it was said that she threatened to throw the twins out of the third-story window if her husband did not meet her current demand—these Sunday dinners were unpleasant, and even roast hare and Trauttmansdorff rice could not save them. But Grandmother Annemarie warbled on as before—in her world impregnated with music and lyrics it probably escaped her that disunion prevailed under the table—and her two dogs, the fat dachshund and the ill-humored Pinscher, were still wearing big silk ribbons and giving off an unwholesome fragrance combining dog hair and eau de cologne.

They went to Pätz for Easter, and Erich hid a dozen eggs so thoroughly and thoughtfully, that many of them could not be found, and he, who couldn't let it alone, kept looking for them late into the evening.

Karin, who had turned into a still more strapping, genuine German young woman, came along, and Else felt uncomfortable in her company. Karin was far ahead of Angelika in physical development, almost no longer a child, and it couldn't be long before she became suspicious of Else's features "foreign to the species," discovered her friends' un-German behavior, and overheard remarks that intentionally or accidentally repeated in her milieu, might put them all in danger. People no longer dared to speak freely in front of her, anxiously closed doors, gave her warning looks, were constantly on their guards, and were aware, with anger and fear, that this little Aryan bovine had more power than all of them put together.

Angelika, whom Else cautiously questioned to find out if Karin sometimes said or asked things that she didn't wholly understand, had no idea what her mother was talking about, and said that Karin was her best friend and that she understood everything she said. It was one of those situations from which there was no way out, and in which one could only trust in God and hope that things went well. Fortunately, Karin stayed only a week. She traveled back to Berlin with Erich, and the two of them were hardly out of the house before Peter appeared with Liena. He had long arranged his visits in such a way that he never saw his stepfather. His hostility to Erich grew in proportion as the disenfranchisement and persecution of Jews increased. His relationship to his own father, whose indifference had always hurt him, he now saw only from a political point of view, and this enabled him to express his bitterness.

Else recognized that her son's personal resentments were combined with objective criticism, and tried to draw his attention to the fact that Erich and Fritz hated the Nazis no less than he did.

Or did he perhaps intend to reproach his father and stepfather for being Aryan?

What he reproached them for was that they had stuck their heads in the sand or in their books. Sitting in castles in the air and hating and considering themselves unimpeachably pure because of this hatred was a little too easy and perhaps even worse than collaborating in the filth out of conviction. All around them their Jewish fellow citizens were being done in, and they had nothing to oppose to it but their damned hatred. One of them was continuing to build houses for the dirty bastards while the other continued to write films and books for them, but for them the main thing was that they were against the Nazis and whispered that into each other's ears behind closed doors and windows.

What else should they do, Else asked, mount the barricades and get themselves shot dead?

Resist—passively, for all he cared, since he could hardly imagine Fritz and Erich as activists, but at least resist! Not go on collaborating! Every job they did for these monsters, no matter of what kind, every mark that they got paid by them, was collaboration. If everyone who was allegedly against Hitler's dictatorship also put up a passive resistance, things would already look different. But they didn't. The money that "decent" Nazi opponents were paid by the Nazis was far more important to them than their ethical principles pushed *ad absurdum* and the fate of the Jews.

He was still very young, Else said, and was able to engage in passive resistance because of his working father's and stepfather's activities, which was probably why he wasn't doing anything. He hadn't really thought through all this stuff he was spouting off about. Big words, and nothing behind them! As if one could overthrow a dictatorship by passive resistance! Ridiculous and a waste of time, this discussion! He was the last one who could allow himself to give speeches like that. He was leading a thoroughly privileged life, doing only what amused him, looking on just as inactively as Jews were being done in, and then presuming to sit in judgment on others, and in particular on the people who were helping them, his mother, his sisters, and now also his grandparents, survive. Wasn't he going to blush for shame?

No, Peter said, he wasn't, because he was drawing the consequences from his position and was going to leave this shitty country, just as every so-called decent German had to do.

What would happen to passive resistance if all the decent people left the country, Else asked, and how would it help Jews if everyone who still supported them disappeared and only the

Nazis remained behind? Didn't he see what rubbish he was talking? And besides, where would he go if he left Germany, and wherever he went, how would he make a living, he who had never done a lick of work, had no idea what work was, and had nothing to offer but what he'd learned at school? Or was he counting on financial support, that is, the filthy lucre his father earned by working for the Nazis?

No, Peter said, he was certainly not counting on that. He knew how both men felt and that he wouldn't receive a brass farthing from them if he had the impudence to shame them by not sharing their opportunism and thus showing that he adhered to his principles more than they did. People didn't like being shown that by an unprincipled layabout. He would get along somehow, she could count on that. He was young, healthy, not exactly dumb, and maybe not even untalented, spoke three languages fluently, would quickly learn others, and had such a sunny disposition that people jumped at the chance to help him.

He laughed, took his mother in his arms, and said that it was true that he sometimes talked rubbish and spouted off, but on the whole he was right, unfortunately. And in this case he was certainly not eager to be right or proven right. It was just too bad that he couldn't convince her that she had to leave the country. He prayed God that she would recognize the necessity of doing so before it was too late.

Else didn't take him seriously. He was still so young, her little Peter, and just as vehement and unshakeable in his emotions as she was. He lumped everything together—Nazis and Germans, childish idealism and unresolved jealousy, bitterness, opportunism, inevitable constraints, demands on others that didn't make sense, and necessities that suited his requirements. But he was, thank God, too smart, too comfortable, and too much in love with Liena to carry out his idea of emigrating. If he'd been trained in a profession and were in a position to stand on his own two feet in another country, she would have had nothing against his leaving Germany. But as things were—he had no training, no profession, nothing at all—she saw the danger to him in another country and certainly not in Germany. What could happen to him here? Just as little as could happen to her daughters. Nothing happened to half-Jews whose father was a citizen of the German Reich. And sooner or later he would have to come around and see that it couldn't go this way. Or one of his many talents would make a breakthrough, and he would concentrate solely on that. Ach, she knew her children inside out: Peter, who had always been unruly, Angelika, who was complicated, and Bettina, who was good-tempered and would never cause her any concern.

It was quiet in Pätz that spring. Many of Else's close friends had left Germany, including Wendtausen and his wife Ibi, and Walter Slezak, who, though not a Jew, had emigrated to America, explaining that the Third Reich was not his country. Ellen had gone to London for a few weeks with Jack Blackwood and decided to remain there with him for the foreseeable future, and Fritz Rotbart was about to emigrate to America.

Else remained behind, and every new farewell was like a bloodletting. She felt herself becoming weaker, lonelier, and emptier. When, how, and where would she ever see her friends again, friends who were such an essential part of her life? Would she ever see them again?

I knew nothing of all this. That's all I can say with certainty. I didn't have even a glimmer. How far I may have sensed something, the way animals become uneasy before an earthquake, I can't say. But I believe that I must have done so, because one of my nightmares suggests it. I've often talked about it, and even described it in one of my books, and have always been careful not to add anything to it but to reproduce it just as I dreamed it: my mother, my father, Peter, Bettina, and I are standing together on the top step of the low stairway that led from the house in Hohenzollernstraße down into the garden. The light is a sulfurous yellow and flows down on us out of an invisible sky, the trees are black, unmoving, and sharply outlined. There is a deadly silence. My father says to us: "When the hearse drives up, we all have to run to it as fast as we can and get in. Anyone who succeeds in doing so will be saved, and anyone who does not will fall dead."

The hearse drives up, a long, black, shiny car. It's only about thirty meters to the street. My father runs off first, then my brother, then my sister. Halfway there, they fall dead. My mother grabs my hand and pulls me behind her down the stairs to the narrow, graveled path. We run, but don't get even as far as the others. My mother falls and pulls me down with her.

This dream expresses my fear and sense of a deadly danger so clearly that I don't understand how I could have been unaware and unsuspecting. But that's how it was. Nothing made its way into my consciousness, or else I blocked it at the threshold. If the latter was the case, I succeeded very well. I have sifted through the last years in Berlin again and again looking for clues, but I haven't found any from which it might be concluded that I knew something. My parents had spread their fine-meshed safety net so broadly that only their own uneasiness and anxiety could have been communicated to me. I lived in an enclave, and everyone who came into close contact with me was told never, ever to talk with me about certain things. These certain things were Jews and Nazis. Under the circumstances, God knows it was better to leave the child in the belief that there had been no Jews since Jesus and that Nazis were people like all others. The confusion and damage that one would cause her by confronting her with the true situation just now would be devastating. One thing I'm sure of: whatever they did, whether wrong or right, they did it out of care and love.

I lived in games I thought up myself and in books. *Little Lord Fauntleroy*, Brentano's tales, or Selma Lagerlof's *The Wonderful Adventures of Nils*—that was my world. Naturally I knew who and what Hitler, Goebbels, and Göring were, but I knew them mainly because the first one had a brush under his nose, the second had a clubfoot, and the third was fascinatingly fat. In addition, we sometimes met Goebbels's five daughters, who lived not far from us and whose forenames all began with H, like Hitler. They were pretty, neatly dressed girls in whom I could, to my dismay, discover no trace of a clubfoot. And there were postcards of Göring on which he was depicted with a litter of young lions in the zoo, and was holding one of them in his arms. But what these three strange figures did otherwise interested me just as little as what Karin did in the League of German Girls. Contrary to my mother's fears, Karin had no desire to spy on us or even to find out what was up with our family. I was her friend, in whose beautiful, exciting world she was allowed to participate for hours or days, and I can even imagine that she would have paid no attention to the designation "first-degree crossbreed." But this was never put to the test.

Whether in 1938 my parents exposed me to the danger of school because they wanted to maintain a certain "normality" and thus prove to the children and perhaps also to those who knew us in Wannsee that everything was all right with us, I don't know. In any case, things were not all right for long, because two months later by pure chance I happened to kick the ball into the goal at school and thus won the game. Nothing is more important that winning, no matter how mediocre the domain. My schoolmates, from whom I had up to that point been able to keep my distance, ran up to me with blazing enthusiasm and asked me the be-or-not-to-be question: "So why aren't you a member of the League of German Girls?" It was completely incomprehensible to them that such a killer girl, a girl who could kick a ball into the goal, did not belong to the League of German Girls. I found them repulsive, these flushed, sweaty, insolent soccer players, and answered them loud and clear: "Because I think it's stupid."

They drew back from me in horror, and my mother, whom I told about the incident, seemed no less horrified. From that day on I no longer needed to go to school. I might have wondered about all this, but I certainly couldn't have made the connection between the ball kicked into the goal and my classmates' question, on the one hand, and my answer and not having to go to school anymore, on the other.

When did Else's breakdown begin? It didn't come suddenly. She broke down bit by bit, always a little more, until she reached the foundation and lay in her own ruins and cried and howled like an animal that has been caught, thrown on its back, and hog-tied.

Up to that point she'd been rather calm, too calm, as if she were somewhat benumbed, dependent on other people's help, and it didn't matter what they had in mind for her, good or bad, so long as they didn't let go of her hand.

She was no longer the same. Sometimes it looked as if her spirits were returning, as for example when she lay in the sun or went swimming in the Wannsee with Enie or took a walk in the forest with her daughters. Then she crept out from under the bell jar that separated her from the world and life came back into her face, her voice, and her movements. But it never lasted long.

That's how it was that summer. Her last summer in Germany. She sent her daughters to Pätz to be with Ellen, who had returned from London. In the state she was in, she didn't want to see again the place where she had always been so happy. The memory of the past would make the present even more unbearable.

She remained alone in Hohenzollernstraße. She took strong sleeping pills to get to sleep, and there were rainy days on which she didn't get up at all. She read, without understanding what she was reading. She thought, but her thoughts dissolved before they had sunk in and yielded a meaning. Many of them sliced into her like a knife, and she cried out in pain: "I can't! No, I can't do it anymore!"

What was it that she couldn't do anymore?

She couldn't laugh and she couldn't cry, she couldn't lie to herself and couldn't ignore the truth, she couldn't let herself fall completely and she couldn't get up again, she couldn't stay and she couldn't go away, as a Jew, she could no longer feel that she was German, she couldn't live and she couldn't die.

Enie came and shouted at her: Collapse, sure, that would be just like her! She was, God knew, not the only one who was suffering. Hundreds of thousands of people were suffering, were getting through much harder things than she was, were in need and acute danger. And she, who could still move about freely, who did not constantly have to reckon with the possibility that the last chair under her hind end was going to be taken away, she was going to collapse!

She no longer knew where this was going, Else said.

Ah, no! As if anyone knew! No one knew, apart from the Nazi bastards, the wretches. She should pull herself together, for God's sake, get up and take a bath. Or didn't she know where that was, either?

Else got up and went into the bathroom.

Erich came and gave her a long-winded lecture on the history of religion, whose gist was religious faith, which abided in every person and was merely waiting to be discovered, whose power to overcome the world provided inner support and peace, and without which one could not survive in a time when the highest human values were being trampled in the dirt and corruption raised to an article of faith.

Erich showed her the way, with the help of his friend Professor Werner Sombart's wife, whom he admired. Corinna Sombart, who had been born into the Rumanian Russian Orthodox faith, was a lady who had a high degree of cultivation and an even higher trust in God, and who painted icons with a group of like-minded women friends. They met for this purpose twice a week, painted, carried on edifying religious conversations, drank tea out of a samovar, and feverishly awaited the arrival of Father Johann.

Father Johann's arrival was the culmination of these meetings. He was a White Russian pope of aristocratic descent with the face and figure of a Christ painted by El Greco and the charisma of a "holy man."

I quote from a letter Erich wrote to Corinna Sombart in 1949: "Seeing Father Johann again was for me a very great pleasure. He was completely unchanged in appearance and radiated a pure and wonderful humanity that I have had the privilege of seeing in only a very few people. Truly a holy man . . . " Father Johann had in the meantime become a bishop in New York.

I doubt that Father Johann's influence on the well-off and no longer quite young ladies of this group was purely holy. There must have been some element of Rasputin-like eroticism in the holy man's aura that made the ladies compliant. This was certainly so in Else's case. She had by now met many men, but never one in a black, loose-fitting robe with a big cross on his breast, long hair tied back in a knot, a cerebral face and such a world-overcoming power of belief.

I am convinced that otherwise she would have gone to Corinna Sombart's little gathering once and never appeared again, because handiwork, even if it involved painting icons, tea, even if it came out of a samovar, and edifying conversations were not for her, even when she was in the deepest despair. But when Father Johann glided into the room, extended to her a small, waxy hand, looked at her out of the softest, most beautiful of all doe's eyes, and said to her with a melodic Russian accent: "Praised be Jesus Christ," she made up her mind to follow him into belief.

Did she love him, revere him, worship him? I don't know. Did he fascinate her as a man with the charm of being impossible to seduce or as a priest with a direct line to God? That, too, I don't know. It was probably all of that. But what seems to me much more important is the question whether at that time she actually found religion, as she claimed in a letter she wrote to Fritz Schwiefert after the war. One of Peter's letters from 1939, which was a reply to her announcement that she had converted to Christianity, seems to me to suggest the opposite. In this announcement she must have spoken about her conversion with a certain irony, and described her motives as opportunistic. When her outraged son told her that her change in religion was twice as unforgiveable because it was not made out of conviction, she corrected herself and explained that she had come to believe.

To be sure, it was insecurity and justified fear of her son's reaction that made her write this way from time to time. But in addition her motives, which arose out of chaos and despair, must not have been unambiguous. She clung to the new religion as life preserver, and probably admitted to herself only later on that there was a hole in it through which the air slowly but surely escaped. But I am sure that at first she did everything she could to find religious belief and thus an inner support. There was no longer any other.

When did Else and Erich discuss the subject of emigration for the first time that year? It cannot have been only in November, after the pogrom that was given the beautiful name of *Reichskristallnacht*. In early January she was already married to Dimiter Lingorsky, a Bulgarian who first had to be found and imported to Berlin. It's impossible that this feat was accomplished in only two months. Therefore I assume that

Else and Erich finally discussed the idea, which each of them must already have toyed with for some time, by the end of the summer at the latest.

Unfortunately, they had waited too long. Else could no longer leave Germany by the normal route, and even if she had succeeded in doing so in one way or another, no arrangements had been made for her reception in another country. She didn't even know which country might be possible, might give her a visa and grant her exile. And no matter which one it was, how would she earn her living, or how was Erich to hack his way through the jungle of extremely stringent currency exchange regulations and transfer to her, perhaps for years, the money she would need? And what was to be done with the children? In the event that an appropriate country could still be found, should they be separated from their mother? Should they be sent into emigration with their mother? It was all too late, and it was all impossible.

Else must have said: "You see, Goody, we aren't getting anywhere. No matter which way we turn, there are traps everywhere. So let's drop it. It's awful to live here, but if they stick to the existing regulations, at least we're not in danger."

They didn't stick to the existing regulations.

The Prussian aristocrat and his eldest son put massive pressure on Erich.

Did he want to get them all in trouble, they asked, did he still not see where all this was leading? Every reasonable Jew had already left Germany, everyone who still had a chance of doing so had gotten out as fast as he could. But he and Else hadn't done anything, and were apparently relying on God alone. It was one minute to midnight, and if the clock ran out and Else had still not left, the game would be over for her and for him as well. As the husband of a Jewess, he could hang up his construction company and retire, that way he would be left alone. Had he ever thought about what disastrous effects his marriage with a Jewess might have on the Schrobsdorffs' firm? It was an unprecedented irresponsibility on his part.

In reply, Erich asked whether they expected him, for the sake of the firm, to act irresponsibly toward his wife and daughter?

God forbid! Responsibility had always been the highest law in their family. The only thing they expected of him was that he get his wife and daughter to safety, and they would help him in every way.

If they had an unobjectionable suggestion as to how to help Else, then they could talk about it. But he wouldn't get involved in discussions about how to get rid of Else in the quickest and most opportune way.

Erich was yielding not only to pressure from his family but also to panic and the insight that he couldn't cope with the situation, that he was powerless to confront it. So he gave his practical, energetic and moreover influential brother and father permission to take the matter in hand, on the express presupposition, of course, that they would come up with an unobjectionable suggestion.

Did he thereby make himself blameworthy? No, I would say, because wasn't he trying to get Else to safety, and didn't he have to allow himself to be helped when he himself was not in a position to do that? Furthermore, Else had in principle agreed to leave Germany, where conditions had become untenable for her. In other words, he acted on the basis of what he knew and his conscience.

Else's fate lay in Erich's hands, and she trusted him blindly. His weaknesses, his unworldliness, his eccentricity—qualities that had worried her at the beginning of their relationship, and even often disappointed her—no longer mattered to her. What outweighed them was his goodness, his decency, and his sense of responsibility, on which she had ultimately always been able to rely. If there was one person who would not let her down in this fateful situation, it was Goody, and she was sorry, deeply

sorry, that she had hurt him through her recklessness and egoism and lost him as a husband. She was the last person who
would have reproached or blamed him. She blamed and
reproached only herself.

Thus the Schrobsdorffs undertook to help Else and thus
save their government contracts. Walter was by now thoroughly familiar with the Nazis' regulations, ways of thinking,
and plans for the future, and getting rid of Else was not at all
the problem. The problem was Erich, who would not, for
moral reasons, agree to a divorce, unless a reason was found
that convinced him that a divorce was necessary.

And they found one. Who found him, I don't know. Maybe
Dora Taslakova, the Bulgarian physician and friend of the family, who frequently participated in the consultations, whom
Else liked, and who, unlike the others, had no ulterior motives
in wanting to help her.

The only way to smuggle Else out of the country and into
another one, for an unforeseeable length of time, was to get her
a new, non-German passport. And the only way to get such a
passport was by marrying a citizen of the country under consideration.

The country that was under consideration, for good reasons, was Bulgaria. The good reasons were Dora Taslakova,
whose three brothers lived in Bulgaria and could look around
for an appropriate marriage prospect, the Bulgarian people's
friendly attitude towards Germans, which would make it possible for Erich to establish business relationships to ensure
Else's financial security, the country's general sloppiness, which
would result in certain irregularities not being noticed or not
taken so seriously, the wonderful climate, with long summers
and a great deal of sun—precisely the right climate for Else—
Bulgarians' hospitality and cordiality, which would help her
cope with many things, the pretty capital, Sofia, in which one
could live comfortably.

If that wasn't an unobjectionable suggestion, what was it, then! It was presented to Erich, and he, pacing up and down the room, mumbling to himself, and then summing up the outcome of his thoughts in a "so, so, aha!" asked for time to think about it.

At half a minute before midnight, Walter said, there really wasn't any more time to think about it.

They could put out some feelers, Erich replied, but a decision could not be made until he'd thought everything through thoroughly and discussed it with Else. They put out feelers, and Erich thought everything through thoroughly, and I assume that this went on until *Reichskristallnacht*.

I didn't notice that my mother was no longer the same woman. At most, that she was different, quieter, more reflective, and simply not so loud and boisterous, but I actually liked that. She no longer screamed at me and Bettina so often. When we'd done something stupid, she shrugged and said: "If it's no worse than that," and when I complained about something, for example that I would never be able to put my hair into a long, thick braid, she said: "I'd like to have your problems and Rothschild's money!"

I was somewhat sad that she didn't go to Pätz with us, but she'd explained that she had important things to take care of in Berlin and that it would be just as nice with Ellen. It was in fact very nice with her, and we "fooled around," as my mother said, the whole time.

At the end of July we returned to Wannsee, and I still didn't have to go to school. Karin no longer came as often as she had earlier, because she had a great deal to do in the League of German Girls, and my mother always had something important to do in Berlin.

My father gave me a raccoon with a long, silky, black coat, a tiny, pointed face with a silver-gray mask, and an outrageously bushy tail, whose tip was also silver-gray. We named him Bingo, built him a big kennel in the garden, and put a washbasin in it. I sat in the kennel with Bingo for hours.

He washed every bite with his little black hands before he ate it, and I wanted to see if he might also wash a handkerchief. I gave him one, and he began to wash it, but then he noticed that it was not edible, and angrily tore it up. Finally, he'd had enough of me and the kennel, and dug under the fence at night. A woman found him in the Hohenzollernstraße in the crown of a tree, and we had to call the fire department. They spread a rescue net and shook Bingo into it. He was not hurt, but I couldn't stop crying, because it had suddenly become clear to me that the poor little fellow longed so terribly for freedom. So then we gave him to the zoo, where he would at least have company.

Twice a week I took ballet lessons with Tatiana Gsovsky. She was even more beautiful than her daughter Liena, taller, very slim, with a fine, small face and a mass of black curls. It's strange, but I don't remember any of the other ballet pupils, only Liena and Tatiana—perhaps because they were both so striking that everyone else paled in comparison.

I can still see the big hall with mirrors on its walls and the bars and Tatiana with her black leotard and a little baton in her hand. And I see Liena with a very gloomy face and sloppy posture doing exercises at the bar and her mother going up to her and giving her a slap on the small of the back. I also often got little slaps on my legs, because my positions no. 1 and no. 5 were seldom perfect.

Peter frequently came, stormed into the hall, interrupted the lesson, embraced and kissed Tatiana, Liena, me, and then disappeared into the adjoining apartment. He seemed to be completely a part of their family, more than of ours.

Once my mother took me into his room. It was in the attic, was very large, and had slanting walls and wooden beams. Blankets, pillows, rugs were lying all around, and the walls were covered with posters, photos, and pictures that he himself had drawn. I found it very beautiful, so colorful and comfortable. He had a Siamese cat with blue eyes and a squint. Peter said she was wild and scratched, but a few minutes later she was lying in my arms and purring. My mother and my brother stood at the window, their backs turned to me, speaking in low voices. Nonetheless, I heard that they were talking about money and a trip that Peter wanted to take. And then my mother said, and I remember this very exactly: "Peter, one can't simply take off and say: after me the deluge."

It was raining hard that day, and I was very worried. On the way home I asked my mother whether the deluge was going to descend on us. She said no, of course not, and how did I always come up with such silly ideas?

At this time I understood little of what adults said and did. The business with Father Johann was also strange. He lived in an apartment on the fourth floor of a tenement, and while my mother and I were climbing the stairs, she told me that we were going to see a Russian priest, a holy man. I asked how one could be holy, and she replied: by being kind and benevolent. I was very eager to see him and was not disappointed when the door opened. In his long black robe, with his curly beard and a hairdo such as only women wore, Father Johann really didn't look like an ordinary man. He could have been Jesus, with his wan, handsome face and pallid hands. What bothered me was his surroundings, which didn't go with him at all. We were standing in a small, disorderly, gloomy, musty-smelling ante-room, and he laid his pallid hands on my head and blessed me. That was all. But it was apparently enough for my mother. Three minutes later, as we were going back down the stairs, she was silent and reverent, and I didn't dare ask her why the Russian priest had blessed me in that musty anteroom.

During this period, I seldom saw Grandma and Grandpa Kirschner, and when I did, only for a short time. They no longer came to Wannsee at all, and never went for walks with me any-more. I was very sad about that and asked my mother if I could sometime spend a whole day at their home and even sleep overnight there. She said I could no longer do that, because my grandparents were already old people whom one had to avoid overstraining. I promised that I would cause them no trouble, but she got annoyed and said I should let her alone.

I had doubts about all this, because my grandparents were always terribly glad when we came, and it was very clear to me that they would have liked us to stay with them. But they never said a word about it.

The parakeet was very funny, flew and hopped around in the room, jabbered and fluffed up his feathers or made himself long and thin and shrieked at us. Grandma and Grandpa said he was like a child, and that's how they treated him.

Why didn't I sense their infinite sadness and weep, weep as I did for my raccoon, whom people had deprived of freedom and who floundered in the rescue net and screamed. But that was just it: they didn't scream, they smiled when we came and showed a loving interest in our joys and cares.

In October 1938, two new regulations were issued:

Jewish passports were to be stamped with a "J."

About 15,000 "stateless" Jews were to be deported to Poland.

On November 7, Herschel Grynszpan's attack on the diplomat vom Rath took place in Paris.

On November 8 there were major riots directed against Jews. Erich called Else in Wannsee and asked that she take the children and go immediately to the Schwieferts and remain there until it was safe to return to Hohenzollernstraße. He'd already discussed it with Fritz and Enie, and they were expecting her.

Else packed the necessary items in a bag. Her hands were trembling. At every unusual noise in the street she held her breath and listened. For the first time she felt physical fear, in her gut, in the hammering of her heart, in her parched throat. She told Bettina and Angelika that the Schwieferts had decided to rent the large studio that they liked so much and to move them in there for a few days. It would be fun to live so close to Papa Fritz, Aunt Enie, and Didi. The children thought so too, and were delighted.

The studio was an extravagant structure that was in the big garden, a few steps from the apartment building. It was furnished with old, rustic furniture and consisted of a huge, beautiful room with a fireplace in which an adult could stand up, a bedroom with an adjoining bath whose big marble tub, which was sunk deep in the ground, was reached by a couple of steps, a small kitchen, and a second bedroom that was located high up under the roof, and was reached by a spiral staircase. No wonder Bettina and Angelika found their mother's idea marvelous and were enthusiastic about moving into the studio.

A day later, on November 9, vom Rath died as a result of his wounds, and that night the pogrom took place. The next morning, November 10, the streets of central Berlin were covered with broken glass and household effects and the air was heavy with smoke. Nine of the ten large synagogues had been largely destroyed, hundreds of Jewish businesses had been vandalized, 10,000 Jews were arrested and taken to the Sachsenhausen concentration camp, 91 Jews were beaten or shot to death, and countless others beaten and severely wounded.

Peter ran to the Kirschners, Erich drove to Wannsee to pick up Else and the children.

You have to get out of here, Peter told his grandparents. You mustn't stay another day in this hell. Daniel and Minna, who had not slept at all that night and had been frightened to death, said that he should be reasonable. They were old people, and for them there was no longer any "out of here."

Peter, who could not bear their resignation, screamed that there was always an "out of here" if one really wanted it and believed in it.

They lacked a Moses, Daniel smiled, and Minna said she no longer wanted or believed anything, and her sole concern was Else, him, and the girls. But it was said that half-Jews and Jews who were married to Germans would not be harmed. Didn't he think so too?

He didn't think in terms of categories such as half-Jews and Jews who were married to Germans, Peter said. On grounds of conscience alone anyone who had a drop of Jewish blood had to get out of this sewer called Germany. He at least would be out of it as soon as he could get his papers and a little money together. That might be in just a few days.

What did his mother say about that, Minna asked, with a sigh.

His mother considered him crazy because he wanted to leave Germany, and he considered his mother crazy because she wanted to remain in Germany. They would see which of the two of them was right.

Erich told Else that there was no longer any alternative to leaving Germany, and there was no way of leaving it except that of a fictitious marriage with a foreigner. He'd thought everything through with care, and that was the only way out. If she agreed to it, he would get everything underway as soon as possible.

Did he want to divorce her, Else asked.

He didn't, but he had to, because otherwise this plan could not be carried out.

Had he had this plan for a long time? And who thought it up for him? His family?

She had her priorities wrong, Erich said, the question was not whether he and she should divorce, but whether he wanted to make her safe. In view of that it was unfair of her to ask these suspicious questions. It was true that his father and brother Walter had made this suggestion a few weeks ago, but he had considered it only as a last resort. He had hoped with all his heart that it would not come to this, but now it had, and he begged her to remain objective and fair and not attribute any ulterior motives to him.

She certainly didn't attribute such motives to him, but she did to his family. Now they finally had an opportunity to get rid of her, and even on the moral pretext of wanting to save her. No, she wouldn't give these fine people such a fabulous break. She'd rather croak here than be sent away in that miserable way. Why were Anja and Ulli able to remain in Germany with their husbands and not be "saved" by the Schrobsdorff family? Maybe he could tell her that? If not, she could tell him. Because in one case Walter, and in the other Anja, did not allow themselves to be humiliated and were in addition so clever that they led even the Nazis by the nose. But in her case they had an easy time of it. He, Erich, was weak and she was stupid, and they had both lost their heads. That was what she had to think. She made him no reproaches, and she didn't blame him—she had no right to do that. After the way she'd behaved with regard to him, it was only too comprehensible that he didn't want to be swept into this abyss along with her as well. She had, after all, left him in the lurch for years, had responded to his decency with her indecency, and thus could not now, in this infernal situation, expect him still to do everything he could, and had to be glad that he wanted to make her safe. But now he could spare himself the trouble.

Erich stood there, where Else's outbreak had surprised him and nailed him to the floor, a few meters away from her, next to Fritz's piano, on which stood a photo of Enie and Else from the time in Dahlem. An expression of enormous confusion had come over his face. He looked like a sleepwalker who, awak-

ened by a call, realizes that he is on the outer edge of a windowsill five stories above the ground. Else had always hit the
bull's-eye with frightful accuracy, and thoughts that he had
never dared think, not to mention admit to himself, had
suddenly become concrete and penetrated into the most sensitive centers of his being. His intention to get Else to safety in
another country was not selfless. It meant making himself safe.
And even if he had a right to do that, on the grounds she had
mentioned, the injustice it involved could not thereby be extinguished. For here it was no longer a question of his personal
rights with regard to Else, but rather of the collective injustice
being done to her people, the Jews.

Else glanced at Erich, and when she saw him standing there
with his arms hanging loosely and his bewildered face, it
occurred to her that he might be even more defenseless than
she. What had she expected from him, after all? That he put
himself in a life-threatening situation with her, saying: what
happens to you also happens to me—he who would collapse at
the first physical or psychological step? That he emigrate with
her—he who was incapable of living without the financial support of the Schrobsdorffs' construction firm? Would it help
her to have a man at her side who was not in a position to
muster the strength, the practical skills, and the financial
means to support her and the children? Hadn't she always
known that he was a gentleman, but not a man, and could not
cope with problems in existential hand-to-hand combat, but
only in the noble, reflective manner suited to him? Had she
expected him to suddenly turn into a Zeus at the age of fifty-
four, and in an apocalyptic situation? No, certainly not, but
perhaps she'd expected that he might face up, if not to the situation, then at least to himself.

"Erich," she said, "this is the hour of truth, and we can no
longer wriggle out of it. The only thing we can still do is stop
fooling ourselves and try to help each other so far as it is in our

power to do so. I don't expect you to be a saint, and please don't expect me to be objective and just at a time when my life is being destroyed. Maybe I'll be capable of that someday, and maybe I never will. Maybe I'll remain here in this hell, and maybe I'll allow myself to be sent away to the desert. At the moment I no longer know anything."

Erich sat down in an armchair, put his fingertips to his forehead and passed them down his face, which had gone gray and slack from one minute to the next. "I know no more than you," he said, "the decision is yours. If you want to remain here, of course I won't get a divorce, but the way things are going I can't say how long you will be protected being married to me. If you want to leave the country, I will immediately make all the necessary preparations. As I said, the decision is yours."

"You'd prefer that I leave the country, wouldn't you?"

"Yes," Erich said, "under the circumstances I'd prefer that."

In Wannsee there was no *Reichskristallnacht*, and had there been, my mother would certainly have come up with a plausible explanation: "You know, it's just a new game that Germans are playing now . . . "

Many years later, I no longer know when and on what occasion I learned about the pogrom and tried to dig up some reference to it in my memory. But I didn't succeed. *Reichskristallnacht* passed me by without leaving a trace.

When I think back on the two and a half months that we lived at number 20a Am Kleinen Wannsee, this time is covered with a shroud of deep sadness and awakening realization. Something had changed, decisively changed, and could no longer be concealed from me. It proceeded from my mother, who had become still quieter and was at the same time driven by an electrifying uneasiness. Even when she was not wandering aimlessly through the house and garden, but instead sat in an armchair with a book or a puzzle magazine, it was as if she were expectantly waiting for someone or something. If I looked over at her, I discovered that she was not reading or doing a puzzle, but only staring into the void and picking at her hang-nails, a new habit she had acquired that I didn't like at all, because sometimes she picked so long that her fingers bled.

It was a November with cloudy, overcast mornings, lightless days, and darkness that came on early. I was often alone in the big studio, sitting at the long table that was not far from the fire-place and stood behind the chintz-covered sofa. For hours, I played games alone—dominoes, Parcheesi, pick-up sticks, soli-taire—and built countless houses of cards. Karin had moved out of Wannsee, a relief for my parents, but a great loss for me. I could have used a friend right then, a robust, fearless girl who would have protected me from my dawning recognition, just as Karin had earlier protected me from my schoolmates.

My mother often spent time with Enie in the other build-ing, and Bettina went more and more her own way. She was now sixteen years old, had lost the weight she'd gained from her eating and bed rest cure, and was about to develop a wom-anly figure. She was essentially still a child, but compared with me, five years younger and another five years behind her in development, she was already almost an adult. I still don't know to what extent our mother had explained the situation to her. Her memories of this time are very different from mine, and a great deal seems to have been buried and repressed. She was going through puberty, showed the first signs of taciturnity and rebelliousness, and was focused more on what was going on in her body than on the events around her. Naturally, she knew more than I did, but certainly not everything. She was probably told half-truths, carefully sifted and diluted to spare her a shock. She was not the kind of person who asked a lot of questions, and what she knew and was not supposed to say, she kept to herself. I don't recall ever hearing her say anything that

might arouse suspicion or having received an answer to a tricky
question such as "Why can't I go to Berlin anymore?" that
might have led somewhere. In such cases she became gruff and
muttered something like "What business do you have going to
Berlin!" But there were also times when we played together
peacefully or told each other stories as we lay in bed in the
evening. We shared the attic bedroom, which was wildly romantic, with its low ceiling and slanting walls, its low couches and
bright-colored carpets.

I also often played in the garden with Fritz and Enie's son
Didi, but he was only five years old, and I couldn't play any
real games with him. The best I could do was get up to mischief, and that got on Aunt Enie's nerves. She had a special
fondness for working in the garden, weeding, tying up stalks,
or raking up the leaves that were ankle-deep on the ground. I
can still see her, small and energetic, in long pants, a kerchief
over her head and tied at her neck, the rake in her hand.
Nothing escaped her swift, sharp eyes, and her cry, "Didi,
Angeli, I'll spank the daylights out of you if you do that again!"
reached us in the most remote corners of the garden. She was
very moody that fall, and at least as irascible as my mother had
been sometimes. I remember, perhaps more because of what
was said than because of how loud it was said, a particularly
bad bawling-out I received. Aunt Enie was digging around in
the damp, dark brown earth like a mole, and my mother had
brought me a sandwich in the garden, which I threw into the
bushes unseen, or so I thought.

"Angeli," Enie bellowed, "you're the worst spoiled brat on
God's wide earth! You play the princess and the pea, you make
your mother's life harder than it already is, and you think it'll
go on that way forever. You can bet your ass that it won't, kid!"

Didi, who was standing near me, made a funny face, took
my hand, and took me away with him.

"She always screams at people," he said, trying to console

me, but I couldn't get the idea of my mother's hard life out of my head. What was so hard about her life, since she had everything one could wish for? I simply didn't understand it.

And then one day, as I was playing with Didi in the garden again, Aunt Enie was raking leaves and my mother had lain down to take a midday nap, I heard terrible noises coming from the studio: sighs and groans, whimpers and howls. I saw Aunt Enie throw down her rake and run into the building. In her haste, she left the door open behind her, and I, in mad fear for my mother, ran after her. But when I stood in the doorway I didn't dare go further into the room, because there, on the broad couch under the window, lay a woman who no longer had anything to do with my mother. She was twisting and writhing, rising up quickly and falling back again, flinging her body from one side to the other. Aunt Enie threw herself on her, tried to take her in her arms and hold her still. When she couldn't do that, she jumped up and ran to the telephone, saw me standing frozen in the doorway, and quickly pushed me back out into the garden.

"Your mother has a terrible headache," she said, "you needn't be concerned. I'll call the doctor right away, and by this evening everything will be all right."

I ran through the garden to the street, which was a dead-end. Our property was opposite a retirement home, and a few of the old people had dared to go out into the street and sit down on the three green-painted benches. I sat down with them and joined them in staring down the street, which was completely empty.

I thought: it will never be the same again; our life will never be the same again . . . and I couldn't stop thinking that, over and over and over, until the notion had become a certainty and the shroud of sadness had become a depressing sadness: No, it would never again be the way it was . . .

One day after *Reichskristallnacht* came the decree that the

Jewish people as a whole had to pay reparations amounting to one billion marks and immediately repair at their own cost all the damage done by the pogrom. This was followed by eight further decrees, including one that prohibited Jews from operating any businesses or craftworks, from attending any theaters, cinemas, concerts, or exhibitions, or being out and about at specific times or places. And others that prohibited Jews from continuing to attend German schools or universities, that cancelled driver's licenses and permits held by Jews, and required Jews to hand over all their securities and jewelry.

Else had decided to leave Germany. With the help of his father, his brother Walter, the Bulgarian doctor Dora Taslakova, and the lawyer Dr. Filier, Erich had managed to get everything promptly underway. Erich and Else got divorced, a formality that required no preparations.

Else had a nervous breakdown. Erich consulted the famed astrologer van Hogerwörth, in the hope that the stars would tell him what could no longer be foreseen by any mortal. Thus Else was treated by a doctor, an astrologer, and a Russian priest: the first of these gave her tranquilizers, the second drew her horoscope every morning, and the third maintained her religious belief. In the evenings, Erich came to see what these therapies had achieved.

And then Peter came.

He found Erich and Else, Fritz and Enie sitting in front of the fire in the studio, and said it was very nice there—just like old times.

All four of them looked at him reproachfully. Did he expect them to be sitting on already packed-up trunks, his father asked him.

God forbid, Peter said.

To what did they owe the honor of his visit, his stepfather asked.

280 · ANGELIKA SCHROBSDORFF

The usual, Peter said, but for the last time. He, in contrast to them, was in fact sitting on already packed-up trunks, had all the papers and now needed only the money for travel to Portugal and a short transitional period.

Why Portugal, Else asked.

Because Jack Blackwood, Ellen's fiancé, had advised him to go there.

Still another reason! Enie said.

And what did he think he would do in Portugal, Erich asked.

Work, whatever he could find.

That's a crazy idea, Fritz cried, and a waste of money! When he'd spent it all in Portugal, then he'd be back and the whole game would start over again.

No, in this even Goethe was wrong, Peter said. For him there was only a path leading ever farther from the land of his forefathers and no return.

Ach, Peter, Else sighed, with a worried look at Fritz's and Erich's resentful faces.

He obviously considers himself as the sole anti-Nazi here, his father remarked.

Not at all, Peter replied, but he did consider himself one of the few who was logically consistent on moral grounds rather than by coercion.

That got a rise out of his stepfather: What he, Peter, called consistency, he, Erich, called irresponsibility. But a big, demonstrative gesture was clearly more important to him than a good, inconspicuous act, taking the risk of leading an emigrant's life more important than enduring the daily grind of a middle-class life. With his admirable moral conceptions had he ever thought about his grandparents, who under these terrible circumstances needed him more than bread itself; about his mother, who was going through the most difficult period in her life, about his sisters, who were facing a nasty realization? Hadn't he noticed that the smugness with which he shouted his moral attitude from the rooftops was nothing more than a way of avoiding his duty to stand by those closest to him?

Peter declared that he loved his grandparents, his mother, and his sisters, but he could not be expected to become a stooge of the system that had undertaken to stamp out the last traces of humanity in itself, to persecute with bestial methods and to deprive of their rights, deport, abuse, torment, and rob hundreds of thousands of innocent and defenseless people.

Everyone who remained in this criminal country and led a so-called normal life thanks to his Aryan descent was making himself an accomplice, making himself guilty, making himself dirty. And *that* he could not bring himself to do, not for his mother, whom he loved more than anything, not for his grandparents, not for his sisters. The responsibility involved here was much larger than the one he owed his family. Here it was a matter of the most sacred law: to be human, and to remain human. And one could not do that in this country.

There was a long, uncomfortable silence, and then Fritz said: In other words, he, Erich, and Enie, to name only three people, were not humans or at least would not remain humans.

That was his view, Peter said, and they had their own.

He really ought to be ashamed, Else said, to play the fool that way and then ask for money.

He couldn't change his position because of the money, Peter said, smiling.

He won't get any money from me, Fritz said, with or without this position.

Erich said that he would continue to be willing to support him, if he entered a professional training program or course of study, but he would not finance a trip without rhyme or reason. That would be a simple cop-out.

Enie declared that she would give him the money so that he could find out that exaggerated nonsense wouldn't get him anywhere.

He should finally be reasonable, Else said, and see that his place was here and that as a half-Jew . . .

They should stop, for God's sake, stop, he interrupted, they all should stop, for God's sake! It was enough to make one throw up! He'd made his position clear, in unambiguous words, but his words ran off them like water off a duck's back. They were treating him like a cretin, and that was certainly the easiest way. Just don't take him seriously, because if they did they'd be running the risk of having doubts. He could do without their suggestions, advice and contortions! It wouldn't be worth listening to this baloney even if he were paid a pile of money to do it, and certainly not for nothing at all. He was now saying farewell to his stepfather, who considered him a slacker, his stepmother, who considered him a blatherer, and his father, whom he had nothing to thank for except his Aryan heritage, a great privilege these days, with which one could, thanks to a German passport, still cross the stinking border. But as soon as he was on the other side of the border, he would go to the closest German consulate and have a "J" and the name "Israel" stamped on his passport. So that he would be done with this damned people, once and for all.

He left without shaking hands with Fritz, Erich, and Enie. Else followed him.

"Peter," she said, "why do you insist on destroying your life?"

"I would destroy it if I stayed here," he replied, "and not by going away. And even if I were to destroy it in that way, it would be the right choice, because I'm one of you people, whose life is being destroyed."

A week later Else accompanied her son to the Bahnhof Zoo. He had received the necessary money from Jack Blackwood and was going to Faro, a small city in Portugal.

In one of his subsequent letters he wrote to his mother: "Do you remember our farewell? Oh, how often it has pained me, that scene at the Bahnhof Zoo. It was all so short, and you were so sad and so brave, and I treated you so badly. I should have been with you night and day for the preceding two months. Ach, Mama, I reproach myself so much for that. I keep seeing your smile as you went up the stairs and there was weeping in that smile, more openly than in any tears. And your hand, as if raised by force, hung like a dead bird in the air. I still had only the memory of a very distant wave, one from before. And I didn't rush to you, even though I knew that that was the only thing necessary, that these were our most irrevocable minutes . . . "

They never saw each other again.

I don't remember the day on which I saw Peter for the last time. He certainly didn't celebrate it as the last time, but did it as if he were just stopping by quickly and would come back the next week. Maybe he hugged me a little longer and kissed me a little harder, or perhaps none of that happened, and I saw him the last time—I don't know when. It's terrible not to have a conscious last time, when afterward one never, ever sees a beloved person again. Peter was like a shooting star in my life, a glimmering little heavenly body that falls toward one and burns out. Physically burns out. Mentally, I came to know him twenty years later, through his letters to our mother.

It took days for me to be able to look my mother in the face again without seeing at the same time that alien, weird woman on the couch. She noticed this, naturally, and was even more loving to me than usual, but she never spoke to me about her "migraine attack." The doctor came often, and once I asked: "Mummy, are you sick?" She said she was not, she was completely healthy, it was just that her nerves were a little frayed, but that was not an illness. She had become calm again, calmer than I had ever seen her, and she listened to music a great deal, with her eyes closed and an almost happy expression on her face. I knew that she was far away. Sometimes I sat down next to her in the chair, and then she told me who had composed the music, and drew my attention to the parts she liked most. She said there was nothing more beautiful than music.

I was allowed to go to Berlin again, with Bettina, to visit Grandma and Grandpa Kirschner. We were driven there by Herr Budau, my father's chauffeur, and then driven back to Wannsee about two hours later.

These were wonderful hours spent with my grandparents. We played word games and "Happy Families," ate little crepes, drank barley malt coffee, and were amused by Pipa, the parakeet. Sometimes Elisabeth came, too. She was still running my father's household and bought my grandparents everything they needed to live on.

"She's a wonderful person," Grandma said, "I don't know what we'd do without her."

I asked if they themselves could no longer go shopping, and she answered that they were old and carrying things was hard for them. I wanted to know whether she was afraid of death, and she said no, on the contrary, she was glad about it. For old people death was absolutely not something bad, but in many cases a release. I begged her not to die for a long time, because without her, being in the world would not be nearly so wonderful for me, and then she took me in her arms and sang Pipifax's song to the little one: "Five times a hundred thousand devils once came into the world, ach, the poor, poor devils hadn't a single penny . . . "

I laughed, but really only to please her. She had become so small and fragile and her voice had, too.

On St. Nicholas's Day my father, Bettina, and I went my grandparents Schrobsdorff's. My mother did not come with us. Uncle Walter and Aunt Ulli were there, along with Uncle

Alfred, Aunt Anja, and the twins. An Advent wreath the size of a freight-wagon wheel hung in the gloomy hall, and the boots full of presents that we were given would have fit a giant. Uncle Walter's face seemed to me more pinched than ever, and I still didn't return his smile. Aunt Ulli, I thought, resembled a slippery, oily otter.

Uncle Alfred and Aunt Anja were nasty to each other, and the twins looked like fairy-tale princes, but they moved only when they were wound up. That's how it seemed to me.

After the meal I went into the Biedermeier rooms with Grandmother. She asked me if I wanted to sit in the green or the blue room, and I decided for the green one, because green is the color of hope. The dachshund Strolchi and the Pinscher Pucki had come with us, and each of them lay down in his little Biedermeier basket. Grandmother suddenly took my hand and said that I was her favorite granddaughter, and she would always think about me and pray for me. Then she read me her latest poem, which was entitled "In the Evening."

"But how strange the room is, / how captured by deep stillness, / and over the familiar things / it floats, restrained, like a melody. / Doesn't the clock rise up with weary strokes / and don't soft steps still send / a tremor through the old armoires? / Awakened by memory, things rise up that have been here and there, / for in gardens the evening walks with tender gestures."

When she'd finished, she put her arm around me and pulled my head to her massive, large-flowered bosom. She began to weep, and I, deeply moved by the poem and her tears, wept with her.

Awakened by memory, things rise up . . .

Every morning Else swallowed a tranquilizer. Then she called the astrologer van Hogerwörth, who had already cast her daily horoscope. There were days on which the constellation of the stars was in a very good relationship to her, and she could fearlessly and successfully undertake and cope with everything that came up. And there were days on which he advised her to remain at home, because the aura was unfavorable. On favorable days she drove to Berlin, either alone, to see Father Johann and to meet the few friends who were still close to her, or with Enie, to go shopping in preparation for her emigration. Bulgaria, one of the few countries about which she had never heard a word, was certainly very backward, and one had to think of everything from books to toilet articles to complete wardrobes.

The three brothers of the physician Dora Taslakova had found the appropriate husband for Else, and described him as a simple man, fifty-five years old, and exceptionally decent and good-humored. For the sum they were offering, he was prepared to contract a fictitious marriage with Else, and was supposed to arrive in Berlin on New Year's Day.

Thanks to her tranquilizers, daily horoscope, and religious ministrations provided by Father Johann, Else was in a balanced condition. Slightly befuddled, but she found that quite pleasant. Whatever she saw, heard, and felt was muffled, as if packed in cotton wool. When she'd finished her errands, she went to a café with Enie, to a meeting with Ellen, or had lunch with Erich in a restaurant. Their relationship to one another had never been so deep, so firm, so inward. Perhaps they now really loved each other—she helpless in the ruins of her life, he defenseless in those of his world—for the first time. Perhaps now, having been enlightened by the hour of truth and caught in the grip of the essential, they for the first time unreservedly accepted and forgave each other: he her faults; she his weaknesses. Perhaps now, when the end had come, they could have had a good marriage.

They talked about what was about to happen: Bulgaria, which had so much sun and fruit to offer; Sofia, in which the air was supposed to be particularly good; Dimiter Lingorsky, Else's future husband, who spoke no language but Bulgarian, but otherwise met all their requirements; Dora Taslakova's brothers, Mitko, who was accompanying the bridegroom to Berlin, Zvetan, who was to bring Erich into his import-export company, and Vesselin, who had excellent connections with government offices and the authorities and who would see to it that things went smoothly in that area. Furthermore, they discussed the idea that Else should complete a little cosmetics training course, because in Bulgaria that sort of thing was surely in demand, and having something to do and a little income on the side couldn't do any harm. It was all carefully thought through and organized, except for the question as to what should be done with the children.

Here Erich and Else began to fall into confusion and perplexity. Should they uproot the adolescent Bettina and the ultra-sensitive Angelika from their native land and transplant them in the Balkans, where living conditions and education were not exactly of the highest quality and where getting their bearings in such an alien environment and language would be difficult or even impossible?

Unthinkable, Erich said.

Should they separate the children from Else and allow them to grow up in precisely the country of their persecutors, to which their mother and grandparents had fallen victim, and in which they were classified as first degree crossbreeds?

Impossible, Else said.

They postponed a decision from one time to the next. There was no hurry, after all. The children were not in danger and could in any case not leave Germany with Else. They would wait and see how Else's life developed in Bulgaria and how the children, especially Angelika, who had coalesced with her mother, got along without her. All that mattered was that they remain ignorant as long as possible—the shock, in any event, could not be avoided, and Else feared that moment more than that of her departure from Berlin, which she experienced over and over during her sleepless nights: the puffing of the locomotive, the call: "All aboard!", the doors slamming shut, the first lurching forward of the train, the slow, creaking, groaning roll out of the railway station, on the right and left the streets, houses, trees, and sky of her city, from which she would be carried away with increasing speed, thrown out, exiled.

They celebrated Christmas in the studio: Erich and Else, Fritz and Enie, Bettina, Angelika, and Didi, the grandparents Kirschner. It was their last Christmas Eve together, and for Daniel and Minna, the first time they had seen Fritz and Enie in two decades. They, who still believed that Fritz was Bettina's father and was alone to blame for the divorce with their daughter, had decided to forgive him his mistake. It was an emotional reconciliation, in which even the children, who had no idea what it was about, participated. Or was it a farewell? The farewell?

The candles were lit on the Christmas tree, and the pail of water stood nearby. They sang, accompanied by Fritz on the piano, "Silent night, holy night" and "Oh, how joyfully; Oh, how merrily Christmas comes with its grace divine . . . "

The grandparents looked at the children and smiled. Enie looked at Else and shrugged. Fritz looked down at the keys with a pained face, and Erich looked pensively up at the ceiling. Then Erich read them a Christmas story: "Behold, I bring you good tidings of great joy . . . " There followed the carving of the stuffed roast goose prepared by Enie, another viewing and examination of the presents, and finally the children's reluctant retirement to bed.

The moment when they had to tell the Kirschner grandparents about their daughter's imminent emigration to Bulgaria and the circumstances connected with it had finally come. Erich filled their glasses with cognac, and those of the grandparents with a liqueur. He was the one who had to begin, and after he had taken a large gulp of the cognac and walked up and down the room, accompanied by the others' anxious looks, he began to speak. In this case as well carefully chosen words and well-formulated sentences were important to him, and thus the bad news took the form of a polished little lecture.

Else, her eyes fixed on her bewildered parents, began to get uneasy, and in a pause in the conversation Enie interjected: "The long and the short of it is that Else is leaving this shitty country, and she's right!"

For a moment there was a silence, reproachful on Erich's part, embarrassed on the others' part, and then Daniel said: "I'm convinced that you are doing the right thing, and I'm happy that Else will be taken to a safe place."

"Yes," Minna said, "thank God, one less thing to worry about! But what about the children?"

"We haven't decided yet," Else said, "we'll have to see how things develop."

"The poor children," Minna sighed, "the poor, poor children."

"It's not forever," Erich said, "we're just talking about a few years to get through . . . "

"Are you sure about that?" Enie interrupted.

"Enie," Fritz said, "don't be so negative, that doesn't help."

"Negative or positive," Minna said, "one helps as much as the other."

"We'll always be there for you," Erich emphasized, "Fritz, Enie, Elisabeth, and I. You're not alone. And we mustn't lose our faith. The faith in the good. The good will win out in the end."

"By that time, Erich," Minna smiled, "if it does come, the worms will have long since eaten me. So I can do without this faith."

"Mother," Else said, "please don't make this still harder."

Minna stood up, went to her daughter, sat down next to her on the couch, and took her hand. "My darling," she said, "I don't want to make it harder for you, God forbid. But I know how hard it is, especially on you, because you've always felt yourself to be only a German, and not at all a Jew. And now suddenly everything is being taken away from you, and for the Germans you are no longer a German, but . . . Ach, I can't even say it. I have always been afraid for you, not because I expected something like this—who could ever have thought anything so dreadful might happen—but because it is false and dangerous to resist what one is, what one was predestined by someone or something to be. One can't simply wipe that away or shake it off or deny it. One simply is it, child, and so you can stand on your head and act in every possible way as if you were not it, but you are it."

She looked over at Daniel, and he smiled and nodded, and said: "Let her alone now, Minna, she'll find her own way." And then to Fritz: "Play us something else on the piano. I haven't heard you play for twenty years, and I always liked it so much . . . you know, the Rosenkavalier waltz!"

One more word, Else thought, and I'll begin screaming and never stop, never again! She quickly stood up, mumbled something about coffee, and went into the kitchen.

"Coffee is just the thing," Enie cried brightly, and followed her.

"Where are your pills?" she asked Else. "Take one and don't spoil the evening for your parents. We should all be utterly ashamed of ourselves in front of these people!"

She blustered and rattled around in the kitchen. A cup fell on the floor and broke.

"Breaking things brings good luck," she said, grimly.

In the studio Fritz was beginning to play the Rosenkavalier waltz.

"That too," Enie murmured and then, putting a hand on Else's shoulder: "Now, go ahead and cry!"

But Else didn't cry. She stood at the window and looked out into the dark, which stood before her like a black wall, and said: "Of course I'm utterly ashamed, Enie, but you know, it was really beautiful!"

That was my last Christmas celebration in Germany. I could say it was my last Christmas celebration, period. We continued to celebrate Christmas for another two or three years, but it was only a pathetic imitation.

It is little highlights that have remained in my memory from Christmas Eve 1938, visual impressions against the background of a heavy, dark love. It had hardly ever happened, especially in recent years, that I'd had the people I loved most, my parents and grandparents, together around me. And now they were all there and deluged me with the happiness of having them, and the fear of losing them. I don't believe it was a premonition, but rather the fear of loss that is contained within every great love. Moreover, the emotional turmoil of the adults must have had an effect on me and in the interplay of solemnity and exuberance impressed me as something unique. In any event, on that evening I became aware that love is a heavy, dark unknown.

It was on that evening, moreover, that my memory of Grandma and Grandpa Kirschner breaks off. A remarkable circumstance, because I must have seen them often over the following half-year, during which I was still in Germany. What happened or took place in me, so that the last visits have been erased from my memory?

The most obvious explanation, or rather supposition, I can offer, is that I sensed some calamity in their apartment, in their life, as I did in that of my mother, something that upset me and influenced my relation to them insofar as they ceased to be for me the quintessence of security. The calamity had inserted itself between us, the spontaneity with which I had loved them had become a feeling of dreadful insecurity, and the last corner of my "safe" world had thus been destroyed.

But in my memory, which breaks off with the Christmas Eve party in 1938, they still embody the safe world, and I see, hear, and feel it for the last time in the studio: Grandma in her black dress, with her enameled brooch at her throat, the big tortoiseshell comb, the familiar melancholy in her small, olive-colored face, the glint of love in her eyes; Grandpa, round and short-legged, my doorbell button, the brown wart, under the right corner of his mouth, the white wreath of hair around his pink bald head, and on his face with the lively, watery eyes the wonderful smile of purest kindness and modesty. They are sitting close together, like birds in a nest, and I feel the happiness of their nearness and warmth, their arms and hands, their cheeks and lips. I hear their voices, Grandma's worried question: "Are you warm enough, with your knees uncovered and your short sleeves?" and Grandpa's never-failing observation: "It's nice to have a birthday, isn't it, little Angeli?"

And my parents come and sit down with us. They're talking and laughing with one another, and I, in the middle, become smaller and smaller until I am only a tiny spot in a sea of love.

And then the fear comes, and I think: Ach, if only I could die before they do.

Else's future husband, Dimiter Lingorsky, who arrived in Berlin on New Year's Day, accompanied by Mitko Taslakoff, was a medium-sized man with a face like a pickle. His nose was long and thin, and the back of his head was flat. He had black, coarse hair that, being cut too short on the sides, grew out of his head like a little bush, brown, somewhat too close-set eyes, and his legs were a little too short, while his torso was unusually long. Nonetheless, he was what people of the Bulgarian lower classes called a handsome man, and in later years I was to witness shy or brazen expressions of love on the part of our housemaids. Mitko was small, wiry, agile, and had a broad, nutcracker face that could, with its distinctive facial expressions, produce a multitude of interesting wrinkles. He was an engineer, had studied in Germany, and spoke German fluently. Dimiter Lingorsky spoke only Bulgarian and had neither studied nor practiced any profession, which was of no importance anymore, because his marriage with Else had ensured him a good income. But he was good-natured and friendly. Else and Erich, who met the two men at the railway station, immediately recognized that they couldn't have chosen better, and approached the bridegroom with good will. Mitko, who had played a major role in finding this fine specimen, rubbed his hands together contentedly and wore a joyful expression on his face. He was to become a good friend to Else, always ready to help her.

The two Bulgarians were booked into a nice hotel near the Kurfürstendamm, and after they had deposited their bags in their rooms, they all ate a welcome breakfast in the hotel dining room.

"My wife and I," Erich said, without noticing his error, "are deeply grateful to you. To your health, Herr Lingorsky."

Dimiter, who hadn't understood a word, smiled in agreement and said, "*Nastrave.*" In accord with the Bulgarian custom, they drank repeated toasts and wished each other happiness, health, peace, and a long life. Else was not to be granted any of these.

Three days after the wedding, she converted to the Russian Orthodox faith. Father Johann conducted the religious ceremony and baptized her Elisavetha. He also conducted the marriage ceremony, because Else had suddenly decided to get married in the church.

What led her to do so I will never know. Even if she had discovered her religious belief at that time, she was not obliged to add a church marriage to the baptismal ceremony. Had she entered so deeply into religious belief that even a fictitious marriage was sacred to her and required the Trinity's blessing? Did she think that the more in conformity with reality the marriage was performed, the safer she would be from possible suspicions? Or was she attracted by a Russian Orthodox marriage, whose theatrical ritual pleased her so much that she didn't want to miss the opportunity to have the marriage crown set on her head to the accompaniment of Gregorian chant? All that may have played a role, and she no longer seemed to notice the absurdity of this enterprise. And neither did Erich. He saw in it only a proof that she had finally acquired religious belief, and he heaved a sigh of relief. She'd found her inner sanctum.

The marriage took place in the Russian Orthodox church in Berlin. The witnesses, Fritz and Enie Schwiefert, held the excessively large crowns over the couple's heads until their arms ached. Erich was smitten with the wonderful chants. Under the richly decorated throne, Dimiter's naïve face seemed to have grown still longer. Father Johann radiated holiness. And Else, kneeling, holding a burning candle in her hand, wearing on her breast the noble cross Erich had given her, and her face very serious, her eyes opened very wide— what was she thinking during these grim hours? Was she thinking: Now I've found my Christian God after all and will enter into exile strong and at peace? Or: I'm going to show them all that I can't be humiliated? Or: We've never played the fools the way we are today!

Afterward they celebrated in an elegant restaurant: Else with her new husband, her two divorced husbands, Enie, Mitko, and Father Johann.

They drank champagne and became quite gay. Erich gave

an amusing little speech. Father Johann and Fritz chatted about Ivan the Terrible. Enie and Mitko drank to each other over and over, so that they shouted "*Nastrave!*" louder and louder and he made increasingly ecstatic faces. Else learned her first words of Bulgarian: "*kack*," "*kackste*," "*kackwo*," and nearly died laughing about "*kack*." Dimiter, who was sitting next to her, saw that her skirt had ridden up a little, and shyly but firmly pulled it down over her knees. Fictitious marriage or not, Else was now Gospodya Elisavetha Lingorska, and she would not be allowed bring any disgrace on him and his name.

Yes, it was an entertaining celebration during which Enie got carried away, raised her glass, and shouted: "So, now let's all drink to the Third Reich, which has granted us this successful festivity and will grant us many, many more!"

One day my mother said: "Sweetie, I have a nice surprise for you! You're moving to Berlin with your father and Bettina. Are you happy about that?"

"And how!" I beamed. "And you are too, right?"

She looked at me oddly, and then cried, "My God, I almost forgot to call Herr Liedke!" and ran to the telephone.

When Bettina got home I said: "We're all moving back in with Papa in Berlin!"

She looked at me oddly and answered: "Yes, I know."

"I can hardly wait!"

"Hm."

"Aren't you happy too?"

"Of course."

About a week later, on a Sunday, my father came to Wannsee with his car and chauffeur to pick us up.

"Let's take a little walk before we go," he said to me.

It was a damp, cold day toward the end of January. Flash, my dog, was very exuberant, raced back and forth, threw fir cones in the air, and grinned at me. I laughed, but my father was particularly distracted on that day. He mumbled to himself and didn't seem to notice anything around him. Suddenly he stopped short and said: "Angelika, you know that we are going to Berlin today and that you and Bettina are going to live with me."

Now it struck me that he had omitted my mother from this sentence, and I said: "But Mummy too."

"No, your mother will stay in Wannsee a few days longer."

"And then she'll come."

"Tell me, my daughter, don't you really want to live with your old father alone for a change? Just to try it out, you know, to see whether you like it. Maybe you'll like it a lot, don't you think?"

"I'm sure I'll like it a lot."

"So, you see."

"And Mummy will come later."

"Angelika, you're a big girl and you have to let go of your mother's apron strings a little. You won't lose her even if she doesn't live with you for a while."

He'd spoken very emphatically, and to prevent him from thinking that I wouldn't like to live with him, I kept silent. That afternoon we left. My father, Bettina, I, and Flash. My mother did not go with us to the car. She hugged and kissed me and said: "See you soon." Then she quickly shut the door behind us.

The building in which my father lived was in Grunewald, on the Johannaplatz, which was round, with few buildings and four streets leading into it. In the middle was a small garden, also round, with lawns, flowerbeds, bushes, and benches. The building was an elegant, three-story structure in a very beautiful area of villas. My father's apartment was no less beautiful and elegant and had a conservatory that I especially liked. Many of the pieces of furniture, carpets, and pictures came from the house in Hubertusallee, but a few of them were new. His library was all there, his canopy bed had been replaced by a very large bed without a canopy, but with a very beautiful, midnight-blue bedspread.

I asked where Bettina and I would sleep, and Elisabeth explained that the three of us would have our own apartment, one story higher up. This was a pretty, brightly furnished attic apartment with a protruding balcony. My father said that we would only sleep there, and during the day we could be in his apartment whenever we wanted.

That evening Bettina and I had supper alone with him. Elisabeth had bought everything I liked to eat: sour pickles, smoked flounder, and Swiss cheese. She'd even baked a layer cake. My father let us drink half a glass of red wine. It was very nice to be with him, only a little unfamiliar because my mother wasn't there. She called later on and asked how we liked living with Papa.

I said: "Very, very much," and told her about the apartment on the top floor and the half-glass of wine and the conservatory.

Elisabeth put us to bed. She laid my big doll Lore, which I'd received as a Christmas gift, next to me, and said that she would be in her room next door all night, and that we could come to her at any time.

My father read us a story and said the Lord's Prayer with us.

He kissed me, stroked my hair, and said, "My little girl, my little girl . . ." And then, with feigned amazement: "No, you aren't my little girl anymore. Now you're my big girl, and we're going to have a very nice life together."

After he had left the room I began to cry. Bettina got up and sat down next to me on the bed. Her face looked shrunken and sallow.

"You're being silly," she said, without sounding harsh, "and really too old to be crying over Mummy."

"Do you think she'll be coming back to us soon?" I asked.
"I don't know . . . should we go to see Elisabeth?"
I nodded and got up.
Elisabeth was sleeping on a couch so wide that there was room for all three of us on it. She took Bettina under one arm, me under the other, and told us a story. Then we went to sleep.

The last weeks in Berlin were a nightmare for Else. Dimiter Lingorsky had gone back to Bulgaria shortly after the wedding, and a few days after the children had left Wannsee she moved into a pension not far from the Johannaplatz. In the mornings, until noon, she went to a cosmetics course, where she learned facial massage, the art of makeup, the use of various beauty products, and manicure—simple things that had never interested her in the slightest. She arranged her afternoons and evenings in such a way that she never had moments of being alone or without occupation. She saw friends, including those who had been close to her in earlier times, but who in recent years had not been part of her circle. She went to have coffee or supper with them, met them in the city to go to the cinema, theater, or concerts. Sometimes she encountered an old admirer or lover and went to dine with him. But it was all only a distant, distorted echo of a time that lay far behind her and would never return. She had already left her friends' world, and could no longer take an interest in their cares and joys, their thoughts and opinions. The tone of their earlier conversations, which had been spiced by silly antics, wisecracks, and wit, made her indignant, and profound intellectual discussions seemed to her a fashionable waste of time. What did she care about abstract art and philosophical issues? What still bound her to these people, who were leading a secure life and thought it important to discuss for hours the scene in the third act of a play that had been interpreted this way by one person and that way by another, and by the critics allegedly not at all? That had also been her tone, which she had found amusing, and into which she had thrown herself with so much verve. Now she found it all simply ludicrous, sometimes even enraging. The questions that interested her were: how does one cope with fear and pain, without being done in by them? How does one live alone in a foreign country, among strangers whose language, morals, and culture one does not know? How does one protect one's children from lifelong mental damage? How does one survive saying farewell to one's parents, knowing that one is leaving them behind in hell, and in all probability will never see them again? How could one ever understand what bestial instincts had overcome the highly cultivated, highly civilized German people, and how could one ever cope with them?

But those were unpleasant questions, questions that aroused embarrassment and perplexity or, still worse, banal recommendations or presumptuous lectures. Apart from the clear-sighted Enie, who understood Else's situation, and the warmhearted Ellen, who instinctively felt it, there was no one with whom she could express herself openly and assume an understanding that went deeper than momentary consternation or irritating pity. Even Father Johann, who offered religious faith as consolation for all problems, fears, and pains, offered her no relief over the long run.

On Sundays she went to the Russian Orthodox church, sank for a while into aesthetic contemplation of precious, colorful objects, beautifully costumed priests, and burning candles, incense and liturgical chants, and then went back out into streets that she perceived as hostile, in which every penetrating glance, every footstep she heard behind her, every approaching SS man terrified her.

But the worst part was getting together with her parents and daughters. The former's resignation and the latter's bewilderment were harder to bear than anything that happened to her personally. She feared every visit to her parents' home, every visit with her daughters, with an intensity that made her physically sick. Whatever were they to talk about, when she saw the misery of the two old people and the pleading questions in the eyes of her children? How could one not break into tears, not scream out the truth? Wouldn't it be better to cry along with them, scream with them, instead of engaging in this grotesque pretense and acting as if everything were all right or at least not as bad as it seemed?

Why couldn't she simply say to her parents: Listen, these may be our last hours together, and so let's talk about the past, about my childhood, which was so happy, about the goodness and love that I received from you, and my regret that I've not paid you back for them.

Why couldn't she say to her children: Listen, I don't want to pretend with you anymore, and so let's talk about the future. We have a very rough road to travel, but if we stay together and stick together, if we love and help each other, we'll survive it.

But then she sat opposite her parents with an unhappy face, and opposite her daughters with a forced smile, and the words stuck in her throat, she could neither get them out nor swallow them, to the point that she felt she would choke on them.

Her timidity with regard to her parents, whom she had too long deceived, and her fear for the children, to whom she had too long lied, were stronger than her tormenting need to tell the cathartic truth. So she continued to talk with her parents about trivial matters and evaded the increasingly reproachful looks of her older daughter and the increasingly fearful questions of her younger daughter.

"Mummy, why are you living in that terrible pension and not with us?"

"Because the apartment is too small, you know that, my angel."

And Bettina's stony silence and Angelika's expectant little face and instead of an honest answer a stuffed animal that seemed to distract attention from what was happening. And when the visit was over, there was exhaustion and despair and bitter self-recriminations: "I was a bad daughter, I was a bad mother. What is my suffering compared to that of my parents, who are vegetating like lepers in their apartment, compared to that of my children—Peter in Portugal, hardly able to keep his head above water, Bettina and Angelika between Germany and Bulgaria, between mother and father. And I, with my hands tied, my tongue ripped out, and all possibility of setting things right taken from me."

The days passed, and the departure date approached. Else began to long for it. Better to live in exile in a foreign country than in exile in her own country. Better to give the children an undisturbed chance to get used to the new situation than repeatedly to upset them by her glum visits to them. Better no longer to see her parents than to sit stiffly with them and be unable to offer them any consolation, any hope.

Better to walk through the streets of an unknown city, of whatever kind, than through Berlin, in which she always had to take care to stifle memories.

She no longer allowed herself any memories, any sentimental moods, any self-pity. It was over, and that was good. The people to which she had once belonged, the country that was once hers, and the Else whom she had once been, all belonged to the past. And the past was dead, just as she was dead inside.

She said farewell to her friends. Many of them threw their arms around her neck and wept. Others wished her luck, saying: "Our Schnuff will be able to handle it!", spoke about the end of the gang of criminals, of seeing each other again and celebrating. Else had no tears, no words. She smiled, nodded, and said: "Adieu."

She went to see the Schrobsdorff grandparents, just as she

had gone the first time, with her head held high and a slight ironic curl to her mouth. Only this time she was not the conqueror who held Angelika in her arms like a trophy, she was the defeated one, retreating with empty hands.

The Prussian nobleman sat in his study, in his brown leather chair. He shook hands with Else and said: "No hard feelings, Else, and the best of luck." Annemarie, his wife, hugged Else to the ample, soft cushion of her bosom. She wept.

"Don't worry about the children, there's no better place for them than here. And I'll take care of your poor parents, I'll go myself to see them. They will lack for nothing!"

"Nothing . . . " Else said, smiled and nodded.

She said farewell to Fritz and Enie.

"I'll miss you very, very much," Fritz said. "And if I can ever be of help to you in any way . . . "

"Not me," Else interrupted him, "the children. Write to your son, call Bettina now and then, and be a father to her a little."

"And if you don't hold up, I'll kill you!" Enie cried, flung herself on Else, and kissed her face, sobbing and cursing all at once.

The day before her departure Else went to see her parents.

"Let's make it brief, little Else," her father said, "we aren't seeing each other for the last time."

"That might suit her," her mother joked.

She tried to imprint them on her memory, as they stood there, two small, wearily smiling figures surrounded by the heavy, dark furniture that had grown old with them, in the faint light of a gray afternoon.

Her parents in the apartment in which she had been born and had grown up, and which she had stealthily left one morning in order to discover the "completely different," in order to conquer the beautiful, broad, Christian world.

That evening, after it was dark, she drove with Ellen to the

Johannaplatz. They climbed the stairs very quickly, very quietly—intruders into the beautiful, broad, Christian world.
The children had been expecting her visit and were very
excited.

"Are you staying with us, now?" Angelika asked, fear over-
shadowing hope in her face.

Else looked at Erich.

"First of all, let's all go into the living room," he said, "sit
down and just listen to me for five minutes, if you can . . .
Elisabeth, please come with us."

They sat down. The children looked up expectantly at
Erich, and the adults kept their eyes fixed on the floor.

"Well, then," Erich said. He spied a bit of lint on his sleeve
and carefully removed it. "Well, then, I have a big surprise for
you. We're all taking a trip to Bulgaria. It's a very pretty country in the Balkans . . . tomorrow I'll show it to you in the atlas.
There are fields of roses there, huge fields of roses. And from
the rose petals they make attar of roses, and that is . . . "

"Goody," Else admonished him.

"Your mother is a very jittery again, so I can't tell you right
now what attar of roses is used for. The main thing is that we're
all going there, not together, but one by one . . . that will make
it more exciting. First your mother will go, and then a few
weeks later Angelika and I will go, and then Bettina will come
with Ellen. When we're all there, we'll sail together across the
Black Sea, in the south, for a holiday. And now don't tell me
that isn't wonderful!"

Ellen thought it was heavenly, and was beside herself with
joy. Bettina as well. Else smiled. Elisabeth kept silent.

"Is the sea really black?" Angelika asked, and Else, who
was prepared for anything, but not for this innocent question,
breathed a sigh of relief.

"She's still a child," she said to herself, "God be praised and
thanked that she's still just a child!"

The next day Herr Budau, Erich's chauffeur, took Else to the Anhalter Bahnhof. She'd insisted on going there alone. It was the first sunny, warm day of spring that year. Green buds were already breaking out on the trees, and women were wearing light-colored clothes. Spring was in the air, on people's faces and in the speed with which they drove.

Else sat in the back of the car, smoking a cigarette and looking out the window. She'd experienced spring in this city forty-six times, and each had seemed to her more beautiful than the last. She loved spring very much, the reawakening of nature, the delicate light that made everything look beautiful, the warmth on her skin, the expectation inside her, the feeling of loving more intensely, of being loved more intensely. Berlin in the spring, Pätz in the spring, her children in the spring, whether she would ever . . . She closed her eyes and stifled the thoughts.

They stopped in front of the railway station. Herr Budau got the bags out of the car, hailed a porter, gave him instructions. Else tried to say good-bye.

"No, no," Herr Budau said, "I'm not leaving you here alone."

He accompanied her to the train, found her car, and waited until the porter had stowed her bag in the compartment. "Well, that's it," he said, took Else's hand and shook it: "Have a good trip, Frau Dr. Schrobsdorff, and I want to tell you again that I'm very sorry to see you go. But everything turns out all right in the end, Frau Dr. Schrobsdorff, and this will too!"

"Thank you, Herr Budau," she said, and felt a lump in her throat and her eyes beginning to burn, "farewell." She turned quickly around, climbed the two steps into the railcar, and then turned around again to him. He was still standing there, his fat, red face under the navy blue chauffeur's cap serious and concerned.

She waved briefly to him, and he shouted, emphasizing every syllable: "*Auf Wie-der-sehen!*"

And now Else wept all the tears that she had never wept on

saying any farewell. She sat hunched in a corner of her compartment and wept into her much too small, thin handkerchief
and listened to the puffing of the locomotive, the cry "All
aboard!", the doors slamming shut and the chauffeur's words:
"But everything turns out all right in the end, Frau Dr.
Schrobsdorff, and this will too . . . "

The separation from my mother was terrible, but the circumstances under which it took place were even worse: not
knowing what was happening, not understanding why Bettina
and I were living with my father, and she in an ugly room in a
pension, in which we sat around as if we were at the bedside of
someone who was seriously ill, self-conscious, uneasy, not having any idea what people were talking about, what was to be
done about the sick person and myself, which questions could
be asked and which ones would provoke that bewildered,
despairing look on her face. I noticed, of course, that there was
a secret, a terrifying secret that made my mother infinitely sad
and that was not to be revealed to us. The secret was always
there, whether we were doing a jigsaw puzzle, going to the
aquarium, or buying a new stuffed animal. It depressed me
more each time and finally became such a burden that I began
to fear our visits to her. When she came to our apartment and
my father told us that we were all going to take a trip, but that
she would be leaving first and that we would follow her a few
weeks later, it was almost a relief. It seemed better not see her
face at all for a while and then find our old Mummy again than
to see her as she was in that room in the pension.

During the four months that I remained in Germany without her, I didn't suffer from her absence; instead, her absence
spared me pain. To be sure, I longed for her and had to be constantly reassured that it was very certain that we would follow
her to Bulgaria, but life with my father was so wonderful that
the happy times far outweighed the sad ones, and I believed I
could never forego them again.

It was the first time that I'd lived in intimate closeness with him, and he gave me a love and attention that went far beyond any he had given me before. Earlier, I'd worshipped him from a certain distance, but now I adored him as my all-powerful father. Whether he was standing in his elegant pajamas in front of the bathroom mirror, shaving himself and putting a dab of shaving soap on my nose, or doing calisthenics in athletic shorts with Herr Sommer, the gymnastics teacher, or sitting in his underwear on the edge of the bed, fastening his garters, he was and remained an adorable man.

I was allowed to go into his bedroom in the morning and lie next to him on the duvet, I could help him choose the suit he was to put on, and tell him which tie to wear with it; during our copious breakfasts, I was allowed to cut the sprats into small, boneless fillets for him, and sometimes to go with him to his office, from which Herr Budau drove me back. I was even allowed to go into his library when he had visitors. The visitors were always men—the huge astrologer, Herr van Hogerwörth, for example, the stringy Herr von Löpa, who owned an estate, or the light-blond, rosy lawyer Dr. Filier, who, Papa had told me, came from a Huguenot family. When I appeared at the door, my father said: "Ah, there's my daughter. Come in, Angelika, and sit with us for a while."

Then I nodded, said "*Guten Tag*," and quietly sat down on the edge of a chair. But I had really come only to hear the words: "Ah, there's my daughter."

I spent most of my mornings alone with Elisabeth. I played in the living room or the conservatory, and often with her, in the kitchen, which was too small for such large woman. She seemed to me to have grown still fatter, but also much gentler. When I spilled red ink on the table or nibbled on a biscuit for half an hour, she sighed, but did not complain. And sometimes she sat down beside me with a glass of schnapps, a cup of coffee, and cigarettes, and talked about the "good old times."

Bettina continued to attend the art school, and didn't get home until 1 P.M. Since our mother had separated from our father, and under the influence of Ellen, who spent every afternoon with us, she had turned into a young woman. The transformation seemed to have taken place overnight, and had changed my relationship to her. With her pretty legs and breasts, her shoulder-length hair and clear, ivory-colored skin, she was for me the grown-up sister and had therefore become a person to be respected. Her curt taciturnity, which had become more marked in recent months, had now turned into an openness and constant cheerfulness that had beneficial effects on me. The afternoons and evenings that I spent with her and with Ellen are among my last childishly carefree memories.

Ellen, who combined in herself vulgarity and naïveté, feminine cunning and human generosity, had the rare talent of making every day a unique event and making a festivity out of things we found repulsive. Washing my neck, which I considered an unnecessary torment, became a common, relaxed bathing festivity; putting away my toys became a major cleaning festivity that even ended with my actually putting my shelves in order; swallowing a horrible-tasting tonic became a general drinking party, in which Ellen put down twice as much. And strolls through the city that we took together, shopping for the upcoming trip, eating sausage at Aschinger's, the excursions into the country! I was never afraid when we got into the suburban railway and the door slammed shut behind us because Ellen immediately made a magic sign that protected me from the shortness of breath that afflicted me at such moments.

During those last four months, I was protected from everything, even more thoroughly than before, and with greater success. I had been so stuffed with indulgence, love, and pleasant living that I no longer even asked questions. The happiness of the last months in Germany became an additional unhappiness during the first years in Bulgaria. It was an inauspicious preparation for the bitter life in exile, made the contrast even more painful, the nostalgia for the lost paradise even greater.

Today, I'm still seeking memories from the last days before I left Germany that are more meaningful than the trivial ones that have remained: the new, black-lacquered trunk with the yellow monogram that Herr Budau carried into our apartment one day; the photo that my father had taken of me as a farewell picture: I in a blue plaid dress, with my arm around Flash, both of us in profile, looking very intently at something interesting that must have been happening in front of us; the horoscope that van Hogerwörth cast for me and that my father showed me, so that from then on I would consider myself a first-class individual; the visit to the roof terrace of the Eden Hotel, where my father had taken me to meet some acquaintances, and where I, dazzled by the elegance, enchanted by the dance music, wanted to sit all night.

Years later, the photo with Flash fell into my hands again, along with the astonishingly accurate horoscope and the many letters that I wrote to my mother during this time in which I described with childish enthusiasm my adventures with Ellen and the hours spent with my father, constantly emphasizing to her that my joy at the prospect of seeing her again and going on the wonderful holiday on the Black Sea was enormously, enormously enormous.

They wanted to spare me the farewell, and they succeeded in doing so. I have no last memories that might have framed the picture. I didn't say adieu and thus could not arrive at closure. I'm still seeking it.

Elisabeth stood at the window, and completely filled it. She wasn't smiling, she didn't move. I called: "Take good care of Flash until I come back!" and waved. She slowly raised her hand and moved her fingers.

Herr Budau held the car door open for us: "hello, Herr Dr. Schrobsdorff," he said seriously, "hello, Angelika."

I left Germany like a sleepwalker, holding my father's hand and in my arms, my big doll Lore.

FIASCO

A letter of Else's from Sofia, Bulgaria, to her friend Ilse Hirsch in Jerusalem, Palestine:

July 1939

Dear Ilse, my sincerest thanks for your letter, which pleased me very much but also bothered me at certain points. What I noticed is this: people outside Germany are just as badly oriented and informed as they are in Germany. You see as black what is still gray, and we saw as gray what was already black. We learned too little, you too much. They lied to us in Germany, and you are lied to abroad. Basically, it comes to the same thing: no one knows what is really going on.

Now that I am outside Germany, I discover with astonishment that even intelligent and politically experienced people have no idea what has actually happened in Germany and what has not. And you, too, have no idea. Otherwise, how could you be surprised that our friend Fritz Rotbart had to leave the country without a penny in his pocket? He is, God knows, no exception, but rather the rule. And why do you refuse to understand that there are people who do not want to emigrate to Palestine as enthusiastically as you and Walter did, especially since there, too, neither calm nor peace prevails and it is impossible to speak of security? And how can you maintain that my Peter would have fallen into the same distress had he acted reasonably and not insisted on being treated as a full-blooded Jew? I am of the opinion that he is behaving like an idiot. I can accept his leaving Germany. He would have been recognized as German just as his sisters now are, but he didn't want it that way, it was his attitude, his right, he was too proud of it. Fine, but why declare himself to be a full-blooded Jew, to convert to Judaism, have a "J" stamped on his passport? He's not religious, he's not a Zionist, and he's certainly not thinking of emigrating to Palestine. So why and for what purpose, for God's sake? Why is he making a hash of his life, and even endangering it? His conviction, his rebellion, his solidarity—simply dishonest drivel, and fifty percent convenience. Working a steady job was too demanding for him and too bourgeois, he'd rather starve to death in Portugal, it's in any case more interesting and even has a flavor of martyrdom and heroism. I know Peter like the back of my hand, I know his proclamations, his demonstrative gestures, his self-admiration. We love one another, but that does not diminish my anger at his foolish escapades. So much for Peter . . .

A letter from Peter to his mother, written in Faro, Portugal:

Dear Mummy, in response to the two terms you used, "proclamation" and "display," both of which designate an extreme that does not entirely correspond to the truth, I want to say the following to you: There are times in our lives that force us not only to be clear about what we think, but also to express it. You forget that I'm not propounding my standpoint before the consulate, but only trying to make use of the means at my disposal to liquidate a legal decision. In addition, I don't believe that I'm acting wholly unjustly if I'm in a position to show in my own person what a Jew is—or perhaps what a Jew *also* is in a time that condemns him to inferiority.

Perhaps you now understand me somewhat better. I haven't made my decision in order to become a different person (I know that I'll never be a Jew as you imagine Jews to be), or to make use of anyone, or even to fight. All that has absolutely nothing to do with it. You completely misunderstand me: I don't do that in order to change something, as you do. I don't assume anything, I'm not changing paths. I'm a JEW, and say so, just as I always have. Is there anything special about that, anything new? People know it about others—it doesn't need even to be said. People don't know it about me, so I have to say it. All this is self-evident, Mummy, because no matter what you do you can't erase the fact that I have Jewish mother. And is it supposed to hurt me not to hide what I am? Why should I reflect on it for a perversely long time—what does reflection have to do with it? It wasn't that I finally managed to make up my mind, I never had the choice. I did what was for me the most natural thing in the world to do, what seemed the most obvious thing to do. Inner clarity—outer clarity. It's over. I've remained the same, Mummy, and that's what matters. Because how could I, please tell me, how could I count myself a Jew one time, and not the next, because it was more advantageous for me? What you say about my country [Palestine] is completely false. It's not my country and never will be. To try to form ourselves into a nation is to underestimate our value and the self-evidence of our history. Not to speak of the fact that for me the concepts "my country" and "homeland" mean absolutely nothing, and since I am stateless without the slightest feeling of regret or loss, I will never be tempted to decide for either my "homeland" [Germany] or Palestine. To Germany I owe only my language, but that is a great deal. For that reason it's the only thing I can retain and want to retain. I owe Palestine nothing, and Zionism is a bad plagiarism of all the futile efforts of our time. What would be achieved by our becoming "a nation"? Nothing more than going backward instead of forward. Now if you can endorse my decision as a stateless Jew and see that it is necessary—just as I see that your decision [the conversion to Christianity] was necessary for you—then what would be achieved for us would be nothing more nor less than an unlimited respect for our opposed goals . . .

The continuation of Else's letter to Ilse Hirsch:

So far as I'm concerned, everything is still unclear. Nobody could foresee the catastrophe that occurred in early November, when the so-called *Reichskristallnacht* swept over us. It took me by surprise as well. Up to that point I doggedly thought: I can do it, I'll remain and survive it. It was sometimes hellish, and increasingly often I had only one wish: to get out of Germany, to be free again, to be able to breathe again. And yet, now that I'm outside Germany, I know that Germany is my country, and that my life is there alone, and I should have continued holding on, and I would have done it. You speak of degradation, and you'll probably say now that my position is untenable. Perhaps you're right, and yet . . . I regret having left, regret it bitterly. Not so much for my own sake as for the children's I should have held on, because I've thrown them and myself into disorder, doubt, and chaos.

We no longer knew what to do, Erich and I, it seemed that conditions in Germany were unbearable for me. So we made the decision that was so infinitely difficult for both of us: we got divorced, and for three months I've been here in Bulgaria, married to a Bulgarian. Today I know that we could have stayed, because neither the children nor I would have been affected by the laws issued in November. I acted under the pressure of fear and desperation, and I curse myself for doing so. I'm only now realizing what I lost in Erich, although—inwardly I have not lost him; with my decision to leave Germany, I have instead won him back. But my parents, what will become of them? They're alone, old, and can no longer get away.

I'm not suffering from any hardships. Erich has a share in an export firm here, and we are being cared for financially. Tomorrow he's arriving with Angelika, and two weeks later Bettina is coming with Ellen. Then we're all going to the Black Sea. Compared with the hardships and great misery of countless people, I have it good and have no reason to be desperate. But I still have the bitter feeling that I'm allowing myself to be driven, forced, humiliated. I've always gone wrong when I've followed the advice of others and not my own feelings and instincts.

What will happen now, I don't know, as I've already said. Everything will be decided only in the fall. Maybe I'll go back to Germany; since I now have Bulgarian nationality, I can do that. Maybe I'll stay here and keep the children with me. For them—at least for Bettina—Bulgaria is not a good place to be, because here she can't study the subject that suits her best. Angelika, as spoiled and demanding as she is, wouldn't like it at all. And all the less because she's been living these last months with her beloved father, who dotes on her and, of course, gives her everything she wants. But it might be good for her to get used to a more modest way of life. It's just that everything is so hard here, God, you've probably got it even harder, nowhere are things as comfortable, as orderly, as clean as in our . . . well, let's not go into that!

Bulgaria was in fact not as comfortable, orderly, or clean as the Third Reich, nowhere was it as comfortable, orderly, and clean! How could my mother have failed to see the irony of her words?

Bulgaria as the trash can of Europe. I don't know why it was so backward. It still constantly happens that people who talk to me about it say: "When you were in Yugoslavia (others say Romania) . . . " And I indignantly reply: "I was in *Bulgaria*!" And they say: "Yes, of course, that's what I meant." But they can't even get the name of the country right. Even today, when Bulgaria is mentioned their only association with it is the longevity of the people who live there, thanks to garlic and yoghurt.

There was a lot of garlic there, that much is right, and an outstanding yoghurt made of sheep's milk that was so high in fat that it could be cut with a knife. But there were also the Rhodope and Rila mountain ranges, with a beautiful monastery dating from the tenth century, and there was the Black Sea with its endless, yellow-gold beaches, there were forests and rivers, meadows on which handsome flocks of sheep grazed, and plains full of the most marvelous fruit and vegetables; there were vineyards with the best grapes I've ever eaten, and the fields of roses my father had mentioned; but there were also fields of tobacco, maize, and sunflowers, attractive little towns and villages that had the kind of originality people call primitive; there was the capital, Sofia, a pretty, lively city at the foot of Mt. Vitosha, in which a little oriental, a little middle-European, and a great deal of Balkan are mixed and which offers a large number of stately buildings, such as the university, the Academy of Sciences, the National Museum, the National Library, the National Opera, and the National Theater, and in addition the castle and the Alexander Nevsky Cathedral. It was a beautiful, fertile, agricultural country with a peasant population of great warmth and hospitality—Slavic souls on which 500 years of Turkish rule had put an Islamic stamp, people who took pleasure in eating and drinking, singing and dancing; pretty, vital women with heavy manes of hair, very masculine men with a marked sense of honor and dignity. At the summit stood Boris, a small, gentle, very liberal and beloved king who, people say, was killed by his German allies in 1944 because he refused to hand over his Bulgarian Jews.

That was what Bulgaria was for me between 1939 and 1944.

The continuation of Else's letter to Ilse Hirsch:

As always, I'm doing nothing at all. When one has indulged in a life for a long time, when one has been spared everything unpleasant and difficult, one is probably incapable of suddenly beginning to work and build a life for oneself. I'd like to do that, but I won't be able to. And first of all I have to find myself again, I have to get clear about the situation, I have to get hold of myself. Then my loved ones are coming—Erich and the children; and then I'll have another reason for not working. Basically, I'm lazy and frivolous, and my energies and gifts have always remained undeveloped or developed along the wrong lines. There has been no one who could have set them on the right lines.

I have many friends here, I'm well-liked and also loved from time to time. Now I'm already so old, and yet people still address me as "Fräulein," fall in love with me, find me amusing and intelligent. I'm a real dazzler, after all!

I've just reread our two letters and I'm afraid that mine will not please you much. Or have some things now become clearer to you? Ach, so much has happened that it can't be expressed at all clearly. Probably one can take stock of it only gradually. In your letter I'm still astounded by the notion that people "without money" had to get out. There must have been many who lack your health, straight limbs, and clear intellect but have nonetheless managed to get out. And some who didn't get out at all, because they'd already been murdered. Who suffered so unspeakably at home that they became totally indifferent to everything material.

Good-bye, my little Ilse. Forgive me if I have said anything that displeases you. It seems to me that you're already far more established than we are. Our nerves are still exposed, and sometimes we scream with pain.

Your Else

My mother on the railway platform in Sofia: the image that has imprinted itself on me is that of a young, deeply tanned woman in a white muslin dress, with a broad-brimmed straw hat on her head and high-heeled sandals on her small feet, a luminescence in her face that I recognized from earlier times, her eyes again dark suns—the old Mummy!

She ran toward us, her arms widespread, laughing, rejoicing. Oh, the happiness of seeing her again, of having her again, of feeling her soft body, her arms that pressed me to her so firmly, her lips that covered my face with wild little kisses, the hands that brushed the hair of my forehead. Hearing her warm, dark voice again, the deep laugh, the pet names: my little bunny, my monkey-tail, my fawn, my birdie. Breathing in her fragrance, sun-drenched earth with a hint of perfume.

Oh, the happiness of having found the old Mummy again!

We took a taxi to the hotel. It was an old vehicle that had stained seats and was falling apart. The driver talked to himself in a very loud voice, probably cursing. It was boiling hot and the city was an inferno: cars from the early 1930s that had never been washed and seemed to have already been involved in a few collisions; decrepit tramways that limped more than they ran and screeched earsplittingly on the rails; horse-cabs, which are there called phaetons, with coachmen on the box cracking their whips and jingling horses wearing blue chains around their necks to ward off the evil eye; asses packed high and carts bearing hazardous, swaying loads and drawn by mules or oxen, honking busses and trucks recklessly forcing their way through the chaotic traffic. A seething mass of people, men in shirtsleeves with mustaches who, to my astonishment, often walked arm in arm or, still more astonishingly, walked with their little fingers hooked together, hatless women with bare legs that were sometimes covered with black hair, who held hands and seemed to have much to say to each other; peasant men with white puttees and red bellybands and peasant women wearing brightly colored costumes and carrying big baskets and bulbous jugs; young men with shaved heads and girls with thick braids and wearing black apron dresses or the uniform of their school; soldiers, also with shaved heads, in shabby uniforms and smug officers in neat uniforms; cadets in smart gentian blue with red lacquered belts, on which silver sabers flashed. Apartment buildings, none higher than five stories, with worn façades and unwashed windows, little houses with disorderly front gardens, many shops, bars, and stands that made a bedraggled impression.

"This is a funny city," I said.

My mother explained that this was the city center and that there were very beautiful buildings and churches in other parts of the city.

"Is it always so hot and loud here?" my father asked worriedly.

My mother laughed and asked if he didn't like it.

"Oh là là," he said.

The light-blond, rosy Dr. Filier, who had accompanied us to Bulgaria and sat in front next to the cursing driver, turned around. His face was violet and dripping with sweat. He smiled wearily, nodded, and said: "The Balkans, that's it all over."

The Hotel Bulgarie—the name was pronounced with a French accent—was the best and newest in the city, a large, ponderous structure that might almost have been found in Berlin. In addition, the area in which it was located was not so Balkan. The street was wide and paved with yellow cobblestones, the façades of the buildings did not yet bear the marks of neglect. Directly opposite the hotel was the castle. It was surrounded by high walls over which only part of the roof and the massive crowns of broad-leaved trees could be seen. A few steps farther on, on the same side of the street, was the Russian Orthodox church, whose gold roof decorated with little cupolas reminded me of a lacy hat with pompoms.

We had two spacious bedrooms on the third floor, connected by a sitting room. From the window I could look down on the castle. It was a friendly, white building—not much bigger and less pompous that my Schrobsdorff grandparents' house—surrounded by pretty, natural grounds.

I tried in vain to catch a glimpse of the king or at least a member of the royal family. I already knew their names, and—thanks to a large painting that hung in the hotel lobby and the countless postcards that were sold everywhere—what they looked like. I found Prince Simeon, a plump toddler with a blond cockscomb, charming, and I identified with the eight-year-old Princess Marie Luise, who wore her hair bobbed like mine and also wore similar clothes. They were an un-Bulgarian family.

The Bulgarians who came to our sitting room, either to make business deals with my father and Dr. Filier or to pay us a friendly visit, did not appeal to me. They had big bones, round or broad angular faces and simply too much hair: on their heads, on their legs, and, in the case of men, on their cheeks, which, though shaved clean, always had a dark shadow. Moreover, they had no manners. They fell upon me, embraced, caressed, and kissed me, and I, who had at most exchanged a handshake with people whom I didn't know, was so upset that I couldn't even resist, but simply played dead, like a beetle.

"These are odd people," I said to my mother, and she explained that they were warm, cordial people who showed their feelings openly.

When my father had things to do, my mother showed me around the city: the Alexander Nevsky cathedral, a colossal structure, wider than it is high, built around the turn of the century. Its size, numerous protuberances topped with gilt cupolas, and colorful, arched windows elicited respectful astonishment in me; the monument to the saber-swinging Alexander Nevsky high on his horse, who freed the Bulgarians from the Turkish yoke; the mosque, with its high, slender minaret, which looked like a balled fist with one raised index finger; the Turkish bath, in which the Bulgarians, who for some incomprehensible reason had no private baths, scrubbed their skins raw with brushes, and finally the market, which I found the most exciting thing Sofia had to offer. This was the Orient, the "Thousand and One Nights," rich in life and color, odors and sounds, exotic figures, foreign behaviors, and unusual objects for sale. There were mountains of fruit and vegetables that one could only buy in large quantities, because a pound of them cost less than the smallest coin; there were sheep and hog carcasses cut in half and hanging on hooks in the heat, enormous casks of white sheep's cheese, huge wheels of Lukanki, a very hard, highly spiced kind of salami; there were new and old articles of clothing, spun and unspun wool, embroidered quilts, colorful kilims, large kettles made of copper and painted jugs made of clay; there were all kinds of junk and kitsch, live chickens, geese, and lambs, which one slaughtered oneself at home; there were storytellers who skillfully recited endless tales in a whining singsong, Bosa sellers with richly decorated jugs on their backs, stands at which *shkembe chorba*, a soup made of entrails, was sold, and peasant girls, half children still and half slaves, who sold themselves as servants at starvation wages.

"These are very odd ways of doing things," I said to my mother, and she explained to me that they were Oriental ways of doing things, which struck only us as odd, and which the people here found quite normal.

I went on phaeton rides with my father through the Borisova Gradina, a large, beautiful park that was named after the king, visited many churches with him, and listened to him read from a tourist guide interesting things about the country and its people. In the evenings, I went out to dinner with my parents, Dr. Filier, and a few Bulgarians who couldn't be shaken off. I considered Bulgarian cuisine, which offered a very limited choice of dishes, an imposition. These dishes were either dripping with oil or cooked in a simple sauce of onions, garlic, and sweet red peppers. I didn't touch them, of course, and preferred to go to the popular joints where shashlik and kebabs were grilled on a smoking, sizzling grate, a great deal of slivovitz and red wine was drunk, big loaves of white bread were torn into bits, huge quantities of meat and salads were consumed, and people shouted, laughed, and sang. Little children ran around, babies were discreetly nursed, old, black-clad women sold flowers, and sometimes a three-man orchestra appeared with a bagpipe, drum, and violin to play Bulgarian folk songs and dances.

"This is really a very odd country," I said one evening as I already lay in bed and was thinking over what I'd seen that day.

"A very spirited country," my father said, and my mother added: "You mustn't always compare it to Germany."

They looked down at me with tenderly concerned faces, and I laughed and insisted: "But it's very odd all the same!"

Bettina and Ellen arrived in Sofia, and the family traveled

together to the Black Sea. We were all in a gay, holiday mood, because everyone had what he wanted: Else had her two daughters and Erich, Bettina had a new self-confidence that she owed to her prettiness and the looks men gave her, Angelika had her parents, Ellen had the prospect of a new layer of tan and little adventures, and Erich had the feeling that up to that point everything had gone according to plan and that he'd provided well for his family, within the limits of his capabilities.

There they found a cloudless sky, radiant sunshine, and a bluish-green sea. They stayed in St. Constantine, a few miles outside Varna, in a former monastery that had been converted to a hotel; though not very comfortable, it was very romantic. It was surrounded by a green wilderness, almost a small jungle, that abruptly turned into a fabulous sandy beach visited by only a few bathers. They found an out-of-the-way group of rocks that offered shade for Erich, who was subject to sunburns, and a place to play for Angelika, and spent the whole morning there. Else, in a navy blue swimsuit, with the excessively large, precious cross that expressed her religious faith around her neck, and Ellen, in a white swimsuit that daringly emphasized her figure and her tan, lay in the sun for hours; Erich walked meditatively up and down the beach or read a book in the shady rock grottos; Bettina spent most of her time in the clear, warm sea; and Angelika, a large straw hat on her head, played by herself or let her sister teach her how to swim.

What more does one need to be happy, Else thought, than the presence of people you love, the sun, and the sea? And she could now hardly understand what had driven her for so many years from one pleasure, one love affair, one adventure to another. In the afternoons, they took excursions to Varna and a village two miles away, where time had stopped in the Middle Ages and she drank red wine and ate cheese in one of the farmhouses. Erich rented for Angelika a donkey named Florinka, which was supposed to console her for certain drawbacks such as Bulgarian food and the times when she had to go to bed early and stay alone in the hotel—for in the evenings, there was dancing under the stars along the shores of the Black Sea, with its ruffles of white foam.

What more did one need to be happy than warm nights, a couple of liters of wine, and love. Else loved Erich, whom she believed she had inwardly won back by deciding to leave Germany; Ellen was having a romantic affair with the handsomest man in the place, the dark brown, muscular lifeguard, Johnny; and the seventeen-year-old Bettina had fallen in love with Mizo Stanishev, a teaching assistant in anatomy, who was fourteen years older than she.

And so they danced the tango, English waltzes, and slow fox-trots, and Angelika sat in her nightgown on the steps of the hotel and waited with breathless anxiety for her loved ones, who she thought must have either run away or been murdered.

Else and Erich still did not know what to do with the children, and the harmonious ambiance allowed them to delay repeatedly a decision that would inevitably have led to upsets.

Who knew when they would ever be so happily and peacefully together again? How could they destroy Bettina's first happiness, which was blooming under the increasingly serious courtship of an absolutely acceptable man? Wasn't it of the greatest importance precisely for her, who had always been overshadowed, to acquire the self-confidence she had so long lacked, and to acquire it through the admiration of a mature, good-looking man who combined Balkan dignity and warmth with a Western education? And Angelika, who was so happy to have both her father and mother around her again, and who saw in Bulgaria nothing but an "odd" country in which one occasionally took short holidays—how could they frighten her by suggesting that she might have to live there for a while? In addition, Else was actually toying with the idea of returning to Germany, now that she had Bulgarian nationality. On the evenings when they did not go dancing but instead walked up and down the beach, Else and Erich had long, perplexed conversations whose only outcome was the decision to wait a little longer.

On those occasions, the night was dark, the breeze off the sea was cold, and the idyll they were living was a farcical intermezzo between the nightmare of the past and that of the future.

"My little, sweet Mummy," Peter wrote, "now you are in Varna, you have your children and Goody with you again, and—what more do you want, really? It's all too comic—as in a puppet show: coming together, happiness, staying together, separation, farewell, pain, a new coming together—all of it as if it were on strings . . . "

Yes, everything as if it were on strings, and one were oneself no more than a marionette, helplessly responding to tugs on the strings.

The die was cast on September 1, five days before their return to Sofia.

Ellen and Bettina were out with their suitors, and Else, Erich, and Angelika had gone to the beach with her donkey Florinka. It was a radiantly sunny day, but for the Bulgarians the bathing season was over, and no matter how hot it got, they no longer went into the water. There was no one else on the beach until suddenly a man appeared in the distance. He was running as if he were being pursued, coming toward them very quickly, and shouting something.

"What's wrong with that man?" Angelika asked.

"Maybe a sunstroke," Else replied, and stretched out on the bath towel.

As the man approached them he slowed down, raised both his arms in the air and cried as loudly as he could: "*Woina!*" Then, when he noticed that they had not understood, "*Guerre . . . Krieg . . .* War!"

Else and Erich stared at each other—she with wide-open eyes, he with a slightly open mouth.

They had intentionally not followed political events, and that was made easier for them because in St. Constantine there was neither radio nor foreign newspapers, and they would learn bad news soon enough.

"Where is there war?" Angelika asked her petrified parents, "here in Bulgaria?"

Else sprang up: "No," she cried with a voice and an expression as if she were announcing good news, "not here, my bunny, but in Germany. In Germany there's war!"

"Please, little one," Erich said, standing up slowly and wiping the sand off his arms, "ride on ahead of us to the hotel and find out where Bettina and Ellen are. We'll come right after you."

Hardly had Angelika moved away than Else threw herself into Erich's arms. She wept, she laughed: "This is the punishment," she stammered, "do you see, Goody, there's an compensating justice! Now the Nazis will be smashed. We're saved!"

He remained silent so long that she became impatient. He was so slow to understand! She shook him and cried: "Do you hear, Erich, we're saved!"

"I'm afraid," he finally said, "that you're seeing things a little too simply. In the end, you may be right—God grant that you are!—but in the short run the war is a catastrophe. The Nazis wanted it, for them it is not terrifying retaliation but rather a welcome challenge to finally crush the others. They're armed to the teeth, Else, and convinced that they'll win."

That was the first time Erich had a moment of clear-sightedness, and the first time that Else did not believe him.

The next day we went back to Sofia. I remember my astonishment at the crowded, noisy train, which stank of goats and garlic: peasants, soldiers, tourists, children and more children, hens, lambs, and baby goats with their legs tied together. Fortunately, we had a compartment to ourselves, but some people had nonetheless overflowed into our car, where they squatted on their suitcases and bundles, made a racket, ate, drank, sang, and slept. Somewhere Ellen had picked up an officer wearing white gloves, and he now sat in our compartment and flirted with her. Bettina's admirer, Mizo, who had the face of a faun and the mustache of a Hitler, traveled with us to Sofia and fed my sister bread, sheep's cheese, and grapes. It must have made an indelible impression on me, because I still see them before my mind's eye: he is breaking off pieces of bread and cheese, sticking them into her mouth and his, and shoving the grapes in after them.

"That's how people eat here," he said with a pride that would have been appropriate had he made a pathbreaking discovery. Bettina ate without protest whatever he put in her mouth, but when he briefly left the compartment, she giggled and said: "You know, he reminds me a little of our teacher, Dr. Richter . . . how about you?"

I said: "Maybe a little, but otherwise he's awfully nice."

My parents sat by the window and spoke to each other so softly that I couldn't understand a word, although I tried very hard. My mother was smoking one cigarette after another and picking at her hangnails, and my father had a book open on his knees, but not to read it.

"Well, this time we finally got something for our money," he said as we arrived in Sofia eight hours later.

We stayed again in the Hotel Bulgarie, and early the next morning preparations for our trip began. I was very excited about being able to go back to Germany. Bulgaria had been something new, but now I'd had enough. Everything was much nicer in Germany, and nicest of all was the idea of living there again with my parents, just as we had earlier. The war made absolutely no impression on me.

My mother packed Papa's trunk, and he stood by with a worried look on his face and said that the way she was doing it the things would arrive completely wrinkled.

My mother said: "I'd like to have your problems and the Rothschilds' money!" and laid a suit on the shirts, which was naturally not right. The shirts were supposed to go on top.

I asked when we were leaving, and my father said that the train would leave the following afternoon at 5:30.

The decision as to whether I should share a sleeping compartment with my mother or my father was a difficult one for me, and so I asked them for advice.

My father walked around the room, looking for his silver cigarette case. He seemed not to have heard my question. My mother asked whether I would rather be in Germany at war than in Bulgaria in peace.

I said I would.

One could think that only if one had not yet experienced a war, my father said, and God forbid that you ever experience one.

I would experience it now, I said.

He'd had enough of the chaos here and my mother's packing methods, he said, and asked whether I'd like to take a little phaeton ride with him.

Of course I would.

We drove down the broad Czar Osvoboditel Boulevard, which was paved with yellow cobblestones. It led from our hotel to the square on which the Alexander Nevsky monument stood, and then on to the park that bore the king's name. My father pulled a handful of coins out of his pocket, counted them very carefully, then put them away. He often did things that served no obvious purpose. We had almost arrived at the park when he said: "I have to talk to you, my daughter."

Had I suspected something? No, certainly not.

Dread struck me, undiminished by any anticipation, with its full force. I listened to the tapping of the horses' hooves, the jingle of their bells, the crack of the whip, and fervently hoped that he would change his mind and say nothing.

But he did, and even more quickly than he often did, and without the usual pauses: "You and Bettina are going to have to stay a while longer in Bulgaria with your mother. That's not a tragedy, Angelika, but rather your good fortune. Germany is at war, and it may get very, very bad. Here you are safe, and that is worth more than anything else that you may miss."

"And you're going to stay in Germany, when it gets very, very bad?"

"I have to, my child."

"I don't want to stay in Bulgaria, I want to go back to Germany with you."

"And leave your mother alone here?"

"She can come with us."

"No, she can't."

"Why? Because there's a war?"

He couldn't lie, the poor man, and he said: "For that reason, too."

There it was again, the secret, the terrible secret!

"What's wrong with Mummy?" I asked.

"There's nothing wrong with Mummy. She's just the same as she's always been."

"No," I screamed, and began to cry.

He put his arm around me, held me tight, and said: "You have to trust us, Angelika, whatever we do, we do for your good. Maybe now you will go through a time that won't be very easy, but everyone has such times in his life, and if he gets through them, than he becomes much stronger and wiser, and is much better able to appreciate the good times. You're twelve years old, and thus no longer a child. You have to help your mother now, she needs you and Bettina more than anything in the world. You love your mother so much, and now you have a chance to show her that you do."

"But I love you, too," I said, and felt a little embarrassed, because I'd never told him that and it seemed to me importunate.

"I hope so, my daughter," he said, "and I hope . . . " and after a pause, "that you'll continue to love me no matter what happens."

They moved into a hideous furnished ground-floor apartment in the Ulitsa Mussala, a tiny street in which a few old houses stood.

Bettina looked around and shrugged. Angelika turned up her nose and asked how long they would have to live there.

She'd have to ask God about that, Else replied, and in any case they would both be well-advised to get off their high horses as soon as possible. Times had changed. Both girls were silent, Bettina looked angrily at her mother with her lips tightly closed, Angelika with an expression like that of a little lamb that has strayed from the flock. Else took her in her arms. It was only temporary, she said, and now they had to all stick together and make it easier for each other rather than harder.

With Erich's departure, the Germans' lightning advance through Poland, and the recognition that her agreeable provisional situation was threatening to become a dismal long-term one, Else's life became a trapeze act. She was always about to fall, whether out of helpless desperation or out of uncontrollable accesses of rage, or out of panic fear. But whereas there had earlier been a safety net into which she could fall, now there was an abyss, and no one who could pull her back. She alone was responsible for her life and those of her daughters, and if she fell, her daughters would fall with her. To be sure, there were people who tried to help her; Mitko Taslakoff, Zvetan Taslakoff's German wife, Wilma, who had come to Bulgaria at the same time as they had, and who had become a good friend, Leo Ginis, a White Russian Jew who had fled to

Germany along with his family to escape the communists, and then to Bulgaria to escape the Nazis, and who had fallen passionately in love with Else.

But since Mitko was often away on business, Wilma was kept on a short leash by her jealous husband, who considered Else a dangerous person to frequent, and Leo Ginis had to care for an almost blind wife and a sister-in-law with serious stomach problems, they were seldom available when Else thought she was going to go mad out of despair, anger, or fear.

How was she to cope with everyday life in Bulgaria, where everything was so primitive, so unreliable and superficial, and every chore, errand, and even the smallest action threatened to become an insoluble problem, and all the more so because she couldn't speak more than a dozen words of Bulgarian and the language was so alien to her that she abandoned all hope of ever learning it before she had even made the attempt. How was she to turn an apartment in which everything was ugly and rotting into a comfortable home where they could feel good and find a compensation for the daily troubles and adversities that the new situation forced upon them? How could she make do with an amount of money that was lamentably small compared with the financial means that had been at her disposal in Germany? And how, above all, could she deal with her daughters, with Bettina, who had closed herself off again, and Angelika, whose suffering was so obvious that it became a constant accusation? She had to provide security for them, the motivation to make the best of a situation from which there was no escape and that could be overcome only with goodwill, determination, and solidarity. But how could she provide security for them if she herself had none, motivation, when Angelika was not even acquainted with the cause of the situation, determination, when she was discouraged, or solidarity, when she, instead of reacting to the girls with patience and understanding, constantly lost her temper?

She was anything but a good example, and she knew it, hated herself for it, and yet was not capable of changing her disastrous behavior.

"Mummy," Peter wrote to her, "you have to be patient—patient with yourself and with others. For once, you have to stop complaining and take responsibility for the destiny of others. You have to finally accept the facts as facts and not as infinitely lamentable changes. They aren't so bad, after all. You're ungrateful, Mummy, and don't know how lucky you are not to have to live in Germany, in that spiritual morass and filth. And moreover, I want to answer you with your own words: just think how many people, how many Jews, there are who are far more unfortunate than you are, who are starving and who don't know where they should hole up. Who haven't seen their children in years. Who have seen those closest to them murdered or who have been injured by the 'elemental event,' as you call it. You're ungrateful, Mummy! And when you say that you've made yourself unhappy and shouldn't have done it, just imagine what would have happened if you hadn't. What then? No, no, Mummy, I know everything and take everything into consideration, and I understand you very, very well. You have it hard, harder than many people, but not nearly so hard as you could. Mummy, my love, hang on and don't be unjust. Listen to me and listen well: we both, you and I, we're going to make it. Be calm and remember that I love you more than anything in the world. And: salvation, inner salvation, always comes from us alone . . . "

Big words, serenely expressed. Inner salvation! She had no inner salvation, only worn nerves, and she was anything but calm, anything but sure that she would make it.

She hired a maid at the market, not an adolescent but a mature creature about twenty years old and surprisingly ugly. Her name was Ivanka, and she had a face in which everything, except her drooping cheeks and her nose like a chicken leg, was too short, and a body whose bosom reached from her collarbone to her belly and her behind from her waist to her knees.

Bettina and Angelika couldn't believe their eyes and began to giggle. Ivanka, a wonderful person, as we very quickly discovered, laughed along with us, and her laugh sounded like a turkey's excited gobbling. Else screamed at her daughters to behave themselves and not insult the poor girl, and Ivanka, who never spoke less loudly than Else screamed, considered that the normal tone and went on gobbling.

With Ivanka a treasure came into our house. She slept, as was usual in Bulgaria, on a folding cot in the kitchen, learned very quickly and with pleasure how one used a toilet and a bathtub, cooked at least four of the approximately twelve Bulgarian dishes, did the laundry, cleaned the apartment, understood Else's sign language, and was unfailingly cheerful.

Dimiter Lingorsky came to lunch once a week, which Else hoped would convince the neighbors that she was really married, made Ivanka happy, annoyed Angelika, and caused Bettina to indulge in wisecracks. Else screamed at her daughters to be polite and not treat this very decent man with scorn and hostility. Her elder daughter pressed her lips together, and her younger asked "Why does he always come here when you can't even converse with him?"

Else had no answer to that question.

She worried terribly about Angelika, who had once again become emotionally very clingy, and physically a finicky eater to the nth degree. She vacillated between threats and pleas, raged against the child's unreasonableness and blamed herself for the pain she had caused her. The more she threatened and pleaded, the more disturbed Angelika became.

On the other hand, under Mizo's influence Bettina began to become more stable, and to move farther away from her mother, against whom a latent resentment emerged. Mizo was the one who coped with the damage Else did, and with his love gave Bettina a foothold and with his ambition to make a real Bulgarian of her, a goal. He now taught her not only Bulgarian eating habits but also the Bulgarian language, and he did so very thoroughly and with great success. When Bettina agreed with his ideas and wishes, he decided it was time to seduce her, a risky enterprise because it took place on the couch in the living room, while Else and Angelika were sleeping in the big bed next door and Ivanka on her folding cot in the kitchen.

Bettina, as she later admitted to me, didn't think much of lessons of this kind. But they were now part of it and were a further, fairly secondary step towards a new realm of life. What was crucial was that she loved a man who was so much older, more respected, and so superior to her in knowledge and education. She began to attend the art school, made friends with other students, was introduced to Mizo's family, and acclimated herself with a rapidity that both relieved and upset her mother. She was, Else thought, still not really grown up, had not yet really been in love, and was she now not to be a young woman and enjoy this short, wonderful phase of life, but rather to jump immediately into the role of a serious, dutiful wife and conform to the principles of an older, authoritarian man with firmly established habits?

Else like Mizo, considered him a decent man, and did not doubt that he loved Bettina, but it was also clear that he was inflexible and would not give her any room to develop into an independent woman with her own thoughts, ideas, and aspirations. Should that be her daughter's lifepath—to stand once again in the shadow of someone, to ungrudgingly grant him priority, to adapt herself to his wishes and demands? Was she so completely her father's daughter, the daughter of that man who had recognized no nuances, who had been as unwavering in his love and in his hate? Wasn't it his eyes that looked up so devotedly at Mizo, his face that looked at her, the mother, with her lips pressed together and hard eyes? Would she lose her daughter? Had she perhaps already lost her?

Grandpa Kirschner died in October 1939 of a pulmonary infection. Grandma wrote to her daughter: "He died as he had lived: with a smile."

Peter wrote to his mother: "No, Mummy, I think that he died very, very unhappy, because there was no one with him but Grandma. None of us whom he loved and for whom he'd lived his life. What wouldn't he have given to have us with him once again, to look at us once again, to say something to us once again . . . "

That is certainly right. And yet I'm grateful that he was allowed to die in his own bed, with Grandma at his side, of a pulmonary infection. At that time Jews died other deaths.

A short time afterward my forty-five-year-old father was drafted into the army with the rank of lieutenant. My mother, who had never reckoned with that possibility, was flabbergasted: "I don't understand how that could happen," she said, time after time.

For me, this meant first of all that he wouldn't come to visit us at Christmas and on my birthday, as he'd promised. I had put together a little calendar for myself that ended on December 24. Every evening I crossed off another day. Now I took the calendar down from the wall and tore it up. From then on, the only thing that hung over my bed was a quotation from Schopenhauer: "Since I came to know people, I've loved animals."

However, a short time thereafter Bettina's visa was not renewed, and that meant that she had to leave Bulgaria. Two days before her departure my mother put her stark naked on the glassed-in, ice-cold verandah. She stood there for an hour, shivering, barefoot, her arms wrapped around her upper body, her face getting smaller and smaller. But the hoped-for pulmonary infection, which would, for starters, have prevented her departure, didn't emerge. She didn't even catch cold.

On the other hand, an incipient tuberculosis of the lung was discovered in me; I was feverish every evening and had lost weight; I was down to sixty-two pounds.

My mother lost her head; her father was dead, my father was in the army, Bettina was being forcibly expelled, and I was becoming consumptive. She said she had to travel with me to Germany, and I was delighted. Who prevented her from doing so, I do not know; in any case, the trip was put off from one week to the next and finally abandoned altogether.

I must have been fairly ill for about nine months, but of course I didn't know what was wrong with me, and suffered mainly from my mother's persistent attempts to stuff me with food.

I believe my mother's transformation began with this series of misfortunes. It was her first collision with reality, the first real confrontation with herself, her first attempt to take stock of her situation: what did the problems of everyday life, the ugliness of the apartment, the limited financial means matter? What right did she have to complain, pity herself, mourn for the past, and deceive herself with regard to the truth? Now it was no longer a matter of the amenities of life, but solely of survival, of saving her children.

From that time forward, I never heard her complain or weep again.

Thanks to Dr. Filier's ingenuity, Bettina was granted a new, unlimited visa, and she was in Sofia again for Christmas. It became, despite the scant supplies, a festival of joy—at least for Else, Bettina, and Mizo. Angelika thought that had little to do with Christmas Eve.

During the meal Bettina talked about her stay in Berlin. No, it hadn't been lovely, in fact quite sad. Grandmother Kirschner, with whom she had stayed, was happy to see her, because she was now so terribly lonely and had even said now and then that the only thing she still wished for was a peaceful death. Elisabeth, who drank a great deal of schnapps and coffee, cared for her in a touching way, and Papa, before he was drafted, had gone to see her once a week, and even Grandmother Schrobsdorff visited her sometimes and took her many nice things. But Grandma no longer took much pleasure in anything. Papa had come only twice on weekend furloughs, and looked bad. He was having stomach problems again and was soon to be sent to Poland.

Papa Fritz was doing well. He was writing screenplays for films and was enjoying great success with them. Aunt Enie was unchanged, but often suffered from headaches and constantly complained about the Nazis. And yes, Ellen had married Jack Blackwood and was now living with him in London. It had really been quite sad.

They went to mass at the Alexander Nevsky cathedral, and Angelika prayed for her family, lighted candles, and put them in a holder. Then she lighted a candle for her dead grandfather and planted it in a vase full of sand. She was already familiar with Russian Orthodox rituals and believed in the power of burning candles and prayers.

Soon thereafter they moved into a different apartment that was larger, lighter, and better cared for. It was in an elongated, four-story building whose roughcast, dark gray façade made a gloomy impression. But Oborishta Street, which led from the enormous square in front of the cathedral directly down to the canal, was pretty and had a good reputation. Immediately adjoining our building was the French embassy, a stately villa surrounded by a large garden, and diagonally opposite it a lovely small park.

Wasn't it much better here than in the earlier apartment, Else asked Angelika.

It was, she replied, but she would much rather live in the French embassy building.

Would she ever get used to the new situation? her mother asked herself.

The apartment was unfurnished, and Else rented all the furniture from an acquaintance who considered durability more important than beauty. They were colossal, polished black pieces that were reminiscent of coffins and limited freedom of movement. Else shared the bedroom and double bed with Angelika, Bettina slept behind a glass door in a room that was as small as the convertible sofa bed was large, and Ivanka set up camp every evening in the kitchen. There was, in addition to these spaces, a small entry hall and a living-dining room that threatened to collapse under the weight of the furniture—buffet, china cabinet, table, and chairs. But there was a bath with an enameled tub, a wooden chest that was filled with blocks of ice in the summer and kept food cold, and an iron coal stove that kept the rooms warm in the winter. Compared to what was to come, the apartment was a palace.

It was a very cold February and the city lay under a deep carpet of snow. Angelika's condition had not improved. She lived chiefly on Ivanka's crème caramel, played like a small child with her stuffed animals, fed the stray cats in the courtyard, and was happy when, with enormous care, she was able to win their trust. When Else lay next to her in the evening, she felt her daughter's anxiety, the restless movements of her arms and legs, and heard her strained gasping for air. Else couldn't bear it. The child was intentionally making herself still sicker that she already was, ate nothing, didn't sleep, made not the slightest attempt to change her behavior and to adapt to the new conditions. She screamed at her, then immediately took her in her arms and begged her not to worry her so much and to finally become "reasonable."

"I can't help it," Angelika said. "Mummy, I swear, I can't help it."

Bettina had resumed her earlier life, attended the art school, met with her girlfriends, and learned Bulgarian with Mizo. He came to dinner almost every evening, was cheerful, charming, and a bright spot for the whole family. Bettina loved him, Else appreciated him, Angelika was infatuated with him, and Ivanka was fascinated by him. It's lucky, Else said to herself, that Tina met this man.

Peter's letters, which up to that point had arrived regularly and, thanks to a steady position as a clerk in a sardine exporting firm, were full of confidence and humor, now came at longer intervals, and their all too emotional tone did not please Else. He wrote only about his love and longing for her, about his belief in the just cause, about holding on and hoping, about the misfortunes of others, compared with whom they could consider themselves fortunate. He repeatedly insisted that he was fine and that she had no reason to worry about him. But he no longer said anything about his current life, his work, his tomcat Ariel, the people he met, and the acquaintances about whom he had earlier so wittily written.

And then one day she learned the truth about his situation from a friend who had emigrated to Holland and who corresponded with her and with Peter. What she had foreseen and tried to prevent with warnings, pleas, and appeals to Peter not to make himself and her unhappy, had happened. Now he had fallen into the trap, and it was up to her, once again, to get him out of it. She wrote a series of letters to friends, acquaintances, and relatives who were scattered over the world, leading the life of emigrants, and begged them for help. One of these letters was addressed to her cousin Bruno Kirschner, who had emigrated to Palestine with his wife Paula and his children, and who now lived in Jerusalem:

Dear Bruno, here's a brief summary of the situation:
Peter was in Portugal for a year and a half, and declared to the authorities there that he was a full Jew, and was there-

upon expelled, and, because he didn't have the money to travel further, spent four months in prison and was sent, at the expense of the local Jewish committee, to Greece, the only country that still accepted refugees. I've reimbursed the committee, foregoing the financial donation of a friend in Rio. For months, Peter has kept me in the dark regarding his situation, and it's only now, from his last letter, that I've learned the full truth. The letter is grim. He has no money at all, no work permit, no residence permit. All that is not unusual in these times, but he's my son! I don't know what to do, I'm powerless and terribly desperate. Could you help? He only wants to live in peace somewhere and be able to work. I'm so dreadfully afraid for him and have no way of helping him. It's impossible for him to come to us in Bulgaria, because then we would all go down with him. Here it is still touch and go, and I can't expose the two girls to an additional danger. The people from the Jewish committee have done all they could for Peter. They wrote me that they are very impressed by his attitude and his courage. Therefore I thought that perhaps something could be done for him from Palestine.

I'm writing confusedly and illegibly, but I'm very upset. I've been tormenting myself with this for weeks. You also have it hard, I know, and I'm sorry to burden you with this, but I have to try everything.

I often think of you, and of Paula—you have to help me!

Your Else

PS: It's lucky that Father no longer has to go through all this.

In early April the German army occupied Denmark and Norway, and on May 10, 1940, the attack on Holland, Belgium, and France began.

Peter wrote to his mother from Athens:

I know that I can no longer calm you—unless by saying that I am resilient and on the whole not so easy to kill. I have a relatively fortunate temperament for enduring adversity, and moreover I no longer make any demands. I have learned to be extremely modest. If we add that I find people everywhere who accept me and help me, there is really no reason for genuine concern. I have to get through it, and I will get through it, and I am not going to be destroyed by it. That's for sure! My only goal is to get out of Europe. I never lose sight of that, constantly think about it . . .

No, he couldn't calm her anymore, and her anxiety about him overwhelmed all her others.

Bruno and Paula Kirschner, who were powerless to help, as were all the others to whom she had written, had given her the address and telephone number of a certain Herr B. who lived in Sofia and might be able to be of assistance.

Else wrote to Paula Kirschner:

Dear Pauline, I thank you and Bruno for your help. So far I haven't been able to reach Herr B.: I called him six times, wrote, and finally made an appointment. Who didn't come? Herr B. Now I'm going to keep trying, but it probably isn't a way out for Peter. I'm terribly worried about him—as always—and he doesn't change. He doesn't learn. He beats his head against the wall, against reason, for beautiful words. He's like me. We deceive ourselves, pressure ourselves, with beautiful thoughts and words. I, who have now endured so much bitterness and have arrived at the nadir, have finally realized that that doesn't help anyone.

Father's death was a great heartache. I still can't believe that I'll never see my beloved, cheerful Grandpa again.

And my poor mother! That had to happen to her! All alone, and I can't go to her. During the worst time a married couple took care of her—they must be wonderful people. Then Bettina was with her, and afterward she finally found a renter who helps her pass the time a little and gets along well with her. A week ago the man suddenly died. No one knows anymore what to do with the poor woman. Otherwise, she has no problems, she is well provided for. Apart from all serious concerns, the uneasiness and the fear of what else might happen, Peter is the one who worries me the most. I'm trying to go to him, but that too is extremely complicated. Today everything is extremely complicated! And all the poor people about whom one hears such appalling things or no longer hears anything at all. One looks around and doesn't know how one is supposed to bear all this, one looks for a glimmer of light and finds none . . .

What wouldn't I have given to be reasonable—as my mother called it—and not to cause her any concern. The last thing I wanted was to cause her, whom I loved more than anything, concern. But I couldn't eat, I couldn't sleep—for fear that she would notice it—I couldn't accept the new conditions, because I didn't know their origin and was always waiting for this grim masquerade to come to an end. I didn't know what was going on around me, and I didn't know what was going on inside me. I was so confused that I considered the most impossible things possible and possible things impossible.

I remember a day on which I once again complained to Bettina about Dimiter Lingorsky's visits and she—whether because she'd had enough of this playacting, or because she wanted to put one over on our mother—let the cat out of the bag. She said: "Now, just listen here, he's married to Mummy." For a while I was even more upset than usual, but accepted it as the most impossible thing that was nonetheless possible.

And on another occasion, when I asked my mother for a wrist-watch and she cried: "If you go on having such demanding wishes, someday we won't have another piece of bread to eat!", I was convinced that we were now all going to starve to death. I no longer even tried to understand what could be true on what grounds, and what not. I accepted it as a fact and then sought to exorcize it by means of a ritual of oaths and prayers that became a compulsion. Every time, the ritual culminated in the quick prayer: "Dear God, let me die before my mother!"

I had no other authority to which I could turn, and my mother apparently didn't, either. Every evening before she went to bed she knelt down, bowed her head, clasped her hands, and prayed. On her night table stood a photo of Father Johann, in which he looked seriously and mildly sad and reminded her of her religious belief.

When in March spring abruptly and impetuously swept over nature and people, many things changed in Oborishta Street and thus contributed to the rapid improvement of my condition.

My mother's terrible anxiety was no longer directed toward her ill, unreasonable daughter, but rather toward the imprudent son, who was in far greater danger, so that my complicatedness no longer seemed so serious and less attention was paid to me. Since Else erroneously assumed that I might suffer from this and feel neglected, one day she came home with a young tomcat with a salt-and-pepper coat and put it in my arms. I buried my face in its silky fur and in my hands I felt the vibration of a still inaudible purring.

"Mummy," I said, "now I'm happy again!"

And from then on things improved.

Paul, as I named my cat, was not only a substitute for everything I missed, he was an autonomous personality with wit and powers of thinking. I, who have lived with cats of all kinds in the course of my life and observed them with unflagging interest, know that there is no other cat like Paul. He quickly learned to open every door by hanging on its handle, used the toilet as humans did, which required a balancing act, was always inventing new games to play with me, and returned my love so impetuously that my cheeks were covered with tender bites and my hands and arms, up to the elbow, with passionate scratches.

In a short time I had almost become a normal child again, and my mother brought another achievement home: Frau Dr. Wudy, a delicate, blond Viennese Jew who had emigrated to Bulgaria with her Christian husband and a little daughter. She taught at the German Catholic convent school, Sancta Maria, which, in contrast to the secular German school, did not ask about one's ancestry. Dr. Wudy had declared that she was willing to prepare me for the local entrance examination.

She combined warmth with authority and thus won my trust. I almost looked forward to the daily lessons, the nearness of the teacher, who always looked so smart and fresh, her tender looks when I was trying to give the right answer. And had it not been for mathematics, one could say that her efforts were completely successful.

With spring Leo Ginis also came. He picked up my mother and me every afternoon at our building and went with us to the Café Royal. That was the most fashionable café in the city, and was located on Czar Osvoboditel Boulevard, where the promenade took place as dusk came on. Tables and chairs were put out on the sidewalks, and people sat in the sun-sprinkled shade of massive chestnut trees.

Leo, whom Bettina and I called Grandpa Ginis, not realizing that he loved our mother like a young man, was a stubby, very well-groomed man with white hair, whose soft face was not quite so cheerful as Grandpa Kirschner's, but still reminded me of him. I liked him very much and felt good in his company. He always spoke softly, listened to me attentively, radiated calm and even understanding when I no longer wanted to eat the ice cream that had begun to melt. He understood that it had to be rock-hard, and ordered me a new one. He talked with my mother in the same empathetic tone as with me, and now and then they talked about Berlin, where he had lived for twenty years, about theatrical performances they had both seen, concerts they had heard, people they had been close to. I listened carefully, less to the words than to their voices, which sounded as if they were telling each other fairy tales.

Once I asked Grandpa Ginis if he had come to Bulgaria because of the war. Yes, he said, that was the reason.

Sometimes my mother and I were invited to his place on Saturday evenings. He lived with his wife Rosa in a two-story house that was furnished with very old, quite worn furniture. It came from Russia, Ada told me.

Ada had a cameo-like face and was as small, pale, and delicate as a ghost. I never saw her sitting or standing. She lay, elegantly dressed, on the bed in her small, dark room, and I sat by her in an armchair and listened to her tell me about Baku, her home town. I liked her stories from Russia, which sounded like legends from another world, another, distant century.

Her sister Rosa was no less elegant, but much more robust. She had the small, somewhat pushed-in features of a Pekinese. Despite her thick, highly polished spectacle lenses, behind which her eyes were nearly invisible, she could hardly see. For the most part she lay, supported by many pillows, on a chaise longue in the living room, in which there was a large bookcase with books in seven languages. She spoke each of them fluently, and every day of the week a different woman came to read to her in one of the languages.

Two or three other guests were always there for dinner, men with very elegant manners and Russian names and accents. They spoke mainly French at dinner, and ate peculiar dishes, of which the *blinis* with black caviar were the only ones I liked. When we had said good-bye, Grandpa Ginis accompanied us to the nearest corner, where the phaetons were waiting, and gave my mother a bank note to pay for the ride. He never forgot, because he knew that for me this was the highpoint of the evening and that we could not afford this luxury. I asked my mother if he was very rich, and she said: "He used to be, like so many others, but he's still getting along quite well."

I liked going to see Wilma Taslakova even more than I did Grandpa Ginis. She came from Cologne and was a pale blond, full-bosomed, blithe spirit. Sometimes, however, the lids of her colorless eyes were red and her face puffy, as if she'd been crying, and once I heard my mother say to her: "Why did you have to go and marry him!"

Thus something was wrong there, but it was seldom noticeable. She had German phonograph records that I was allowed to play, and homemade German cake, which I ate only because it was German, and her apartment was a German home, dazzling white and so impeccably furnished that even the little napkins were the same color as the flowers on the drapes. In Germany I would have found the apartment cloying, but here in Bulgaria, and especially in comparison with ours, it seemed to me wonderfully pretty.

Wilma even had a car, and in it we sometimes went shopping in the market or took excursions into the Vitosha mountains, where we lay in a meadow of wildflowers and talked about Germany. She told me about the Cologne carnival and I told her about Pätz.

I also started attending a ballet school again, where the lessons were given by an elderly little Russian woman whose hair was dyed carrot-red and who had holes in her leotard. I could hardly imagine that she had once been on the stage as a graceful ballerina in a tiny tulle skirt, but when she danced for us every step, every movement was perfect, and I hardly noticed her shabby appearance. She told me that I was talented, and since I no longer wrote poetry and acquisition of an estate seemed to have become a distant prospect, I decided to become a prima ballerina first.

It was true that I was making good progress on all fronts, and I owed that entirely to my cat, Paul. "You see," my mother said, "if you want to, you can do it."

She was wrong about that.

At least three times a week I went to the Alexander Nevsky cathedral, which was just a few minutes away from our building. I lit candles for my family and prayed for their protection. Then I looked up at the ceiling, in whose high, concave cupola ceiling someone had painted the Lord God. He looked down at me, white-bearded, white-maned, blue-eyed, and well-fed, and looked like an elderly Wotan.

"Dear God," I said, "let us very, very soon return to Germany."

Else's anxiety about her son never left her. She felt it like a dull pressure around her heart, whether she was alone or among others, whether she was reading or was in the city doing errands, whether she was awake or asleep. Her first thought in the morning was for Peter, her last thought in the evening was for Peter. He haunted her sleep, pursued her into her nightmares, woke her up with the thought of him.

When the postman came and brought no letter from Peter, she panicked, and when the postman brought her a letter from Peter, she panicked as well. What dreadful news would she now learn? She tore open the letter even before she had closed the door, scanned the lines. Thank God, no new bad tidings, but also nothing that might have calmed her anxiety.

"Everything is much better in every respect," he wrote. "In the one week I've been in Athens, I've followed out all the connections, all the tips, all the encouragements and I've also achieved something: a major businessman who has very good relations with the Portuguese consulate is willing to help me by making me a broker in sardine sales. This is how it would work: I get the offers from Portugal and then hand them on to the gentleman in question, who has contacts with Greek firms. The way people treat me is really touching, they're doing all they can for me, and we'll manage it . . . "

Typical Peter! They'll manage it, he'll manage it! The one thing he'd managed to do was to get himself expelled from the country where he could have survived and now, without valid papers, without a roof over his head, without a penny in the pocket of his sole pair of pants, he was waiting to become a sardine broker.

She read: "The people from the Jewish committee continue to support me, but can't do anything because of my residence here, since I'm half-Jewish (they act only on behalf of full Jews!), and they can't register me and represent me with the police. They say: See how you can manage, we can't do anything, even if we wanted to . . . "

Oh God, the boy's falling through the cracks! First he gets into hot water because he declares himself a full Jew, and now he's getting into hot water again because he's a half-Jew. Have they all gone mad? And I'm supposed to remain sane with all this?

She read: "Naturally, it would be great if I got a little extra help from you, since I'm getting along only by the skin of my teeth with what I've got now. But I hope that the sardine business works, and if it starts up well I might be able to open my own office. The space has already been made available to me at no cost. So you see what all people are doing for me . . . "

Office space! As if that were the most important thing in his situation! Maybe the boy is already crazy—it would hardly be surprising, given all that he's been through. What's he babbling about! Is he doing all this just to upset me, or does he really believe it—has to believe it, because otherwise all his hopes are dashed? He's always been unrealistic, but never this much!

She read: "Don't worry at all about Bulgaria. First of all, I won't do anything before I've spoken with you about it, and second, even if things are as you say, it's still better here. So, Mummy, I'm not coming to you in any case, and won't bring 'disaster' upon you. But I repeat once again: come here, so we can talk things through from the ground up. Come as soon as you can, if possible before April 25, because a certain time limit is up then. Come right away, what's keeping you in Sofia? The children can handle a few days without you. But by far the most important thing is that we see each other now . . . "

Oh God, her boy! She had to help him, come what might! She immediately sent him money, made up her mind to take the next plane to Athens, and told him she was coming. That was on April 15.

He wrote: "It makes me madly happy that you're coming so soon. You can't imagine how much I want to see you, my love! So I'll be at the airport at 6:30 P.M. on Tuesday, April 23 . . . "

She told her daughters that she was flying to Athens for two or three days to see Peter. Bettina accepted this calmly, but Angelika threw a hysterical fit. She screamed, she cried, she pleaded with her mother not to fly to Athens. She'd never come back, she just knew she'd never come back, and she'd rather die first.

O God, her little daughter! She'd just recovered so well, and now it was going to begin all over again. She distrusted them all, and rightly so. Farewells, separations, and trips had become a trauma for her. There was always something horrible, inconceivable, irrevocable behind them. And what if something really happened to her, Else, as it always could at a time when any imprudent slip might lead to catastrophe? What if the local officials became suspicious and started reviewing her case? What if she were no longer allowed to come back to Bulgaria or if she could no longer get out of Greece? Everything was possible, and was even to be expected under the present circumstances. They were living on a razor's edge and could survive only if they behaved with the greatest care and prudence. And now she suddenly wanted to endanger herself and her daughters, take risks that might lead to their undoing, and sacrifice the delicate balance of her little girls to a short visit with her son? No, in her anxiety about Peter and her longing for him she had acted carelessly. She sent him an express message to tell him that she had to postpone her trip. The message arrived too late.

Peter wrote: "Tell me, what's really going on? This is the second evening I've waited for you, and you haven't come. Has something happened to you? Are you sick? Why haven't I heard from you? I no longer understand anything and I'm worried. Tell me immediately what has happened and when you're coming . . . "

No, she couldn't disappoint him this way, couldn't leave him alone in his distress. She had to go to him! But she had to be wary, proceed prudently, and examine every step with the greatest care.

She asked Mitko Taslakoff to make inquiries. First of all, it emerged that getting a visa would cost 5,000 leva. She didn't have 5,000 leva, but Leo Ginis would certainly be prepared to lend her the money. She informed Peter that she would come at the beginning of May.

He wrote: "Naturally, I'm disappointed that you can't come now. But it's not so bad if you come at the beginning of May. Just get the 5,000 leva as fast as you can and then come! I'm fine, and my only problem is that I can't work. Your 1,000 leva are already spent, almost all of it for the most urgent mending, laundry, postage, debts, etc., and if one wants to eat at all decently, the money from the committee is gone in a flash. Please be sure to let me know in time exactly when you will arrive. I don't want to wait in vain again. It's terrible to be so full of joy and expectation and then be disappointed . . . "

She immediately sent him more money and asked Leo Ginis for the 5,000 leva. He was, of course, prepared to lend it to her, but he had major reservations about the trip. In her situation, he said, it was probably a little risky, since her son, after all that had happened, was probably under surveillance. Else became insecure, asked other friends for advice, and everyone expressed the same reservations and warnings. She told Peter about them in a letter.

He wrote: "I think you're getting a little strange. Now you suddenly don't want to come again, because there are people there who are putting bees in your bonnet. So, my dear, I'll make it short: You're going to come, and as soon as possible. I want to finally see you—and you want to see me, too! I don't give a damn what your horoscope says, and you can tell your people that they should keep their noses out of things they don't understand. Because they can't possibly understand how important and imperative it is that the two of us meet now. What do we have in this world except our love? How can we go on living if we have to put pressure on ourselves in such matters? And now there's an end of it, because it's getting almost laughable to go on engaging in ponderous reflections as to whether two people who haven't seen each other for years and are only a few hours apart, should or should not get together."

Else was at a complete loss: here were her daughters, there was Peter, on the one hand the urgent need to see him, and on the other the fear that she might thereby bring disaster on them all. Moreover, upon further inquiry new bureaucratic hindrances were constantly emerging: certificates she was reluctant to hand over to the authorities, a currency-exchange permit, or, if not that, a notarized invitation.

How was she to overcome all these technical obstacles, her friends' warnings, and her own fear? She wrote Peter a long, despairing letter in which she described her situation once again, but did not entirely exclude the possibility that she might come later.

He wrote: "Unfortunately, I understand very well that you can't come yet, but you must take into account that things can happen here, too, at any time and then a trip will of course be out of the question. What I'm asking of you is to see to everything that is necessary, so that when the time comes you won't have to lose a moment. And furthermore, Mummy dear, you mustn't worry so much about me and imagine such silly things. What you said, that you always thought you were to blame for everything, is really completely absurd. I know that you are not to blame for anything, and have I ever accused you of it? No, listen to me, blame has nothing to do with this. I know very, very well how difficult your situation is, and if I sometimes brush it aside in my letters, I do so only in order to take the initiative, so to speak, because you're so anxious. You've become a huge fraidycat, Mummy! But I never, ever do it because I don't understand that you're in a difficult position."

In June 1940 the granting of visas for travel to Greece was temporarily suspended.

Peter wrote: "On the one hand, this helps us avoid a certain calamity, namely reproaching each other. On the other hand, I am waiting with longing for the prohibition to be lifted again and you can finally, finally come! . . . "

The prohibition was not lifted again.

Half a year after he was called up, my father was discharged from the army. He'd had a nervous breakdown in Poland and he had bleeding stomach ulcers and was taken to the military hospital. My mother was radiant with joy when she told me this.

I said: "But it's terrible that he's so sick!"

"It's the best thing that could happen to him and to us," she replied, "don't worry, he's already back in Berlin, and he's much, much better. Soon he'll come to us."

"Are you sure?"

"Completely sure."

I ran to the Alexander Nevsky cathedral and lit a candle for him. Then I looked up at the elderly Wotan and prayed: "Please let him come soon and take us all back to Germany with him."

A few weeks later Mizo came to dinner. He had a big smile on his face, kissed my mother's hand, and announced: "Paris has fallen!"

"Am I supposed to consider that good news?" my mother asked.

"I think it's great!" my sister said.

My mother threw her a mute, cold look, and Bettina pressed her lips together.

All this aroused a very unpleasant feeling in me, and so I kept still. Besides, Paris did not interest me at all.

Shortly afterward my father arrived in Sofia. He seemed smaller and his hair had turned a little silver at the temples. I hadn't seen him for nine months, and was so overcome by his handsomeness and elegance that I didn't dare to run to him shrieking with happiness. He came to me, taking something out of his jacket pocket, stood in front of me and said: "Now, my daughter, your joy at seeing me seems to be very restrained." He bent down to me, and then I threw my arms so passionately around his neck that his panama hat flew off his head.

He said: "Oh là là," hugged me, and kissed me on the cheeks and mouth.

"You still have the same eau de cologne," I said, happy to have found his familiar fragrance again, and he said: "Yes, and I still feel every one of your ribs. But you've grown as long as a Midsummer's Eve . . . "

We drove to the Hotel Bulgarie. He'd brought three large suitcases, which contained chiefly presents for us. He said he'd unpack them later, because I couldn't see certain things that were intended for Christmas and for my birthday. That also meant that he wouldn't take us back to Germany with him, and wouldn't even come back for Christmas. For a moment I hated the elderly Wotan in the cathedral.

We rode home in a phaeton. On the way my mother said: "I'm afraid, Goody, the apartment won't be entirely correspond to your aesthetic feeling."

She laughed and my father replied: "Lately my aesthetic feeling has had to cope with more difficult problems."

But when we walked into the apartment, I was very ashamed of it.

My father naturally pretended not to notice and said, "I see that you have everything you need, even a bathtub in which Angelika can wash her neck—which she so much likes to do."

Ivanka stamped out of the kitchen, and when she saw my father and he shook her hand, she was so shaken that she got a lump in her throat and couldn't say a word. I called Paul, and he came with leaps and bounds, flew up to my breast, put his forelegs around my neck and covered my face with tender bites.

"So this is the famous Paul about whom you've written me so much," my father said. "He looks to me like a real Bulgarian with a great deal of spirit."

We remained a few days in Sofia, and it was one big festivity. Suddenly there were flowers in our apartment, and Ivanka wore a black apron dress with a white collar. Everyone came to greet Herr Dr. Schrobsdorff, to invite us, to go to dinner with us, and my father had the right gift and the right thing to say for everyone.

We drove through the city, and I pointed out and explained the sights to my father. Whenever he heard me speak Bulgarian, the same look of incredible amazement came over his face.

"You're already a real Bulgarian," he said once, and I protested: "No, never, ever!"

We went into the Alexander Nevsky cathedral, and I

showed him where one put the candles for the living and where one put them for the dead. He took a single candle and stuck it in the sand. I asked for whom it was. He said, for all the innocent people who'd been killed in the war. As we were leaving the church, I asked him if it had been very bad in the war. He said, yes, it was indeed. But it will soon be over, I said, because the German army is the strongest in the world and would be victorious everywhere. Who told me that, my father wanted to know. Mizo, I said, he had told me that the German army was occupying one country after another. Did he also tell me what it meant, to occupy a country? No, he hadn't told me that.

It means, my father said, forcing me to stand still by taking me so firmly by the upper arm that it hurt, taking for yourself a country that does not belong to you, and doing violence to the people who live in it. It means willful destruction, plundering, repression, and misery for that country and its people. I asked whether the Germans were doing such things. Yes, he said, they were, not in every case, of course, but in more than enough, and I therefore had no ground whatever to be proud of the German victories.

His voice sounded very sharp, and his face looked angry in a way I had seldom seen. Perhaps now he was angry with me because of the war.

I said: "I'm sorry, Papa, I didn't know that," and he said, in a way that was already friendlier: "But now you know it, little one, and please never forget it."

Then we all traveled to the Black Sea: my parents, Bettina with Mizo, I with Paul, who sat under a net in a shopping basket and meowed for seven hours straight. This time we didn't stay in the hotel in St. Constantine, but rather on the lower floor of a secluded two-story house.

There were three modestly furnished bedrooms, a shower room, a terrace, and a large, wild garden, in which Paul enjoyed freedom for the first time. I remember an enormous number of flies, which my mother hunted with a hand towel. The flies she had not swatted entirely dead I gathered up and nursed back to health.

"Angeli," my father said, "can you explain to me the point of what you're doing there?"

"I'm glad when they fly again."

"Your mother will certainly be glad, too," he said, laughing to himself.

These were beautiful, peaceful days. Mizo, who lived in another house, often went out with Bettina, and so I had my parents to myself. Every evening they sat on the terrace until late at night, drank a bottle of wine and talked to each other quietly. I didn't understand what they were saying; only once did my father raise his voice, and it sounded completely broken, like a voice on a phonograph record that turns slower and slower and then stops dead: "I saw it, Else, with my own eyes . . . They're are not rumors, it's the most infernal . . . "

And then my mother's voice: "Hush, Goody, please keep your voice down, the little one . . . "

At that time I repeatedly wondered what he'd seen with his own eyes and had been so terrible that his voice broke.

Two of the most beautiful photos of my childhood have remained from this last summer on the Black Sea. One shows me sitting on the terrace with my father; he in a white shirt open at the neck and gold-rimmed onyx cufflinks, I in the pale blue smock with the little salamander made of granite at my neck: he's looking down at me with the trace of a smile, I'm beaming up at him, both of us in profile, his classically handsome, with a big, straight nose, mine deeply tanned and already marked by my mother's high cheekbones. The other picture shows me with my cat Paul in my arms, both of us looking into the camera: I'm laughing and wearing an enormous straw hat, and he's very photogenic

with his large, slanting eyes that look as if they'd been outlined with charcoal and the black beauty spot on his little
white nose.

The part of my childhood characterized by innocence ends
with the two pictures.

It seemed to Else that her children had allied themselves
against her and were now showing her, each in his or her own
way, the mistakes she'd made with regard to them.

"You reap what you sow," she said, using her mother's
words, and from then on she said it more and more often. It
was late August and hellishly hot. Erich had returned to
Germany, Else had gone back to Sofia with her daughters.
On September 1, Angelika was supposed to take her
entrance examination for the Sancta Maria convent school.
She was in good health and had become much more independent. The worst seemed to be over. But one afternoon,
which she had intended to spend with her beloved Wilma,
the pale blond blithe spirit from Cologne, she came home
early. When she came into the room where her mother was
writing a letter, Else knew immediately that something serious had happened. The girl was quiet, too quiet, and her
eyes were hard and wary in an unchildlike way. Else had
never before seen Angelika's eyes look like that, and it made
her feel uneasy.

Why had she come home so early, Else asked, and hoped it
would all turn out to be a trifle.

Because Wilma had other visitors, two German women
who'd gone up the stairs in front of her, and so then she'd
turned around and come home.

Well, thank God, the child was disappointed, that's all. She
took up her fountain pen again.

"Mummy," Angelika asked, "what kind of people are Jews?"

Else held the pen in her hand and looked up from the half-written letter. Don't let her see anything, act as if it were the most normal question in the world, something like: "Mummy, what kind of cat is Paul?"

She said: "They're people like any others."

"No."

"They have a different religion, that's the only difference."

"No."

Else laid down her pen and looked up: "Angelika," she said angrily, "if you already know everything, you needn't ask me."

"If you were a person like anyone else, we wouldn't be in Bulgaria."

"*Who* told you *what*?"

"Nobody told me anything. I learned it by accident, from the two women on the stairs, who were one story higher up and may have thought I couldn't hear them. They must have known who I am."

"What did they say?"

"One of them said: That's the little Schrobsdorff, and the other one said: Yes, an attractive girl, too bad that her mother's Jewish, and then the first one said: The poor child."

"And you're taking all this silly nonsense seriously!"

"Yes. Because it's true."

"What do you mean?"

"If you were a person like anyone else, none of what has happened would have happened, and that's why it's too bad that you're a Jew. And because you're a Jew and all that had to happen, I'm a poor child."

Else stared at her little girl: the long, brown, matchstick legs, the long, thin arms, the flowered peasant dress, the interesting face, whose upper half resembled that of her Jewish mother, while the lower half resembled that of her Aryan father. And in addition the hard, wary eyes of a wild little creature watching people from its hiding place.

No, that wasn't going to work. Else realized that Angelika

would no longer allow herself to be deceived, to be fobbed off with evasions and half-truths—that was over!

"Angelika," she said, "we wanted to protect you and spare you suffering and fear as long as possible. That's why we haven't told you everything, and not because it is terrible to be a Jew or because that would make you a poor child."

"If it's not something terrible, why did you have to protect me from it, and why did we have to leave Germany?"

"Because a dictator named Hitler came to power in Germany and along with him a group of people—or rather monsters—called Nazis. And they have now decided to persecute Jews and to drive them out of the country.

"Why?"

"Unfortunately, I can't tell you exactly."

"Then inexactly."

"Because Jews have a different origin or, as the Nazis say, belong to a different race than Germans. So they have to leave, because the Nazis want an all German, Teutonic, Aryan Reich."

"Jews come from Palestine, don't they?"

"Yes. They lost their country two thousand years ago and went to other countries in order to settle there. There are Jews in every country, and they belong fully and completely to those nations, and have sometimes for centuries; they speak their country's language, have adopted its customs and culture, and fought in its wars, and they love their country and don't want to live in any other. You can see that in me. Did you ever think of me or Grandpa and Grandma as anything but Germans?"

"No."

"Well, then!"

"And don't other countries persecute Jews and drive them out?"

"That has also happened, and unfortunately, God knows, again and again."

"Why?"

"Honey, that's really too big a question. And anyway, I'm not sure I can explain it to you."

"Mummy, I don't know what to do anymore!"

"What do you mean, my little fawn, come here to me."

Angelika went to her, and Else took her on her knee.

"If I now hate the Germans, Mummy, and there's nothing else I can do, Papa's one of them."

"Angeli," Else said slowly and emphatically, "you have to make a distinction between Nazis and Germans. Your father is the best, most wonderful person in the world, and there are still many people of that or a similar kind in Germany."

"How many? More like him or more Nazis?"

"I don't know."

"But I do. More Nazis, many more."

"Perhaps."

"Am I a German or a Jew?"

"You have a German father and a German-Jewish mother. You were born in Germany and lived there until you were twelve years old. Your language and culture are German. So you're German. The law that says you are a half-Jew was made by the Nazis."

"Are Bettina and Peter also half-Jews, and is that why Peter left Germany?"

"Yes."

"Are there many half-Jewish children?"

"Countless."

"Are we allowed to choose which side we belong to?"

"Angelika, no one is asking you to make such a choice!"

"I don't want to belong to the one that is persecuting you and Grandma and driving you away."

"I've already explained the difference to you. There are Germans like your father, and there are Nazis."

"Will the Germans win the war?"

"God forbid!"

"I hate the Germans," Angelika decided, "they occupy countries, and they persecute and drive out Jews. I hate them—with very few exceptions."

So I'd chosen the Jewish side. For me, this went without saying, because I loved my mother. It had absolutely nothing to do with the awakening of a Jewish consciousness or even a feeling of belonging to the Jewish people. I was much too young for that, and besides, I had not even a glimmer of what Judaism is. I also felt no need to learn any more about why my mother declared the subject of Jews to be taboo and repeatedly told me not to say anything to anyone about what we were: I was German, Bettina was German, she was a native German recently married to a Bulgarian, and the word "Jewish" was never to cross my lips. Otherwise I would put us all in the greatest danger. She made me swear it, and I never broke my oath.

Her prohibition had such enduring success that years later, after it was all over, I still couldn't say the words "Jew," "Jewess," or "Jewish." I had a deathly, insuperable fear of them.

My sister chose the other side, and at that time I couldn't understand why. How could she take the side of those who were persecuting her nearest and dearest? My mother was certainly at least partly responsible for this. She should at least have told the older Bettina the plain truth, hammered into her every detail of the Nazis' crimes, until she was immune to the temptation to take the side of the powerful. She shouldn't have looked on passively as Bettina fell more and more under Mizo's influence, but instead made it clear to both of them that taking the side of the Nazis was tantamount to spiritually murdering her, Else.

I believe that Bettina, a very young, disoriented girl who was, moreover, going through a phase of protest against our mother, neither reflected on her behavior nor was fully aware of all its consequences. She thought, said, and did what Mizo thought, said, and did. But he, a mature, educated man, must ultimately have known. He was the father figure whom she had probably lacked all her life. She loved Mizo, was devoted to him, and was therefore prepared to go through fire and water for him. For her, it went without saying that she would take his side. Just as I had chosen the Jewish side because of my mother, she chose the Nazis' side because of Mizo.

Mizo came from a family of physicians highly respected in Bulgaria. His father was a doctor, one of his brothers was a doctor, and his uncle was the most famous surgeon in the country. The fact that they were all fascists and enthusiastic supporters of Nazi Germany bothered no one. On the contrary. People expected the Germans to march in any day, so to speak, and were not against an alliance with them. In that sense, the Stanishevs were on the right side, though that changed neither Mizo's behavior nor his attitude toward my mother. Whereas during the whole time that he waved the Nazi flag and expressed incredible views and made propagandistic statements, he was as warm and polite as ever, appeared every evening for dinner and took an interest in her personal cares and problems. Looking at it that way, Bettina probably also believed that there was no connection between the two things, and that one could remain true to the Nazis and to our mother at the same time. An absurd idea that took absurd forms.

I still remember one downright crazy incident in every detail: one evening Hitler was to give a speech on the radio, and it was, of course, to be broadcast on Radio Sofia. We all sat in the living-dining room, the table was already set, but Mizo was too excited to eat before the great event, which was to take place at 8 o'clock. Bettina turned on the radio; German marches were being played. My mother picked at her hangnails. Mizo lit a cigarette and waited for the beginning of the broadcast with a deep seriousness that was expressed in his wrinkled brow and pursed lips. My cat Paul, to whom the tense atmosphere must have been communicated, was particularly skittish on that evening and suddenly jumped on Bettina's leg with his claws out. She squealed like a stuck pig, and my mother said nervously: "Angeli, please put the cat out."

I had just put Paul outside the door when the radio announcer bellowed that Adolf Hitler, the Fuehrer of the German Reich, would now deliver a speech. "Deutschland, Deutschland über alles . . . " thundered forth. At the same moment Mizo stood up, followed by Bettina, and they both raised their arms in the "German salute." The sight of them standing there in front of the set dining table, with their iron faces and outstretched arms, was so comical that I could hardly keep from laughing. But then I saw my mother's contorted face, and my merriment disappeared.

"Come, Angeli," she said, and we left the room. As the "Horst Wessel Song" was being played, I shut the door, but not without taking another look at Mizo and Bettina. They were still standing there like monuments, in the same pose.

That evening the usual scene did not take place. It consisted of my mother raging and screaming and Bettina, stony-faced, letting the storm flow over her without saying a word, and then, at the crucial moment, making some outrageous statement that functioned like a *da capo* for my mother. This time Else left the house with me, and we went to a cinema in which a romantic drama with Zarah Leander was playing. That was a sensational event for me, and I wished all Bettina's outbursts could have such results. When we came home, my sister was very wisely already in bed, and she had hardly gotten up before my mother said to her in an eerily calm voice: "Bettina, you disgust me. Get out of the house."

Bettina, after giving her an astonished look, made a scornful face and disappeared. When she was not back as dusk came on, my mother became uneasy and started to telephone around looking for her. She reached her at the house of some girlfriend or other and said she should come home. Bettina did not come home until the following evening, and had thus proven that she was not following her mother's orders.

The rows were repeated at irregular intervals for two years. Sometimes there was a relatively long period of peace, and then they occurred one after the other again. I assume that the crises ran in parallel with the victorious advance of the German troops, which did, however, occasionally stop. It was a bad time, in which my mother, with her desperate screaming, and my sister, with her stubborn displays of her attitude, worked their way into ever-deeper discord, and poisoned life for themselves and for me. I hated quarrels, tension, and grim, daylong refusals to speak, and I found Bettina's performances just as idiotic as I found my mother's reactions unbearable.

Now that I finally knew the truth, a circumstance that provided me with a certain relief but at the same time threw me into new, conflictual situations, I could have used Bettina's support, the certainty that there was no path other than the one I had chosen, and closed ranks against the common enemy. Instead, we had the enemy in our own house, an unimaginable event that completely confused me.

"Mummy," I asked one day, "haven't you told Bettina that she's a half-Jew?"

Else was grounded between her three children: Peter, who wanted to be a full Jew, Bettina, who had gone over to the Nazis, and Angelika, who couldn't understand either of the other two. All right, Angelika had always been a complicated child, Peter had been a problematic young man, but what had happened with Bettina, the uncomplicated, unproblematic girl, she no longer understood at all?

Was the misfortune they'd already encountered not great enough? Did each of them also have to jury-rig his own misfortune, choose one side or the other, get wound up in fundamental decisions that could cause them all to suffer and have fatal consequences? She chose her children, and she suffered, no matter whether from Bettina's false choice or Peter's right one. Or was the danger in which her son found himself, the fear for him that she endured, thereby diminished or even erased by the fact that he was on the right side? Not for her, she wasn't a heroic mother and had no interest in being the mother of a hero. She didn't want to lose him, and everything else seemed unimportant to her.

Peter was still in Athens, but the danger of being expelled from Greece increased in the same proportion that his chances of finding another country in which he could take refuge decreased. A large part of Europe was occupied by the Germans or about to be occupied by them. America and England were now accepting almost no immigrants, and certainly not someone as problematic as Peter. One had to wait for months to get a visa to enter Latin American countries, and the voyage cost a few hundred dollars. He had neither the time nor the money. Palestine, where he would now have been prepared to seek refuge, was closed to him because of his German passport, which continued to lack the "J." The trap had snapped shut.

In Greece, he had to go to the police station every month to have his residence permit extended, a procedure that panicked him because it was never certain whether the police would grant him another thirty days or demand that he leave the country within forty-eight hours, though he did not know where he could go. He didn't receive a work permit. The Jewish committee had withdrawn its modest financial support. All the nice, touching people he'd met and who had promised him the moon, seemed to have disappeared and with them the sardine deal and the job as a chauffeur, tutor, or language teacher in wealthy homes. The only thing that was keeping his head above water was the money his mother scraped together and sent to him.

His calls for help became increasingly pressing:

"Thank you for the money, which came at the very last minute. To be honest, I was actually counting on a thousand. It's so difficult here, and I can't go beyond my means . . . "

"And tell me, what's happening with the money you were going to send me? Is it causing difficulties? I'm seriously short of cash and I don't know what will happen if I don't receive anything from you . . . "

"Your letter has still not arrived. Incidentally, I need the money very urgently."

"Tell me, wouldn't it be possible to receive a little allowance every month from America, from Walter Slezak, for instance? Ten to fifteen dollars would be enough . . . "

It broke her heart. Her boy, her handsome, talented, spoiled boy who had loved life, love, beauty, and freedom so much and who was now wandering down and out through the streets of a foreign city, always suspected, persecuted, never knowing when this last right might be taken from him as well, when he might be expelled or imprisoned. Perhaps he was hungry, no longer had a decent shirt to his back or a roof over his head. He always emphasized that he had enough to eat, a room, as she could tell from the return address, and even an overcoat, not a very good one, but something, anyway, and that she shouldn't, for God's sake, constantly have these unnecessary worries about him, he was doing fine. But she didn't trust him. Hadn't he even succeeded, by having his letters forwarded by an acquaintance in Portugal, in keeping her from discovering that he'd been in prison for four months?

"Mummy," he wrote, "I'm worried about you again. Your letters sound so desperate. I can't give you any specific answers, but I do want to tell you one thing: Think about the great sufferings of others, and compare them with ours! I never believed it, but now I know it's true: that changes things and helps."

It didn't help her. She could always see only Peter the beloved son who was in need and in danger, and couldn't get the image of an emaciated, exhausted Peter out of her mind. The great suffering of others was for her an anonymous suffering, but she felt her own child's suffering like an incessant pain in her entrails. There were still moments when in her desperation she tried to get him to return to Germany, to convince him that there was no longer any other way out.

"There's only one world in which I can live," he wrote back, "and if that world dies, I will die too, if there is no longer any escape. But I will never consider even for a moment the idea of returning to Germany or attempt, on the basis of practical considerations and the popular 'What-else-can-I-do? There's-no-other-way-and-I-can't-miss-the-boat,' to find my place in the new regime. Nothing revolts me more than all these people who are beginning to come to terms with the new regime . . . "

They still had long, violent arguments, in which she called him a wrong-headed Don Quixote, and he reproached her readiness to compromise and her "half-measures." They also discussed Bettina's case, and on that subject he wrote:

> I think you are not at all to blame and it's mainly Bettina's youth and her rather hard, unreceptive mentality. So it's a little worrying. I think the complete lack of inner measure and an outer yardstick is to blame. The vague, peasantlike closedness in her, as you say, is the real problem. Forgive me if I say this, but don't you also think her father comes out in this, too?

Despite the plight in which he found himself, he was always ready to take an interest in his mother's problems and sympathize with her, offer her his assistance and moral support. His love for her, which filled whole paragraphs of his letters, grew along with the length of their separation and the improbability that they would see each other again in the near future. He asked her for photos of her and of his sisters. He wrote to Bettina and Angelika, to his grandmother, to Liena Gsovsky, the great love of his short life. He wrote not a single line to his father.

In November 1940 Bulgaria declared war on America and England. The postal service was interrupted for a time. Else spent almost a month in terrible fear for her son. Then finally a letter from him arrived:

> "Since the declaration of war I have heard nothing more from you. I hope very much that you are all well and ask you most urgently to write to me immediately. Things are still going well for me, health-wise and otherwise. Here everything is completely peaceful, and you needn't worry about me . . . "

On September 1, 1940 I passed my school entrance examination. I think that had less to do with my performance than with the nuns, who had been asked by Frau Dr. Wudy to be lenient: "The poor child really is not to blame for the fact that her education has been interrupted over and over!"

I was put in the second year of high school and was suddenly surrounded by many Bulgarian girls of my own age. What a difference from my German schoolmates! I was accepted by everyone with the greatest warmth and cordiality; they embraced me, took my arm, held my hand, and taught me the names of the nuns and my schoolmates. I never encountered any rudeness on their part, never heard them say anything spiteful or vulgar to me, never saw a malicious look in their eyes. Their behavior toward one another was also marked by a feminine comradeship. There were groups of friends, but no cliques, their games were boisterous but not aggressive. We wore black apron dresses with white collars and long, black stockings. The only thing I didn't like was that we were not allowed to wear our hair uncovered. I was going through a first phase of vanity and was particularly proud of my hair, which I put in rollers every evening, a difficult task because there was no curler and I had to use tightly rolled strips of newspaper. It pained me to look and my beautifully curled locks in the mirror in the morning and then destroy them with clips and ribbons.

I made friends with Elena and Lily, and this friendship survived years of separation, and both the fascist and the communist regimes.

Lily, who was small and trim, was a model of diligence and honesty. She had beautiful black braids and eyes, and the collar of her never frayed or soiled skirt was white as snow. Since her father was the administrator of the castle, she lived in a house within the royal domain and was often invited to visit the princess and the little prince.

Elena, who was the opposite of Lily and a closer friend of mine, was an unusually intelligent girl who, to the horror of her solid bourgeois parents, ignored all rules and conventions. Although she was lazy and careless, she was the best student in her class, which she cared about as little as she did her appearance. I never saw her in a clean white collar or stockings without runs, and the two buttons that were missing from her wrinkled skirt remained missing from the first to the last day that we were in school together. She had a feline face with broad cheekbones, a short nose, eyes at the height of her temples, and a thin, rubbery body. The *femme fatale* was already discernible in her.

With Elena, I wandered through the city, the lively downtown with its bars, shops, and cinemas, the market, the fashionable neighborhood adjacent to Czar Osvoboditel Boulevard, the outlying districts, the Gypsy area, which we were strictly forbidden to enter, the park. We went indiscriminately into museums and churches, the lobbies of public buildings and hotels. We sat on benches, stairways, and walls, watched passersby and commented on their appearance, their clothes, the way they walked. When Elena had some money, we rode from one end of the city to the other on the streetcar, sneaked into a cinema, sat in a café and pretended to be a pair of lovers—Elena was the man, I the girl.

When I came home again, delighted and cheered up, and told my mother about the innocuous part of our day, she shook her head and said: "You and Elena can do nothing but fool around! No wonder you found each other."

She didn't like it when I roamed around the city with Elena, but on the other hand she was glad that I no longer clung to her apron strings like a little child, but instead showed the first signs of a normal development. My stuffed animals and dolls no longer interested me, the ritual oaths and prayers in the evening had given way to wild games with Paul, and I went to the Alexander Nevsky cathedral only once a week, in order to light candles for the most urgent cases. The most important things to me now were my hair and my books. When I was not with my girlfriends, I spent hours reading through my mother's bookcase with great concentration. I read Wedekind and Strindberg, for whom I had a special liking, Scandinavian novels, which were fashionable at the time, the novellas of Schnitzler and Stefan Zweig, Goethe's *Sufferings of Young Werther* and, since I liked that so much, I moved immediately on to *Faust*, parts I and II. I must have had a thoroughly satisfying grasp on complicated texts, because the fascination with which I read was genuine. I remember that I sometimes came across erotic passages that I, as the most naive of all adolescent girls, found very disconcerting, and that I did not understand nearly so well as I did

Faust, part II. They puzzled me greatly, and I never figured them out, because I couldn't ask my mother what Wedekind meant by "a woman's breast for gracious play." Sometimes she asked me what I was reading so eagerly, and when I told her, she was either impressed and full of unjustified hopes or shook her head and said that that was not for me. But that was it. She was a very liberal mother, she just wanted nothing to do with questions about sex and requests for explanation. It was simply painful for her.

The year 1940 was coming to an end. We celebrated Christmas and my birthday with the presents that my father had brought with him the preceding summer. I was now thirteen years old. Apart from my hair, there was nothing that satisfied me, because I was still flat as a board. I went to Ivanka in the kitchen. She was already lying on her cot, and under the covers the mound of her bosom bulged from her neck to her waist.

"Ivanka," I asked, "when does one become a woman?"

"When you begin to bleed."

"What? Where?"

"Down there," she shrieked.

"You always talk nonsense," I said, "and this time you're disgusting to boot."

She gobbled, and I left the kitchen.

In January 1941 the German air corps landed in Sicily. In February 1941, the German Africa corps landed in Libya. On March 1, 1941, Bulgaria became one of the Axis countries. On March 2, 1941 the Germans marched into Bulgaria.

On March 4, 1941, Else received her son's last letter from Athens:

My dearest Mummy, another attempt to tell you that things are still going well for me in every respect, and that in future you should not worry about me at all. I am always with you with all my heart and I know that you're near me as never before—and that gives me more strength than all my resolution. I thank you, thank you for everything, what you are, what you are for me: more than my mother, the greatest, the highest . . . Kisses,

Peter

On April 6, 1941, the German army occupied Yugoslavia.
On April 11, 1941, the German army occupied Hungary.
On April 30, 1941, the German army occupied Greece.

When Else looked out the window, she saw German soldiers—gray-green uniforms, shiny waxed boots, the swastika in the claws of the imperial eagle. When she left the building, she encountered them on the streets. When she went to the Café Royal with Leo Ginis, they were sitting at the tables.

"What now?" she asked her friend.

"We have to wait."

In the cinemas, German films were playing. On the radio, German marches and hit songs were broadcast, in newsstands German papers were sold.

"Angeli," Else said, "I forbid you to have any contact with the Germans! One false step and we're all done for."

Angelika stared at the soldiers, stopped to examine them, sometimes walked close behind them like a lost dog hoping to find a new master.

"Have you gone mad? What are you doing!"

"I just want to hear how they speak German."

In the evening, Else locked her windows and doors and turned on the German language news broadcast on the BBC. She sat very close to the radio and picked at her hangnails. Angelika sat next to her. The English city of Coventry had been leveled by a bombing attack. London was under the German "Blitz."

"Dear God," Angelika prayed inaudibly, "let the Germans lose the war."

Bettina came home with a red V on her chest. The badges people wore to show their solidarity with the victorious German army were sold on every street corner. A great many people wore them.

Else threw a screaming fit of rage: She had to take the filthy thing off immediately!

She had no intention of doing so, Bettina said, with a stubborn look on her face.

Then she should get out right now.

Bettina got out. She showed up a day later with the V on her chest.

Else said nothing. For three days she said not a word to her daughter, and every day the expression on Bettina's face grew more refractory.

"I think she's not quite normal," Angelika said.

"Neither of you is quite normal," Else said, "she wears a V for German victory, and you run after German soldiers."

Peter's last letter lay on Else's night table, next to the photo of Father Johann. Every evening she read it, and every evening she prayed for him. Where was he? Had he gone underground in Greece? Had he escaped to another country? But which one? Without money, without papers, and with the German army everywhere!

She lived with the pain and fear, she got used to them. You reap what you sow, she said to herself, all of it! You can get used to everything, she told herself, everything!

One day she found three German soldiers standing at her door, simple men with friendly faces. Herr Dr. Schrobsdorff had given them his address, they said, when he had been their officer.

They sat in the living room, were delighted to have a chance to be among German-speaking civilians again, drank slivovitz and talked about Herr Dr. Schrobsdorff.

It had been so funny, the way the Herr Doctor had commanded them! He'd always said: "Gentlemen, could you please turn right . . . "

The three soldiers were doubled up with laughter. Angelika stared at them steadily without speaking.

"Were they Nazis?" she asked her mother when the soldiers had left.

"I don't think so," Else said, "but you can never tell."

A short time afterward Dr. Richter, her daughter's former private tutor, came to the door. He was wearing an SS uniform.

He was sorry, he said with a sheepish look at his uniform, but he had no civilian clothing with him. He was working for Organisation Todt[3] and was on his way to Greece.

Else smiled a little smile that was half-sarcastic, half-patient.

He should come in, she said, the girls were sure to be glad to see him.

The girls were beside themselves with joy. They absolutely insisted on showing him around Sofia. Else thought that was a good idea; there was no better excuse.

They rode through the city in a phaeton. Dr. Richter with his broad swastika armband, Bettina with the red V, and Angelika with her curls.

"Dr. Richter," Angelika asked him, "are you a Nazi?"

"Here we go," Bettina said, "she asks everyone whether he's a Nazi. And she doesn't know at all what that means."

"Better than you do, otherwise you wouldn't be one."

"Children," Dr. Richter said in the admonitory tone of their former private tutor, "that is really not a fit subject for discussion!"

They returned home in a good mood. Mizo was already

---

[3] Organisation Todt: A Nazi organization that undertook large-scale civil and military engineering projects. It came to rely increasingly on slave labor (concentration camp prisoners, prisoners of war, etc.). [Trans.]

there and was pleased by the prestigious visit. They all ate dinner together.

"Please, no politics," Else said, when Mizo began to ask questions about the current situation.

"I would prefer that, too," Dr. Richter said.

As he said good-bye to Else at the door, he asked how she was getting along. Could he help her in any way? He felt a need to help her.

Else shook her head. They had everything they needed, she said, perhaps not for life, or for what she had imagined that to mean, but for survival. He kissed her hand, and she watched him go, the cute SS man who had once been her lover.

The German soldiers put me in a terrible dilemma. With the best will in the world—and I had that—I couldn't hate them. They attracted me irresistibly, not as present-day German soldiers, but as German people of the past. They had those light faces without dark shadows on their cheeks, they looked so well-scrubbed, and, above all, they spoke German. When I walked close behind them I picked up a few expressions that I hadn't heard for a long time. But very ordinary sentences such as: "Man, Fritz, I could sure use a real German beer!" also made my pulse race. I longed for nothing so much as to speak with them, to tell them that I also came from Germany and that German was my native language. Maybe I'd happen on someone from Berlin, who knew the Grunewald and Wannsee, the streets on which I'd lived. Wouldn't it be wonderful to reminisce with him about my life at that time, to find things we had in common, similar feelings and impressions! But of course I couldn't do that, and I realized that and scrupulously kept my promise. I didn't say a word in school, either. My schoolmates talked a great deal about the German troops, and asked me whether it wasn't nice for me to have so many of my countrymen here. I said yes, that was very nice, and a few of them had already come to visit us. I was allowed to say that sort of thing.

I was particularly taken with the officers. Many of them were very good-looking, and dozens of them passed our house between one and two o'clock in the afternoon on their way to the officers' mess, which was located at the lower end of our street, directly on the canal. Then I always took my plate and stood at the window, and my mother made no objection, because I had sworn to eat everything if I was allowed to see the officers. I still ate very little, and she was prepared to do anything to get me to eat.

We went to see every German film that was shown at the cinema. I know them all, the profound or clumsy tendentious ones, the idiotic amusing ones. I haven't forgotten any of the names of the actors and actresses of that time, from Kristina Söderbaum to Theo Lingen; nor have I forgotten any film, from *Hitler Youth Quex* to *I Accuse*, a particularly cunning film that argues in favor of euthanasia. I can still sing the encouraging hits of the war years: "Homeland, Your Star" and "Everything Passes, Everything Goes Away," etc. Not to mention Zarah Leander's "It's Not the End of the World," a view that she was able to express with utter conviction. Beethoven's Ninth Symphony, to the accompaniment of which the German newsreels unrolled in sound, image, and words, celebrating the German army and a German homeland delirious with joy at the victories, has also lodged itself forever in my memory and still makes a cold shiver run down my back. I hated the Germans in the newsreels and prayed for their death, but I loved the Germans in the films and identified with them.

For me, the former were a life-threatening present, the latter a transfigured past.

And then one day what I longed for so earnestly came to pass, without my having provoked it, without my having broken my promise. I was strolling home from the Alexander

Nevsky cathedral, in which I had prayed for the Germans' defeat, when a German soldier suddenly passed me, stopped, turned around to me and said "*molle*"—it's pronounced "mol-ya" and means "please"—holding out to me a piece of paper. There was an address on it, and evidently he wanted to know how to find the street. What was I to do? Give him directions in Bulgarian, which would be completely unintelligible to him? Even my mother would not have demanded that of me. I looked at the soldier. He was very young, very thin, and had a nice face with hazel eyes.

"Rakowsky Street is in the opposite direction," I told him in German, "so go back to the cathedral and then turn left . . . "

"*Mein Gott*," he interrupted, beaming at me, "you speak German fluently! Are you from Germany?"

"Yes," I said, from Berlin."

He took my hand and shook it. "What a stroke of luck," he cried, as if he had just won the jackpot, "my name is Paul Scholz, what's yours?"

"Angelika," I said, "and I have a tomcat whose name is also Paul."

"I absolutely have to meet him," he said, laughing, "and your parents, too. You know, it's so great to find a German family in a foreign country with whom one can sometimes sit as if at home and talk about home."

I nodded. I understood him with all my heart: a German family, with whom one can talk about home.

"Do you live near here?" he asked.

"Yes, a little farther on, but my whole family isn't there. My father is in Berlin, and I am here with only my mother and my sister."

"That makes no difference," Paul assured me, "I'll walk you home."

The pleasure of being walked home by a German soldier

outweighed my fear of my mother. Besides, I hadn't done anything wrong, as she would have to see.

She opened the door for us, and in order to nip her horror
in the bud, I hastily said: "Mummy, this is Paul, he asked me
how to get to a street, and he's homesick."

To my relief she smiled, shook hands with him, and said,
"Come in, Paul."

Perhaps she was thinking about Peter.

From then on, Paul Scholz, the nineteen-year-old, unpre-
possessing boy from a city in northern Germany, visited us
every week, brought us German delicacies from the packages
sent him from home, ate dinner with us in the evening, told us
about Germany, and listened with me to German hit songs on
the radio, such as "Whoever loves the homeland, as you and I
do . . ."

Paul had found a German family, and I had found a
German soldier.

Bettina was still wearing her "V," and Else put up with it.
Just as she put up with Angelika's two- and four-legged Pauls.
Paul the soldier was far less of a problem, because Paul the
tomcat was growing up and announcing, with powerful spray-
ing and an unbearable odor, that the apartment was his territory. Sometimes there were still quarrels with Bettina, but they
were like a play that has been staged too often. And sometimes,
when a visitor declined to cross the threshold, Else decided to
get rid of the cat. But shortly afterward she said to herself that
none of that was important. Let Bettina wear a "V" and the cat
spray all over the apartment. All that was better than her son
being lost without a trace.

In the spring of 1941 Else, who was now forty-eight years
old, became acquainted with the twenty-eight-year-old
Lieselotte Schröder. They met at the home of Wilma, Zvetan
Taslakoff's German wife.

Lieselotte, who was called Lilo and came from Berlin, was a beautiful person—tall, slender, with long, perfectly shaped legs, a tiny bust, and broad, somewhat angular shoulders. She had a delicate face, deep blue eyes, and a very large, full-lipped mouth. Her blond hair looked like a dust-whirl in the sun.

Else had always had a predilection for good-looking people, and since Lilo had not only an aesthetic appearances but also naturalness and a certain sparkling charm to offer, she approached her with an openness of which she had hardly been capable in recent years.

On the other hand, Lilo, who came from a solid bourgeois family and had an unsatisfied penchant for Bohemian life, was fascinated by Else's ready wit and intelligence, her life experience and unconventional way of thinking. Here was a woman with whom she could, in her disagreeable situation, speak freely and frankly, and from whom she could seek advice. Lilo's marriage to a huge, vital, inwardly and outwardly uncouth man was on its way to breakdown. He was a representative for a large import-export firm who had been sent to Sofia two years earlier, and his wife had followed him there very reluctantly. They had a five-year-old daughter, a sickly child whom she had left behind with her parents in Berlin because a husband who got on her nerves and a foreign country she didn't like were bad enough. She was a cool and not very tender mother.

It happened that Else and Lilo lived only three minutes apart in the same street, and nothing prevented them from getting together daily. Since Else avoided contact with Germans, whether soldiers or civilians, and always had to reckon with the possibility of meeting such guests in the Schröders' apartment, Lilo went for the most part to Else's home. The two of them sat for hours in the room with the coffin-like furniture, and Lilo was bothered by neither the smell of cat urine nor Ivanka's shrieking. For her, their conversations were a revelation, for Else they were a diversion and a change of pace. They discussed very normal problems: a dysfunctional marriage, weariness, physical repulsion, boredom, longing for a new great love, fear of the final break. Else offered advice based on her extensive experience, and as she spoke images came back to her from far away, as if she were looking through the wrong end of a telescope: the loves, flirtations, affairs, the mad happiness, the abyssal pain. Had that actually been her life? She could no longer relate to it, it no longer awakened anything in her. Only when she talked about Erich did her eyes shine and her words sparkle, because he alone still lived in her.

You will soon meet him," she said to Lilo, "and you'll fall in love with him on the spot."

She laughed and her young friend laughed with her.

With her beautiful figure and deep blue eyes, Lilo had many admirers who were crazy about her, but she wasn't crazy about anyone. She liked being courted, she flirted a little, but she remained cool and passive. When she was sixteen, she'd taken part in a beauty contest, had won, and, to the dismay of her ultra-conservative parents, had her picture as a beauty queen plastered on advertising pillars all over Berlin and been offered parts in films. Though she was neither excited nor talented, she'd taken acting lessons, met Helmut Schröder, become rather infatuated with the big, awkward lout, married him, had a child, and then realized that she could have done without either of them. She'd never been in love, never felt passion, never given warmth. She admired Else, who had always lived to the fullest.

Erich arrived in Sofia in early June. This time they did not go to the Black Sea, because he stayed only two weeks.

There were many things to take care of and to settle, he told Else, because the situation looked bad. After all their victories and conquests the Germans were not going to stop now. It was rumored that their next goal was the Soviet Union. Tensions were mounting. It was no longer easy to get a visa.

Elisabeth had sewed valuable jewelry into the lining of his suitcase: rings, brooches, big crosses made of semiprecious stones.

"Goody," Else said, "please don't do that. If they caught you . . . "

"You need a reserve fund," he said.

Angelika proudly showed him her curls and Bettina the "V" on her breast.

He looked at both of them: the curls with a certain doubt, the "V" with repulsion. He told Angelika that the hairdresser seemed to him a little too wild, and Bettina that she should instantly take the badge off and take care never to put it on again.

Erich told Mizo, who arrived in the evening in the most cheerful unself-consciousness and left in deep embarrassment, that he could not approve of Bettina's behavior toward her mother, and politely asked both of them not to show their support for the National Socialists in their home.

He took Angelika and her two new girlfriends to eat ice cream in the Café Royal and asked the two girls to help his daughter, to encourage her in the school, and to teach her that curls were less important in life than learning and knowing. Elena and Lily were deeply impressed by him.

Lieselotte Schröder was no less impressed by Erich, and what Else had predicted with a laugh came to pass: Lieselotte fell in love with him on the spot.

Erich was not unaffected by Lieselotte, either. Basically, she was what he'd had in mind back then, when he was still living with his poets and thinkers in his parents' house, and showed very little interest in women: a cool, passive blonde, who suited him and did not disturb his thoughts, with whom he could lead a quiet, peaceful life, talk about the fine arts, go to the theater, and read a book by the fire. A tall, svelte woman, with long, slender hands and feet, with eyes that reminded him of very still, deep waters.

They saw each other often during Erich's stay, but never alone. Else noticed that in Erich's presence Lilo lost her usual naturalness and displayed the decorous behavior of a proper young lady. She listened with disconcertment to what Erich said about his life in Berlin, about good theatrical productions, first-class concerts, and an interesting circle of friends that consisted of well-known actors, directors, and scholars—people of his kind, Nazi opponents—clever, decent, clean. That was the only way one could survive this inhuman time, he said.

Good heavens, Else thought, only that way!

The conversations she had with him were of a different kind. Here it was really a question of surviving, of the chances of those who already had a noose around their necks that could be tightened at any time, people who were being persecuted, like her son, her mother, relatives, friends, her daughters, herself. What would happen if the Germans continued to win all along the line, extended their persecution of the Jews to all of Europe, the connection between them was broken, money ran out, she, Else, were no longer protected by her marriage to a Bulgarian, or the girls' visas were not renewed?

Questions upon questions, to which they knew there were no answers. Possibilities that were weighed and rejected again, a little flicker of hope that was quickly extinguished. Discouragement, resignation, perplexity, the miserable feeling of total impotence.

Erich said he would come again at Christmas, and then they would examine these questions further. The situation couldn't change fundamentally in six months, he thought.

On June 22, three days after he left Bulgaria, the German assault on the Soviet Union began.

What I remember about that summer is chiefly the swimming pool, a rather pathetic, unappetizing facility—no meadow in which one could lie, no trees or parasols to provide shade, only cement surfaces, hard packed earth, and a pool with cloudy, seldom-changed water.

My mother, with her eyes closed, and Lilo, constantly talking to her, lay next to each other on deck chairs, and sometimes they stood under the shower, because the water in the pool was too dirty for them. My mother had the cross around her neck, and the indispensable little handkerchief tucked into the neck of her dark blue bathing suit, and Lilo had breasts about the size of green apples and was oiled from head to foot. I was in the water all the time, and now and then my mother called to me: "Angeli, come out now, you're going to get a bladder infection."

I thought this bathing facility was wonderful. Earlier, when I still measured everything against the German yardstick, I had refused to share a few square meters of ground with countless almost naked, sweating people and a pool in which children peed. But now even I was no longer upset by a dirty privy or a caravan of bedbugs on the wall next to my bed. The Bulgarian present had won out over the German past. I had also gotten used to the German soldiers. I no longer saw them as an exciting union of light faces and German language, but instead distinguished, with a sharp eye and ear, which of them were good-looking and spoke High German, and which were not worth paying attention to.

Around noon the German army came to the swimming pool, soldiers and officers who'd obviously already adapted to the situation in Bulgaria and liked nothing better than dirty water. Among them was Lieutenant Commander Dahle, one of Lilo's admirers, with whom I had become infatuated. Since then I had only one goal: to bewitch him with my curls—I still had nothing else to offer. When he arrived at the swimming pool, punctually at 1:00 P.M., an attractive, large, round-faced man in a pearly-white uniform with gold buttons, I was so dazzled by his appearance that a reflection of me even fell on his black tricot swimming trunks and his somewhat flabby, sallow body. Love made me blind and his presence, an occasional caress, or even a kiss gave me such happiness that I could live off it for days, reveling in romantic dreams. I imagined us dancing across a ballroom, he in his white uniform, I in a beautiful evening dress of silver lamé—in the image of Irene von Meyendorff, the most ladylike representative of German film. But when I looked at myself in the mirror, I was overcome by deep despair. I still had no hint of breasts or hips, and my unwashed neck, which I rubbed with eau de cologne from time to time, was as long and thin as that of a plucked goose.

I asked my mother whether there were children who always remained children, and she said no, unfortunately there were none, and she considered it a blessing that I was still a child.

She did not see that for me it was a curse, because Lieutenant Commander Dahle would definitely not wait another two or three years for my breasts to grow.

The desire to be grown up, to be a woman or at least a young lady, dominated me more and more, and made all others fade into the background. Naturally, I still wanted the Germans to lose the war, us to return to our beautiful former life in Germany, finally to receive news about Peter, my father to come to Sofia for Christmas, and naturally my love for my mother and the fear of losing her remained undiminished. But these desires and feelings no longer stood with obsessive urgency at the center of my life. I had also stopped praying: "Dear God, let me die before my mother," because I wanted to grow up and dance across a ballroom with Lieutenant Commander Dahle before I died.

That summer and fall, I heard on BBC news that the German army had conquered the Ukraine and taken Rostov.

"I think they're winning the war," I said to my mother.

"Don't meet trouble halfway," she replied sharply.

In November we heard that the Russians had retaken

Rostov and that the German army's offensive had stalled before Moscow.

"Perhaps they're not winning after all," I said.

"Now they're done for," my mother said, and we hugged each other.

Shortly before Christmas my father came back. He brought Dr. Filier with him. "If we lose contact for a while," I heard him tell my mother, "at least you're protected by the new agreement with Zvetan Taslakoff. And if worse comes to worst . . . " Since he didn't finish his sentence, I did not know what would happen then.

He had brought a great deal of jewelry with him, and not only my mother and sister, but even I was allowed to wear it. Every day I hung a different cross around my neck and was very proud of it.

My father wore a black armband and a tie, because his old man, as he called him, had recently died of a third stroke. The loss of my grouchy grandfather, from whom I had never received more than a brief kiss of greeting, did not move me at all. My mother said it was good that her father didn't have to live through all this, but her poor mother!

My father nodded. Yes, it was sad for the two old ladies to be suddenly left alone, especially during this terrible time. Bombing attacks and food shortages, and that was just the beginning. He planned to move his mother to Pätz, and thought it would be a very good idea for her mother to go to the Jewish retirement home. There she would have at least someone to talk to and would be taken care of. Whereas she was helpless and really very lonely in her apartment. Elisabeth did go there twice a week, and he went as often as he could, and also his mother would visit her again from time to time . . .

Was she still allowed to do that, my mother interrupted, now that Grandma had a star on her door?

"What kind of star?" I asked

"Please Angeli," she said, "don't constantly interrupt us."

"That was the first time," I said, hurt.

There were still danger zones from which I was kept away. I first learned about the yellow star only eight months later, when it was introduced in Bulgaria as well.

There was, as always when my father was there, a great deal of activity. I found it very exciting and became a little infatuated with Dr. Filier, though my love for Lieutenant Commander Dahle continued unabated. I fell in love with every big, well-groomed man who spoke High German.

Lilo gave a large evening party for my father. My mother didn't go—but I was allowed to help with the preparations and later to be there for a while. Lilo put mascara on her eyelashes, a process that I observed with fascination, and then she put on a tight-fitting, strapless evening dress, white with big wine-red flowers that had black stems and leaves. She looked so tall, slender, and beautiful that she overshadowed even Irene von Meyendorff.

My father and Lieutenant Commander Dahle also thought she looked very beautiful. Since I had found out what love was, I sensed such things. I had spruced up for this evening and also received many compliments, but they made me more sad than happy because they were for a child who was not taken seriously. Even the lovely apartment decorated with flowers, the cold buffet with delicacies I hadn't seen, not to mention eaten, for years, the festive atmosphere, the soft music, the fragrance of various perfumes and kinds of tobacco made me sad, because they all reminded me a little of the parties in Hubertusallee.

I looked over at Papa, who was talking with the beautiful Lilo and two distinguished gentlemen. Yes, my aristocratic father with his tailored suits and manicured fingernails fit into this context, and certainly not into ours. For the first time I became painfully aware of the abyss that separated his life from mine. His was a smart misfortune, ours a dismal one. For the first time I felt that he was an outsider who showed up briefly and then disappeared again, who took care of us, but did not suffer for us, for whom I had remained the child he'd left in September 1939, and who didn't know, would never know, what had happened in me over the past two years, what had broken in me over the past two years. I quickly and quietly left the apartment.

How was it, Bettina asked me when I got home.

"A little the way it used to be at home," I said, "and Lilo had an evening dress on and looked very beautiful"

"I can easily imagine that," Bettina said, "she wore it for Papa."

"Ach, you're crazy! She's married and doesn't really know Papa."

Bettina laughed through her nose, as she always did when she was really ungracious. "We'll see how long that lasts," she said.

Dr. Filier went back to Berlin two days before Christmas, and we celebrated Christmas Eve and my birthday with Papa. We didn't know where to put the Christmas tree, and finally had to completely rearrange the living-dining room so that it could be placed in a corner between the clunky furniture. Dimiter Lingorsky had brought us a live goose from the market, and it swam in the bathtub, because no one, not even Ratka, our new maid, wanted to kill it. I no longer remember what happened to the goose, but in any case we didn't eat it. Ratka wore fashionable black stockings, and when she brought the soup into the living-dining room, Paul jumped on her plump calves, and she shrieked and almost dropped the tureen. My father didn't like such incidents and he said angrily: "Is that necessary?" I tried to explain that Paul wasn't to blame but rather the black legs, which he might have taken for those of an animal. We lit the candles on the tree, but they dripped and melted away like snow in the sun.

My father read the Christmas story to us: "For unto you is born this day in the city of David a Savior, which is Christ the Lord . . . " Then he wanted us to sing "Silent night, holy night," but I refused and said that it would sound terrible without piano accompaniment. The gifts consisted primarily of practical clothes that my father had brought with him, probably for the time when worse came to worst. There were many pairs of panties, and he must have forgotten my mother's size. She shrieked with laughter when she saw the things, ran into the bedroom, put one on and called us. The salmon-colored cotton panties reached from her knees to her armpits, and she looked really terrible. I was very embarrassed for her. How could she let a man like my father see her looking like that? Grandmother Schrobsdorff had also sent me two books, silly young girl's stuff I had long since moved beyond.

But the worst were Grandma Kirschner's crepes, which she had baked for us and packed in box that must have earlier had soap in it. I can't forget those crepes, crumbled and smelling like soap, the symbol of a happy childhood, a sign of a world in ruins, last proof of love given by my painfully dying grandmother, who had been deprived of the right to be a human being. I didn't know that then, and I didn't know why I was crying. There was just a boundless desolation in me, the feeling, which could not be expressed in words, that nothing was right in this world, that everything was wrong and that there was no longer anyone, not a single person, whom one could count on.

"What's wrong with her?" my father asked, when I ran out of the room, and my mother answered: "Just the moodiness of puberty."

Three days later we took my father to the railway station. It was snowing, and the wind drove the snowflakes onto the platform. My father counted his bags, he counted them three times. My mother said, "Goody, they're all there." He nodded and politely asked the porter to put them in his compartment. I translated for him. It was ten minutes until the train was to leave. I followed the hand on the big clock, which sprang from one minute to the next, and wished it would skip a few. It was painful to wait for the departure of someone one loved. My mother and sister felt the same way. I looked at their frozen faces; they couldn't manage even a forced smile.

Papa said to my mother: "There will always be a way to keep in contact," and to my sister: "Bettina, your highest duty is to stand by your mother," and to me: "Angelika, please try to study hard and with pleasure, don't cause your mother any additional problems, and don't disappoint me," and then, to us all: "Someday we'll be together again in Germany."

He hugged and kissed us, got on the train, and went to the window. He had difficulty getting it open. The three of us stood there and watched his awkward efforts. My mother finally signaled him to let it go. One minute before the train left, he finally got the window open. I can still see him standing there in his navy blue cashmere coat and the red and green patterned silk scarf. He had taken off his hat, and his hand with the signet ring lay on the windowsill. He looked down at us with an expression of dismay.

"Let's spare ourselves that," my mother said. "Please, Goody, go into your compartment."

"You mustn't lose your belief in the good!" he said.

"We're going now," my mother said.

Then there was the shrill whistle and the sound of the doors slamming shut.

"Angelika," my father said as the train started to move forward. His lips moved, but I could no longer understand what he said.

I wanted to run alongside the train, but my mother held onto me. "Come," she said, "there's no point in doing that."

I still saw the white handkerchief and raised my hand to wave to him. Probably he could no longer see it.

"Will he never come again?" I asked my mother.

"Of course he'll come again."

But he never came again.

In February 1942 Else received the first Red Cross message from her son: he was in Palestine with Ilse and Walter Hirsch, he was healthy and happy to have left Europe behind him. He lacked for nothing. His only concern was for her, his sisters, and his grandmother. He asked her to reply immediately to the Hirsches' address in Jerusalem.

Else's relief and delight were so overpowering that they drove her out of the cramped apartment into the streets, to the homes of her friends, to her daughters' schools.

"Peter is alive!" she shouted. "Peter is saved! Peter is safe!"

She laughed, she cried, and her friends laughed and cried with her.

Else spent the evening with her daughters. They were happy and loving. Peter had brought them together. They talked about him, about Ilse and Walter Hirsch, about Palestine.

"Does the land belong to the Jews again?" Angelika asked.

"No," Else said, "but many of them live there."

"Can't we go to Jerusalem to see Peter? I'd like to go to Jerusalem."

"Maybe we can go there some day."

"That would be wonderful," Bettina said.

"It will be wonderful again, my sweets, I promise you, it will be wonderful again!"

For the first time in years Else was warmed by a feeling of confidence: we're going to make it! We'll get through! We're going to begin a new life—afterward. My children and myself. For the first time in years she dared to dream of a future: she and her children, finally at peace and in safety, closely bound to each other and made stronger, more mature, wiser by their hard fate. A life in a beautiful place, no, not in Germany, which would always be haunted by the ghosts of the past, in a country where she could feel good again and that could become their new homeland. A country with sun and sea and warm-hearted people. A life without fear. The love of her children, the nearness of her children, the happiness of her children—she longed for nothing more.

When spring came a new offensive began on the Eastern Front. The German army pushed far into the north and south of the Soviet Union. In Libya it reached Tobruk.

Else received only a few anodyne lines from Erich: he was healthy and had a lot of work. The news from her mother, who had in the meantime moved into the Jewish retirement home, was similar: she was healthy and had good company. Since every letter coming out of or going into Germany was opened and censored, one could no longer write anything meaningful. Thus Else had no idea what was really going on. She heard on the BBC that the bombing raids on German cities were increasing and more intense, that more and more food items were rationed. She heard rumors about the deportation of Jews to concentration camps. Now that she was relieved of concern about her son, she worried about her mother and Erich.

In early May Lilo told her that she was going to divorce her husband and return to her daughter and parents in Berlin. Else was surprised, because up to that point her friend had tentatively played with that idea, but never seriously considered it. However, Helmut Schröder was a good-natured and generous man who offered her, a passive woman without a profession, a comfortable life. Was it wise, at a time like this, for her to leave a man just because she didn't love him?

No, Else said, and knew what she was talking about.

But she, Else, had done it.

Because the next one had always already been standing at the door. And since in Lilo's case the next one was not standing at the door and she really liked leading the good life, she should think twice before taking such a step.

But Lilo had made up her mind.

"There's nothing worse," she said, "than sharing table and bed and bath with a man you can't stand."

"Without one it's also not easy," Else warned her, "especially during a war, when bombs are dropping all around you."

"Better alone with bombs than without bombs and with Helmut."

"Fine," Else said, "*tu l'as voulu!*"

Lilo left Sofia.

"You're the only one I'm going to miss," she said on taking leave of Else, and Else laughed and said: "You'll soon find something better."

At the end of May, Else was called by a man who spoke in a light Bavarian dialect and introduced himself as Dr. Hartmann. He said that he had just arrived from Berlin and had brought mail and gifts from Herr Dr. Schrobsdorff for her and her daughters.

Else, delighted, asked him to come by that afternoon. He came—a broad, thickset man with a bull neck, bulldog face, the Nazi party insignia on his lapel, and a briefcase in his hand.

For a second, Else lost her composure. She stood in the doorway, stared at the man and thought: has Erich gone mad, sending me this prototype of a Nazi, or is the whole thing a trick and this guy is from the Gestapo?

Dr. Hartmann guessed her thoughts, shook his head and said: "Madam, everything is all right.

Else smiled sheepishly and stepped aside: "Excuse me," she murmured, "but for a moment . . . "

"I can't blame you!" He gave a short laugh, a kind of bark that went well with his face.

She led him into the living room, and he pulled letters, gifts, and an envelope filled with banknotes out of his briefcase.

Herr Dr. Schrobsdorff, he said when he had laid everything on the table, would not be able to come to Bulgaria in the fore-seeable future, because people who were neither party members nor in the military were no longer granted visas.

Had he known Erich Schrobsdorff for a long time, Else asked.

No, he was sorry to say that he had met him only recently, through a mutual acquaintance who had told Herr Dr. Schrobsdorff that he was traveling to Bulgaria. That was how their connection had come about. They had talked half the night, and he felt the greatest respect for her divorced husband, and was glad to be able to help him and her by doing them this little favor.

Else kept silent. She really had no idea how to deal with this caricature of a Nazi. She didn't know what he knew about her.

He said: "Madam, to make the situation clear: I was one of the first whom Hitler in person decorated with the Blood Order medal, I have continued, as you see, to belong to the party, and Herr Dr. Schrobsdorff has told me everything. If you trust him, you can trust me."

"Can you also trust yourself?" Else asked.

"Yes, I can: I know exactly what I'm doing and why I'm doing it. But I prefer not to offer you any further explanations. Coming from me they would sound false and embarrassing, and I prefer to spare you and myself that. Would you like to have dinner with me tonight? It would be a great honor and a pleasure for me." He took off his party badge and put it in his pocket.

Dr. Hartmann stayed a week, and not a day went by when he did not call Else, invite her out, bring her flowers, or go on a walk with her and allow a sidewalk photographer to take a picture of them, arm in arm.

Else was forty-nine years old, and still an attractive woman with a fascinating personality. Her heavy, curly hair had not gone gray, her plump body had not grown fat, and her deeply tanned face had, thanks to her high cheekbones and large, luminous eyes, retained its original boldness and shape. Dr. Hartmann had obviously fallen in love with her.

Angelika disapproved of the burly man with the dented nose and asked her mother the obligatory question: "Mummy, is he a Nazi?"

"He has all the attributes of a Nazi."

"Then how can you go out with him?"

"He is helping us and people like us."

"Then he's not a Nazi."

"You see, that's what I think, too. I don't know what he is. Maybe he's a Nazi-mensch."

"There is no such thing."

"You'd be surprised what all there is in the world."

Dr. Hartmann, who wore the Blood Order medal, was the last man who was to fall in love with Else, because in July of that same year her face was disfigured by a paralysis of the facial nerve.

She had paid no attention to pains behind her right ear and at the back of her head. They had not been particularly bad, and headaches were nothing unusual for her. That evening she had gone to bed around eleven P.M., had read a little and slept well. The next morning, half-asleep, she sensed that the right half of her face was like ice—cold, stiff, insensitive. Her eyelid no longer closed, and saliva was running out of the corner of her mouth and down over her chin.

Maybe a poisonous spider had bitten her, maybe she had an infected tooth. But she had no pain and her cheek was not swollen, and besides, she didn't believe it. She didn't know what had happened to her, but she knew it was serious. She stood up and went to the mirror, slowly and with increasing anxiety, her hands pressed against her cheeks, the live one and the dead one, in order not to be struck immediately by the full force of her appearance.

And then she stared at the wide-open eye with its motionless lid, and her crooked mouth opened to let out a silent, horrified scream. She wanted to shut her eyes, but only the left one obeyed her command, the right one continued to stare frantically at her. And then she let her hands fall, looked long and hard at her ruined face, and thought she understood.

"I saw and still see my illnesses down to the bottom," she wrote in one of her letters, "and I recognize their meaning."

My mother's face—the beautiful, beloved, familiar face, the tip of her nose soft as silk, her eyes under their high lids, her cheeks like gentle slopes descending from her cheekbones to her chin. A face so full of life and expressive power, warmth and intelligence, humor and impetuousness. A face that I had first recognized as that of my mother when I was two years old and had last seen the night before had overnight become a travesty.

She held a handkerchief over the paralyzed side of her face, but even that way she could not conceal the disfigurement. Her left eye, which suddenly seemed small in comparison with the wide-open right one, looked at me as if begging forgiveness. I wanted to run to her, but I couldn't move, I wanted to say something consoling to her, but I couldn't get a word out, I wanted to spare her my dismayed look, but I couldn't keep my eyes off her.

She said, articulating unclearly, "Angeli, my love, don't be so terribly shocked. We'll find out what I have, and cure it."

I nodded and wept bitterly.

Mizo went with her to the best neurologist in Sofia. He diagnosed a paralysis of the facial nerve, which was unfortunately very severe and could not be cured. In time, the tension in the right half of the face would abate, and she would be able to move the muscles a little. She'd get used to it.

She didn't tell me what the doctor had said, only that it was a tedious business. I began again to go to the Alexander Nevsky cathedral to light candles, to address fervent prayers to the white-bearded, white-maned, blue-eyed, well-fed God. I prayed in the evening, I prayed in the morning before I opened my eyes to look at my mother: "Dear God, make her face the way it used to be."

Then I quietly sat up and looked over at her. She was sleeping, but her right eye, only a little covered by the lid, was staring into the void, and the right corner of her mouth was raised as if in a painful grin. I cried, I cried often in those first weeks.

Everyone else seemed already to have gotten used to her face, but I thought I would never get used to it. How much suffering her appearance must have caused my mother, how ashamed and dismayed she must have felt when she looked in the mirror, how embarrassed when she couldn't pronounce certain sounds correctly, or when she drank, had to fear that the liquid would run down her chin.

"Angeli," she said one day, "it's not as bad as you think, and it bothers me much less than it does you. Naturally, I'd rather be healthy again and have a normal face, but after all, I'm almost an old woman already, and how I look is no longer so important to me. For a young person it would be a tragedy, but for me it's just a misfortune. I've already had everything out of life, more than most people, and now it's my children's turn. If you're healthy, beautiful, and satisfied, then there's nothing that can still make me really sad. I swear it to you, my little fawn, a crooked face is no longer a disaster for me."

"And it will get better again, won't it, Mummy?"

"Maybe yes, maybe no. In any case we shouldn't wait every day for it to get better. We have much more important things to wait for."

In August 1942 the Jewish laws went into force in Bulgaria. They were no different from the German ones, and included the compulsory wearing of the yellow star, the handing over of all assets, and dozens of prohibitions that limited Jews' freedom of movement to a minimum.

Else trembled. If she was subject to these laws, things would be even worse for her in Bulgaria than in Germany. She would be exposed to the same threats and humiliations as in Germany, and moreover she would lose her daughters.

But now it turned out that the conversion to the Russian Orthodox faith, which she—for whatever reason—had made was her salvation. The Church was very strong in Bulgaria, and the laws were not applicable to it.

She thanked God, but unfortunately too soon. Because there was Viktoria, who had been Dimiter Lingorsky's beloved for years, who wanted to marry him, and thought the right moment had now come to use the newly introduced laws to get rid of the obstacle represented by Else. She went to the police and denounced her. As luck would have it, she couldn't hold her tongue and triumphantly told Dimiter what she intended. He, who had neither the intention to marry Viktoria nor the indecency to hand Angelika over to destruction, promptly threw Viktoria out the door and hurried off to warn Else. She should not leave her apartment or open her door to anyone until he had called her. He would go immediately to the chief of police with a friend of his who was a lawyer and sort the matter out.

Else trembled. Angelika, the only one who was at home, asked what would happen now. Else was too upset not to tell her. She asked her to go to Wilma and wait there for her call. But Angelika refused: what happened to her mother should also happen to her, she said. Else said that this was no time for heroics, and her daughter replied that she didn't want to be a heroine, she just didn't want to live without her mother. Else no longer had the strength to argue with her. She went into the bedroom, knelt down next to the bed, within sight of Father Johann, and prayed.

"At that time," she wrote in a letter, "I had the 'intimate feeling' that God existed . . . "

This intimate feeling helped her to get through the hours until Dimiter called.

Everything was all right, he said, not a hair on her head would be harmed.

"Angeli," Else called, "I prayed, and God heard my prayer!"

"He didn't hear mine," Angelika answered, bitterly.

One afternoon, just as my mother and I were about to leave the apartment to go to the cinema, the postman came and brought an express letter.

My mother went very pale, tore open the envelope, and when she put the letter down on the table the color still had not returned to her face.

"From your father," she said. "Come, we're going."

We were already in the street when I dared to ask: "What did he write?"

"Grandma has been taken to Theresienstadt, along with the other residents of the retirement home," she said in an expressionless voice.

"Where is Theresienstadt?"

"He writes that it is in Czechoslovakia. Near Prague."

"Why was she taken so far away? What is she supposed to do there?"

"You know that letters are censored. You father couldn't give any further details. I assume that Theresienstadt is a camp."

"What kind of camp, Mummy?"

"A concentration camp. Those are camps in which Jews are imprisoned."

"They're imprisoned in camps?"

"Yes."

"And what is done to them?"

"I don't know, child."

"And Papa doesn't know, either?"

"I also don't know that. I told you, he can't give us any details. He saw her before she left. She was very calm and said: 'When you're eighty you don't expect much more out of life.' She sent us her love."

"Would we rather not go to the cinema?"

"Do you think that will make it better? It doesn't matter where one sits or what one wears. Mourning has no outward marks."

"And she's also not dead. It would be completely different if she were dead. Maybe the camps are not so bad, and she will be fine, and after the war we'll see her again, won't we, Mummy?"

"Yes, my bunny."

It was a film with Zarah Leander, who sang "I know someday a miracle will happen . . . "

Sometimes I looked over at my mother. She looked at the screen the whole time, with an unmoving face, but I was sitting on her right, the paralyzed side.

The next day I asked Bettina whether Mother had told her what had happened to Grandma.

She nodded.

I asked whether she thought that she was all right in Theresienstadt. She screamed: "Stop, stop, stop!" and ran out of the room.

A short time later I walked through the little park that lay diagonally across the street from our building and found Grandpa Ginis sitting on a bench. It was a damp, cold afternoon, and he sat huddled, his head down, his collar turned up. On his breast, sewed to his coat, the yellow star gleamed. It was the only bright spot on that gray day.

Grandpa Ginis saw me only when I stopped in front of him. He smiled wearily, looked to the right and left, and said, "Hello, Angelika, how are you all doing?"

"Well, thank you."

"That's wonderful. Say hello to your mother for me. Goodbye, my child."

I sat down next to him on the bench.

"Angelika," he asked me, visibly terrified, "please don't sit here, you'll catch cold."

"I haven't seen you for a long time," I said, "and now I know why. But it doesn't bother me. I'm glad to sit here with you. I would go anywhere with you, even to the Café Savoy. Shall we go there?"

He glanced to the right and left again, and when he saw that no one was nearby, he put his hand on mine.

"Child," he said, "I'm no longer allowed to go into the Café Savoy, and you mustn't stay sitting here. It's too dangerous for you, you see! You must now be much more careful than before, and you don't want to harm your mother, do you?"

"Won't you come to see us anymore, and won't we go to see you anymore?"

"Not in the near future, but sometime later."

"I think this is all mean!"

A couple, a man and woman, came toward us, and Grandpa Ginis quickly stood up.

"Farewell, Angelika, it was very nice to see you . . . you're a good child."

The couple was only a few steps away from us, and he turned around without shaking my hand and quickly went away, his back bowed.

I looked after him for a while, then went home. A terrific wrath raged in me.

My mother was sewing a button on some article of clothing. I asked: "Mummy, why don't you wear a yellow star?"

"Because I converted to Christianity."

"Why did you convert to Christianity?"

"Because I believed in it."

"How can one believe in it?"

"What?"

"The Germans are Christians, aren't they? The Bulgarians are Christians, all of Europe is Christian. What kind of Christianity is it that torments Jews this way?"

She had stopped sewing and stared at me as if I had suddenly pointed a pistol at her.

"I think you're confused about everything."

"Oh, no, not I, you!"

I turned around and went out of the room, left the apartment and walked directly to the Alexander Nevsky cathedral. A few people were kneeling, praying, lighting candles. A pope with a little topknot on the back of his head was doing something at the high altar. I stopped under the highest cupola, in which the aging Wotan had been painted. I looked up, smirked spitefully and whispered: "Dear God, you know what? You can kiss my ass."

Then I left, elated and feeling a great inner freedom, never to return.

In October 1942 the German army had advanced as far as Stalingrad, and taken over parts of the city. In November the Russian counterattack began.

Else sat breathless in front of the radio: "This is the beginning of the end," she said, and a tear of joy ran over the paralyzed side of her face. She did not feel it and dried only her left eye. Christmas came. Angelika declared that she wanted to celebrate just her birthday a little, she didn't care at all about Christmas. She was very delighted with the Christmas package her father had sent, the new dress fabric her mother gave her, and the cake with the fifteen candles. That afternoon her friends Elena and Lily invited her to the Café Royal.

On New Year's Eve, Mizo went dancing with Bettina and Else went with Angelika to a ballet performance. She was proud of her daughters. Bettina, with her ivory skin, long black curls, and pretty legs, looked lovely, and Angelika, in a suit and wearing silk stockings for the first time, already looked almost like a young woman.

At long intervals calming Red Cross messages came from Peter in Palestine.

Else thanked God. Her children had managed so far, they would make it to the end. Bettina had radically changed her attitude toward her mother, and there were no more quarrels. Angelika began to develop physically and intellectually, and to surprise people with her first curves and critical opinions. Peter was safe.

Once again, she had thanked God too soon.

In early March, Mizo came to us terribly upset: his friend at the German embassy had told him that Bettina would soon be ordered to return to Germany. The document had chanced to fall into his hands, and he, although a convinced National Socialist, had thought it is duty as a friend to inform Mizo of it. If Mizo wanted to save his girlfriend from a labor camp, his friend had said, he had to marry her immediately.

The hastily and poorly prepared wedding took place scarcely a week later.

It was a windy, cold, rainy day in March. Bettina wore the pale blue taffeta evening dress that she had bought for her first ball in Germany, to which she had not been able to go, a borrowed stole of white rabbit fur, and a not quite new veil that fell down over her face in front, while the train was carried by Angelika, crowned with a wreath and playing the role of bridesmaid. Mizo wore a black suit, Else a fur coat and a hat whose violet-colored veil concealed her half-paralyzed face, and Angelika a delicately flowered organza dress that would have been suitable for a hot summer day.

The wedding was performed by an archimandrite, a friend of the Stanishev family, and the witnesses, Mitko Taslakoff and his sister-in-law Wilma, held the crowns over the couple's heads.

Mizo looked serious and dignified, an expression he knew exactly how to produce, and Bettina looked very pale and distraught. The members of the Stanishev clan, who thought they owed the hasty marriage not to Bettina's ancestry but to a slip on Mizo's part, had all shown up, crossed themselves, kneeled down, got up, sniffled, smiled, and said, "Amen."

Else thought: My poor little girl, only twenty-one years old and still hasn't really come into her own! Ripped out of one life, thrown into another! Hasn't truly lived yet, perhaps hasn't truly been in love, even if she thinks or imagines that she has. But my God, I know what love is! I've never seen bliss and fulfillment in the features of her little face or in the movements of her pretty body, never heard her either rejoice or sob. There was always only that willingness to ask of a man, of love, of life, nothing more than a little, modest happiness.

They came out of the cold church—the bridal couple in front, holding candles in their hands, then a procession of freezing people who bravely smiled at the wintry, gray day. The wind put out the candles and tugged on the long veil that Angelika tried to control with one hand while she clung to her crown with the other. A photographer literally flew up to them in order to take the wedding photo, come what might: in the middle the bride and bridegroom, alongside them the witnesses, the mother, the father, and behind them, on their tiptoes and craning their necks, the grinning brothers and sisters.

They went to a restaurant with gypsy music. The musicians played both the fiery and the melancholic styles at the same earsplitting volume. Food, which the Bulgarians were bravely and loyally delivering to their German allies, was now in short supply, and the meal was correspondingly meager. But there

was a great deal of rakia, slivovitz, and red wine, and that suf-
ficed to relax everyone. Toasts were constantly being drunk to
the young couple, people laughed and joked, embraced and
kissed one another. Else kept looking over at her daughter, the
second of her children, who would now soon leave her and
lead her own life. Now only she and Angelika remained—
Angelika, the little one whose development, which had earlier
been slow, was now advancing at breakneck speed, and who
was at the same time also beginning to move away from her.
No, that wasn't how she'd imagined it would be.

Neither Peter nor Bettina had undergone an organic development, a gradual transition from childhood to adulthood. The
violent break in their lives had robbed them of their youth and
forced them, from one day to the next, not only to grow up but
to grow old. At fifteen, Angelika would perhaps be the only one
who might be able to enjoy her youth after the war was over. Else
felt responsible for the fate of her children and suffered from it.

The newlyweds spent their wedding night in a shabby room
in a pension, and Bettina was glad when it was over.

Later she once confided in her mother: "You know,
Mummy, I really didn't enjoy it," and Else answered: "Doesn't
matter, Tina, it will still happen someday."

With my radical farewell to God and my development of a
feminine figure I began to undergo a transformation. It was the
first step in a new, critical attitude towards life in which signs
of negation and hardness became discernible. I now very often
said: "I've had enough!" or "Not me!"

In school, where my performance had been barely average,
I sank further and further down. My mother asked me if I
wanted to go through life as an ignoramus. I said I didn't care
how I went through life, and I had had enough of school.

She said that someday that would hurt me, and I replied
that I would no longer bank on "someday." She said I'd been

abandoned by God, and I replied no, it had been the other way around.

I now very often stood at the window, because in the building opposite ours lived a boy who also very often stood at the window, and flirted with me across the street. He was somewhat older than I, blond, delicate, and always very elegantly dressed. Sometimes he was picked up by a black limousine with a chauffeur and a Romanian flag on the mudguard. I found out that he was the son of the Romanian general consul, and that increased the excitement of flirting with him still further.

When I was not standing at the window, I roamed around the city with Elena. We still fooled around and behaved like children, but our ideas and observations were no longer so naïve.

One time I asked Elena if she believed in God. She said that depended on her mood, and sometimes she did, sometimes she didn't, but it was in any case more comfortable to believe in him.

Another time, when we met a man with the yellow star on his chest, I asked her what she thought about that.

She said she always felt like throwing up when she saw it, and the Germans were to blame, those stiff louts who had no business being in her country.

I asked her if her parents were also of that opinion. She answered that she didn't care what her parents' view was.

I said that was how it was with me, too.

Shortly thereafter I received a letter from my father, in which he told me that he considered my confirmation to be of the greatest importance.

I said to my mother: "Papa is crazy. He wants me to be confirmed. Not me!"

"If your father wishes it," she replied, "you will be confirmed."

I cried: "You don't seriously think that I'm suddenly going

to start studying with a Protestant pastor and then have him confirm me?"

The next day I received a letter from my mother:

A day comes for all my children when they receive a serious letter from me. This day has come for you, and the letter is a sign that you are now no longer entirely a child and I am very worried about you. It is possible that despite all my love I may not find the right tone to talk to my children, that has to do with my nervousness and my temperament. As your mother, I admit gladly and without shame my mistakes and omissions, but I ask in return that you do the same.

I'm sure that you are secretly more honest and critical with regard to yourself than you let on. It's impossible for such a young person to have more confidence in herself than in adults, who all say the same thing and are not unsympathetic or stupid. And it's impossible that you don't see that you can be master of your fate, which is not an easy one, only through strength, hard work, and decency, whereas with vanity, superficiality and moodiness you are making it so much worse that fate will become stronger than you are and shatter you. In this letter I also want to warn you against annoying your father. For if you continue to do that too long, we might lose him and thus the best person, our last protection, and the possibility of returning to Germany someday. I have known your father for twenty years now, and therefore I understand him a little better than you do. I know that he is the kindest, finest, and most patient person, but he also has a limit. He was very proud of you, had great plans for you, and wouldn't be able to get over the disappointment that you would cause him by being disrespectful to him, not wanting to go to school and, even more than Tina used to be, being against me more than with me. You might not notice it, and Papa might not show it, but inwardly something would be broken in him. And you can't know whether, discouraged, agonized, and psychologically overburdened, he might suddenly say: "Do what you want, I've done my duty to the utmost, but now I've had enough of struggling with you all the time, now I'm going to live my own life." And if it ever comes to that, then there will be nothing, nothing at all, that can be done about it. Then you will have lost him. Forever. Believe me, I know that for sure, because I too lost him by being unreasonable, selfish, and addicted to pleasure. I considered only what was good and easy for me. He worked, and I amused myself. He never said anything, but inwardly he was bitterly disappointed, and he no longer loved me as much as he had earlier. I could never get back what I had lost.

Papa worships duty, kindness and decency. Now you must, in one way or another, do your duty, and the harder it is for you, the better you will become, and I and all serious people will respect you. You must be decent and kind by helping us, who are suffering greatly, both inwardly and outwardly, as best you can. We all want to remain close together, survive this hard time, and not have to reproach ourselves later on for having failed. Let's badger ourselves, torment ourselves, be unhappy, but let's retain our morale. The reward will certainly come. The more effort we make, the more God will help us. When I was thinking only of myself, he abandoned me, but now that I recognize my mistakes and shortcomings, and am trying to change myself, he is helping me. Life is hard. That you have already had to learn that at such a young age should not harm you, but rather benefit you. Reflect and trust me and your father. Overcome yourself and go along with us. Schiller said: "Triumphing over oneself is the finest victory." That's what you have to do now. Fight everything that is bad in you and conquer it. I'm very sure that you find school disagreeable, and I remember very well how one feels about it when one is fifteen. But I am also sure that overcoming what we find disagreeable leads to satisfaction.

I did not agree with this letter. I found it laughable and impertinent. Let her become happy with her quotations from Schiller and with her God. In her case it had been going on for forty or more years and would probably never have changed if the Nazis hadn't laid into us, and she was demanding that at the age of fifteen I be strong, upstanding, serious, dutiful, helpful, kind, and so on. Why all this? And why should I trust her and Papa? I'd had enough. My mother was suffering, my father was tormenting himself, and I was supposed to master my fate. Not me!

My mother asked whether I had anything to say in response to her letter.

"No," I said. "Nothing at all."

On January 31, 1943, the German Sixth Army surrendered in Stalingrad. The BBC reported that there had been enormous losses at the front and massive bombing raids on German cities.

Angelika grabbed her cat Paul, who was lying on the windowsill, and danced on the table with him. She sang: "We're flying, we're flying, we're flying against Naziland, hurrah!"

But Else, who was just as happy as her daughter, immediately said: "Angeli, please, be careful! Don't show anyone how glad you are and don't blab! The war won't be over for quite a while yet, and we're still in danger, perhaps even greater danger. If the Germans start losing, they'll get even more ruthless. And besides, think of your poor father. He's also in danger now!"

Angelika sighed: "Of course I'm afraid for Papa and I don't want anything to happen to him, but what am I supposed to do? Cry because things are finally beginning to go badly for the Germans?"

Else looked at Angelika silently, almost anxiously. The girl was half a head taller than she herself was, but still very slender and delicate. Her face was that of a strikingly pretty child, but the expression in her eyes betrayed a precocious hardness and inapproachability that frightened her.

I'm going to have an even harder time with her than with the other two, Else thought, because she has neither Peter's capacity for love nor Bettina's willingness to sacrifice. Someday she'll stop at nothing.

Spring came.

Bettina had moved out of Oborishta Street and now lived with Mizo in a large furnished room with kitchen and bath privileges. She was already pregnant and was earning a little money by working part-time as a kind of secretary in Zvetan Taslakoff's export firm. Bulgaria had been thoroughly plundered and there were shortages of everything that one needed for everyday life. Bettina was already thinking of nothing but her child. How could it grow strong and healthy if she couldn't nourish herself properly, and how was she going to swaddle, dress, and wash it?

Erich sent one package after another, Wilma Taslakoff, who in the meantime had given birth to a son, gave her articles of clothing her child had grown out of, and Else scoured the city to find a little fruit and vegetables. Bettina hoarded everything like a squirrel and was delighted with each newly acquired diaper or bib.

Else was moved by her pregnant daughter and her marked maternal instinct. She recalled her own pregnancy during the First World War, during which she had experienced hardships and fears like those Bettina was experiencing now.

Bettina had never been much like her, and she had given her, if the same amount of love, much less attention than to her talented eldest and her peculiar youngest child. Now that she no longer shared the same apartment but rather the same experience with her daughter, and recognized herself in her concerned, loving motherliness, Bettina was the one closest to her, and her virtues—willingness to make sacrifices, loyalty, modesty—outweighed the attractions of her other children.

In May 1943, the battle of El-Alamein took place in North Africa and ended with Montgomery's breakthrough and the retreat of the German Afrika Korps. On the Eastern Front the Russians began a new offensive.

A Red Cross message came from Peter in Jerusalem: the page had been turned! He was doing exceptionally well. He was full of confidence and with her and his sisters with all his heart.

Bettina came to lunch in Oborishta Street almost every day. Else was occupied solely with providing her daughter with food that would strengthen her and that Maria, the new maid, cooked rather incompetently. Maria was a small, misshapen person whose only interesting aspect was her attacks of unmotivated flurries of activity, during which she swept through the room followed by the concerned Else and the frightened cat.

At the end of August, as they were sitting at the dining table, the sirens sounded for the first time. Angelika jumped up from her chair. Bettina laid both hands on her swollen belly. Else said: "That's all we need!" Maria rushed into the room and cried: "Alert!"

"What do we do now?" Bettina asked.

"Good question," Else replied.

The Bulgarian government had forgotten or prudently decided not to prepare the population for possible bombing raids. There were no public or private bomb shelters, no blackouts, no emergency services, no guidelines. People were left to find safety however and wherever they could.

Maria turned on the radio. For a minute there was an ominous silence, and then we were informed that a bomber squadron coming from the West had flown over the Bulgarian border and was heading for Sofia. The population was asked to keep calm and go into the cellar.

Angelika was trembling with fear, but she refused to go into the cellar, in which she would inevitably be buried under rubble. Else and Bettina, who shared her visions of horror, did not try to persuade her of the necessity of this questionable security measure, and all the more since the cellar was full of coal. The voice on the radio threateningly repeated the exhortation, and Maria, with a madwoman's obsession, shrieked: "I'm going up to the roof!"

"Idiot," Bettina cried, "the man said cellar, not roof!"

"I know," Maria laughed, "but I'm getting on the roof. I want to see the bombers."

She ran out the room, and Else tapped her forehead, stood up, and walked to the window. The street was empty, nobody there, just a few cars left abandoned at the curb. She thought: I never considered the possibility that we might be killed by our saviors rather than by our persecutors. What madness!

She returned to the table. Angelika was holding Paul in her arms, Bettina was still holding her belly.

"Children," Else said with a strained smile, "nothing is going to happen, they have more important things to do than bomb Sofia."

In this case she was right. After an eternity of about twenty minutes, the announcer's voice informed us that the bomber squadron had left Bulgarian airspace and flown on over the Romanian border. The radio then broadcast a triumphal victory march. The sirens signaled the all clear.

"Mummy," Angelika said, "I swear, I won't be able to stand that a second time."

But I stood it many times, all through September, October,

November, and half of December. At least three times a week, at precisely 1:30 P.M., there was an alert and then at 2 P.M. the all clear. They were American planes flying to Romania to bomb the Ploieşti oil fields there. My mother wondered whether she shouldn't delay lunch until 2 P.M., because as soon as the sirens sounded my throat seized up and my mouth became so dry that I could hardly swallow or move my tongue. I told my mother that it felt like my mouth was full of wood shavings and no matter what I did couldn't get another bite down. She said: "If you keep that up you'll never get your period," and was fully aware that that was not the reason. She had taken me to the doctor, who had examined me and determined that I was in perfect physical condition, and asked my mother whether I'd had a bad shock at some time.

"At least five hundred of them," I answered before she could get a word out, "not counting the alerts."

The doctor looked at me wide-eyed, and my mother quickly explained: "The child is oversensitive." That might have been the case, but it didn't make things any better.

Bettina had long since gotten used to the alerts. She no longer came to lunch so often, because her belly had become enormous and she didn't want to haul it the twenty minutes from the export firm to our house every day. But when she was there and the sirens sounded, she went on eating with stoic calm; after all, the baby had to be fed. My mother acted as though the alerts no longer concerned her, and every time Maria ran up to the roof and came back disappointed, because she never saw an airplane. I was as sick of the whole business as anyone could be, and wished that the Allies would hurry up. On the Eastern Front the Russians had already driven the Nazi gangs out of Kiev, and in North Africa the Germans were steadily retreating. But it was still a long way to Germany.

In the second half of December, the Americans went after a new target: Sofia.

Bettina had not come on that day, and at 1:30 P.M. there was no alert. But at 2 P.M. the sirens suddenly wailed, and that was so unusual that I immediately knew that something terrible was about to happen. My mother also made a strange face, went into the bedroom and got the big bag with our papers and the last jewelry that we had not yet sold.

I asked: "Why are you doing that?" And she said. "I don't know, either."

And then we heard for the first time that low, horrible droning in the air, and as it came nearer and the windowpanes started to rattle very softly, she shouted: "Put your coat on and come!" We already heard whistling and crackling as the German antiaircraft batteries began to fire with an awful racket, and we ran to the cellar, along with all the other residents of the building.

The cellar was divided into small compartments provided with latticed doors, in which the families kept their coal, and everyone dived into his cage, in which there was hardly any room. Those who had large stocks of coal crowded into the compartments of those who were not so abundantly provided, and we were among the latter. Suddenly there were seven of us in our coop, but whether seven or only two of us would be buried under the ruins of the building was no longer important. Outside and inside the scene was hellish, and I only hoped I would faint from fear. My mother held my hand, and her hand was as cold as mine was hot and damp.

At 3 P.M. the raid was over, and I threw up. My mother insisted that I lie down, and brought me a hot-water bottle. Then she immediately called the export firm and, when no one answered, Wilma Taslakova, whose apartment was in the same building. She answered and said that everything was all right. Bettina had been with her all during the bombardment and had now left. The center of the city had been hard hit, and she was worried about Mizo, who had not gone to the university that day, but instead remained at home. She would certainly soon call us.

Bettina, who could not be reached because she had no telephone in her apartment, called about 5 P.M. I heard my mother shriek, and when I ran into the room, she had already put down the receiver. Her face looked as if the other side were now paralyzed as well.

"Mummy, what is it?"

"Mizo . . . " she said.

"Mizo what?"

"Mizo was buried under the ruins. His uncle is operating on him right now. They don't know whether he'll make it."

Else hurried with Angelika straight across Sofia, because the hospital was at the other end of the city, almost in an outlying district. There was no public transportation, no taxis, no horse-cabs. In many parts of the city there was also no electricity. In the center, which they could not avoid on their route, all hell had broken loose: burning buildings, collapsed buildings, buildings whose tops had been blown off, black smoke, glass shards, piles of rubble, debris, craters, dead people, wounded people, people screaming, weeping, running amok, the crackling of the flames, the roar as parts of buildings crashed down, a small contingent of firemen and ambulances that were not up to dealing with the chaos.

"Come on!" Else cried every few steps, "hurry . . . we have to hurry! . . . hold the cloth over your nose and mouth . . . don't look around . . . watch out, for heaven's sake . . . stay in the middle of the street . . . ! We'll soon be there . . . "

It took them an hour and a half to reach the hospital. And there they found a chaos not unlike that in the streets.

"Ask about Mizo," Else shouted at Angelika, "about the nephew of Professor Stanishev, who has just been operated on!"

"Whom should I ask, Mummy?" They're just pushing people away!

Else blocked the way of a man in a blood-spattered gown. "Second floor, ward 22," he said, and hurried on.

It was a ward with at least thirty beds, from which were coming groans, wails, and gasps. In a corner, hunched over her belly, sat Bettina. She sat next to a bed on which there seemed to be nothing except a pile of grayish-brown blankets. Else ran to her, stroked her head, and said softly: "I'm here, my child, I'm here with you . . . "

Bettina didn't move. She stared at the bed, on which Else now saw Mizo's head, a tiny little head with a yellowish-green face covered with cement dust. His eyes were open, but he was not conscious. His teeth constantly clattered against one another, making the bed shake.

Suddenly Bettina began to talk, hastily, in a toneless voice: "He didn't go to the cellar . . . everyone who was in the cellar is dead. He was in the apartment, and when the building collapsed, part of the ceiling of the room remained hanging there . . . he was buried up to his neck in rubble, and I tried to dig him out of the ruins . . . with my hands . . . a few people helped me . . . and there was no ambulance. Someone called here, the hospital, and said that the professor's nephew was seriously injured, and then somebody came. His uncle operated on him immediately. His whole left side is kaput . . . his leg is broken in six places, his gall bladder and liver are bruised . . . one of his kidneys has already been removed . . . "

"He'll make it, Tina, he's young and strong and his uncle is the best surgeon in town."

"My poor baby," Bettina went on, "do you think anything has happened to him? The shock, you know . . . and nothing is left, not a diaper, not a bar of soap . . . "

Why does all this have to happen to my children, Else asked herself, why do they have to suffer so much? Why is their life being destroyed? I'd rather have to cope with anything, anything, anything, rather than my children's suffering! Isn't there some way of punishing me other than by destroying my children?

"Bettina," said Angelika, who up to that point had stood motionless and silent next to Else, "you can have some of my clothes to put on."

"Yes," Bettina said without standing up, "they'll fit me, for sure."

"You won't always have your belly."

"I wish I'd have it for a long time yet, so that the baby wouldn't be born into this misery."

Else looked helplessly from one of her daughters to the other.

And we older people, she thought, allow our children to be made unhappy, exposed to war, sent to war, killed . . .

We were back home by about 9 P.M. Kyril, Mizo's brother, who had gone to the hospital with his parents, had given us a ride in his car. He was a doctor and said it looked very bad for Mizo.

I was deadtired and couldn't get the terrible images of the destroyed and burning buildings, of the dead and injured, out of my head. I just wanted to sleep and lay down on the bed fully dressed. My mother came and asked if I'd lost my mind, going to bed with all my clothes on. I said I was afraid to get undressed, because there would surely be another alert.

She said: "Angeli, please, we can't live constantly expecting another bombing raid. Think about your sister, how incredibly brave she's being . . . "

"Yes," I interrupted, "and think about Mizo, how incredibly kaput he is."

"You always have to make things more difficult for people than they already are," she sighed and began to get undressed. She was in her underwear when the sirens began to wail and the electricity went off. I jumped out of bed and stood there, shivering all over.

People were clattering down the stairs and shouting. Doors slammed, and someone yelled: "Candles out!"

It was a clear night, and the moon was almost full; there was a spooky light in the room. My mother pulled on her fur coat over her underwear, grabbed the big bag, and said, "Come on, Angeli!"

Maria was standing at the door in her nightgown; she laughed madly and said she was staying in the apartment, because from the window she could see the bombs falling.

The cellar was packed full of people and pitch-black. We stood somewhere jammed between human bodies and piles of coal. One woman was praying, a child was crying, and all the rest were silent. They were probably just like me: their mouths had gone dry, they could no longer move their tongues.

Then came the first explosion, a second, and then a third. One followed another, faster and faster, and it was as if the world were breaking to pieces, with crazy thudding and clattering, splintering and whistling. The building began to shake, and then to sway like a ship on high seas. We stood there, up to our ankles in coal, while other objects stored in the cellar flew around our heads. People were shouting, wailing, praying. It was inconceivable that we would ever get out of this inferno alive, since the building was about to collapse any second.

My mother grabbed my arm and began to pull me toward the door: "We have to get out of here, Angeli, come on, come outside, quickly!"

In the doorway we collided with a man who was coming into our cellar from the street, seeking shelter. He was carrying a flashlight, and I could see that he was a German soldier.

"Goddamn it," he shouted at my mother, "where the hell do you think you're going?"

"Out!" she cried.

"Do you want to get yourself and the kid killed?"

He took me by the shoulder, pulled me back into the cellar and took me in his arms.

"Calm down," he said when he felt me trembling, "just be calm . . . it'll soon be over."

And in the arms of this unknown German soldier I calmed down. I felt his hands on my back, holding me tight, his breath on my forehead, the rough material of his coat on my cheek, and I closed my eyes.

I don't know how much longer the attack lasted. Perhaps ten minutes, perhaps half an hour. When it grew quiet, the sirens sounded the all clear, and the light went on, he let go of me and disappeared.

I never saw his face, I could only feel his warmth, his hands, his breath, and the rough material of his coat.

After the massive raid, which the Americans had carried out with great accuracy, all of Sofia was in flames and normal life came to a standstill. It was unlikely that the city would begin to function and people to go about their everyday business again once the rubble was cleared up. All the more because these two raids would surely not be the last. Two years earlier, Bulgaria, in the proud certainty that it was allied with a victorious power, had declared war on England and America, and did not count on things going so badly for them. The residents of Sofia fled in all directions, by the hundreds of thousands.

Elsa stood in the cold, drafty apartment. The telephone no longer worked, most of the windows were broken, a bomb had landed in the courtyard and left a deep crater, the ground was covered with shrapnel. We escaped this time by the skin of our teeth, she thought.

"I'm not staying another day in Sofia," Angelika said, "I have no intention of letting myself be buried in rubble, not me! I've had enough!"

"And where should we go?"

"I don't care."

About 10 A.M. Dimiter Lingorsky appeared like a rescuing angel.

"I was worried about you," he said.

Else and Angelika threw their arms around him.

A man! Thank God, a man! He would know what to do, he would straighten out this dreadful mess, he would organize things. He had no back to his head and he was no genius, but he had a heart and practical sense. Else's affection and relief knew no bounds.

Dimiter took Angelika, who thought every unusual sound was an air-raid siren, to the home of his brother and his wife, and accompanied Else to the hospital. Mizo had survived the night, but he was no better. Bettina sat next to him on a folding cot that had been brought in for her, and was eating cornmeal mush. Else gave her the two apples she had found in the kitchen and Bettina hid them under her pillow.

She said that the following day the hospital would be evacuated to Kjustendil, a small city in the provinces, and that she would, of course, go along. Else thought that was a good solution. She couldn't be separated from Mizo now, and she no longer had an apartment anyway, and in the hospital at least she was under medical supervision.

Else went with Dimiter to see Wilma Taslakova, who gave her a suitcase with clothing and food that would keep, and she returned to the hospital with it. Wilma said that she was going to leave Sofia that afternoon and go to hole up with relatives of her husband in a small town. For God's sake, Else should also get out of Sofia!

She picked up Angelika. Dimiter's brother Mirtsho was an active communist, small, robust, with an intelligent face and a black beard. His wife Stella, in contrast, was a buxom, heavily made-up person who seemed to prefer a solid bourgeois life. Her black-and-white polka dot dress was made of silk and her apartment was full of plush and bric-a-brac. She served Turkish coffee and slatko to her guests and said, in a shrill voice, that in her street two buildings had been destroyed and twenty people killed. She intended to leave the city as soon as possible and go to Bukhovo, a village not far from Sofia where her husband, Mirtsho, had good friends. If Else didn't know where to go, she continued, she should come along, she would certainly be able to find a safe place to stay for herself and for Angelika.

"Oh, yes," Angelika cried, "please, Mummy!"

And so it happened that on December 24 Else, along with Angelika and the three Lingorskys, set out on foot for Buhovo.

We walked through ankle-deep mud on an endless trek— men, women, children, old people, bearing bundles, baskets, bags, little suitcases. Some people pulled a small cart behind them, others pushed baby carriages.

The weather was the most unfavorable we could have had for this walk, with the temperature around freezing and a uniformly grayish-white sky so deep that one couldn't tell where it stopped and the grayish-white fields on both sides of the road began. If it now began to rain or snow, we would be lost.

I'd had to leave my cat Paul with Maria in Sofia, and that was a heartbreaking moment that I'd already often experienced. My mother said we'd have someone bring him to us, but I no longer believed such statements. I wailed all the way to the edge of the city.

Dimiter had tied a little suitcase to my back, and my mother, in her fur coat and with a kerchief on her head, carried a bag in each hand. Stella, in a black Persian lamb coat and matching cap, her face carefully made up as if she were going to a reception, and the two men, Dimiter and Mirtsho, were burdened like pack animals.

"God, we look funny," I said.

"Very funny," my mother replied, "pull your hood up, all we need is for you to catch cold! Are your feet wet?"

"No, Mummy, I'm wearing my galoshes."

I didn't have wet feet, but I had a cramp in my lower abdomen, a strange, unfamiliar feeling that I didn't tell my mother about. She would have been capable of turning back.

Because of the mud, we made slow progress, but we had certainly already walked eight kilometers. It was another twenty to Buhovo.

"Today we'll go as far as Vrazhdebna," Dimiter said. "In two hours it will be dark, and then we won't be able to go any farther anyway."

"And how far is it?" I asked.

"About four or five kilometers."

I was now very uneasy, because suddenly I had the feeling that not my feet, but my knee-length woolen underwear was wet. I couldn't understand how that had happened, and decided to ask my mother.

She stared at me, taken aback, and then said: "Typical! And now what are we going to do?"

"What do you mean, what should we do, then?"

"Child, as I see it, you've begun your period, today of all days."

My mother consulted with the two men and Stella and then disappeared with her and with me behind a bush at the roadside. As luck would have it, one of them had a large handkerchief, and the other a sewing basket with scissors. As they were cutting up the kerchief, they talked about my menstruation, which had certainly been triggered by the shock of the bombing raid.

"Well," my mother said, "it was high time. The child has already turned sixteen, after all."

"Just today," I said, "and as for the shock, it was the five hundred thousandth."

When I saw my blood, I was overcome by a mixture of pride and disgust.

"Now I can have children, right?" I asked.

"God forbid!" my mother cried.

We spent that night in the village of Vrazhdebna, and found a place to stay in one of the small, comfortless houses. My mother and I even got a room with a fairly large bed, with one paillasse to serve as a mattress and another as a blanket. She immediately took off her coat, skirt, and shoes and got into bed.

"Let's hope we don't have to share it with bedbugs and fleas," she said.

I looked down at her, and suddenly I felt that I could under no circumstances lie down next to her. It was such an unprecedented and unexpected feeling that I didn't know how to explain it to myself, much less to her.

She asked: "Do you have to go outside once more?"

"No, I've already been."

"Well, then, hurry up, you must be more dead than alive."

Slowly I took off my coat and shoes and sat down on the bed.

"How can both of us lie there?" I asked.

"As we've been lying for the past two years."

"Those were always double beds."

"Angelika, we're not in a hotel where we could ask for a room with a double bed. Be happy that we've gotten a bed at all, and even a fairly wide one."

She moved over a bit.

I was desperate. I couldn't overcome my resistance to lying down next to her. I could have lain down next to Stella, and perhaps even one of the farm girls, but not next to my mother.

"I can't do it," I said.

"What can't you do?"

"Lie down next to you."

"You know, Angelika, you've always been a very peculiar child, but what you're doing now is simply abnormal. Can you explain what's wrong with you?"

"No."

I was able to explain it to myself only many years later, and even today I don't know whether my reaction was normal or, as my mother said, abnormal. It must have been directly connected with my first menstruation. Now I could have children, now I was a woman, and my life, which had, for better or for worse, coalesced with that of my mother, belonged to me alone. It was not a gradual process of detachment, but rather an abrupt break that separated me from the person whom I had most unconditionally loved, on whom I had been totally dependent for sixteen years. There was no hostility, as in the case of my sister, nor even resentment; there was only the unconscious impulse to free myself from her and thus no longer have to suffer under her. Because loving her meant suffering.

My mother had been looking at me the whole time, annoyed and aghast. She didn't understand, I didn't understand. The break had come too abruptly, too violently.

"Do what you want," she finally said, "stay sitting here, lie down on the floor, stand on your head—I'm too tired to cope with this silliness." She turned over on her other side.

I lay down next to her, but in the opposite direction—with my head at her feet.

The next day we arrived in Buhovo. It lay at the foot of a forested range of hills, about a hundred houses, randomly scattered over the area, without trees or even connecting streets, only muddy paths that didn't always go as far as any given house. Slapped together from clay, these houses had tiny windows, small doors, flat roofs, and uneven walls that were neither stuccoed nor painted. Each house stood in a courtyard that had nothing to offer other than an oven for baking bread, a wooden shack in which the toilet, in the form of a small hole, was located, a shed for the sheep, and a vicious dog.

In the middle of the village there was a large, unplanned square with a spring, from which water was drawn in fat-belied earthenware jugs and carried home on long poles slung over the shoulder. There was also a school to which one could go when one wanted to or was not otherwise needed, a tavern in which rakia and slivovitz were dispensed, and a church, in which a grubby pope with a matted knot of hair performed his services.

"It's a poor village," Mirtsho needlessly observed, "most of the villages in this area are very poor. It's a scandal, the way our farmers are exploited."

"What do they live on, actually?" Else asked.

"They have a few corn and wheat fields and sheep. They're wonderful people, these Bulgarian farmers, as generous as they are poor."

Else and Angelika found lodging with a family of eight consisting of five sons, aged six to eighteen, a twenty-two-year-old daughter, a father, and a tiny, bent grandmother. They lived in two small rooms and a still smaller anteroom with an open fireplace where the cooking was done.

"This is entirely impossible," Else said, "we can't take one of these people's two rooms. Where are they going to sleep?"

The family stood around the newcomers, expectantly smiling, the young ones with broad, Slavic faces, light-blue eyes, and straw-blond hair, the father, a good-looking man with a bushy, salt-and-pepper mustache, the grandmother with a kerchief pulled back and a thin, gray braid that lay on her back like a sleeping snake.

Suddenly Jonka, the daughter and supreme commander, stepped forward and said: "Our house is your house. You will have the nicer, larger room, we all sleep in the other one anyway, where there are two large beds. Here you have a stove and a bed with a mattress and we will give you another one. Also a table and two chairs. Welcome to our home."

Else hugged Jonka, and Jonka hugged Angelika, the grandmother giggled with delight, the father said to his sons: "Hurry up, get to work, everything has to be ready before it gets dark here."

Everything was ready before dark, and there was also a piece of sheep's cheese, two large crocks of water, and wood for the stove. Jonka lighted the stove, swept the bumpy clay floor, put coarse but clean sheets on the bed, brought in a tin washbasin, earthenware plates, and wooden spoons. She said to Else: "From now on you needn't worry about anything," and to Angelika: "You can go out only if I accompany you, otherwise you'll get a bad reputation."

Else laughed at the look on her daughter's face, and delighted in the aromatic, homemade bread. She felt comfortable and warm in this little room with the crackling stove, among these simple people with big hearts.

Over the following days Dimiter brought her a cart full of the things from Sofia that were most important to her: books, writing materials, the radio, two large suitcases with clothes, coffee, and money from Zvetan Taslakoff's export firm. It was only half of what she was supposed to receive according to the contract. Else was not surprised. She'd always sensed that she couldn't count on Zvetan, who was prejudiced against her. What were they going to live on, if he kept turning down the tap?

She shouldn't worry, Dimiter said to console her, there wasn't much left to buy anyway, and there was still plenty of money to buy a handful of white beans.

It was not hard for Else to get used to Buhovo. She read, wrote letters, not knowing whether they would ever reach their addressees, listened to music on the radio, and in the evenings, to the BBC. Often she sat with the family, watched Jonka and the grandmother spinning thread, and talked with the father and his sons in her inadequate Bulgarian.

None of them ever made fun of her. They treated Else with respect and affection, called her "Mummy." They knew no more about her than that she came from Germany, was married to Dimiter Lingorsky and had three children, and that her son lived in a distant country. And they asked no further questions. She was Mummy, a friend, who shared their joys and concerns. They never exchanged a sharp word, never an unfriendly look, never a comment that implied that this long-term visit, for which they sacrificed a room, washed laundry, provided firewood and water, was not welcome to them. When there was a piece of meat in the white beans or in the cornmeal mush, a dish of it was brought to them as a matter of course. And if they ran out of ink or sugar, heaven and earth were moved in order to find these rare commodities.

In a later letter to Peter Else wrote: "We lived in a village for nine months, ten people—after the eldest son got married, eleven—and in the winter also the lambs, in two small rooms and another even smaller one. It was very dirty and extremely primitive, no running water, hardly any furniture, and we did our cooking on an alcohol stove. But since I am always much happier and more peaceful in the country than in the city, and prefer simple people to the so-called 'fine' ones, I did not suffer from this . . . "

For me, Buhovo was a revelation. Never before and never afterward have I been closer to life than I was there, never have I felt so free, so secure, so mentally and physically healthy, so lightheartedly happy. Buhovo taught me what life is in its original form, what people who live in accord with their hearts can be. Never before and never afterward have I experienced such selfless generosity as was shown us by these poor farmers, never seen such a noble attitude towards strangers about whom they knew nothing other than that we needed help, never such profound and genuine sympathy. I saw the brothers again two years ago in Buhovo. The eldest, Vassil, still remembered after forty-six years the exact date of my brother's death, which he'd learned from my mother later on, during one of her visits to Sofia. When he said, "He was Mummy's only son!" he had tears in his eyes.

I have met countless people in my life, good, helpful, warmhearted people, but I have never met another Vassil or Jonka. She was a loving sister, an ungrudging friend, a strict teacher, and a courageous defender. We were foreigners, we lived in their house, and therefore it was for them self-evident that they would assume responsibility and duties for us—not out of calculation or ostentation, but solely out of the need to help us and spare us unpleasantness. They were people who acted with an innate sense of tact and an unfailing instinct for what was right and decent. I realized all that only later on; at the time I simply had the feeling that I had landed on an island where nothing bad, nothing mean, nothing underhanded could happen to one. Everything was clear, simple, genuine. I, who had constantly been ill, struggled with fears and idiosyncrasies, been disgusted by little things, and been closed to everyone, suddenly became both outwardly and inwardly a stable, happy person who loved life. Whether it rained or stormed, whether we ate white beans at noon and again in the evening, whether I had to go to the outhouse on icy nights or had to stomp through the mud to get water, whether my clothes were too tight and my hair got wet and stringy, whether a fly was floundering about in the yoghurt or little Gosho's hand, with which he passed me a piece of bread, was stiff with dirt, I could not be dislodged from my cheerful equanimity. I looked like blooming life, and I felt that way, too.

"Angeli," Jonka said one day, "this can't go on like this any more. The men are staring at you. I'm going to sew you a brassiere."

Who would have thought just a year earlier that I would need a bra and would be stared at by men? And who would ever have thought that I would find Boris precisely in Buhovo and experience with him the first love of my life?

Boris was a man who was eight years older than I, a law student in his last semester, the son of a retired general who, like us, had fled the bombs with his family. Boris was smart and gentle, he spoke German and French, played the piano and the accordion, had a strikingly high forehead, a large, violet-colored mouth, and a good figure, which to my dismay he did not show off as well as he might have because his posture was poor. Boris fell in love with me, and after I had come to terms with his poor posture and the old sheepskin jacket that he wore all winter, I fell in love with him, too.

I've forgotten many events, many men in the course of my life, but Boris has remained intact on the film of my memory. I still see the broad sweep of his brows, the thick eyelashes, the bewildered, amused, tender look in his dark eyes; hear his deep, soft voice, his slow laugh, the accent with which he spoke German, the melodious "Angelina" with the emphasis on the third syllable; feel his beautiful hands that were so soft and so discreet until one day he rightly boxed my ear, and then I felt their power. Could I ever forget the first kiss, the first time he said "I love you," the first recognition of the yearning demand in a man's eyes, the first discovery of my power over him?

We were inseparable, and since we had nothing else to do, loved each other from morning to evening—for eight months.

"Angelina," Jonka said one day, "this can't go on like this. People are talking about you and Boris, you're going to lose your good reputation if you go alone with him outside the village."

"But we don't have a room of our own!"

"Good Lord, that would be even worse! So either you get engaged to him, or this has to stop."

"We're already engaged."

"Well, then, that's different!"

Jonka informed Buhovo that I was engaged to the general's son. Buhovo was delighted.

"Angelika," my mother shortly afterward, "please don't do anything stupid with Boris."

I guessed that when she talked about stupidity she was talking about THE stupidity, the one that produces children. But I had no idea how children were produced, and perhaps this was time to learn something about it.

I asked: "What kind of stupidity?"

"Don't pretend to be dumber than you are," she said.

"I swear to you, Mummy, I don't know anything about this stupidity."

"So much the worse! Then it can happen without you even knowing it."

"Boris says that I'm much too young and the times too dangerous."

"He is a very decent, sensible boy. I trust him."

I asked a farm girl to explain it to me. Her explanation was so graphic that I was scared of Boris for a week.

He asked: "What's wrong with you, anyway?" I answered: "Svetlana explained everything to me, and I will never get married."

He laughed and said: "I just had to fall in love with a child!"

My annoyance at this remark dissipated my fear of him. I'd show him that I was no child. But the highly decent, sensible boy never used my demonstrations to take advantage of me.

Kyustendil, the small city to which the hospital was evacuated, along with Mizo and Bettina, was heavily bombed. The

Bulgarians seem to have overlooked the fact that the city was a rail junction and therefore a potential target for the Americans. Else set out the following day. The birth of the child was in any case imminent, and she wanted to be with her daughter when it came.

The trip lasted twelve hours. Else arrived in Kyustendil exhausted. Bettina had rented a room for her in a private home. She herself was still staying in the hospital. She spent all day in the ward where Mizo lay with eleven other patients, and slept at night in a small room in which a cot had been set up for her. Since the hospital's staff was too small, she took care not only of her husband but also of a few other patients who had no relatives nearby.

Mizo was doing better, but when Else saw her daughter, she was shocked. She'd had her hair cut short, and that made her pale face look at first glance very young, but when one looked more closely, the faint lines of premature decline could already be seen. She was still wearing the same dress that she'd had on two months earlier during the bombing raid on Sofia.

"It's the only one that can still be let out," she said, "I can't get into Wilma's dress anymore."

"You have to spare yourself, Tina, you need your strength for the birth and the baby."

A nurse had told Else that Bettina was a heroine and a saint. During the bombing raid on Kyustendil she had not left the ward. They had all run to the cellar, but she had lain herself over her husband in order to protect him from falling rubble.

"She shouldn't talk such nonsense," Bettina said gruffly, "heroine, saint! Was I supposed to lie there helpless and let his face be destroyed too?"

She's the best, Else thought, she's Hans in every way. He would have done the same, and she, his daughter, doesn't even know that he exists.

A week after Else's arrival Bettina began to have labor

pains. They lasted for hours, then let up, came back, reached a level that Bettina seemed unable to bear. She who had never shown physical or psychological pain in front of others, screamed until her voice broke and she could only whimper.

"I can't stand it anymore, Mummy," she whispered, "and the baby can't either. It has to come out! Why doesn't it come out?"

The midwife patted her cheek: that was always how it was with a first birth, she said consolingly, and for some women it's even worse.

Else ordered her to get the doctor immediately.

He diagnosed a breech position and asked Else to leave the room. Her panic was infectious, and Bettina now needed all her strength and concentration.

Else was glad to be sent out of the room. Bettina's pain and her cries were like torture for her. She walked down to the farthest corner of the corridor, saw a bundle of dirty linen, sat down on it and buried her face in her hands: "Why can't anything ever go easily for my children?" she asked herself.

The baby was born about an hour later. "A boy," the doctor shouted to Else, "as big and stubborn as a calf!"

Bettina and her newborn were taken back to the little room where she slept. There she lay with her son in her arms and tenderly stroked his black-haired little head with her fingertips. She no longer had enough strength even to smile. Else sat beside her and had to struggle to keep back her tears. Her first grandchild, her daughter was a mother. And no pretty little jacket for the baby, no decent nightgown for Bettina, no nutritious food, no flowers, and all the people close to her who might have been able to share in her joy were far away, unreachable, or dead. Poor little thing, so terribly young and so terribly brave.

A few days later Bettina got up and divided her day between her husband and her child. A gray veil had come over the pupil and iris of her right eye. The scar that the tuberculosis had left had broken open again during the difficult birth, and Bettina discovered that she was now blind in that eye.

"It's not the end of the world," she said to her weeping mother, "I still have the other eye and my son, too."

He was given the name André.

In the meantime the Russians had reached the former border of Poland, and in March the Ukraine was in their hands again.

"Mummy," I said, "now it's going fast! I think the war will soon be over."

She nodded and smiled. She had an absent, blissful look on her face, as if the war were already over and we were on the way to seventh heaven.

I never failed to listen the news on the BBC with her. Now that I'd broken away from her and made myself independent, this half-hour was our strongest bond. That and the subsequent conversations about the great day of our liberation. Simply wonderful things would follow it: seeing Peter again—that was always first—the immediate re-establishment of contact with my father—we hadn't heard anything from him for months—a speedy departure from Bulgaria—with Bettina, Mizo and little André, of course—and the free, secure, happy life that we would all then live together.

"But where, Mummy?" I asked.

"Where would you like to go?"

"I don't know, I know only Germany and Bulgaria."

"Would you like to go back to Germany? To your father?"

"To Papa, yes, but to Germany . . . "

"Well, we'll see. We're not that far yet."

Sometimes I felt almost afraid of the day of our liberation. We'd already invested so much, and I'd forgotten how to think about the future. For me, only the present still counted, and the present was Buhovo and Boris, love and springtime, the meadow to which I accompanied Angel with the flock of sheep, the convent and the wooded range of hills to which I hiked with Boris, the springs where I drew water with Jonka and joked with the farm girls; it was Vassil's engagement to Mara, the weddings at which I danced the choro in a circle with the villagers, the birth of twins in the Andreovs' house and the burial of the 102-year-old grandmother Zanka; it was the fresh-baked bread that Jonka took out of the oven, the first cowslips in the meadow where I lay with Boris, the lambs that were born; it was the Easter holiday, the highest holiday of the year, for which the whole little house and all its inhabitants had to be scrubbed, eggs had to be decorated, sheep slaughtered, and new clothes sewn. On that holiday we ate and drank and danced and greeted one another with the words, "Christ is risen—He is truly risen."

I was completely happy in this present, and the future, no matter how beautifully we imagined it, aroused my distrust.

"What do you think," I asked Boris, "how will it be after the war?"

"Horrible," he said, "we'll have the Russians here."

"Nonsense, what would they be doing here?"

"Occupying us, beating communism into us."

"But after the war there won't be any more occupation."

"Angelina, I love you very much, but you're abysmally stupid."

In June, D-Day came, the Allied landing and invasion of Normandy. Winston Churchill gave a speech. My mother hugged and kissed the radio.

The next day a policeman went through Buhovo and sealed all the radios. Ours as well. We could listen only to Radio Sofia.

My mother sat slumped on bed, with an unhappy look on her face. For the first time it occurred to me that she'd lost a great deal of weight and was no longer curvy at all. Her hair was more gray than brown, and her fingers looked slightly hooked. Her face, still heavily tanned because she often sat in the sun, was flat and taut on the right side because of the paralysis, and drooping on the left side. Despite the damage, it was not an ugly face, only an infinitely sad one.

"Mummy," I said, "you've gotten so thin."

"Well, finally! I was fat long enough!"

"Is something wrong with your hands?"

"Probably arthritis, that happens to you when you get old."

It seemed to me that it was more difficult for her to speak clearly than it had been earlier.

"But you're not sick?"

"I'm exhausted."

I went to the radio, turned the knob, and broke the seal.

"Angeli, for God's sake, you've broken the seal."

"That's what I meant to do. No one is going to take away your last joy. I've had enough of this swinishness!"

Three days later the same policeman made another round through the village to make sure that the seals were intact everywhere. I was very scared and at the same time annoyed.

"Who did this?" he asked.

"The Holy Spirit," I said.

"Fine, Missy, then you'll get to know him at the police station." He stamped furiously out of the room.

I received a summons to report to the police station, which was located in the schoolhouse. My mother was beside herself with anxiety: "I know you did it only for me," she said, "but it was really very thoughtless of you. Now, in the last weeks, you've put everything in jeopardy."

Jonka could not be prevented from accompanying me to the police station. In front of the door stood a long line of farmers who had evidently committed similar offenses against the authorities.

"Let little Angelika go ahead," Jonka commanded, "if she isn't home quickly, her mother will go mad with fear."

They were only too glad to let me go first.

"What have you done," they asked.

"That doesn't concern you," Jonka said, "is one of you already inside there?"

"No, we've already been waiting for half an hour."

Jonka took me by the hand, opened the door without knocking first, and walked in with me. Four men, two of them in police uniforms, stared at us. One of them, in civilian clothing, a thickset, brutal-looking fellow, sat behind a table.

"What does this mean?" he shouted at us. "Just coming in here like that!"

"When we're summoned, we come," Jonka declared. "Here's the notice, and this is the Germantsche—"little German"—who accidentally broke the seal on the radio."

"Accidentally, ha!" the fellow said, and looked me up and down, "how does one do something like that accidentally?"

"Haven't you ever broken something accidentally?" Jonka asked.

"Will you keep your big mouth closed? I'm talking to the Germantsche." He reached under the table and suddenly had a wire in his hand: "Do you know what this is, Germantsche?"

"A wire."

"An electrically charged wire. Will you accidentally hold it in your hand?"

I was terribly afraid of electric shocks, and he saw that. He laughed, looked me up and down again, and said: "Pretty girl, the Germantsche," and then raised his voice: "The next time, I swear you'll hold the wire until you're black. Get out!"

They forgot to seal the radio again, and I asked my mother: "Well, wasn't that worth it?"

"Angeli," she said, "please be careful. They're still in power and we're still in danger."

"Someone will always be in power and think up new disgraces."

She looked at me and shook her head: "Child," she said, "how can one be so negative at your age?"

In mid-August Else went again to Kyustendil. Bettina was now living with her child and husband in a private room near the hospital. Mizo still had to go to the hospital every other day for outpatient treatment, and he was thin, weak, and careworn: "It's not getting any better," he said. "The game's over."

Bettina said nothing, and Else tried to encourage Mizo: "That's nonsense, Mizo. You were more dead than alive when they pulled you out of the rubble, and now look at you! So you're going to limp for a while and feel a little miserable, but if your uncle says that you're going to be fully functional and healthy again . . . "

"Let it go, Mummy," Bettina interrupted, "he thinks only of himself and likes to wallow in his suffering."

Mizo made a scornful grimace, and Bettina pressed her lips together in the old familiar stubborn expression. She was now wearing one of Wilma's dresses, which was too long and too wide for her, and made a gaunt, careworn impression like that of her husband. Only when she turned to her son was her face transfigured to radiate joy and warmth.

André was a strong, very pretty boy with a shock of black hair, dark brown, lively eyes, and dimples in his plump cheeks. He balanced out the misery of his parents by having an enormous amount of character and blooming good health.

"You've got to stop nursing him now," Else said, "he'll suck the last strength out of your body."

"The main thing," Bettina replied, "is that he's doing well."

"We won't be able to protect him against what's coming," Mizo said.

"What's coming?" Else asked.

"The Russians."

They were already in Romania, and Else, although she counted the Russians among her liberators, became uneasy. She decided to return with Angelika to Buhovo as quickly as possible, because as a German citizen, the girl might now be in danger. On the way back they joined the exodus of many Germans who were leaving the sinking ship as fast as they could.

From Buhovo, where it was still calm, fortunately, she wrote the following letter to Bettina:

My dear little Tina, I'm writing to you with a pencil, because I'm sitting by my pond again. It's not as beautiful as the river where you are, but there's still water and sun and a blue sky without a cloud, for days now. And at night the moon, and all that we can now suddenly enjoy without the years-long fear that has already become our second (perhaps even our first) nature! Can you grasp it? I can't! It's still as if I were dreaming, during the day I wander around like a sleepwalker and at night I sit up in the bed wide awake with excitement.

Well, my little Tina, our departure was very hard for me, and I constantly think about you, even more than about your sweet baby, because you are after all a little closer to me. My beloved, how are you? Just don't worry—you're prettier than ever before. No, pretty isn't the right word.

The love and kindness in your face makes you almost beautiful, and it's a beauty that never goes away. You don't want to hear such things, I know, and I'm going to stop now. I'm consoled only by the idea that I will soon come back. I want to wait a while to see what happens, because we have to be very careful so far as Angeli is concerned. She has her German passport, but I'm afraid that she now needs a special residency permit. In addition, it's still not clear whether German civilians and the embassy will leave the country. If that should happen, she would be in an extremely critical situation, and then Dimiter will have to adopt her. But I hope and believe that that won't happen.

Diplomatic relations between Bulgaria and Germany haven't been broken off, there's only a state of neutrality. However, the wind is now blowing strongly to the left and one can't tell whether the neutrality will continue. Yesterday, for example, we were listening to the news on Radio Sofia in French, English, and Russian! German is dead and now pops up only in hit songs, because if they stopped playing them, they'd probably have to go off the air for lack of "Allied" records. Yes, indeed, one always has to take precautions.

Angeli went to Sofia with Dimiter and Boris for a day, and was very enthusiastic about her excursion. The destruction was not so catastrophic, she says. She dined in the Hotel Bulgarie at lunch and later had ice cream in the Café Royal, and after nine months of village life for her that was the great, wide world. She also visited Captain Dahle, and she says he couldn't believe his eyes, which I can easily imagine, because she has now really become a fully developed, very pretty girl. Apart from that, Dahle, the poor fellow, will also now have to leave, and thus the last possibility of contacting Papa will be lost. On the other hand, it occurred to me last night that we are now free to rejoin Peter, and that was such a happy idea that I awakened Angeli and spoke with her about it. One grasps the situation only gradually, sees the great possibilities that are opening up, the new problems that are emerging. It has all gone so fast and is still so new.

My trip back was very eventful. The train was crowded, and I was afraid that we'd have to stand in the corridor all night. But sometimes I fall on my feet just by luck! I got into a compartment in which a young woman, a student from Paris who has been living with her mother in Bulgaria for the past four years, very charmingly gave me her seat. Then we were sitting more on top of one another rather than beside one another, nine adults and a child, including two German ladies who had fled Varna. They told me what had happened: all the Germans, whether civilian or military, left the city in haste, leaving all their baggage behind, and didn't know where to go. They were trying to reach the Bulgarian border before it was closed, which apparently is imminent. The German fleet stationed in Varna was scuttled. The train, I later learned, was full of German officers and their wives and children. My heart was heavy when I saw the officers, unarmed and completely distraught. It was an uncomfortable but very interesting trip. One of the German ladies fainted, and two Bulgarian women felt ill. All that in my compartment. One of them groaned, the other vomited out the window, and the third was halfway brought around with cognac and eau de cologne. I dozed on a seat with the little French student for only about three hours, and was nonetheless not tired, I'm no longer tired at all, it's as if I were drunk and not yet capable of forming a clear idea—except this one: our hour has come, we've survived, and we're free! I thank God . . .

On September 5, 1944, Russia declared wear on Bulgaria. The population was thrown into panic. The rumor was that if the Soviets marched in as a military power, the worst would have to be expected.

My mother burned my German passport and told Jonka, Vassil, and the rest of the family that I was not a "Germantsche" but a Jew, a racially persecuted person who had had to flee Germany with her and Bettina. Her eighty-year-old mother had been deported to a concentration camp, and her son was in Palestine.

I don't know how much of all that our farmers understood. At that point they probably hadn't yet heard about the atrocities committed by the Germans, but that didn't prevent them from being appropriately upset, lamenting our fate with us, and rejoicing in our salvation.

We had nothing to fear from the Russians, she emphasized, they were good people. They had already once liberated the Bulgarians from Turkey, and now they were liberating them from the Germans.

The good news that I was not a "Germantsche" but instead an "Evretsche"—a young Jew—rapidly spread through Buhovo, and many people came to express their surprise at my metamorphosis and to celebrate it. However, there was still another and better reason to celebrate, and that was that in only four days the Bulgarians had made peace with the Russians and thus avoided the apocalypse of an armed invasion.

From one day to the next the people switched sides: Germany is dead, long live the Soviet Union! The government was overthrown, its members killed or incarcerated in camps and prisons, and some of their family members, fellow travelers, and supporters met the same fate; in the haste, many thousands of them fell victim to doubts or errors. One saw more and more red, in both the literal and figurative senses of the word. On the radio, Russian marches and songs were played. People raised clenched fists instead of raising their arms in salute. They remembered with emotion the Big Brother who had already once freed them from the yoke of foreign domination, namely from the Turks, and with whom they shared the Slavic race, the Slavic language, and the Slavic soul. What was more obvious than now to share its ideological principles as well? In Buhovo jubilation, excitement, and gaiety prevailed.

The partisans, of whom there was suddenly an abundance, came down from the hills and were received with pride and joy. Almost every family had a partisan to whom they were closely or distantly related, and if not, one with whom they were at least friends. There was singing and dancing. My mother and I were invited to every party, because after all, we were Jews, persecuted people, who had been eagerly awaiting liberation just as they had.

"Do you think they were really waiting for it?" I asked my mother.

"People are always waiting for something, and when it's presented to them as what they've been waiting for, then they have in fact waited for it."

"But that's all crazy!"

"Crazy or not, in any case it's lucky for us!"

Overnight, Boris had left Buhovo with his parents and returned to Sofia. The little, excited village was an unsafe place for a general of the former Fascist army, even if he was retired.

"We'll see each other in Sofia, then," I'd said to Boris as he was leaving. "No, Angelika, we'd better not do that. It's too dangerous for your family."

So it was starting all over again! It used to be too dangerous to sit on a bench with Grandpa Ginis, and now it was too dangerous to be with Boris.

"I'm sick of people," I said, "I'm as sick as anyone could be. I'd like to have nothing more to do with them."

"I'm afraid," Boris said with a sad smile, "you won't be able to avoid them for very long."

"Yes, I will," I replied, "they can be avoided! I won't let them get near me . . . here."

"Wait until you meet someone whom you really love."

"I'll never really love anyone again."

"Ach, Angelina, what nonsense you talk!"

That was the end. The end of Boris, the end of Buhovo, the

end of a phase in my life in which for the first and last time I felt free, secure, healthy, and completely happy.

Else returned to Sofia with Angelika. She had had to give up the apartment in Oborishta Street, because she could no longer pay the rent, and Dimiter had packed up all her belongings. They fit into three suitcases and a crate.

Now she lived with her daughter in Murgash Street, a narrow lane with dilapidated houses, some of which were hardly fit to live in.

From there she wrote the first letter to her son, who she thought was in Palestine:

Peterkin, it's like a dream that I'm sitting here writing to you—a real letter, a letter that will reach you. I'm sure that you'll now do the same and I'll soon be holding a letter from you in my hands. When the overthrow came, suddenly and unexpectedly, and we could hardly grasp the full significance of the new situation, I woke up one night, waked Angeli, and said: "Angeli, now we rejoin Peter!" And I was filled with so much happiness!

Peterkin, the photo of you at nineteen, which you had made right before your emigration, is still hanging on our wall, and everyone who sees it asks: "Who is that handsome young man?" How do you look now? Still as handsome and elegant as in this picture?

Your mother isn't pretty at all anymore, and I'm already afraid that you will be shocked and disappointed when you see me. My hair has gone a bit gray, and by my handwriting you can see that I'm in urgent need of glasses, and an inflammation of the nerve on the right side of my face doesn't exactly make me more beautiful. But none of that is important, we love one another, and our joy on seeing one another, our happiness at finally being together again after six long, terrible years, will certainly not be diminished by such external things. I have only one wish: to be with you soon, to love and pamper you, to be able to care for you. We would come immediately to Palestine, Angeli and I, but we don't know how or even whether it can be done, because everything is still unclear and confused here. But now it is only a question of time, and not of inhuman laws. After twelve years I am free, I can live again without fear and torment and constant uncertainty as to whether we will survive or not.

I have so infinitely many things to say to you, but how can I say them in this first letter? It still can't be done, it's too much. The despair, the hell of these pasts years! I'll never see my mother again. She was deported to Theresienstadt, and we have never heard from her since. All our other relatives are also dead, have been murdered. But I have you three! Angelika is sitting next to me, she's seventeen and so pretty that you'll be proud of her. Our Tina has suffered a great deal. Her man was buried under the rubble during a bombing raid on Sofia and for four months it wasn't clear whether he would live or die. They have a little boy; his name is André and he's enchanting. The birth was so difficult that Tina's optical tuberculosis, on account of which she'd had to stay in bed for a year in Berlin, broke out again. I'll probably never lack for things to worry about. Tina has become such a good person, mature and kind. Entirely different from you and Angeli. She herself says: "I'm not talented and interesting, I am and can do nothing at all." But I see what she is and can do: she can love, and she is good-hearted and willing to sacrifice herself.

Because of the heavy bombing raids we lived in a village for nine months, but now we're back in Sofia, living with a sister of Tina's husband. We have a little room, a kitchen, even if it has no stove, a hall, a verandah and a real toilet—and what has to be emphasized is that in the village we didn't have all that. It isn't easy for us, but the worst is now over.

And you, my Peter? How are you living, where, with whom? What work are you doing? With whom do you spend your time? Do you like it there? And Paula and Bruno, Ilse and Walter, and all the many people who are there and whom I have known so well and so long—what are they doing? Are you still writing? Do you speak the five languages that you know, and now also Hebrew? What have you seen and experienced? Have you had to endure many hardships? I know nothing about you, nothing at all! I'm very lonesome here, I see very few people, and Tina, and soon Angeli, are going their own ways. This is still something new for me, that no one any longer seeks me out and loves me. It's hard to get used to that when one was once at the center of things and as cosseted and courted as I was. At the time I never made anything positive out of that, never did my duty, always thought only of my own pleasure. And with regard to you, my children, I was impatient and nervous, shouted at you and didn't make an effort to understand you. How infinitely heavy my heart is, when I think about that, and then I say to myself about everything terrible that has happened to me: I had it coming. I've often caused my daughters to suffer, and there was a time when Bettina no longer loved me, and perhaps Angeli doesn't love me even now. You never had to live with me, and so you love me the most, and perhaps also because you are the most like me and understand me best. I have changed a great deal in the meantime, but I'm also already old. What I miss is friends. Perhaps I might have been able to make a few here, but language is such an obstacle. Ultimately, I can express how and who I really am only in German. French is not my language, even if I speak it well. And as for my

Bulgarian—you should hear it! Tina and Angeli, who speak it fluently, shriek with laughter when they hear me, or are ashamed of me.

You see, Peterkin, I could ramble on for hours. But regarding what has gone on and is going on inside me, what I've thought and felt, I can't even begin. That has to come slowly, first it has to settle and become clear.

Say hello for me to everyone who still thinks about me, and write to me, my son, nothing would make me happier than a letter from you. I kiss you, my beloved, big Peter, and I remain forever

Your mother

PS: Angelika says hello. She wants to write to you, but she doesn't dare. Everything is so new for her and so difficult to grasp, as it is for me, too.

Yes, everything was still so new and difficult to grasp, but I was not happy. I was impatient, angry, bitter. When one has waited for years for the day when one will be free, has constantly consoled oneself by thinking about it and imagining it in the most beautiful colors, with an excess of fantasy and a dangerous lack of realism, then the event itself is inevitably a disappointment, even under the most favorable circumstances—not to mention under unfavorable circumstances! So now we were free, and this is the way it looked:

We were living in an attic apartment on the verge of collapse, which was, except for the toilet without a seat, the cold water tap in the kitchen, the rotting wooden floor, and the little cabinet, no better than our lodging in Buhovo. We now had enough money for only a handful of white beans, because Zvetan Taslakoff had told us that he himself was penniless—which was certainly not true. We had sold all the jewelry with the exception of a diamond ring—our last emergency reserve, and neither my sick mother nor I, who was now stateless and at the mercy of arbitrary bureaucratic decisions, could work. There was still less to eat than there had been in the village, because there we had at least good, home-baked bread, whereas in Sofia there was a damp glop of cornmeal that got moldy inside within a few hours. There was even less to wear than to eat, which was not important since we couldn't have afforded to buy anything anyway. We went about in our old, threadbare clothes, wearing artificial silk stockings with runs and shoes with wooden soles. My mother still had silk underwear, three elegant dresses, and high-heeled sandals, but not much could be done with them in the life we led. We washed ourselves with a bar of soap that no one would have used even to scrub floors, and we also used it to clean our teeth. Every month Vassil brought us a cartload of firewood from Buhovo, without which we would have frozen during that particularly cold winter.

Every month I had to go to the militia to get my residence permit renewed, and going there made our bodies tremble and our teeth chatter. Being deported wouldn't have bothered me, but they could just as well have put us in a camp or a prison. We had hardly any friends left. Grandpa Ginis, who had been sent to the provinces with the rest of the Bulgarian Jews, had disappeared without a trace. Wilma Taslakova, who was under her repulsive husband's thumb, no longer dared visit us, and her brother-in-law, Mitko, had fled to France shortly before the overthrow. We hadn't heard anything from my father in over a year, and wondered whether he was still alive. Because all postal service to Germany had been broken off since Bulgaria declared war in January 1945, we had to wait without being able to do anything.

Bettina had gone back to Sofia with her husband and son, and was living, no better than we, in Mizo's parents' squalid house. The whole family, except for the older, married sister in whose house we were living, had flocked together there: his parents, two brothers, one of them with his wife and daughter, the younger sister, Bettina, Mizo, and little André. They were eking out a miserable existence there, constantly expecting the militia to come, behind barred doors and locked windows, and my poor sister had become a mere shadow of her former self. Sometimes I went for a walk with her and the baby. Someone had given her an old buggy with squeaky wheels, and together we pushed it though the big park which now, God forbid, no longer bore the king's name, but was called the "People's Park."

"We'd all imagined it somewhat differently, hadn't we, Bettina?" I asked.

"I think a curse has been laid upon us," she replied.

"The curse is humanity," I said.

When the Russian army came into Sofia, my mother forbade me to go out on the streets. I said, "But Mummy, they're our liberators, and surely they won't bother victims of fascism."

She said: "Save your cynicism for better times and do what I tell you."

I didn't do what she told me. I sneaked out of the building, ran to Czar Osvoboditel Boulevard—which could still bear that name because the Czar, though he was also a Czarist, was nonetheless a Russian—and watched the troops march in.

I have seldom seen anything as imposing as the endless lines of Soviet troops in their gray uniforms, with wide leather belts around their waists, heavy boots, and caps with a red star. They were marching in columns, with an officer in the lead who sang in a clear, metallic voice the first lines of a song, followed by the soldiers in a strong, beautiful chorus. They were elite troops, as I later learned, the best that the Soviet Union had to offer. Their conduct was exemplary. To me they seemed to be visitors from another planet, unapproachable, unreal creatures whose functions, needs, and modes of behavior must certainly be different from our own.

Shaken, I returned home.

"That was something," I told my mother, "no wonder those German jumping jacks lost the war."

"Angelika, do you really want to tempt fate by unnecessarily exposing yourself to danger?"

"Am I supposed to spend my whole life in hiding, so as not to tempt fate?"

"Your life has just begun."

"Yes, but how!"

She looked at me with that pained, helpless expression on her face and immediately I felt sorry for her. And that was exactly what I wanted to avoid. I suffered from nothing more than from sympathy, especially when it involved my mother. It was a terrible feeling, as if I were psychologically seasick. I felt weak to the point of keeling over, I choked and my heart pounded so hard I thought I would throw it up. This feeling of psychological seasickness now came very often, almost always when I paid close attention to my mother. She'd become so tiny and fragile, and she was harder and harder to understand. She now often swallowed wrong when she ate and drank, and then coughed until tears ran down her face and she could hardly breathe. Something no longer functioned properly, she'd lost control of the muscles for speaking and swallowing. I noticed how she struggled to pronounce words in a comprehensible way, how careful she was when eating and drinking, and that made things even worse. She knew as well as I did that something calamitous was going on, and tried to hide it from me and from herself. But I didn't dare speak to her about it, and acted as if the calamity didn't exist. It was a game of hide-and-seek, and neither of us helped.

"Don't you think," I asked Bettina one day, "that Mummy's condition is getting steadily worse? Sometimes I can hardly understand her."

"That comes from the paralysis."

"She got the paralysis two years ago, and up until six

months ago, she could still speak well. So if that were the cause, from the start she would have spoken just as badly as she does now. Besides, she's constantly swallowing wrong, and there's something wrong with her hands as well."

"Angeli, stop with this pessimism. As if what we're going through here weren't already bad enough! If Mummy didn't have to suffer so much and finally had rest, care, and good food, she'd be healthy again right away. It's her nerves."

I was only too glad to allow myself to be reassured by her words, but I wasn't convinced.

In March 1945 English and American "missions" arrived in Sofia. Altogether there were about a hundred men, soldiers and officers—infinitesimally small in comparison with the Russians, but something nonetheless.

For me, the Englishmen were, thanks to the BBC and my mother's veneration of them, demigods. The Americans, with whom I had not been in connection every evening at seven o'clock, interested me less. I was determined to get myself a demigod in low shoes. The latter impressed me very much. Only demigods could go to war in such footwear.

My first step was to learn English, and since I worked hard to achieve my goal as quickly as possible, within a month I could manage colloquial English. The second step was to stalk the Englishmen and to become familiar with their ways of behaving. I took along my friend Elena, because she was bolder than I. We hung around in front of the buildings where they lived or worked, and although our observations had to be limited to the minimum, I thought I had gained a certain insight.

"They're gentlemen," I declared.

"How can you tell that?"

" They don't try to flirt with us."

"That's not because of their gentlemanly behavior, but because we look so scruffy."

The third step followed, and consisted in digging out my

mother's three elegant dresses and high-heeled sandals, and adorning myself with them. They were black dresses, one of them with a sparkling diamanté collar.

"You can't run around in broad daylight dressed like that, especially at your age," my mother protested.

I strapped a broad belt around my waist and put on lipstick. "This is just a dress rehearsal," I said.

"Good Lord," my mother sighed.

As luck would have it, a party was given for the British soldiers by the "English Speaking League" in which I was studying the language. I was invited, put on the dress with the sparkling diamanté collar, and went with a wildly beating heart and the terrible fear that I would have to sit all evening unnoticed in a corner. It turned out to be a triumphal debut, from which I emerged with Bert Littman, the most splendid man in the group, the demigod of the demigods.

He became my second great love.

In March 1945 the Allies reached the right bank of the Rhine. In April 1945 Russian troops were on the eastern edge of Berlin. On May 2, 1945, the German troops capitulated in Berlin. On May 7, 1945, at 2:41 A.M., Germany signed the unconditional surrender.

Else sat with her daughters and grandson in their small room. "The war is over," she said. "We survived."

The girls said nothing. They were both wearing the same blue-and-white checkered dresses that they'd had made out of bedsheets. On their young faces their mother discerned an expression of immemorial resignation.

We survived dead, she thought.

On June 30, 1945, Else turned fifty-two. When she awoke that morning she felt so weak and sick that she felt she would never be able to stand up again. She thought, I have to go to the doctor. This can't go on like this, the children need me!

Angelika, in a faded slip whose seams she had already burst in several places, stood up, went to her mother's bed, and kissed her. Since she had fallen so passionately in love with Bert Littman, and he no less with she, she had become warmer and more accessible again. Else regarded the relationship with the young Englishman as a great boon. It meant protection for her daughter, and with him she might even attain the highest of all goals: a British husband and passport. That she had also met a particularly handsome and refined Briton was more than Else had dared to hope. The girl had to be given one thing: she knew how to get the right men.

She had wonderful gifts for her, Angelika said, coffee, cigarettes, and chocolate, all made in England. Did she have any other, very special wishes?

"Only one," Else said. "A letter from Peter."

One hour later there was a knock at the door, and the postman brought her a letter from Peter, the first in four years.

"Oh, Angeli," she said, and pressed it to her cheek, "and now say there is no God!" It was a twenty-page-long letter that began with the following words:

Mummy, Bettina, Angelika, my beloveds—I'm crouching in a tent in the middle of a forest. I have wound my blanket around me, I'm cold, it's raining, it's autumn. The forest is in France somewhere on the Western Front, and in front of us are the Germans. From time to time, we can see them in the distance, about two or three hundred meters away. Now and then a few shots, and in between the thundering of the artillery. But in general it's quiet. It's quiet, it's raining, I'm cold, and I'm writing you my first letter . . .

And so Else learned the truth, a truth that he had kept from her for four years and had spared her, and of which she'd had not even an inkling.

Since the beginning of the war he had made many attempts to join as a volunteer, first the British army, and when he had been rejected because of strict security rules, the French army. The French had finally enlisted him in General de Gaulle's army for the duration of the war.

At the end of March 1941 he had been taken to Egypt on the last ship to leave Greece, and sent as a soldier to the front. For more than three and a half years, he had fought in all the theaters of war: in Syria against the Vichy army, and in Libya and Tunisia against the Afrika Korps. Then in Italy, where he was wounded north of Rome and had to spend a few weeks in a field hospital. And finally in France. The landing, the invasion, the fighting to advance toward Toulon, and then the battle for Toulon. The steady advance up the Rhone valley, passing through countless villages and towns in Provence. Attacks, counterattacks, patrols, nocturnal vigils, destroyed places, forests, rain, cold . . . but the end was in sight.

Four years of war, battling against inhumanity, putting his life on the line for "the just cause"—twenty pages in which he tried to recuperate a whole word and the language, tone, and elan of an earlier time; in which, full of love for his mother, full of faith in the victory of humanity, he yearned for the end of this life of misery, the day of the final liberation; in which he spoke with contempt of his father and with tenderness of Ilse and Walter Hirsch, with whom he had spent his furlough in Jerusalem, and with infinite sadness about the fate of those who had been tormented, murdered, systematically eradicated, and cold-bloodedly annihilated by the Nazi brutes. Twenty pages, which he had written over several days, at different parts of the front, and which, buried in snow at 700 meters altitude, he had now finished with frozen hands:

. . . But no, I don't regret anything—I am now closer to you than ever before. The war is coming to an end. Oh,

Mummy, I feel that it won't last much longer, that I will soon, very soon, see you, Bettina, and Angelika again . . . Farewell, my much-beloved, and wait just a little longer. Now you are safe—I can be calm, can't I? Tell me, Mummy, that I can be calm! Auf Wiedersehen, my beloved, I tell you auf Wiedersehen . . . For now it won't be much longer. It can't be much longer! We've held out many years, we've held out well—now it's time for it to stop. Auf Wiedersehen, my beloved, everything is forgotten in an immense hope . . .

I love you all, I kiss you a thousand times—you, Mummy, you, Bettina, and you, Angelika—

Peter

When Else read this letter on her birthday, June 30, 1945, her son had already been dead for six months.

She immediately answered him:

Peter, my little Peter, I've never received such a beautiful and distressing letter. I'm mad with love, admiration, and longing. I felt: you're my son, you belong wholly to me. You think my thoughts, feel my feelings, speak my language. My daughters whom I love just as much as you, are different. I'm afraid they don't love me the way you love me, don't understand me the way you understand me, in any case they're both different from me—in their natures, their temperaments, their views. They have no great respect for me and are justifiably annoyed when I'm nervous and grumble about things. Even with you I used to grumble and yell, and I regret every word that wasn't a word of love. If I'm nervous today, perhaps it can be understood and forgiven. But earlier, when I still had everything anyone could wish for—my children, my friends, music, books, love, a carefree life, everything—then I was nasty, spoiled, and ungrateful instead of being happy, kind to everyone, and grateful. And one has to pay for that, Peterkin, and it is just. Why am I writing this to you? Because, after reading your letter, I want to ask you to forgive me. Because I'm afraid that you love me too much and I don't deserve it. Because when I think about past times I see only my mistakes, and they are a perpetual torment to me, Peterkin, for they cannot be redeemed.

Enough about me, I want to talk about you, about you who have become a man, who has suffered more than I, who has proven that he can not only speak and write fine words but is prepared to sacrifice his health, his life, for his ideals. You, who have shown that you are very deeply bound to your mother and your grandparents—whose love for us was so great. How small I feel myself in comparison to them and to you! You haven't learned what they did with Grandmother? They put her in a concentration camp like all the others, and since August 1943 we've never heard from her again. The first who were deported were Marie and little Eva, then the Habermanns and Engels, and so it went on until none of our relatives was left. Ernst Saulmann and his mother committed suicide, many people did that.

I understand your anger, Peter, and I share it. But you have to understand that your father and Enie have helped wherever they could. They were decent and have greatly suffered. And Erich, whom you don't even mention, was very good to us and to my mother. You reproach me on her account. How can I make you understand this? I couldn't bring her to live with me in Bulgaria, Peterkin. There was no possibility of that. I myself could leave Germany only because I made a sham marriage to get Bulgarian citizenship. We no longer had passports, and they would never have let my mother leave. I can't explain everything in this letter, Peterkin, someday we'll talk about it, won't we? I'll never comprehend how all this could happen. I can no longer understand people. I know only that those who have committed these crimes will be punished, so mercilessly that one cannot even imagine it. But that will not bring back the millions they have killed.

I've imagined countless times the end of the war, the end of the Nazis. And now it has actually happened as I dreamed it and longed for it with all my heart. And like you, I have imagined how I would someday take my revenge, revenge on all those who have insulted me, humiliated me, done such terrible things to me. Who have taken everything away from me—my son, my mother, my husband, my country. Who made my children unhappy, who have forced me to make my children unhappy—my children, whom I love like nothing else in the world. That was the worst! Nonetheless, I want to fight the wish for revenge, and I want not to hate anymore. What I would like is peace and a little rest. I beg for only one thing: not to be afraid anymore, not to have to live alone in a foreign country. And above all I'd like to see my three children saved, secure, and happy. I'd like to have them around me, that is my prayer, every morning, every evening.

My Peterkin, I embrace and kiss you, I'm proud of you, my son.

Mummy.

PS: The children send you hugs. Angelika asks that you come to visit us. Will you come, Peterkin? Sometimes I feel I can't go on. It was too much. Everything seems dark within me. But if you could come . . .

Peter, my big, courageous brother, our savior, with whom we lived, who would make us happy again. I'd go dancing with him, in a white dance hall with Chinese lanterns, under the open, starry sky, at the seacoast, dancing the tango, as he'd once danced it with our mother in Switzerland. What a lovely couple we'd be, what a happy couple! We were like one another, we'd understand each other, love each other, and never again allow anyone, any fear, to torment us.

In the meantime, I'd broken off my relationship with Bert Littman. At some point I'd confessed to him—I no longer know how, because I couldn't say the word—that I was half Jewish. He had reacted with an enthusiasm that would have been appropriate for glad tidings, but not for such an unpleasant revelation. Thereupon he confided that he was a full Jew. It was a shock, but one that had a delayed effect. I didn't immediately feel it, and when he asked if I would marry him, I said yes. He went to England to see his parents and came back with their blessing and gifts. In the interim it had become clear to me that I could not love a Jew, and certainly not share a life with him, because that would mean fear and torment, danger and humiliation. I no longer believed in the triumph of the good. Humanity was like a Hydra, if one cut off one of its heads, ten new ones grew in its place. Thus I had told both Bert and my mother that the marriage was off, and always gave the same answer to their despairing questions: that was how it was, and nothing they said or did could change my mind.

I had chosen Bert's superior, Captain Benson, as my next conquest, because I sensed that he posed no danger to me. He seemed insignificant, obviously had not a drop of Jewish blood, and was just as deeply in love with me as I was bored with him. Through him I gained access to the circle of the upper ranks, to parties and excursions, to the officers' villas and clubs. I was afraid that they were all masochists, because otherwise it was impossible to understand their willingness to give me everything I wanted—me, a reckless little hussy.

Since I liked all of them better than Captain Benson, I

kissed, danced, and danced with them rather than with him. He suffered, but took that in stride as well. Only once did he lose it and almost strangle me. Afterward he asked me to marry him. I laughed and said I was interested only in a fictive marriage.

Bert had had himself transferred a few weeks after our separation, and my mother, who'd probably still hoped that we'd get back together, was very unhappy about that.

"I really don't know what's going on in you," she said, "and I no longer know what I should do with you."

"Nothing," I replied.

"You've got to get out of here as soon as possible."

"I've had to do that for the past seven years."

"If your father knew all this!"

"But he doesn't know. And he may never know."

My eyes were burning, my throat hurt, but I couldn't cry.

"Angeli, the war has been over for just two months, and there must be such terrible chaos in Germany that it's entirely normal that we haven't yet had any word from him. But now we might be able to get in touch with him through the British mission, what do you think?"

I asked Captain Benson, and he said yes, he thought that would be possible and would immediately take all the necessary steps.

About two weeks after the arrival of the first, long letter from my brother the postman brought a letter from Palestine; the sender's name was Ilse Hirsch. I brought it in.

"Mummy," I cried excitedly, "a letter from Ilse! Just imagine, now the mail is coming in from Palestine again!"

"You see," she said with a happy smile, "now we're beginning to see that the war is over."

I gave her the letter, and she took it to the window.

Oh, God, why can't I invent that moment now, cobble something together out of little fragments of memory? Why didn't it disappear instead of now unreeling before me again, in slow motion and with cruel clarity, after forty-eight years?

I'm standing behind her and looking over her shoulder, in order to be able to read the letter at the same time as she. She opens the envelope and takes out the letter. There are two pages, each one folded separately. She unfolds the one that lies on top. A ray of sunlight trembles on it. There are only a few lines, written in French on a typewriter. I read, "Madame," and understand nothing more. I ask: "Mummy, what is it?"

She does not answer, takes the two steps to the table, lays the pages on it, sits down on a chair. Oh, God, why can't I forget her face, which looks as though several centuries have passed by, have hollowed it out and left it empty, completely empty.

I sit down on the other chair. My thighs are trembling, only my thighs. My lungs are like concrete, I can hardly breathe. It's terribly hot in the room, no air is coming into it. I stare at the two pages, I'm afraid to touch them. I already know it, anyway.

I say, "Mummy, I'll be right back."

She does not react.

I ran the short distance to Bettina's apartment. She was feeding her child. Mizo lay stretched out on the bed.

"Peter is dead," I said.

They both immediately jumped up. Bettina opened her mouth, but nothing came out. Her face was waxy yellow. For the first time she forgot her child and ran to the door.

"Take André with you," I cried, "he's the only one who might still help."

My mother hadn't moved. Even her hands were still lying in the same position in her lap—the fingers slightly hooked. She glanced up at us with her washed-out eyes, with that terribly empty look.

Mizo went into the kitchen and came back with a half-full glass of water. He dissolved two tablets in it. "Please drink this, Else," he said.

She drank, swallowed, coughed. He clapped her on the back, carefully pulled her up from the chair and led her to the bed. She lay down.

We stood there, mute, even little André made not a sound. He sensed that something unspeakably awful had happened in this sunny little room.

My mother lay on her back, her head turned toward the wall. Over her hung the photo of her dead son.

Sofia, July 17, 1945

Dear Ilse, I thank you for everything. A hope is dead— my boy whom I was supposed to finally see again soon. He suffered for seven years, and when it was almost over he died. He survived all the dangers for four years in order to fall four months before the end of the war. I have already felt his hand and his hair and his skin—soon, I think, I will hold and kiss everything. No Peterkin any more.

I envy you very much, you saw him and spoke with him again shortly before his death. I have not seen or spoken to him for seven years, and that is why there is no physical void for me, he is just as near or far as before. My handsome, gifted son. I wanted to live with him.

I can say all that only to you, because you're now the closest to me. I would like to see you and embrace you, because something of Peter is still in you. Ilse, tell me about him, tell me everything! You write: he looked so wonderful. How did he look? Describe him very exactly. Was he still as cheerful and lively as before? Did he have a girl? Do you have any photos of him? Send me everything of his, Ilse, please.

It's so hard for me, so many have survived, why not he? He deserved to survive. Did he speak about the possibility of dying? Did he have a premonition that something would happen to him? Was he happy? I reproach myself for so many things. How often I scolded him, doubted the sincerity of what he said. Did I disappoint him? Was he very unhappy when I didn't go to Greece? He was already waiting for me at the airport, and I could perhaps have managed it, had I been more energetic. But I was so insecure and afraid for my daughters. If only I had gone anyway and seen him one last time. I was never really afraid for Peter, only during the last few months I felt a kind of void within me. Was he often sad? Did he suffer? You have lost him too, but it doesn't hurt you so much. Children, even after they have grown up, are still connected to their mothers by the umbilical cord, and they tug and tug on it, whether they know it or not, and that goes straight to the heart. My mother lost her son in the last month of the First World War, and she never recovered from it.

I really don't know what will become of me. My son has already been gone for six months, and I didn't know it. He was killed two days after his twenty-seventh birthday. It never occurred to me that Peterkin could be killed in the war. Now, half a year too late, I am beginning to cry. It is all so wrong. No one was with him when he died, his Mummy was not with him. I am good for nothing, nothing at all. I can bring everyone only unhappiness. Ilse, write to me and receive many greetings,

Schnuff

PS: Ilse, in what language did you speak with him? How long was he in Jerusalem? Did he live with you? What kind of uniform did he wear? How often was he on furlough? Did he receive only the Red Cross messages from me and not my letters and cards? Didn't you know earlier that Peterkin was already dead? Did you not know how to tell me? Why did he love me, anyway? I never did anything for him. In my answer to his long, beautiful letter I was able to tell him for the first time how much I loved, respected, and admired him, and ask him to forgive me. And now he'll never learn all that. He died for me, and he didn't know how much I loved him.

Three days after we received the notice of Peter's death my sister contracted a pulmonary infection. She had no more reserves, and she was very ill. My mother spent almost all her time with her and cared for her and the child. I think that helped her get through the first period. Sometimes I went for a walk with her and the child. I told her that now word might soon come from my father and that then we would go back to him in Germany. She nodded and said: "Yes, where else should we go?" I replied: "Germany is now entirely different, and it will be very, very wonderful to be with Papa."

He was our last hope.

When Bettina was almost healthy again, she was picked up by the militia at four o'clock in the morning and loaded onto a truck with a certain number of other women of German descent. They left the whole fascist Stanishev brood alone, but they had to take away my sister, who as a half-Jew had barely escaped landing in a German work camp. Mizo tried to throw himself between them and ran after the truck on his six-times-broken leg, but of course in vain.

I feared that my mother would now not be able to survive this, but it is incredible what strength can still exist in a broken person. She spent all day with the authorities, trying to get Bettina out of the camp, which was located somewhere in the mountains. Because she was terribly afraid that the same thing could happen to me, I was no longer allowed to sleep at home. Captain Benson arranged for me to stay sometimes with one officer, sometimes with another. Most of them lived a few kilometers outside Sofia, in the former American College, but the upper ranks had apartments or at least a room in the city. I moved every night with my toothbrush and one of my mother's silk nightgowns and was very embarrassed to be dependent on the generosity and sympathy of the Englishmen.

A short time later I got to know the Americans. The occasion was an English party to which the American allies were, for once, invited. The reason must have been an imperative one, because the two victorious powers—not to mention the third—scrupulously avoided one another. I immediately saw that the Americans wore more becoming uniforms than the English, and that their behavior was less impeccable. As a result, they were more amusing. I danced all night. A very attractive Air Force colonel offered me a job in the American mission. I asked him what I could do there, and he said that given my good looks, something would certainly be found.

I reported the colonel's offer verbatim to my mother.

She said: "Call the man immediately. If you are working for the Americans, you'll be protected."

"No matter what work I'm doing?"

"It doesn't matter! Even if you're washing windows!"

She hadn't understood. Or maybe she had understood and it didn't matter to her anyway? The main thing was that I was protected? Not me! I knew what I'd be getting myself into, and it disgusted me. Loads of young women and girls who didn't shrink from anything went to bed with the worst of the Englishmen or Americans for a pair of stockings or a chocolate bar, for protection or a marriage certificate, feigned passionate love, chastity, suicide attempts, and pregnancies.

"I'm not going to call the colonel," I said.

"Angelika, my mother said, "I can't stand any more, don't you see that I can't stand any more? My Peter is dead, Bettina is in a camp, and you are in constant danger. Am I to lose all my children?"

I called the colonel and was given a job at the American mission the next day—an absolutely respectable job in the translation office, which was directed by Sergeant Kitai, an elderly Viennese Jew who was very ugly and very kind. I typed long political reports from eight in the morning to five in the afternoon, using two fingers and making many mistakes. My mother breathed a sigh of relief. I was allowed to sleep at home again, because I was now protected by the Americans. At least one of the children had been saved.

Not long afterward Bettina was released from the camp. She looked like she had just climbed out of the trash can, but when she took her son in her arms her face lit up as mine had not lit up for a long time, and then she looked like a pretty gypsy girl.

"I told you, Angeli, there's a curse on us!"

"And I told you, Bettina, that the curse is humanity."

Dear Ilse, your letter with the photos gave me great pleasure. You are so unchanged that I can hardly grasp it. Ten years have passed, and you're still exactly the same Ilse—I heard your light laughter and saw you dancing and flirting. You're just happy, that's all. I look again and again at your sons. They seem so smart, happy, well-groomed. And all three of them around their Mummy. Fortunate Ilse, don't lose a minute, enjoy every one you are with your children. When one is young, one is so profligate with happiness, doesn't have any idea what one has, and then later . . . If only I still had my Peter! You write that he certainly had a hard time because he doubted himself and everything so much. But whether he would have succeeded with writing or not, whether he would have gone to America or to Australia, really doesn't matter. He would have survived and would have certainly preferred even so difficult a life to death.

Yes, I would be only too glad to see you, and Turkey would be halfway between us. But in addition to everything else I am now also financially at rock-bottom, and couldn't even afford a pair of shoes—if there were any. Earlier, when something went wrong for me, Walter always said: "Schnuff is never defenseless." But now I'm permanently defenseless. I have no idea where I find the strength to keep going on.

Do you speak German or Hebrew at home? I can't imagine how one can show who one really is in a language other than one's native language. We are so intertwined with language, it's more expressive of our personality than anything else, just as it's more the key to a people and its culture than anything else. One can learn words and grammar, of course, but never what is in and behind the words. With a different language, wouldn't one have to become a different person?

"I'd like to have your problems and Rothschild's money," you'll think, so now I'll pass quickly to my daughters. Here are the photos; when you look at them, think back to Walter's prophetic words: "Bettina looks like a little devil and is an angel, and Angelika looks like an angel and is a little devil." Now these words, spoken twelve years ago, have proven to be amazingly correct.

In the picture my little Tina has just turned eighteen, but she was already in love with her Mizo. That is probably the reason for her lyrical expression, which she generally does not have. Unfortunately I don't have a more recent photo, so just ignore the lyricism and the retouching. Moreover, at the moment she's not so beautiful. She has already had so much unhappiness in her life. She has been married for a year, and her little apartment was destroyed by bombing and, what was much worse, her husband was seriously injured and almost died. Tina, whose pregnancy was far advanced, sat at his bedside day and night for months and cared for him—tirelessly, without thinking of herself, without complaining, without crying, stubbornly. Erich once said: "Tina takes only one-way streets, straight ahead. With her, there are no intermediate colors, only black and white. She doesn't reflect much, just feels, sacrifices herself, says little, acts."

Then came the turnaround, the great hour of liberation, the salvation. And this is how it looked: Mizo lost his job as an instructor of anatomy and shortly after I learned of Peter's death, Bettina was interned in a camp. As an emigrant and the daughter of a Jewess, during the German occupation she was been in constant danger of being sent back to Germany and from there to a labor camp; her mother had barely escaped, her grandmother was murdered in a concentration camp, her brother had died in the battle against fascism, and then she was interned because she had emigrated, at the age of sixteen, with a German passport. Thus poor Tina was in a camp and I nearly went crazy. I wrote heaps of petitions and explanations, I ran from Pontius to Pilate, waited for hours and hours in dark, cold corridors in front of closed doors, but it was nonetheless six weeks before I was able to clear up the appalling mistake and get her released. Now our misery is finally over, but we still have not had a single moment of peace—we're still anxious, persecuted, tormented, still, still!

In the meantime Bettina's husband has gotten his job back—possibly to make up for the embarrassing mistake—but otherwise the two of them have nothing, not even a toy for their baby. When I see my little Tina sitting in her dreary room, at the end of her rope physically and mentally, and yet so brave, then I wish all the people who have caused my children so much pain were dead. Fortunately there is little André, a curly-headed child who has big, dark eyes and is so cute that he allows his mother and grandmother to forget their misfortunes a little.

The two other pictures, as you will easily guess, show Angeli in all the splendor of her seventeenth year. She's still living with me—even if I hardly ever see her. A delayed and then explosive development made out of the thin, shy, little girl a beautiful young woman with a mind of her own and tore her away from my apron strings, to which she had firmly clung so long that people called us Siamese twins. She is a fairly astonishing egoist and is very intelligent, though she doesn't take advantage of her intelligence. But with her, anything could still happen. She may even be gifted, I can't yet tell. She, Peter, and I are all alike. However, Angeli also takes after Erich to a large extent. She works at the American mission, which is a blessing because first of all she is protected by the Americans, and secondly she receives a small salary and a hot meal every day at noon. Invaluable advantages given the general food shortage and our particular shortage of cash. In addition, she has a rather extensive group of admirers, Englishmen and Americans, whom she at first worshiped as our saviors, and now treats a little as if they were her personal slaves. Two of them have already made her marriage proposals. She flatly turned down one of them, and made the other very unhappy because she was at first greatly infatuated with him and resolved to marry him, and then, a few weeks later, was the exact opposite. I was very sorry about that, because he was an especially handsome and attractive young man, and by marrying an Englishman Angelika would have escaped all the dangers that threaten her here. I'm afraid I'll have to go through a great deal more with this daughter of mine. But you should just see her when she goes to a ball in a long, décolleté evening dress with a black fur cape over it, her hair done up in curls and with flowers in it. She borrows the things somewhere, the flowers are artificial, her shoes are made of wood. But she has so much taste and charm, she's so young and graceful, that even rags look elegant on her. And then I'm very proud, no matter how silly that is, and I'm glad that she's so beautiful and that people love her and spoil her. She has already experienced more than is good for so young a person, and perhaps she has suffered more than we will ever know.

Ilse, yesterday was the first anniversary of Peter's death; on the fifth he would have been twenty-eight years old. I'm dreadfully sad. It's all so meaningless and wrong. What I'm waiting for now, I don't know.

Old, familiar voices from all over are now making themselves heard again, and I'm glad, but it's all the sadder because we'll never see each other again. One can't live on letters alone. No one is coming back. The children have their lives ahead of them, people like me have become superfluous. Where should I go? What should I do? What should I live on? Where is the country that is my homeland? Where are my friends? Where is Erich? I've had no further word from him for many months. It is all very dark . . . "

Thanks to Captain Benson and the British mission we discovered that my father was in Garmisch-Partenkirchen and sent him our message and address. We received the first, greatly longed-for word from him through the Red Cross in November 1945.

"Angeli, just imagine, we've received a message from Papa," my mother said when I came home from work.

I shrieked with joy: "Oh, Mummy, finally, finally, finally a lovely, splendid message! Where is it? Give it here!"

She picked up her bag, which was lying on the bed, opened it, looked inside, poked around, and finally pulled out a sheet of paper. It all happened very slowly and elaborately, and I was a little surprised by it.

"Give it to me, Mummy," I said, and impatiently held out my hand.

She gave me the sheet of paper with the flicker of a smile, went to the window and stood there, her back turned to me.

The message consisted of the usual twenty-five words, but I saw and read only four: "I have married Lieselotte."

I crumpled up the message and threw it into a corner of the room. "Doesn't matter, Mummy," I said, "it really doesn't matter anymore."

She turned around and said: "Angeli, don't take it so hard."

"I'm not. You get used to it. We've already lost so much and better things, so why not him, too?"

"I forbid you to talk about your father that way," she said, and I saw that every word, which she tried to speak clearly, firmly, and loudly, cost her great physical effort, "your father is the most decent, finest person . . . "

"Will you finally stop that, Mummy! Next you'll be saying that he saved our lives, that he's our last protection, and so on and so on."

"And isn't all that true? Could we have survived without his help?"

"And do you find this help so exceptional that you still feel obliged to fall on your knees in veneration? It was the most natural thing possible, and anyone with a spark of conscience would have given us this help. Or do you think Papa might have let us be killed after it was his people who'd committed this crime, after he'd shooed us out of Germany and sent us off to Bulgaria . . . "

"He didn't do that. It was the last remaining option. We'd waited too long. You have no idea what was going on at that time."

"I don't give a damn what was going on then, I just see what resulted from it."

"That's not your father's fault. He did his duty to the utmost extent . . . "

"I shit on duty!"

"Angelika!"

"And I repeat: it was his duty, and he shouldn't be smug about doing it. Not to mention that duty is the only thing he loves, and for which he does everything. Not for you, not for me—we're just people. He can't love people—I understand, but that's another matter—and so for him doing his duty is a substitute for love."

"He loves you, Angelika, I know it and I can perhaps judge it better than you can."

"What does he love, Mummy? The little girl from the Hubertusallee? That lasted about three years, an hour at noon and in the evening. Or the somewhat bigger girl from Johannaplatz. That lasted three months. The rest was the little Sunday girl. And from the time I was twelve it was all over. So what does he love? Can one love a person whom one doesn't know, about whom one knows nothing? He must love an *idée fixe*, the daughter who becomes what he wants, in whom he can one day take pride: a cultivated, polite, elegant girl, a valuable person who believes in the good and studies philosophy. Well, he was really wrong about that! I've become exactly the opposite, and whether I'm to blame or not doesn't matter. So seeing him again would have been an enormous disappointment, and we're all sparing ourselves that. He's married his young lady, and let him enjoy it. Personally, the two of them make me sick."

"You can't be serious about all that! One can't be so unjust! You know your father, who did everything for you and who will continue to do everything for you . . . "

"Thanks very much! I don't want to have anything more to do with him, with that incredibly decent, proper man who has given us this last kick. While we're stuck here, up to our ears in shit and with a knife still at our throats, he's over there celebrating and getting married. He can go jump in the lake,

Mummy! The only thing he can still do, and it's his god-damned duty and debt and not some exceptional delicacy or kindness, is take care of you. If his wife, your best friend, allows it."

"Angelika, I no longer understand you."

"What did you expect, Mummy, that I come out of this hell as an all-forgiving saint?"

She remained silent, and I knew that she'd now give me that pained, helpless look. To keep from getting psychologically seasick, I started rummaging around in my bag and getting out cigarettes and matches.

"You smoke too much," my mother said, and I answered: "I'd like to have your problems and Rothschild's money!"

Through a Red Cross message, Else had informed Fritz Schwiefert of their son's death. When shortly thereafter mail deliveries between Germany and Bulgaria began again, he wrote her a long letter. She replied:

Pitt, thanks for your kind letter. Had it come earlier, it might have been of some help to me. It took a long time before I realized what pains me so greatly about Peter's death, apart from the thought of not having him anymore. Now you have said it plainly and—as you are so good at doing—expressed it beautifully and clearly.

It was not a void like the usual one when someone dies. There was no illness, no dying. There wasn't anything at all, a void—earlier no Peter, now no Peter. Like you, I'm searching for traces of him, like a dog. Perhaps you are searching more spiritually, I am also searching corporeally, because I am his mother. If only I knew how his hands, his hair felt, if only I could have felt his warmth one last time, his skin, his mouth, if only I could have breathed in his smell once more. I sometimes clutch his picture, something of Peter must still be tangible. But it's cold, and it's also sentimentality. One can do what one wants, it's all useless. He'll never return.

If I could really cry, it might be better. But I can't. With other people I act as usual, and I don't go about in black clothing. It's all such a matter of indifference. Can you perhaps explain to me why I don't perish of it? I should really have perished long ago—after all that. Am I already completely numb, or is it the instinct of self-preservation? If I ever let myself go, I know that I'd scream, scream. But I don't scream. Why don't I weep day and night, like my mother did when her son died? It would be easier, I think, the way it is I choke and choke. But the worst is not that Peter is dead for us, but that he, who was young, healthy, and just beginning his life, didn't get more out of it. It was all in vain. In vain the torment, in vain the longing, the hope that it would end; in vain he showed his great love for us by sacrificing himself. He wanted to begin living, he loved life, the sun, summer, girls. You will understand everything when you read his letter, the first and last I received after four years of silence.

I didn't see it coming, like you I was never afraid for Peter. I thought he was safe in Palestine. When I read the letter and realized that he had already been in the greatest danger for the past four years, then I was so thankful that I'd been spared the concern about him. Because now, I thought, he'd survived everything . . . "

In the death notice it says that Peter was killed by a grenade. He died instantly. His face was disfigured, it says. He'd been decorated, he was one of the oldest members of de Gaulle's army, a brave soldier and a good comrade. He's buried near Strasbourg, and a few things he had with him are in Paris. When you read his letter, then you will get to know your son a little. Maybe rediscover a little. But there's not much.

He wanted to write when everything was over, Ilse

Hirsch says, that was his greatest wish. He was the finest person she knew.

Your letter did me good, and I love you very much, because you're Peter's father . . .

My dear Pitt, you speak of such distant things: theater, chamber music, evenings at the fireside. I hardly know anymore what they are, and when I think about them, I feel a mixture of vague yearning and annoyed incomprehension. And then you also speak about our "transfigured" past. I don't know what you mean by that. What is transfigured about it? You seem still to be living in your ivory tower, and the hardship, which even you cannot have escaped entirely, you probably felt more in your belly than in your heart. Misery and fear of death can be neither idealized nor romanticized. They are the only things that cannot be clothed in fine words. They are ugly and make things ugly, they smell bad, they transform people into harried creatures battling for their lives, and only in the rarest cases into martyrs and saints. Our past was a rat's existence, it was degradation and humiliation, powerlessness and hatred, illness and death, flight and deceit, sweating with fear and chattering teeth, dirty lodgings, darned clothing and white beans. Transfigured past! Pitt, it was bodily, mental, and spiritual destruction, it was an eight-year-long nightmare from which we occasionally awoke with a shout or a whimper and realized that the nightmare was reality. Where were you during that time? In noble seclusion, in your beautiful house in Wannsee, in your beautiful world of ideas, in your lovely dreams? Pitt, millions of people died the most horrible deaths, and we, who survived entirely untransfigured, will never, do you hear, never be able to forget the horror.

You're surprised that I was so eager to receive a letter from Enie, and that surprises me in return. After all, she was for years my closest woman friend, and when I've been lonely I've often imagined I was speaking with her, that I was walking through Berlin with her, sitting with her in the studio in Wannsee. She wrote to me so often, and her letters were the most exciting and the wittiest. But the letter that has now finally arrived, was no longer the old Enie. It was lame, almost a little banal. What happened to her? . . .

My good Pitt, I foresaw your reaction to Peter's letters. I knew it wouldn't deepen your sadness, make your love stronger—on the contrary, it would be a disappointment for you. I was so happy over your mourning for our Peterkin that at first I didn't want to send them to you at all. But in the end that would have been false and cowardly, because as his father you have to get to know his thoughts and the life he led.

I grant that what he says about you is hard, but Pitt, he was still very young, our Peter, perhaps not so much in years as in his emotions. He was still full of enthusiasm and very radical. Besides, I think, something else is involved in what he says there—a bitterness against you that he'd harbored in his heart since childhood, perhaps unconsciously. You were unfortunately not a friend to him at that time, and he was not ready to know you and recognize that you had to be the way you were, or rather that you couldn't be otherwise. Yes, and because he was so completely filled with hatred for the Germans—don't forget that what was done to us caused him to suffer terribly—and because his memory of you was not exactly positive, it somehow did him good to be unjust with regard to you, and he wrote what he did out of childish vengeance. At least that's what I think, and perhaps it's not true at all.

Forgive me, Pitt, you have probably made the same reproaches to yourself, and it's not fair for me to bring them up again here. I, too, can't mourn our Peterkin without the eternal reproach that I neglected my duty to him, and that makes it much more painful still. We were just such unrestrained, immoderate people!

The photo of Peter that Ilse sent me and that I have had enlarged here, is as bad as everything that is made here. Retouched to the point that nothing is left in the face. I have a large, unretouched copy, and in it you can see the person. You write that there is something skeptical and bitter about his mouth. I find it melancholy instead. He probably knew what was coming. Tell me, where are all my photos of us and the children? And the beautiful pictures of Peter in the Russian tunic, with his head held high and his clever, arrogant expression? Where is all that?

You know, I also felt for a few years what you say about the "spiritual" Germany and that it was my country and my language, and that I came from there and belonged there. But I am, after all, a real Jew, and I don't need Germany at all anymore.

What I got from it I still have: the language, which I love, the music, the literature, a few people to whom I clung and whom I understood as I will never understand people from other countries. But it's over. I am now entirely somewhere else. What I would earlier have died for will be a matter of indifference to me. Everything is so terribly unimportant to me, I find so many things laughable, I see and sense too strongly what is hidden behind people and things—an uncomfortable condition. I believe I could live anywhere that is beautiful, where I have my children and a livelihood. But not here, I've never liked it here.

Theater—what is that, really? I have never been in one again and have no desire to be. Being with you two, whom I love, I want that. But I might be embarrassed to be with you, because I can only sit there and hardly make myself understood. Speaking is so hard for me because of my facial paralysis. That was a hard blow for me. So many things occur to me, and I don't trust myself to say them.

Mizo went with my mother to see a doctor. When she came home, she explained that it was as she had thought, the paralysis of the facial nerve had gotten worse as a result of the constant anxiety and agitation she had recently experienced, and the only thing she needed was rest, relaxation, and better nutrition with plenty of vitamins.

I was very relieved and said that our lives could no longer get worse, they had to get better, and then she would also be able to rest more. In addition, my father was really making an effort to bring her back to Germany as soon as possible.

"Not without you!"

"All right, all right, not without me."

The next day Mizo called me at the American mission and asked me to come to see him after work. He had something to tell me.

I went. Bettina was ironing with a big iron full of glowing coals. She looked at me with an anxious face and said: "Hello, Angeli." Little André was not in the room.

"Something has happened again," I said, "but what? Everything has already happened."

Mizo, who had been lying on the bed as usual, stood up, came over to me, and took me in his arms. I glanced at Bettina over his shoulder. She was stubbornly hanging her head and mumbling: "It simply never ends."

"It's your mother," Mizo said. "She's very ill . . . " He let me go and asked: "Do you have a cigarette?" I got the pack out of my bag and we both lit up.

"It's a fairly unknown disease," he went on, "multiple sclerosis. It starts in the central nervous system and proceeds, not gradually, but in phases. Sometimes the paralysis remains local, but for the most part it spreads to the whole body. No one knows yet what causes this disease. There is no cure."

"Are you saying that Mummy . . . "

"Angelika, I'm a doctor, and I cannot and must not conceal the truth from you. Your mother knows nothing, but I've already told Bettina, and now I'm telling you: she doesn't have much longer to live."

There was no longer a shock, a desperation, a pain. There was only a void so enormous that I was entirely absorbed into it, I was weightless, perhaps no longer existed at all.

"Angeli," Bettina cried, and Mizo said: "Come, sit down here, I know that this is upsetting for you . . . for us all! We have to be strong now."

Why didn't they leave me in my void? It was so nice not to feel anything anymore, no longer to have a body, no head, no thoughts, no feelings. It was so nice not to exist anymore.

"Mummy has to go to Germany as soon as possible," Bettina said. "I'm firmly convinced that they can help her in Germany."

"They're more advanced in medicine there," Mizo said, "they might be able to prolong her life by at least a few months."

Germany, the fairyland. It was in rubble and ashes, but its aura remained.

"You have to write to tell Papa that Mummy is very ill," Bettina said.

"You have to be very, very tender with her, but never let her even guess what her condition is," Mizo said.

"Can't you leave me alone!" I cried.

Mizo got one of his tranquilizer tablets from the night table and held it out to me.

"I don't need one," I said. "I need all you've got."

"What do you mean by that?" he asked, severely.

Bettina ran out of the room, but not quickly enough. I still heard her convulsive sobbing.

"If you say that again," Mizo threatened, "I'll hit you. A

seventeen-year-old girl, beautiful and healthy! You've got your whole life ahead of you."

"No, it's behind me. The past is my life."

"Nonsense!"

I went into the People's Park. It was getting dark. The air was very warm and heavy. I lay down on a bench and closed my eyes. Immediately the images were there—images from a distant past, which I had dreamed at some time: my mother in a garden, plump and deeply tanned, her face radiant, her arms outstretched: "Come to me, my little fawn, let me kiss you!" My brother and I singing "San Francisco, Open your Golden Gate." My grandparents Kirschner on the terrace under the red umbrella with white polka-dots. My father and I walking through the woods, hand in hand, autumn leaves on the ground, smelling sweet and rustling. I tried to call back the merciful void. I couldn't do it. A whirl of images and the accompanying voices rose up in me: Mummy is dying, Peter is dead, Grandmother was murdered, Papa is no longer there, Mummy is dying, Peter is dead.

And suddenly the pain over my right eyebrow, a maddening pain concentrated on a very tiny point, a pain that had lurked there for many years and captured all the pains of this world. It devoured all the images, all the voices in me. It devoured me.

I jumped up, pressed my fist to the raging spot, ran over to a tree and banged my head against the trunk, over and over. I had to kill it, this pain, before it killed me. And then the tears came, a deluge of tears, and minutes later, just as suddenly as it had attacked me, the pain disappeared.

I went home. Tears were still running down my face, and I felt wrung out as one does after a serious illness.

"What's wrong with you?" my mother asked. "Have you been crying?"

"Yes, from pain. There was this terrible pain. Here, over my right eyebrow. It didn't last long, but it was unbearable."

She looked at me, worried, anxious, raised her hand with the hooked fingers and stroked the right side of my forehead. "Where? Here?"

"Mummy, it went away a long time ago."

"Don't you want to lie down for a while?"

"No, I'm going to be picked up at eight o'clock, I have to hurry."

She watched me change my clothes, silent, attentive, the way one follows an interesting play on the stage.

She's dying, and I'm going dancing, I thought, and when I dance and drink and am admired, when I feel the men's desire and my power over them, then I'll forget that she's dying, then I'll forget everything and everyone: those who have done things and are doing things to me, who have abandoned me and are abandoning me, who are dead or are dying.

Captain Benson had been transferred and I now moved over entirely into the American camp. I was working for the Americans, I was having fun with them. The difference was that I drank whiskey with Coca-Cola instead of gin with lime, smoked Camels instead of Player's, ate Hershey's chocolate instead of Cadbury's, and I now often had to be wary of my American liberators and protectors. They simply refused to accept the fact that there was a girl in their group who couldn't be bought. It wasn't morality that prevented me from taking the last step, but rather fear, fear of selling myself away and losing myself. Only love justified the hideous act that had been graphically described to me, and I didn't love anyone.

It was June 1946, and the Iron Curtain was already almost closed. I didn't know what was going to happen to me. The two missions were preparing to leave the country. If I remained behind, as a stateless person and a former employee of the Americans I would be in prison before long. And then even the return to Germany that my father was so eagerly pursuing and on which my mother was counting, would no longer be possible. It wasn't that I'd yearned for it, I dreaded it, but when I considered the alternative, Germany was better than a Bulgarian camp. Only under the circumstances, I was no longer to have the choice. In other words, my fate was as good as sealed and amounted to a death sentence.

We had survived—for what?

I danced and drank and let myself be admired. It was so nice to forget—everything and everyone. But when the band played "Good Night, Sweetheart, 'til we meet Tomorrow," I disappeared into a dark corner somewhere and wept. For me there was no "tomorrow." I would never dance, drink, and be admired again. I would never experience love in its consummation.

It was at the end of one of these parties that I danced with the attractive Air Force colonel, the one who had gotten me the job in the mission. He reminded me of Clark Gable, whom I had seen in *Gone with the Wind* and adored. He was thoroughly manly, held me pressed firmly to him, body to body, cheek to cheek. He smelled of Old Spice shaving cream. There was absolutely no doubt, I was fond of him. The band played "Unforgettable," and the colonel said he had now waited half a year for me, and he would leave Bulgaria in a week. Would I come to visit him over the weekend?

I went to visit him and became acquainted with the consummation of love in the form of forcible rape.

A week later, on the same plane on which the colonel left Bulgaria, the last American officer arrived in Sofia to wind up operations there. His name was Edward S. Psurny, and to hear my mother tell it, it was the good Lord in person who had sent him to me.

"If I now come to Germany," Else wrote to her first husband, Fritz Schwiefert, "I'll come without Angelika, because she has gotten married. And if the man is not an Englishman, but an American, and if this step, which is supposed to be permanent, has been taken a little too quickly to be examined in detail, it is advantageous in many respects and was, so far as Angelika's situation here is concerned, appropriate and even necessary. Not to mention that the man is of impeccable character, tall, good-looking, cordial, twelve years older than Angelika, and so devoted to her that I cannot help being worried about him. Because Angelika is and was always very peculiar. In any case, she is now in seventh heaven, is called Mrs. Psurny, and as the wife of an American officer, has every imaginable advantage: a large, splendid apartment, a maid, a car with a chauffeur, elegant clothes and furs, cigarettes, coffee, and chocolate. She is beautiful, content, and in love, and expects life to be easy and merry from now on. At least that's the impression one has. What she really thinks and feels, one never knows. She is unfathomable. Poor Goody was very shocked when I wrote to tell him about Angelika's marriage and she herself didn't add a word. Now he's left standing there empty-handed, and has as good as lost his only daughter. She has completely changed with regard to him, and has presumably never gotten over his remarriage. She was so disappointed and wounded that I couldn't even speak sensibly with her about it. She said she wanted to hear neither about nor from her father. In general, our fate hasn't made her merciful, loving, and tender, but instead wrathful, cold, and hard. So far as she's concerned, I'm prepared for a few surprises and fear that it will be a long time before she has digested the last eight years."

In the spring of 1947 Mizo was appointed professor at the university in Plovdiv, the second-largest city in Bulgaria, and Bettina left Sofia with him and their then two-year-old son.

My mother suffered greatly from the separation with her daughter and grandson.

"I now especially miss Tina," she wrote to Fritz Schwiefert, "she has become so charming and understanding."

Unfortunately, she couldn't say the same about me. I supplied her with cigarettes and food. I sometimes visited her for half an hour or had her picked up with the car and chauffeur and brought to my apartment. But they were painful visits. I couldn't, I wouldn't see her die. Her eyes grew in size and expression as she got smaller and smaller and spoke less and less clearly. One couldn't escape those eyes, with which she begged me for forgiveness, for patience, for love, with which she followed my restless moving back and forth with dismay, resignation, and uneasiness, with which she concealed from me her unhappiness, her loneliness, her helplessness. I couldn't and wouldn't see them, those beautiful, dark suns, in which the darkness was slowly and relentlessly sinking, which made me miserable, drove me to desperation, and aroused the dreaded sympathy, a sympathy so boundless that it turned into rage, into rage at myself, at her, at this damned life. I wanted to be happy, at least imagine that I was happy, I wanted to enjoy this new, pleasant existence, I wanted to shake off the years of hardship, pain, and fear, at least imagine that they could be shaken off. I'd had enough of misery, enough, more than enough, enough for all time. How did she end up persecuting me with her dying, with her eyes, just now, when I finally could lead a life worth living? Hadn't I already loved her much too long and much too greatly? Hadn't I freed myself from her, and didn't I have the right to remain free? Yes, I had that right, and her dying wouldn't force me to give up my freedom again.

"Angelika," said Ed, my husband, who treated my mother with unburdened, unforced affection, "she doesn't ask anything of you."

"But that's much worse," I replied, "why can she no longer complain and scream and demand? Why does she have to make me feel guilty with her eyes?"

"Darling, we'll be leaving soon now, and so will your mother. Then it will be much easier for you and for her."

Ed was transferred, precisely to Germany, and I confronted this unexpected turn of events with uneasiness and doubts. Sometime in May I would leave Bulgaria—the country in which I had changed from an oversensitive child to an implacable woman, in which I had experienced the greatest unhappiness and, at the age of sixteen, in Buhovo, the greatest happiness, the country that had shaped me for the rest of my life.

Sometime late in the summer my mother would leave Bulgaria—the country in which she had found refuge and experienced hell, the country in which she had changed from a beautiful, vital woman to a physically and psychologically damaged creature.

We would leave Bulgaria, she to die, I to live.

"Now I have my American entrance visa," she wrote to Fritz Schwiefert, "I have only the exit visa to obtain. So I'll probably come in early September. It will be hard for me to say goodbye not only to Tina and André, but also to the sun. How cold I'm going to be in Germany—in body and in soul."

She got ready for her trip, sold her last ring, had her hair dyed reddish-brown, and her teeth, which were in bad condition, repaired. She had the clothes that hung loosely on her body taken in and bought material for a suit on the black market. Then she went to see my sister in Plovdiv and stayed two weeks there.

When she was back, she came to have coffee with me. She drank in small, careful sips and told me about Bettina: in what miserable conditions she was living! An ugly apartment, which she had moreover to share with another family. The money that Mizo earned as a professor was barely enough for necessities, but not for a new dress. Bettina worked from morning to night to keep the two rooms clean and orderly, to scrub the floors, wash the laundry, stand in line for food, cook something halfway reasonable. I had to attend very carefully in order to understand her, and forced myself to sit quietly and listen to what a wretched life my sister was eking out. Did my mother want me to feel ashamed of my good life, to feel guilty, to melt with sympathy? Did she hold it against me, that I once again had everything, and my sister had nothing? Was I somehow responsible for that?

"And she is so brave," my mother said, "so upright and willing to sacrifice."

"You see, Mummy, and I'm not at all like that. And I'm happy that I'm not. That's all I need!"

"You're an entirely different kind of person, I don't know what kind."

"And you, Mummy, what kind of person were you when you were young?"

"A person whom I now wish I hadn't been. And you have to be careful that that doesn't happen to you, too."

"I don't care, Mummy, what I'm going to wish thirty years from now. What I wish now, and thanks to a lucky accident I can have, is the only thing that matters to me. Eight years were enough, and now that they're more or less over, no one has the right to tell me how I should lead my life. What I do or don't do with it from now on is nobody's business but my own."

"Angeli, I don't want anything but for you to be happy."

"You don't control that, Mummy, we've now seen that clearly enough."

"But you do."

"Yes, until the next time."

"How can one be so negative at the age of eighteen!?"

"I'll give you three guesses!"

That was the last conversation I had with my mother in Bulgaria, and I could even say that it was the last conversation period, because in Germany I avoided her right up to the end.

I said goodbye to her on the day before I left. I went to

Murgash Street, to the small room in which I had lived with her for two years. I looked at the green tiled stove that I'd lit every morning in the winter, the alcohol cooker on which we had cooked white beans for hours; I looked at the two narrow beds, the rotting floors, the shabby writing pad and penholder on the rectangular, long-legged table, the photo of my dead brother.

"Yes," my mother said, who had followed my gaze, "now this is behind you, thank God."

"You, too."

She remained silent and smiled a terribly sad smile.

I looked quickly away.

"When you go to visit Bettina," I said, "give her a hug for me."

"You probably won't see her again for a long time."

"She'll soon visit us in Germany."

"Do you really believe she will?"

She looked at me, as if Bettina's visit depended on me. I nodded. Naturally, I didn't really believe it—what did I really believe, anyway—but I would also not have believed that I was not to see my sister for eighteen long years.

"Give good old Ed a kiss for me," my mother said, "I'm so happy that you have him. He loves you very much."

"I love him, too."

"I've written to your father to tell him that you're coming."

"You'd have done better not to have told him that. I'm not going to see him."

"You can't forgive us, is that it?"

"What does that have to do with it?"

"We made many mistakes."

"Stop it, Mummy!"

She put her arms around me. "Goodbye, my little one, I'm terribly fond of you."

I felt her emaciated body, her dried-out lips, her hooked hands, and I thought: this used to be my mother.

I left Bulgaria on May 23, 1947. My mother arrived in Germany three months later. She lived another year and a half.

The following letters, which she wrote during this time, document a ruined country, a ruined people, and a ruined person.

AND LIFE WAS BEAUTIFUL, AFTER ALL

Garmisch, September 1947

Bettina, my sweet, today is the eighth, and I'm finally, finally (!) in Garmisch. I had more problems between Salzburg and Munich (three hours) than between Sofia and Salzburg. All the information I'd been given earlier turned out to be false. As a result, I had so much to cope with during my stay in Salzburg that I hardly saw anything of the wonderful city. So many beautiful old buildings and such attractive girls in traditional costumes, and especially everything was so bright and clean and friendly. In the train I sat by the window and gazed out and took pleasure in the landscape, which looks so different from the Bulgarian landscape—so green, soft, and sweet, little houses, each cuter than the last, flowers on the windowsills and in the gardens, the people so neat and clean, the farms so orderly, every hen, every goose looked as if it had just been washed, the whole landscape looked as if it had just been tidied up or painted in a picture book. And up to now that is my strongest impression: this cared-for look. It's as if I've been freed, as if something that has weighed on me for years has fallen away. I see that this German order and cleanliness are as necessary to me as eating and drinking.

I'll move on. I traveled the last stretch from Salzburg to Munich in a little Bavarian train that was packed to the breaking point, in which people complained and scoffed outrageously, about the Americans, the English, the Jews, the regulations, the food shortages, the organizations. Since they thought I was a foreigner and believed I didn't understand a word, they spoke openly. After a while it got to be too much for me, and when someone made a particularly insolent remark, I said: "You'd better be careful, I speak German as well as you do." You should have seen their faces, these stupid, blond, Bavarian faces. So that they would get over their fear, I handed out cigarettes and gave the children candies, and then they were all terribly fond of me. When we finally arrived in Munich, three hours late, they carried my luggage and led me to the gate in a triumphal procession.

I was convinced that Goody had finally given up on me and left, but there he stood, true and loyal and looking in a direction from which I couldn't possibly come. Typical! I called and ran toward him, and everything was as it always was—the same warm, deep relationship, no feeling of estrangement, no inhibition. Papa is unchanged, perhaps a little thinner, a little stooped, and the hair on his temples is white. But otherwise he's the old Goody—dear and kind.

We spent the night at the home of friends of Papa's, and there too everything was pretty and well cared-for, a tiled bath, white washbasin, but no hot water and no electricity because of restrictions on the use of electricity. I was surprised by that, but the next day I was to be far more surprised. Munich is one big pile of ruins, hardly a building in the old center of the city is intact, only the façades are still standing. The streets are full of bomb craters and rubble. People don't look like they're starving, and are also not at all badly clothed, but many of the young people already have white hair. And the honesty, the famous German honesty, is down the drain. Anything that is not nailed down is stolen: suitcases disappear, crates are broken open, trucks robbed. Inconceivable, isn't it?

The next day we continued on to Garmisch, where Papa, Lilo, and her daughter Beate live, eat, and sleep in one room plus a verandah, and everything is higgledy-piggeldy. But the house is very attractive, the garden beautiful, the landscape so lovely—despite the poverty, primitiveness and shortages everywhere, it can't be compared with Bulgaria. I'm staying in a different house, in a particularly pretty room. In the corridors there are fine old pieces of furniture, everything is very tasteful.

Both Papa's landlady and mine are big, blond ladies who have lost their husbands and their money and feed themselves and their children by renting out rooms in their houses. But nothing is squalid or dirty. Three blond girls live in my house, and when I go to the bathroom in the evening, there are three little piles of children's clothes lying there, one piece exactly on top of the other.

I eat with Papa, Lilo, and Beate, who are showering me with love and attention. In Papa's case it is certainly genuine, in Lilo's I'm not yet sure. She looks bad, very emaciated and not at all pretty anymore. Her famous beautiful hands have become raw and broad, because she cooks, cleans, washes, and darns just like women in Bulgaria. Beate, who is eight years old, is cute and affected, is constantly putting on an act, but I like her nonetheless.

I've already gone on long walks with Papa, and we've spoken openly about everything. That is the most positive thing I've experienced here yet. Otherwise, life in Germany is infinitely complicated. Intellectually, I don't like it, and materially it no longer exists. There is nothing, nothing at all to buy and to eat. On the other hand, there are countless offices, authorities, and organizations through which one has to pass before one can even draw a breath. Coming into the country, going out of it, moving in, moving to another place, moving away, everything involves grotesque running around, begging, forms, stamps, and permissions. My head is filled to point of exploding with a jumble of thoughts and questions that I don't pursue all the way for fear of what I will find out. It's all alien, so different, so uncertain and undecided, but sometimes the secret thought surges up: Why did you come here, anyway? What are you doing here? I look for the reason and don't find it. Maybe it's all still too much for me, and first I have to calm down. I could always weep and laugh. It's so sad and then again very funny. I still see, thank God, what is comic in the most tragic things.

If only you hadn't cried so much at the farm, my little Tina. And my little boy, what is he doing? I kiss you all and long to see you.

Garmisch, October 1947

My good, little Tina, finally your eagerly awaited letter arrived. Wasn't it crazy of me to go back to Germany? I am constantly wondering how I can be with you all again—here or there. It can't go on like this forever!

You ask how I'm living here, so I'll describe it to you in detail:

My room, which was around the corner from Papa's, I have had to give up, and now I'm living half an hour away from him in a pension for people who have been persecuted on racist, religious, or political grounds. As "atonement" for what was done to us, here we are given privileges that make everyday life a little easier for us. I had to go to Munich three times and go to various offices in order to get permission to take up residence in Garmisch. I encountered great sympathy everywhere, and now I also have the residence permit, which is completely impossible for ordinary mortals to acquire. Soon I will be moving for the third and I hope last time into a room that will be in Papa's house. That was his wish, and in view of the fact that he will slowly go mad in his own lodging, it is probably also the best solution. Then he can escape to my room and be alone for at least a few hours a day. I have never seen him before the way he is now: impatient with Lilo and terribly unfair to Beate, who has to put up with a great deal from him. When he's in a bad mood, he rants and raves at them constantly, and behaves absolutely peculiarly. The two of them can now really do nothing about the misery. But often he is also charming again and content, and with me he is full of great understanding and helpful goodness. He has gone with me to each of the offices, and there was nothing he wouldn't do. I also find Lilo exceptionally patient, gentle, and brave. She works a great deal, never complains, does what she can for me, and is tactful in every respect.

This is how my day goes: in the morning, breakfast in my room, then errands, shopping, etc., then lunch at Papa's room (potatoes with sauce or sauce with potatoes), then lying in the sun (if there is any) or sleeping, then at five o'clock tea with a slice of bread, then writing letters (mainly business letters for Papa), then supper, then sleep. The food doesn't taste so good, but poor Lilo can't do anything about that, because try cooking tasty food without onions, fat, or pepper. One dish tastes like another and like nothing at all.

At the moment I'm sitting on the balcony, and above me a newborn is bellowing. Slovakian refugees live in the room on our left, a father, mother, and five children, all in one room. In the room to the right of us there is a mother with her ten-year-old son, and above us the parents of the newborn, who are constantly thrashing one another. In front of me is the athletic field. That's where the Americans amuse themselves, drive out to the middle of it in their cars, march with music, belt out the national anthem, and then hop back in their cars and drive away. And all around me lies the very splendid Garmisch, the mountains, radiant blue sky, and sun—it could be very beautiful if one were more beautiful oneself. Often I go to the doctor, who gives me injections, but my face will probably never get any better. I notice only one improvement, maybe: I seem to swallow the wrong way less. My throat eats and drinks better.

The more often I come to Munich, the more upset I am. These conditions! To save electricity, the trams run only two hours in the morning and in the afternoon until eight in the evening, there are no cars, one has to run until one can run no more, sleep sometimes at one person's house, sometimes at another's, no one has anything to eat, there are not nearly enough coupons, everywhere people are lugging their food with them, it's dreadful. I haven't been to the theater even once. At the hairdresser's, one has to make an appointment a week in advance, cobblers, and craftsmen in general, work only for cigarettes, and even then they don't work. The prices on the black market are exorbitant, a pound of onions costs 25 marks, a pound of peas 30 marks, there's no sugar to be had, or eggs either, butter costs 200 marks a pound. No one works, there is no material, no workers. People who have money eat it up, Papa is selling what he has, and is also eating it up. The people's mood is miserable, one sees signs of a recovery nowhere, everybody muddles along without meaning or understanding and steals.

I'm very curious about Berlin. I think another wind is blowing there, even if people say it's no better.

Berlin, November 1947

My little Bettina, now we are in Berlin, and I have so much to tell you. Nonetheless, it will be only part of what I've seen and heard, and then again only part of what has really happened. No one who hasn't experienced it can imagine what took place in Berlin when Germany finally surrendered and the victorious troops marched in. Things happened whose horror we cannot even guess, and that go beyond our powers of conception. There is not a single family that is not mourning one of its members, not a single person who emerged from this hell without being beaten, sick, or destroyed. Whether they are refugees who have watched their family members starve, or people who have lost everything, absolutely everything, or women who've already been waiting for years to see if their missing husbands might yet come back, whether they are mothers looking for their children or children looking for their parents, it's horrible and incredible, and I will never, ever understand how a whole people could have allowed itself to be drawn into such hellish madness. It's all so aberrant that one constantly thinks, this kind of thing doesn't exist in reality. But it is reality, and it's as though I'm still in a nightmare. For the first time in my life I find that I can no longer read. I feel bad and dizzy.

Yesterday I drove through Berlin with Dr. Filier. We drove for two hours, from the West End to the Alexanderplatz, Lützowplatz, Wittenbergerplatz, the Bavarian quarter, the castle, the Tiergarten,

Brandenburg Gate, Unter den Linden, Tauentzienstraße, and along the Kurfürstendamm—no matter how I count it up, it all looked the same. It's a dead city that consists solely of ruins and façades and where one sees into the destroyed interiors of the buildings through empty window frames. Strange silhouettes rise up against the sky, like the pictures that were called "degenerate art" during the Nazi period. The Kaiser Wilhelm memorial church looks like a charred layer cake whose top has been broken off. There is not an intact building here and there, for kilometers there are not any buildings at all, only ruins, ruins that are unrecognizable even for me, a Berliner who lived for fifty years in this city. I could no longer find my way around at all, and had to constantly ask Filier: "Where are we now . . . what is, or rather what was, that?" Once he said: "That's the Knie," and then I could have almost cried. The Knie—you know, where I grew up, where Grandma and Grandpa lived, I didn't recognize it! And the Tiergarten is gone, there is hardly a tree or shrub left, the Tiergarten looks like a grazed-over field, neglected, with burnt trunks, perhaps ten trees still stand lonely and scattered around, and suddenly there is somewhere a bronze deer or a monumental statue without a head. At the Brandenburg Gate, what used to be Victory's chariot lies here and there as if in a junkyard. And yet people are already living in the outlying districts, and all the artists are there, painters, sculptors, writers, theater people. There are the most beautiful theatrical performances, there are concerts, artists' clubs, cabarets, exhibits. The artists say: only in Berlin is there life, only in Berlin is it worthwhile to work, Berlin will become a center again. And I too must say: even if they are ruins, they are Berlin ruins, the Munich ruins will always remain alien to me. Papa thinks the same, but has not yet had the courage to return to Berlin.

I was in the Schrobsdorff grandparents' villa in the West End, in Papa's last apartment, in his office, and in Pätz. When one goes through the old rooms like that, the first thing one notices is how much property the Schrobsdorffs had. Despite the enormous damage, there is still more there than most people have ever owned, and it is still enough for many families. But if you could see the old Schrobsdorffs' villa now! Everything has been destroyed and broken up. The built-in wall cabinets, the wainscotting, the wooden ceilings, the parquet floors have all been ripped out and ruined, the marble basins and bathtubs shattered. The remains of the furniture lie all around in dreadful condition amid building material, crates, wood, stones, roofing paper that Alfred, who then dealt in it, had brought in. He and Walter got rich where and how they could. They behaved like swine in the truest sense of the word, lied and deceived and didn't hesitate at anything. Moreover, because of his glorious Nazi past Walter is scared to death, and both brothers are trying everywhere to take advantage of poor Papa, whose integrity they envy. It's simply inconceivable what filth, envy, and amorality is going on here. Anja, the monster who literally sent her own mother into Lake Pätz and thereby got rid of her Jewish ancestry, is now suddenly a full Jew, living with all four children in southern Germany, and having a good time. Both of Walter's children are with a nanny somewhere in the French zone, while Ulli, their mother, amuses herself with various men in Berlin. Frau Guttsmann, Papa's bookkeeper, with whom I am staying here, lost her husband in Auschwitz and now uses her privileged status to take possession of various valuables that don't belong to her. Not only has an external chaos set in, but also an internal one. There is no longer any mine and thine, everyone does what he wants, and the decline is taking place all along the line.

But now to go on to Pätz and the good Schwankes. We drove there in a car, an ancient jalopy that had a kind of furnace attached to the back. When one heats the furnace, it runs—at least sometimes. We were lucky and arrived in Pätz, but when I saw all that again, the old familiar roads, the village, the lake, and then the gate, the garden, the house, and the two Schwankes, who rushed to meet us, I ran away and went down to the lake, because I had to cry so dreadfully. I suddenly saw you two in front of me—you with the black bob and the red swimsuit, Angeli on her pony, Peter lying on the grass in the sun, father and mother battling the wasps at the breakfast table, Ilse, Ellen, and all the other friends—it was so lively, I couldn't stand it, it was so infinitely painful. Frau Schwanke walked after me, embraced me, held me and wept with me, and then, little by little, I regained my composure.

We stayed two days, and the Schwankes thought of nothing but what they could do for us that was loving and good. In the big room, there was a stove that burned day and night. Most of the time I sat by it, and Frau Schwanke told me so much that was sad and unimaginable. I will never understand how all that could happen, there is no explanation for it, and all that world produced, I believe, was madness.

Grandmother Schrobsdorff died in Pätz under the most horrible conditions. There she lived to experience the Russian invasion, greeted the soldiers in her house with a nod, but was then only on the edge of consciousness. One of the soldiers said to Frau Schwanke: "Mother sick, poor mother." The next day she was dead. None of her sons was with her, even though Alfred and Walter were in Berlin. The Schwankes wrapped her in a sheet and carried her out in to the field in a handcart, dug a grave, and laid her in it. That was how Grandmother ended up, after a life in which she had been able to satisfy her every wish. The wish to see her children again remained unfulfilled. It's a hard thing to be a mother. I recently read in some book: "A mother's love is always an unhappy love." I have also had a taste of that—from Angelika. Only you are my real, good daughter, who loves me.

Papa is charming, moving, and always concerned to offer me whatever can give me pleasure. Lilo is also still nice to me. They live in one room in Papa's office on the Kaiserdamm, and it is now sometimes remarkable to see Lilo play the role that I played for such a long time. I still turn around or answer when someone speaks to Frau Schrobsdorff. But don't be annoyed by that, basically it doesn't matter, and no longer disturbs me so much.

We constantly receive invitations and go out every evening. It's not pure pleasure, since one has to wait for hours in the cold to find any kind of transportation. There are no longer any taxis, and the tramways, which are also a rarity, go back to the 1890s. Tomorrow I'm finally going to Wannsee, which I really have no desire to do. Papa Schwiefert is indignant that I've put off my visit so long, and Enie is in a bad mood because she's had a quarrel with Leon. It's important, all that! There are people who seem not to have been touched at all by the catastrophe. They include Heini Heuser, whom we saw twice. He is just as he's always been, makes dumb jokes, goes out in society every night, is never alone. But what used to amuse me in him, now strikes me as simply silly. I can no longer deal with such people, become impatient and disgruntled.

My little Tina, now I'm going to crawl into bed. It's always so cold here that I'm already quite desperate. There's no question of bathing anywhere, in every apartment only one room is heated, and I sleep in the cold. Traveling is a real pain, and I'm terribly worried about the return trip.

Berlin, November 1947

My sweet Bettina, I'm sitting here by a candle because Frau Guttsmann has gone beyond her electricity quota and is not allowed to burn any light until December 7. People now talk only about electricity and gas quotas—it's revolting! The theater is also in bad shape. Yesterday we went to the most interesting play of the season, Giraudoux's *The Trojan Will Not Take Place*, which I'd really been looking forward to. Before the first act was over, something indefinable fell down on the stage, missed the head of the male lead by inches, and went up in flames. The audience and the actors panicked, the curtain went down, the bundle of flames was taken away, and the play continued. In the second act, in the middle of a fascinating dialogue, the female lead began to sway, which I at first thought was due to an inappropriate stage direction, and then put both hands to her mouth, which I no longer understood, and fell from the stage. The male lead followed her. The curtain was rung down, and the public was astonished. After a while we were then informed that the play could unfortunately not be continued, because the female lead had suffered a heart spasm. I didn't believe the stuff about a heart spasm. The lady was plainly and simply nauseated, and that I completely understand. Under the circumstances prevailing here, one can hardly avoid feeling nauseated. Instead of having had enough of the theater, the next evening we went to a premiere, and in fact with Enie and Papa Schwiefert. At this performance nothing happened, absolutely nothing, neither foreseen nor unforeseen. The play was thoroughly boring. On the other hand, the audience was interesting, many elegant women, many actors and actresses whom I knew from before. The actors have now all become terribly old, and the elegant women look like nuns, their heads and necks draped in black. Enie goes around like that, too. It seems to be the latest fashion, and has something to be said for it: it conceals badly dyed hair and wrinkled necks. After the performance both Papas looked desperately for bar where we could sit down together for a while. Unfortunately, nothing like that could be found; everything was dark and empty, because on police orders closing time is ten o'clock, in order to conserve electricity. I believe that for me this will be the end of the theater season.

Naturally I did something I shouldn't have done: I wandered around in the streets where I grew up and looked for the buildings in which I lived: Berlinerstraße, where I spent the first fourteen years of my life; Grolmanstraße, where I lived with my parents until my first marriage; Bismarckstraße, where you children so often and so gladly went, where our Grandpa died, and from which poor Grandma was driven at the age of eighty-one. Oh, God, the memories of a time when we were hardly aware of how much we had and how happy we were! It's all ruins and ashes, in us and around us. Not a single building is still intact in these three streets, and one can't even go down Bismarckstraße because there's so much rubble in it. But from where I stood I could see the charred façades of the buildings and the two empty window openings behind which Mother's room used to be. I clambered over the debris and wreckage until I got near Mother's room, hoping that I might still find some trace of her, something familiar to me from the past, perhaps a fork, the shard of a broken plate. But there was nothing, only total devastation. I will never understand how a city of millions could be so ravaged. The whole wrath of the Allies was unloaded on Berlin, smashed it, avenging my parents and all the unfortunate people who were tormented, humiliated, and murdered. And as I imagined that, I felt an enormous satisfaction and said to myself: they should feel what we suffered because of them, they should groan and lament, freeze and starve, wait for their missing husbands, look for their lost children! Haven't we millions of innocents lost everything that could be lost?

My little Tina, I had to interrupt this letter again, because I've moved in with Papa Schwiefert and Enie. But I've had lots of practice in moving from one place to another.

Here in Wannsee I now have everything I could want. No one talks about electricity and gas quotas or about saving this or that. The house is lovely and comfortable, nothing is stolen, burned, or bombed, there's a bath with hot water, and the gas and electric heaters are on all day. Enie, as it turns out, is the cleverest, most skilled person in Germany today. She has dug up two American women—one of them is the secretary of the American supreme commander in Berlin—and rented the studio to them. The result: they pay for everything that goes with it and that doesn't go with it. I've just bathed for half an hour and washed my hair, and now I'm going to Rohrbach's—do you still remember our cobbler Rohrbach? Yesterday I went to the shop of Frau Lemmer, the vegetable woman, and also to Dobrik's. You know, the delicatessen. It was moving the way both of them were pleased and still remembered each of us. Then I walked through the forest, along the same path we so often took on the way to your school. There were the pines, the smell of damp earth and leaves and memories, memories, memories.

Tomorrow we're going to see the *Trojan War* again, and just hope that this time no fire will fall from the heavens and that the leading lady won't faint. By the way, it has been raining constantly, and the sky is grayer than I remembered it. Seen from my present point of view, everything used to be sky blue and rosy red—but that's not true.

Garmisch, November 1947

My good little Tina, I returned without hesitation to Garmisch on November 21, whereas Papa and Lilo remained in Berlin somewhat longer. Five weeks in that devastated city were more than enough. Besides, Angeli is in Garmisch at the moment, and I didn't want to miss seeing her there. Who knows how long I'll still have her here in Germany.

The weeks I spent with Pitt and Enie Schwiefert were on the one hand lovely, and on the other depressing. Lovely, because nothing is broken in Wannsee, and depressing because of the atmosphere, which is mixture of French boulevard theater and Strindberg. To tell the truth, I no longer understand. I really tried to find something attractive in this Leon (Enie's lover), but in vain. He hasn't a trace of intelligence or charm or good looks, there's absolutely nothing, and what Enie, a classy, smart woman sees in him will always be an enigma for me. And probably for poor Pitt as well. He makes a rather beaten-down impression—no wonder!—and I have a feeling that he is just about finished, both as a writer and as a human being. He spends his time in an attic room and rarely comes out of it. He cleans it himself, heats it himself, and appears in the kitchen only to make himself breakfast. Enie, on the other hand, lives in the downstairs rooms and concerns herself very little with Pitt and a great deal with Leon. The two of them meet mainly on the stairs—when he comes down to make tea for himself, and when she goes up to take a bath—and the only thing that seems to bind them together is their financial problems. They have more than enough of those, like everyone else. Pitt's plays, apart from the silly *Margherite and her Three Uncles*, are no longer performed, and if he weren't eating up his savings, just as Papa is eating up his buildings, they would go hungry. The prices for food and heating fuel are exorbitant, and if you're not running a racket or at least selling something on the black market—which doesn't suit either of the two Papas—you're soon done for. I'm not exaggerating. When one goes into a railway station in Germany, one finds boys and girls as young as twelve standing there selling things on the black market. Many children have large amounts of money because they steal cigarettes, coffee, and other valuable things or get them some other way, and then sell them at enormously high prices. I can no longer accept all that, and have truly become a foreigner in this country.

The trip back went pretty well. That's because I've learned to take advantage of my privileged status. I've gotten a pile of papers from various offices that prove that I am what I am: a victim of the Nazis, a foreigner, and sick. And so I now travel in a special car in which there is plenty of room, and I don't have to get out of the train at borders, like all the other passengers, who are obliged to wait as long as three hours, crowded together with their luggage, children, and dogs, until their passports have been stamped.

I am now completely content here in Garmisch, and I will not soon go away again. My greatest happiness is the stove, which I heat until both it and Lilo are red-hot. She says that if I keep doing that, we'll run out of wood in two weeks. So then we'll run out, but at least I'll have been really warm for a few days. Poor Lilo, in Berlin she caught the mumps, and now feels terrible and has become still thinner. And on top of all that I offended her terribly by saying, as we were eating sauerkraut and potatoes for the dozenth time: "This is really nauseating!" No one can tell me that this perpetual sauerkraut and potato eating is necessary. Wherever you go, that's all there is. People let themselves be persuaded that there isn't anything else, and since German cooking is and was bad even at its best, they're not fastidious, they accept it. In other countries, the men would have long since beaten their wives to death. One simply can't make a lot of dishes out of stupid potatoes. I told her all that, and Papa laughed, but she was as furious as a cat that has had water thrown on it.

Angeli comes every day, and you can't imagine how sweet she is. She always brings me something, the finest delicacies, so fine that I almost hesitate to eat them. I am astonished by her, and even more, delighted. I believe she is thawing out again after all.

It's enchanting here now that everything is covered with snow. If you were all here too, I would have nothing more to wish for and would never complain again. Please write me soon, I wait for your letters as I do for the Messiah.

Garmisch, January 1948

My dear Pitt, your letter gave me as much as our conversation. No, I was not, as you believed, disappointed that you didn't sacrifice your work time to me, I found that completely normal. One can't talk for hours on end, and I in particular can't, because every sentence costs me a physical effort. But a little can also be a lot—in content, that is. However, our conversations were unfortunately not only short in time but also short on content. You were so conventional and closed, and that was what disappointed me. That's your business, you know why you were that way, and to be sure, I'm indulgent and don't hold anything against you—or against anyone now. But it was nonetheless sad.

In a letter, I once asked you whether God existed. At that time, you said he didn't. But now you seem to sense God. In my case it was the other way around. All during the years of my emigration I could live only because I had the "secret feeling" that God existed. Now I have lost God, or rather I have lost the secret feeling. It's true that I could never believe without asking myself questions. And that I lacked genuine, deep will in matters of faith. So if belief is question of will—and perhaps you're right that it is—then I have certainly made it too easy for myself. My will was always concentrated on the wrong things, and where I should have used it, it was too inconvenient for me. I am really the last person who would contest that or seek to deny personal guilt—whether metaphysical or profane. But it seems to me that others seek to do that all the more.

When you write: don't expect or ask for more than one can give you, then I have to reply: I haven't been expecting anything for a long time, but if I did, I would not be unjust because I asked for too much, but you two would, because you don't want to give enough. I've suffered more than you have, and in this case I am blameless. But you two are indifferent, and want to forget, and I, with my sick inside and outside, am, stupidly, too heavy a reproach, too heavy a burden for you.

My face was not covered with tears on Peterkin's birthday or on the anniversary of his death, either. It's no worse on January 5 and 7 than on any other day, and besides, I seldom cry. I can't avoid self-accusations, but I try to repress self-pity, because I find it pathetic. I don't always succeed—and then I cry. I think your comparison of me to a kaffir who believes in the medicine man and his magical arts is excellent. But there's a difference: the kaffir doesn't have the choice between a medicine man and a physician—and so he believes in what he has. I, on the contrary, had a choice between highly developed science and dark magic, and I chose the latter. It does no harm and costs nothing. In other words, I gave up all hope of getting better. Look, I don't have a bacillus that can be killed by penicillin or the like, or some benign or malignant tumor that can be cut out. I don't have any conventional illness, I simply broke, and what's broken can't be put back together again.

I find it very interesting that you call me a rationalist. Was I ever a rationalist, or is it possible to become one? I think you shouldn't define me. I am, depending on the circumstances and my constitution, sometimes one thing, sometimes the opposite: rational and emotional, generous and vindictive, smart and dumb, old and childish. Aren't we all that way?

Garmisch, January 1948

My little Tina, I've received a message from Prague that I'm copying for you here:

With regard to your worthy inquiry of November 10, 1947, we inform you that the name Minna Kirschner appears on the so-called cremation list for Theresienstadt under the date December 12/14, 1942. Coffin number 6767. Since these lists give only the name and date of the cremation, an identification is impossible. Thus our communication has only the value of an additional proof, in case witnesses to the death were available. We regret that we cannot give you any better information, and sign

With the greatest respect!

Thus we now know that Grandma lived, that is suffered, in the concentration camp for four months, and that she was then burned up, whether alive or dead cannot be determined from this document. It is very important that we know her coffin number!

In addition, my room was broken into and all my Bulgarian cigarettes, my traveling bag, my watch, and all kinds of other things were stolen. At first the police didn't come at all, and when I went to them, I was told that they would check on the black market. That was all. A lady recently had all her clothes stolen while she was asleep. The police said that she should be glad that she was still alive. They have no time for such trivialities, countless murders are being committed, and they are more important. That's Germany! Happy he who doesn't have to see it. It's dreadful everywhere, life in general is dreadful. Our mistake, when we were young, was to think that life is beautiful.

My little Tina, don't be angry about this bitter letter. It's all a little too much for me.

Garmisch, January 1948

Dear Pitt, how can Mother have died a natural death in Theresienstadt? Isn't every death in a concentration camp an unnatural one? Even if the cause of death is supposed to be, let us say, a pulmonary infection, hadn't she already died many painful deaths? Why did I—as usual—survive at all? I who was such a bad daughter and mother. Have I really ever achieved anything that had a deeper meaning and value? Wasn't my life only a series consisting of craziness, superficiality, selfishness, addiction to pleasure, and erotic madness? Do you also see all your mistakes so clearly, and do they torment you as much? Everywhere I see only my mistakes, and nothing, nothing at all, to which I could cling, about which I could say, yes, that was good and decent. And yet sometimes I don't even regret it. It was beautiful after all.

Garmisch, January 1948

My good Tina, why do you say that I must be happy here? Why do you say that you would immediately trade places with me? Aren't you happy and content? "Wherever you are not, there is happiness," said some great man—in case of doubt, Goethe. Write and tell me honestly how you really are, and don't always tell me only nice stories to spare me. Is it longing that torments you? Believe me, I'm just as tormented as you are, and what you suffer, my child, I suffer a hundred times more, because I'm old and sick and no longer have anything, anything except for the wish to see you and little André again, and to keep Angeli with me in Germany for a while longer. Otherwise, nothing interests me, absolutely nothing. Naturally, there are other things that are important: friendship, for instance, freedom, peace, and others that are beautiful: books, music, and nature. But they can no longer make me happy. Happiness would have been being near my three children, the feeling of being needed by them. Only that would have given me a justification for my existence, only in that way would I have known where I belonged. Because surely you won't seriously claim that I belong here in Germany. If I were at least healthy and could speak and move like a normal person, could work and make myself useful. But I can't even do that anymore. And as always, when one is physically handicapped, can no longer participate, can no longer make oneself comfortable, one becomes cranky, senses betrayal and affront everywhere. That is the case for me as well.

Garmisch, February 1948

My sweet Bettina, today I moved to make a change. My new room is magnificent and is in a stately house. But that is still nothing. A girl lives in the same house—God bless her—who has an American friend, and this American, a clever person, wants to have a warm house and hot water. Since the house has central heating, we all benefit from the American's love, live like kings in overheated rooms, and bathe in a tiled bathtub under streams of steaming water.

The move was made with an ancient rattletrap driven by an excessively ill-tempered Bavarian who constantly complained about the "rubbish" (meaning my precious belongings) and then, to top it all off, couldn't find his way. He got so beside himself that not even a handful of cigarettes could calm him. He swore that he would never again drive rubbish to a street he didn't know. I must add that Garmisch is a village and that the man had lived there all his life. When he refused to transport a second load to the same street, which was now known to him but still suspect, we tried to get a farmer who had a horse-drawn wagon to undertake this difficult task. But he said he didn't want to, first he had to feed the "nags." It took two handfuls of cigarettes to make him change his mind. Title: Bavaria!

For the past four days my cousin Claire has been visiting me. She is staying with me, and it is a great pleasure for both of us to see each other again. She was, like Mother, in Theresienstadt, and suffered greatly. Her sister Eva was murdered in Auschwitz. Of our whole large family only four survived. In addition to her and myself, there is also a male cousin who lives in New York and a female cousin who lives in Palestine.

Today I'm continuing my letter. It's Sunday, and the day has not exactly begun well. Claire suffered a circulatory collapse. I called in our doctor, who gave her injections, and then she improved. She is, like all of us who have been through so much, broken. We survived in order now to die, very quickly, one after the other.

I'd like to return once more to your last letter. It sounded so skeptical, Tina, that I fear you don't believe what I'm telling you about the situation here. And how could you, who carry and protect Germany within you as a beautiful, intact memory, imag-

ine that nothing remains of what we loved? And yet it is so, and
even if you had the possibility of coming here, and even though
I long for nothing more than that, I would have to go against my
own interests and advise you wait a while longer. You still have
more to eat than we do. Here you couldn't feed yourselves properly, and that is particularly bad for young children and couldn't
be justified. Children who go to school are given a hot meal by
the Americans. Ever since the children like to go to school.
Beate doesn't miss a day and raves about the cocoa and hotcakes
or pea soup. She swears that there's even fat in it. Since large-
scale graft has caused the whole supply of fat to break down, we
can no longer afford even a few grams of margarine. Prices have
reached astronomical levels. We received a desperate letter from
the poor Schwankes. They—that is, the Russians—want to take
the large and the small house away from them, and the ponies as
well. In other words, the Schrobsdorffs' property in Pätz is
being confiscated. And that means that all the things that were
put there to keep them safe will disappear. There wasn't much.
Clever Papa moved the valuable things, his whole wardrobe and
especially his beloved library, to an isolated sawmill at the end of
the world, and then battles were fought precisely there and
everything went up in flames. Now Papa wears borrowed or
donated suits and shoes. Imagine that!

More horror stories, you'll say, and I don't want to burden
you with them, either, for God's sake. But I still have many pleasures, especially of a heavenly nature. When the sun shines and
the sky stands out deep blue against white snow and the water
in the Loisach is so clear that one sees the pebbles on the river
bottom, then I feel pleasure and consolation. And in addition
there is also music and now and then nice people. If I recently
wrote that life was absolutely dreadful, then you are allowed not
to believe that. It is very beautiful, despite all its ordeals.

Garmisch, March 1948

My dear Tina, today your letter finally came—along with Martinitza (a gift for the beginning of spring!)! What a question, whether I still remember it! Did you think I would forget so soon? I will never forget all that, and the more time passes, the stronger my memories become, and I even find some beautiful ones among them.

Since I left, Bulgaria has come much closer to me. Sometimes I long for it. The original, the natural, the primitive, the people's hospitality, the directness and warmth of their relationships—I miss all that very much.

Ach, child, I'm really not happy here, I belong to you, and if I could be with you and not be a burden, but rather a help, that would be happiness for me. You can't understand it, Tina, but if you were here you would understand everything. The Germans are incorrigible. They have not shed their arrogance, they have not understood anything, have not learned anything. And if anything disturbs them, it's not what they have done, but what is being done to them now. They can't bear being the defeated and the inferiors, they complain and vituperate and are obviously not at all aware that they have gotten themselves into this position through their own fault.

I've been severely disappointed, and by Papa as well. Even Ed, who greatly admires his father-in-law, recently lost his patience and said to him: "If Germans are bitter about the American occupation, then I can only reply: We are two and three times as bitter about the Germans and are only longing for the day when we can get out and leave this country to its fate."

But woe to us when they go away and leave Germany to the Russians! Many people here fear that and tremble and consider plans for getting out as fast as possible and wonder where they can hide. Papa lives in a constant state of panic that infects everyone except me. I'm completely calm, have no fear at all, and see from this how hardened I already am, how used

I am to tolerating whatever is imposed on me. How pointless it is to run away, no one runs away from his fate. We Jews have learned that from perpetual persecution and suffering, we bow our heads and put up with it. But here people are building up rage and feel no remorse and have understood nothing. I'm afraid that before they get wiser they'll have to experience and endure a great deal more. You mustn't think that Papa would let me feel anything personally. Of course he wouldn't. But sometimes, in his agitation and rage, he doesn't hear what he's saying, and I can't bear that. Peter died for us, and millions of people have been murdered. No one must ever forget that.

Otherwise, everything remains the same. We are going crazy in the one room, where I spend the whole day. If now the baby comes too and screams day and night, the frantically maintained domestic peace will break down altogether. I was recently at Angeli's, she hardly eats anymore and is thin as a rail, no longer has her period, has trigeminal nerve attacks over the right eyebrow that began back in Bulgaria. She runs to the doctors who, delighted with such a pretty and lucrative patient, try to treat her with various cures, injections, and the devil knows what else. I don't know how this will turn out, and worry about her and poor Ed. He gives and gives, and she has everything and he has nothing. Nonetheless, like Papa, he's wax in Angeli's hands.

Garmisch, April 1948

Dear Pitt, I've received a letter from Bettina. She was summoned to the French consulate and given the things Peterkin left behind. She writes: "Everything was tied up in a silk cloth: a batch of letters from Liena, from Ilse, from us, with foreign money hidden and sealed among them, his engagement ring, and a little gold pendant from Ellen, "Everybody loves you," various decorations, a little lock of hair from Liena, a small album with photographs of us, Liena, Sergette, passport photos of himself, a bag with insignia from all countries (probably from men who died), including swastikas and imperial eagles, two pocket watches, two prayer books, two books, letters to us, his passport and documents, comb and fountain pen, a silver Star of David.

Garmisch, June 1948

My sweet, on Sunday the currency reform descended upon us—it means that we can throw our old money in the trash can, and the new money that they gave us in exchange is not sufficient for anything. Buying on the black market is now out of the question, and thus we have to make do with our food coupons. Lilo just sits there and calculates. As if that would change anything in the slightest. But it is at least a pretext for not doing something else.

Recently poor Papa felt very badly again. He had felt dizzy and his ears were ringing. The doctor discovered an uneven pulse and much too low blood pressure. No wonder! He's completely overstrained, and Lilo is to blame. In addition to his work, which is as arduous as it is unprofitable, he has to run around and carry things and do everything for her. She very often torments him. But I did too, in my time. One must take care not to forget one's own mistakes and think that one would have done better. It's easy to criticize. And besides, Lilo also has it hard, being as far advanced in her pregnancy and as shapelessly fat as he is. It was crazy of Papa, at his age and under these circumstances, to marry a young woman and then also bring another child into the world. It can't turn out well, I can see that clearly: if only he at least gets his long yearned-for son! That might still save the whole thing.

Garmisch, July 1948

My child, I beg you to be reasonable and not to talk about Papa that way. He is so good to us all, and he is very fond of you. How unhappy he would be if he knew how you reacted to his last letter. No, he no longer conceals anything from me, either in his relation to me or in his relation to Lilo. He is the truest, most reliable friend I have in the whole world, and Lilo is a generous, thoroughly good person. You must be generous and magnanimous, not petty and bourgeois, especially with regard to people who are as good and as decent as your Papa. And you also mustn't speak ill of Lilo. Just look around at people and tell me how many there are who would take in a woman like me unquestioningly and even with sincere warmth. Of course, in both Lilo's case and Papa's, feelings of guilt with respect to me still play a role. But that doesn't diminish their decency—on the contrary. Most people repress their feelings of guilt, rid themselves of them in one way or another. Lilo and Papa live with their personified guilt, have it constantly before their eyes. How many people can do that?

I know, Tina, that it is only your loyalty and your love for me that makes you see the two of them in so false a light, but nonetheless I ask you to adopt a little of my tolerance and become more tractable. It's what is best for all of us.

Garmisch, July 1948

Dear Pitt, when I wrote to you, perhaps I needed you for once, and then it was because of this feeling that I no longer belong anywhere. My existence here is that of a totally dependent person. One gets used to everything, even that, only: should one get used to it? Erich and Lilo are so good and decent to me and relieve me, with the rarest tact, of every care of a financial nature. But should it go on like this? At my age, with my head and my independence, I simply blunder on without knowing where I belong. At first my anxiety was so acute that I wanted to ask you for help. Now it's no longer so acute, but someone has to come and talk to Erich, make it clear to him that he has to make me secure, that I can't live like a poor relation who asks for pocket money and has to go to him when she needs a new coat. But don't misunderstand me! He doesn't make me feel bad, he'd give me what I ask. And if he gave me a so-called security in the form of a larger sum of money that I could live on exclusively, I would probably be less well off. But it would nonetheless be better. I can't tell Erich that. He's goodness itself, and besides with the currency reform he now has serious financial difficulties. And he's so inept that it could make you weep! He earns nothing in the regular way, and he can't do it in irregular ways. Lilo is having a baby, and Pitt, for the whole family we have just one room!

I went again to a new doctor, and he said what I'd expected and what you will not want to hear: there's nothing to be done. The doctor I consulted back then in Berlin was right, of course. I didn't want to take it in, but inside I knew it was true. It's an illness on which no research has been done, it's incurable, and I have only one chance: that it stays as it is, and—I know in my gut—that won't happen. The doctor does consider it possible, but it would be unique—in other words, the famous miracle. I couldn't see why it should happen precisely to me. I was often a unique case, but always in a negative sense. Therein lay my talent. Moreover, I feel that this illness, which is as strange as it is rare, is somehow just. I always plumbed and still plumb my illnesses in depth, and recognize their meaning. Now it's up to me to come to terms with it, and I don't find that so hard. It isn't death that I fear, it's dying. Mother always said: "How one leaves this world is terrible, and not that one has to leave it."

Well, enough of that, other people have suffered far more than I have. And life was beautiful, after all.

I don't understand at all what your sister Luzie is talking about. Bettina and Mizo are not on their way, on the contrary, there is less prospect than ever before that they will be allowed to leave Bulgaria. The regulations are made stricter every day, and soon the Iron Curtain will be hermetically sealed and it won't be possible to do anything at all. That's one reason why I'm so depressed. If Bettina and the child were here, then I would know again where I belong. There are many wonderful relationships among people, but the only natural, firm, and true bond is blood. And without it I no longer have any foothold, I can no longer live, not here, in this country, in which I have become a stranger.

We seldom see Angelika because she is acting in a play directed by Herr Domin, whom you probably know by name. He is supposed to be fascinated by her—whether by her face and figure or by the American cigarettes and coffee or by her talent, I have not been able to discover. In any case she has a new six-seater car, and while her husband is studying up on Russian at the school in Oberammergau, Angelika drives elegantly through Munich and attracts attention.

Forgive me, Pitt, for always burdening you with my fears and hardships, but I've become so helpless. Your tirade did my heart good. I understand you so well! Shit everywhere, and the constant appeals to hang on, to go slowly, but of course also the contrary. Darkness and cold cannot be borne. Moreover, in such conditions I completely lose my composure. Nonetheless, I don't share your opinion regarding the Allies. I am on a very different level than you. The last twelve years have fundamentally changed me, and our attitudes, yours and mine, have been so differently shaped that we no longer have any common language. Besides, I willingly admit that on this point I am biased to the point of narrow-mindedness: I hate only the Germans, and no matter what the victors do, I would always find excuses for them, even if I believed absolutely everything that people reproach them for. They are the ones who saved me and for six long years gave me the strength to go on. When I could hardly get up in the morning, I consoled myself by thinking of the evening, when I could listen to the English news broadcast. And I found Churchill so brilliant and the way the English waged the war and the courage of the English people so grandiose and their attitude toward Jews so civilized that I can never forget what they have done. What is happening now is certainly to be attributed to the Allies' stupidity, but 50 percent of it is also civilized, because these two characteristics obviously go hand in hand. So what should they do, in your opinion? What would you do without the so-called airlift? Why always malicious criticism, when no one has a better idea? The Russians will manage, and it's only a question of time, how long the "golden West" will still shimmer with gold. Moreover, I'm absolutely not against the Russians, but I was sick of Bulgaria and feel very comfortable in a parlor, like simple people better than "refined" ones, and find that the old ideas and attitudes are no longer existentially justified and that people who can't separate themselves from them seem very tense and cramped. Here I'm decried as a "Red," and at first I often had quarrels with Erich, who has, as you all do, an obsessive fear of the Russians.

I find unbearable the people who are literally enthralled by the Russians' crimes and who draw the edifying but false conclusion that "they're no better than we are." Fundamentally, nothing has changed in their attitude. They are already complaining about Jews again, feel that they are being gratuitously mistreated by the victors, and are convinced of their own superiority and of the victors' envy and inferiority. And when the occupation is over, within one year we'll have the same old crap. It's just too bad that I really fall between two stools and that neither the West nor the East is right for me. As a person deprived of her rights I feel myself drawn to the Russians, but by my nature and temperament I am a westerner.

I'm sorry that you must work so hard. Not having any money is terrible, especially when there is still much to tempt one, as in your case. But tell me about it, we don't have any money either, but we do now have a house, which Erich bought, on our backs. That's what Lilo wanted, and poor Erich allowed himself, as always, to get roped into it. Now he has so many worries that he's completely at a loss to know what to do, and all we talk about is saving money, and all that is sometimes dismal. What good is a house if it puts you on the verge of bankruptcy? But we live in a "cultivated" way, as people of our kind are supposed to. Important! Living in harmony would be better. And Gauting is such a crummy place. When I think of Wannsee! You can be happy, Enie, that you haven't lost anything and are healthy. At sixty, you can still enjoy life. I sometimes think about how easy it is to get old when one is healthy in body and mind. I was never bothered by diseases, but now I know what they mean. Another kind of illness! I'm no longer even half a person, so skinny my bones show and so weak that I can hardly walk anymore. Nothing works properly, not even my heart, I can't talk, swallow, or breathe right, and now my hands don't work either. I can hardly move them. But enough of that, it's not interesting.

I just got a letter from Tina. She's such a good person, and I'm always afraid that I'll never see her again. Angelika doesn't give me much pleasure, but she doesn't realize it—I was in fact hard on my mother, too. If only I still had my mother!

Garmisch, September 1948

My sweet, finally a letter from you! Papa read it, including the ironic remark that the birth of the baby is an "enormous joy" for you. He didn't say a word, and maybe he didn't take it seriously. But I don't think so, and I'm very sad for him.

Tina, if now you can't write a nice letter congratulating him and Lilo, then you don't care about me. I told you in my last letter how much I think of the two of them, and asked you to be reasonable. How often do I have to remind you that Papa and Lilo are my only support and that with your ungracious behavior you're clouding our relationship, because they certainly believe that I'm behind it. How can one be so stubborn, Tina! And what can the little thing do about it? You, who like children so much, would melt on seeing her. She's so sweet.

Listen, I'm going to tell you the truth: the business with Lilo and Papa no longer bothers me, it's all over and done with, and often I'm even happy not to be in Lilo's shoes. She undoubtedly imagined it all quite differently. Believe me, it's no fun being cooped up in a room day and night with an irritable, grousing man who is constantly flying off the handle out of nervousness and venting his moods on you. Just now the chaos came to a head, and I wish you could see our room, so that you would never again think I'm exaggerating: Beate, the poor child, is never properly cared for, and has been suffering from a liver infection for weeks; Papa's foot got infected, and now he has blood poisoning and has to have an operation; and on top of all that Lilo's frenetic mother and foolish aunt have arrived. Thus while Papa sits with his bandaged foot in the living-work-dining-bed-children's room, Beate lies in the glassed-in verandah kitchen and goes to the potty opposite the hot-plate. At the same time, mother, aunt, Lilo, and the baby are flouncing around. Everyone is talking, complaining, ranting. There's never any peace, any order—never. That how we live here, and maybe it's a just punishment for having been so spoiled and having taken houses and gardens and cars and clothes and wonderful meals for granted.

For the last time, and in all seriousness: write them both a warm letter of congratulation, and if that's really so hard for you, think that you're doing it not only for them but for me as well.

Garmisch, October 1948

My little Angelika, it's really no longer necessary for you to send us food. First of all there's now plenty to buy in the shops, and secondly I can tell that it's not easy for you and that you're even cutting back on your own food. It would be thoughtless of us to continue in the same old routine and go on the way we earlier did, when you were our only source and I had the impression that it didn't bother you to accept gifts. So whatever you bring will be paid for.

It was very nice in your apartment. You can't imagine how much I enjoyed the good meal, the heated room, the bath, and even the big mirror. I always sit in front of it and try out your fine cosmetics.

As for Lilo, I'd like to tell you once again that you're being unfair. You don't know her good sides and don't want to get to know them. How many women do you think would manage living with me with such tact and patience? Just honestly put yourself in her place for once and ask yourself how you would react. To be sure, at first her goal was to catch Papa, but she has accepted the heavy duties that resulted from her success. Hopefully not only for his sake, but also out of her own inner conviction. However, it would be terrible if, as you believe, another side of her came out when Papa is no longer there.

Garmisch, October 1948

My little Tina, things are happening here! Papa has bought a house, that is, Lilo bought it, with the courage of desperation. Our room was running over, and we were about to murder each other. So while Papa was away for a lengthy period, Lilo seized the opportunity and spent her days and half the night looking for a house. In such matters she is very persistent, and adept as well. She found what she was looking for, and

sent bewildered Papa the purchase contract. And he, as he
always does when someone holds a gun to his head, did what
was asked of him. He signed, without even having seen the
house. Now at least I know how Lilo snared Papa.

In the meantime we'd all gone to inspect the house. It is
located in Gauting, half an hour away from Munich, like
Wannsee, but without a lake and without charm. But Gauting
is supposed to be a nice place, and the house is on its outskirts.
It is right next to a deep and dark Hansel and Gretel forest.
The rooms are very low, because everything is built to fit
beneath the famous Bavarian roof, which is high and pointed.
The room to be assigned to me is small, but nice—well, it
doesn't matter. Nothing matters to me. Nothing. The others
are already making thousands of plans and are surprised that
I don't participate at all in the general excitement. The owners of the new house are completely crazy. They have a dog, a
cat, a parakeet, a hedgehog, many turtles, and geese. When we
came into the kitchen during our tour of the house, we found
an enormously large white plaster goose sitting on a chair, and
when we asked about the deeper meaning of this monstrosity,
the lady of the house confided in us that it was the death mask
of her favorite goose. Then she began to cry and stroke the
shapeless plaster figure. We maintained a pious silence, and
only Angelika, who was also there, snorted with laughter. Papa
said reproachfully: "Angelika, please," and then Lilo and I also
started laughing. We had hardly regained our composure when
another act worthy of an insane asylum occurred. The lady told
us, weeping, that her parakeet had a heart disease and that she
feared that he might have a heart attack during the move in
their small, old car. He—the parakeet—was so sensitive, she
said, and the car made so much noise and would Angelika be
able to take the suffering beast to the new house in her quiet,
well-sprung, warm car?

So you know that I don't approve of this! Millions of peo-

ple have died and a parakeet has to be driven a hundred kilometers in a luxury car so that it doesn't have a heart attack.
Doesn't anyone still know which side is up, where thoughtlessness stops and indecency begins, at what point a person
ceases to be human?

Yesterday I received a very nice letter from Walter Slezak
from Hollywood. He—like a lot of other people—is trying to
get me to write a novel about my life. Fine, if I could write one!
It would be too wonderful to be true, not because I consider
my story so important, but rather because I could earn some
money and make myself independent. Being alone and free
and independent never disappoints. If only I'd known that earlier and hadn't always been so spoiled. Naturally, for a woman
the best thing is to have a husband and a family, but nonetheless she always has to be prepared. Something usually goes
wrong in a family, and if she can then stand on her own two
feet, she is saved.

Gauting, January 1949

My sweet, yesterday was the anniversary of Peterkin's
death, and on February 5 he would have been 32 years old.
How different life would have been with him. I was very
wretched.

Your letter, my child, was not exactly amusing. My heart
ached when I read that you are so worn out and not in the
mood for Christmas. But look, you have your son!

Lilo's mother and aunt have settled down here in Gauting,
and even the cold can't drive them away. In the evening, we wander like startled hens about the house with our bedclothes looking for a place to sleep in the rooms that are heated. There are
two of those, and so we all sleep together on narrow couches
and too-short sofas. The aunt spends restless nights on two armchairs pushed together, and sometimes she falls through in the

middle. Very comfortable! Only Lilo and Papa have a beautiful, heated room, sleep in a wide bed under a down comforter and are constantly courted by the two old ladies. This goes on all the time: "Schrobschen, don't you want . . . " and "Pusschen, don't you need this . . . " and "Diezchen, be careful . . . " and "Schnuckchen, don't overdo it . . . " They fidget and fuss like beetles and suck up to Lilo and Papa. Whether because of her new pregnancy, or because of her proper, good bourgeois position as the lady of the house, or because she has never genuinely changed, Lilo has turned back into the person she was in Sofia, a neglectful, lazy woman lacking in feeling. She takes care of nothing, leaves all the work to others and enjoys a blissful peace. Little Viola is cared for by the mother and aunt, while Lilo has not bathed the child herself for weeks or taken her with her into the bedroom. She comes and says: "Ach, my darling, my sweet little one . . . where's your Mama?" And that's it. I can't understand it, I find it dreadful and constantly see you and me as a mother. You're a much better mother than I was, sacrificing and always there for your little one, but even I couldn't let a day go by without holding my children in my arms, kissing them, feeling, smelling, tasting them. I'm very sad about Lilo, because I was just beginning to be fond of her. And then last Thursday Viola was baptized in the church in Gauting. Angelika was the godmother—with very mixed feelings, I'm afraid—and Viola has thus now been accepted into the Christian community. I hope she likes it.

My room is finally arranged and now, since it is finished and by far the prettiest room in the house, everyone comes running to admire it. It cost me a great deal of effort, because no one helped, and I had to take care of everything myself. Shall I describe it?

There are two beautiful old pieces of Biedermeier furniture in it, a secretary and a corner cabinet, Grandmother Schrobsdorff's little green-upholstered armchair, and a bed-couch with an attractive covering. On the wall are two candle sconces and two little corbels with bouquets of flowers on them, and between them hangs Peter's picture. On my night table there is the beautiful leaf-pattern lamp that Gipkins designed for me. Our house in Pätz, painted by Heini Heuser, hangs over my couch. Now all that is lacking is a little table and a book-case, and then it is all done and ready. But it's already very attractive.

For Christmas, Angelika once again gave me a great many gifts. The highlight was a pair of white felt boots with a triple sole, hand-sewn and wonderful. I can really use them, too. It's so cold that it's better not to go out of the house. Moreover, there's no reason to do so. An incredibly boring place, just old women, not a single decently dressed person.

Papa's business is going exceptionally badly, and he has dreadful worries. The house is much too great a financial burden, and I have no idea how he is to hold out. Now I often think about a time in Berlin in which he also had financial problems, though they weren't comparable to the ones he has now. But he was depressed, and when he came home in the evening, I couldn't bear the mood. I wanted to be surrounded by perpetual jubilation, hubbub, and gaiety. So I went to Pätz and left him alone with his worries. I didn't help him, and paid a heavy price for that.

Garmisch, March 1949

Dear Angelika, yesterday your Papa talked a great deal, but I didn't hear a single word from you. I could have believed that you'd lost the power of speech. I can hardly imagine anyone less adroit than your father, and moreover as he has grown older he has contracted verbal diarrhea. Nonetheless, you mustn't always say that we don't understand you. To tell the truth, I can't see how parents could be more tolerant, but perhaps we are too tolerant, and what you need and unconsciously want is a firm hand. I was always too easy on my children, I screamed at them but didn't guide them, and your Papa probably doesn't dare to, because he feels a little guilty about what happened.

I'm sorry that you went away disappointed. Maybe you wanted to open up, to speak yourself, get a little help from us. But I'm afraid it would have failed anyway, because at the bottom of your heart you reject us, no matter how we are. You reject everyone who argues with you. Then you've always got the same excuse ready: he or she doesn't understand me. For you, understanding you and approving of your behavior is one and the same, for us it isn't.

Another thing: your father is not well, and it's disrespectful and unfair of you to say that he likes to lie in bed. He's the most conscientious man I know, and he toils and drudges for us all at the cost of his own health. You know that he has always had stomach problems, even when he was still young and didn't have to go without anything. Now he's 55 years old, behind him lies hell and in front of him a difficult battle for life. Do you really believe those were and are the best conditions for healing a sick stomach? To be perfectly clear: often when he comes home from Munich, he looks so bad that that I'm shocked, and he has nights during which he can't sleep a wink because of nausea and pain. He really should go to a sanatorium, because one never knows where such ailments can lead, but at the moment he has neither the money nor the time to do it.

Now back to you. I shouldn't have taken the whole matter so seriously, and had also resolved to keep out of it. But there are two things that deeply upset me and for the sake of which I cannot keep silent: first Ed, because he loves you and thought he had a life with you, and you've cut the ground from under his feet; and second, the careless way you have tossed to the wind everything good and beautiful that you could have had. For it can hardly be denied that there's nothing better than a husband on whose love and protection you can entirely rely, and that under the current circumstances America is better than Germany, and perhaps better than all Europe. I'm convinced that Ed's unhappiness does not leave you unmoved, and that you'd give a great deal to know how you could spare him pain without having to give up your pleasures. Believe me, I know how one feels in such situations and understand you very well in this respect. When I recently saw you sitting in your car, so small and helpless in the big machine, I felt terribly sorry for you. You're still a child, and if your father hadn't disappointed you so much by getting married, and if I hadn't driven you crazy with my perpetual fear that the Iron Curtain would close before you got out, you might not have plunged so quickly into a marriage. You were and are much too young for that, and we, your father and I, are to blame.

So what I'm reproaching you for is not that your marriage is breaking down, but how it is breaking down. You have completely confused Ed and scared him away, you have led him around by the nose for months by convincing him that a woman like you has different, higher rights and claims than any ordinary woman. On what basis? Your beautiful face? That's too little, Angelika. You can do something out of the ordinary, only by doing something out of the ordinary. You consider yourself far too interesting, you take yourself far too seriously, you're not honest with others and, what is much worse, with yourself. If you would at least admit to yourself that your behavior is in many cases wrong, then the problem would not be so hopeless. But not only do you not admit it to yourself, you project it onto others and want to convince them that they are the ones who are acting wrongly, not you. You twist everything around, wrap everything up in fine words, talk your way out of everything. As you used to say that all Germans are nauseating, so now you say that all Americans are nauseating, and tomorrow it will be another people. Everyone is to blame for your personal discontent, never yourself. You know how to get people to do whatever you have in mind. You exploit the misfortune we had, you trade on it. Something positive should soon emerge from your fate. The negativity can't go on much longer, it's getting boring. You can't do anything about your marriage and its breakdown, but you can learn from it, you can start over, gain a different attitude. Sitting down on the ruins and saying that life is to blame will do you no good in the long run. No one cares two hoots about a person who isn't producing anything. Beautiful, young, and intelligent as you are, all doors are open to you. If only you knew what incredible treasures this life, this world has to offer. You want to be independent and free, fine, but one has to earn one's own money. That one person pays and the other is free is not the way it is, or should be. Unless the one who pays is a rich father. But that time is past, Angelika.

You've once again gotten what you wanted. You won't—I'm sure about this—separate from M., either. You made that promise to your father only to shut him up and to flee. It didn't shock me. I don't consider separation the primary thing. If you don't wake up, it doesn't matter whether you see M. again immediately or two months from now. And if you do wake up, it doesn't matter whether you live with the one or the other. Because when you finally know what you want, and see a path in front of you, then no one can harm you, and neither can a failed marriage or a new love affair.

You can't be changed by outward pressure, but only by your inner will. I'm still betting on you, I believe there's something in you, though I'm still not sure what it is. Try harder, make something of yourself, I swear to you, it's worth it. Just see how I've frittered away my talent and intelligence all my

life, and now I'm just sitting here. Logical! Consistently—
except for the illness, and even that's part of it. You still have
a long time and, moreover, many more possibilities than I did.
As a woman of my generation I was something new, unusual
and suspect. I fell outside the box, so to speak, and had to be
very strong and make my own rules. No one helped me do
that; on the contrary, I was seen as being at best strange and at
worst degenerate. You live in a period that is already much
broader, much more open. Make use of it, work on yourself,
become more mature, more serious, and especially more honest with yourself.

Angeli, you will be shocked by this letter, but that doesn't
matter. It's better that you be shocked now rather than half a
century too late, as I was.

Gauting, April 1949

My sweet, dumb little Tina, what a shock! I knew it. When
I feel as I have the last few days, then something is going on. I
sense it the way an animal senses a storm coming, I'm restless,
can hardly sleep. What a shame! I would have so much liked
to have a second grandchild, but then nothing could have kept
me here any longer, nothing! My little one, I'm worried about
you, I'd like to be with you, help you. Even if it's all over now,
surgery is no fun, especially without anesthetic. I have had
experience with that, you know, and think it is hardly bearable
when one is fully conscious. What barbarous methods! These
days there are other means and options.

You ask about Angeli. I've already told you a few, unfortunately not very pleasant, things about her. She is making me
pretty unhappy. You, who are far away, are so close to me, and
she, who is close to me, is so far away. But here it is less a question of me than of poor Ed. A short time ago, when I sensed
something but did not yet know what was going on, I found a

letter from Ed to Angeli in her apartment. I read it (please, never say anything about this) because I wanted finally to get things straight. I got them straight, but I also got a terribly heavy heart. How miserable she has made the man, and he still writes to her that she is a marvelously beautiful flower that one can only look at, not touch. But he would have preferred to touch her.

He has treated her with great tenderness and loved her idolatrously—and continues to love her and to suffer. Ellen, who as you know is staying with us in Gauting, is hopping mad at Angelika, because during a trip they took to Switzerland together she stole her boyfriend. Now Ellen is consoling Ed. It's almost like Schnitzler's *La Ronde*.

What is to become of your sister I no longer know. She has spoiled everything for herself and continues to spoil everything for herself. She has a hundred different passions and just as many admirers. But not a trace of ambition. She begins everything—acting lessons with one teacher, ballet lessons with another—and the teachers are all enchanted by her, and she is enchanted by them, but suddenly she's had enough of everything, of both the teachers and the lessons, and she disappears. She proceeds exactly the same way with her men. First it was the Viennese actor M., for whom she left Ed, and now it's the Swiss, for whom she has left M. She goes into everything with flying colors, and comes out of it with evil eyes—as you called her scornful look. Ed has now taken away her car, and given M., unfortunately too late, a terrible blow to the chin in the middle of the street. It would be consistent if M. were to slug the Swiss in turn, because at the moment he deserves it. Or perhaps he already doesn't. Right now Angeli is still living with Ruth in her apartment. Ruth is also a special case. Originally hired as a maid, she quickly became a kind of companion who accepts with slavish devotion and love all the moods, craziness, and bad ideas Angelika has to offer. The apartment looks as if a bomb had gone off in it, because neither of them will risk damaging one of their fine red-painted fingernails by cleaning it up. And it isn't worth the trouble anymore, because after the divorce Angeli will have to leave the apartment. I'd like to know how she will live without an apartment, a car, money, or a profession. I fear that Papa will be the one who will end up paying for everything. He blames himself and me for Angelika's behavior more than he does her, and he is probably not entirely wrong to do so. But he forgives her too much and us too little. He's positively enamored of her. Well, at least no one can say that our daughter is boring.

My little Tina, now you know everything about your sister. She was always a peculiar child, and there's nothing to be said against that, either. It's just that she shouldn't express her peculiarity solely in plain mischief, but also sometimes in an achievement. But perhaps I am expecting too much of her too soon.

My child, please watch out for yourself and don't treat yourself carelessly.

Gauting, May 1949

Little Angeli, unfortunately I can't meet you in Munich. It was crazy of me to arrange a meeting with you at all, because I am very much worse. Recently, on my way to the seamstress's, I suddenly couldn't go on. That should have been a warning signal for me and kept me from going to the theater that evening. During the first act everything went black and I couldn't breathe. I spoiled all of Ellen's pleasure, because she had to take me home as fast as she could. It's so bad that I'm no longer capable of doing anything. My heart bothers me a lot—everything bothers me a lot. When I'm asked where it hurts, I always say that I should rather be asked where it doesn't hurt. That's faster. Now I just sit around, and even for that I need a cup of coffee. Most of the time I lie in bed.

What you took the wrong way in my last letter I really don't know. It was not written so much against you as for Ellen. You've been mean to her, and I wanted to do her justice; I'm fond of her. I recognize Ellen's earlier mistakes, but she has worked on herself with success and has developed into a person who can be delightful. One can't say as much of you, Angelika. You work on others, and work on them until they are the way you want them to be. Ed says what you want to hear. Your father keeps silent, but dances to your tune. I do neither the one nor the other, and you don't like that. And there's something else: never think that we—you and I—are complicated. We are just as simple and insignificant as most people, only we boast more. We're ostentatious, conceited egoists, and lazy to boot. Geniuses are never complicated and never lazy. So far as I'm concerned, I'm more intelligent, analytical, contemplative—as my race is, but that's all. I've also always imagined that I was complicated! I wish!

I will certainly no longer get involved in your affairs, because I have realized that I do so in vain. I'm also much too weak. If you can come to see me, I'll be glad, because only you and Tina still interest me. Everything else is becoming increasingly a matter of indifference for me.

Gauting, May 1949

My good Tina, another letter that seemed so listless that it made me very said. What do you want, then? You still have a husband who puts in an appearance, and—touch wood—a splendid son. You're young, healthy, many people love you and need you, and I'm convinced that you'll come here someday. Don't think that it's because you live in Bulgaria that you have to work so much and so hard. All the women here work just as hard as you do, and moreover they've endured a long, dreadful war, in which they lost a great deal, if not everything. Do you really believe that they all have maids and a happy life again? They have worries and hardships, they're battered in body and soul and nerves. My dear child, you'll never understand what results a lost war can have.

In addition, you complain that you have no opportunity or time to study and read. There I have to laugh a bit. How much you used to resist all that back when you had the time and opportunity, finding reading boring and studying disagreeable. Why does insight always come too late?

I also have to laugh at your reaction to my thoughts about death. You've taken them as a personal insult, and in your sullen reply I clearly hear you say: can't you spare me that at least? But I spoke entirely in general, I was just talking to myself, and I was more positive than depressed. You can't close yourself to that, my stupid little thing, death is nothing bad as long as it doesn't strike young, healthy people. For many people who are old and sick, it is less frightening than living. Be glad that I can say that so clearly and calmly, and don't feel that something horrifying is approaching me.

So my little Tina, I ask you to be reasonable, and not to see in everything that you have to do or not do an injustice and a burden that is imposed on you alone. Don't make your home unpleasant for Mizo, think of little André, who suffers from that, just as you suffered from me. Even with all my love for you children I was impatient and intemperate, I ranted and screamed and drove you crazy. What came of all that? A bad conscience, then and now. I regret so much that I wasn't a better mother. My Peter is dead, you're far away, and Angelika keeps her distance from me; I can never make amends for what I failed to do back then. Think about that. And also keep in mind that one must be glad to be young and healthy, loved and needed. One must be glad about that every day. Life goes by so quickly, and when it's drawing to a close, one asks oneself: why did I waste so much of it?

So now I conclude. Take care of yourself, stay healthy, kiss your two men for me, and always remember that I love you. I just can't bear it anymore.

My mother died on June 5, 1949.

Angelika Schrobsdorff was born in 1927 in Freiburg. She immigrated to Sofia in 1939 with her mother and returned to Germany in 1947. She married Claude Lanzmann, director of the landmark 1985 documentary *Shoah*, in 1971, and, after more than a decade in Paris and Monaco, they moved to Israel in 1983. Today, Angelika Schrobsdorff lives in Berlin. She is the author of ten novels and two works of short stories.